To Christopher, this [...]
with my every Best [...]

THE RAVENS FALL

Richard de Methley

Richard de Methley

First Impression: August 2015
Second Impression: October 2015

www.richarddemethley.co.uk

Copyright © Richard de Methley
Richard de Methley has asserted his right under the Copyright, Designs and Patents Act 1988 to be identified as the author of this book.
A CIP record for this book is available from the British Library.
ISBN: 978-0-9557480-8-0
Cover design by Ingrid Freeman: **ingridfreeman@me.com**
Prepared and Printed by: 4edge, Eldon Way, Hockley ESSEX: 01702.200243
www.4edge.co.uk

Dedication

*T*his book is dedicated to all those who have helped put it together. To Michael Craig and Ingrid Freeman, who have worked with enormous skill and goodwill on the new covers, on the map and advised stalwartly on presentation. And to Rosie Craig for her sharp intellect and her editorial skills...and my own Diana Mary for putting up with me, especially when it was not going well, or the damned computer 'stole' vital bits! Outstanding...and gleaming, all of them!

Especial thanks go also to Diana Lyne-Pirkis who helped create the original story-board when it was known as *Sica*, and typed every word of the original manuscript from which this book has finally flown free.

Thank you all *so* much.

Richard de Methley:

July 30th 2015

OTHER BOOKS BY RICHARD DE METHLEY

THE WHITE ROSE SERIES.

A Medieval tale of love, murder, treachery and adventure in the days of Richard Lionheart.

THE LION AND THE WHITE ROSE

THE WHITE ROSE AND THE LADY

THE WHITE ROSE BETRAYED

THE LION AND THE WHITE ROSE TRIUMPHANT

And, since November 2014, a vibrant tale of survival and revenge in the Viking days of Alfred the Great.

A STORM OF RAVENS

All these books can be viewed and purchased from my website, which I hope you will visit: **www.richarddemethley.co.uk.** You can pay by PayPal, or directly to me through the website. Just follow the instructions. R de M.

Historical Note

*T*his second part of my story begins in Athelney, to where Alfred fled after the disaster of losing Chippenham to Guthrum's invading forces on January 6th, 878. We still don't really know how he escaped. But as the Danes burst over Chippenham's defences, Alfred and his family, including a baby at the breast, together with a small number of his household, escaped from the back of the town the Danes couldn't reach because of the Avon…and finally got to Athelney.

Now in what is known as the 'Somerset Levels', it was then in a huge area of tidal marshes and rivers, more a sea than anything else. Athelney and East Lyng closeby, were small islands in a maze of streams, reeds, waterways and vast meres, all linked to the sea, from where the Danes never managed to winkle him out. There the Anglo Saxon Chronicle (ASC) tells us: '…King Alfred, with a small company built a fortification at Athelney, and from that fortification, with the men of that part of Somerset, he continued to fight against the host…" His biographer, Bishop Asser, writing in 893, just fifteen years after the event, says in his 'Life of Alfred the Great': '…and from it, with the thegns of Somerset he struck out relentlessly and tirelessly against the Vikings…'

So, this is where Alfred established himself, and where the Time Team excavated in 1994 and again in 2003 and near where, in 1693, the magnificent Alfred Jewel was found: now in the Ashmolean Museum, it has to be seen to realise just how stunningly beautiful it is. And while the Time Team did not find any Saxon artefacts, they did find many exciting things: the remains of ditches and earthworks, the foundations of the monastery Alfred later built there and the copious remains of iron workings from the forges used to fashion weapons of many sorts. It was the fortress Asser and the ASC talk of, linked to East Lyng by a causeway that Alfred built, and where there is an excellent pub, the Rose and Crown, that does magnificent beef and ale pies! And if you go to Athelney, climb also to the top of Barrow Mump, where Alfred built a watch tower, and look out across the whole area below, which was once a sea, and imagine what it must have been like in Alfred's day. Like the floods in the winter of 2014!

From here Alfred fought a real guerrilla war against his enemies, bitter stuff, designed to encourage his people not to lose faith. To show them that the Vikings could be fought and beaten, and for them to do their best to follow his example…as Leofric, Brioni, Edwin, Harold and many others did. In fact, he must have built up quite a resistance movement throughout Wessex in those desperate months after Chippenham fell, for his appeal to his people after Easter to have been so successful. For when he sent messengers out, far and wide, as the story says, to come to a great muster at Ecberht's Stone the response was truly remarkable.

The ASC says: '…in the seventh week after Easter {23ʳᵈ March} he rode to *Ecgbryhtessan*, to the east of Selwood, and came to meet him all the men of Somerset, Wiltshire and that part of Hampshire which was on this side of the sea, and they received him warmly…' Asser says: '…There all the inhabitants of Somerset and Wiltshire, and the inhabitants of Hampshire – those who had not sailed overseas for fear of the Vikings – joined him. When they saw the King, receiving him as if one restored to life after suffering great tribulations, they were filled with immense joy…' As you will find they did when you get there in the story.

As for the Battle of Cynuit, the ASC puts it in the same winter as the Danes captured Chippenham: '…And in the same winter a brother of Ivar and Halfdan {Ubbi Lodbroksson} was in Wessex, in Devon, with twenty three ships and there was he slain, and eight hundred men with him and forty men of his retinue…" his hearth companions, the best of his best. And then goes on to talk about the capture of the magic flag, the Raven Banner, that I have called Landravager. Bishop Asser's account is very much more detailed, but I will leave you, my keen reader, to find it. It's worth the effort. For entirely narrative reasons I have put that battle much later, after Easter and before the muster, as I wanted Guthrum's plans to catch Alfred in a Viking pincer to be more disturbed than otherwise they might have been.

Ecberht's stone, however, is a real problem.

Many believe it no longer exists. But at Kingston Deverill there is a hill called King's Court Hill where there were once three standing stones, two upright Sarsens and one capstone, where Ecberht of Wessex, Alfred's grandfather, was known to hold moots and give dooms to his people. These stones were moved by a farmer in the nineteenth century, and then again by successive rectors to a small field near the church where they can still be seen. The capstone was removed because it was considered dangerous, and not by Leofric as my story has it! And it is to these stones that I have Alfred going for the great muster that preceded the climactic Battle of Edington, or *Ethandun*, as it was called in those days.

6

Iley Oak exists, or rather its massive stump does, stuck amidst a fiercely spiky plantation of monkey puzzle trees, where there is a small semi-circular earthwork, the whole marked on the OS map for the area as Robin Hood's Bower! And here the ASC says; '...And one day later he went from those camps {where the muster had been held} to Iley Oak, and one day later to Edington...' All of which is corroborated by Asser in his 'Life.'

And so we come to the most climactic battle of Alfred's life, and an area of much controversy, because there has been great dissension amongst scholars over where this battle was actually fought. Some have put it in Eddington in Berkshire, Minchinhampton in Gloucestershire, Etton Down in Wiltshire, even Abingdon in Oxfordshire...but in modern times it has been firmly established at Edington in Wiltshire. But even that has not satisfied some, very eminent writers, who have put it around the ancient British fortress of Bratton, on the top of the escarpment, about a mile or so away.

I love the Warrior Chronicles of one famous writer and have read every one of them with great joy. But I cannot accept his premise that Alfred's battle was fought at Bratton Camp. For one thing the battle is called 'Edington' by all who refer to it, not 'Bratton'; for another it is on top of a very steep escarpment, almost precipitous in places, where there is now, and was then, *no water!* And no easy escape off it for the Danish host if it was beaten. Those slopes would have been murderous for mounted men in a panic, and Guthrum's army was largely mounted. Four thousand horses! A horse needs between five and ten gallons of water a day, let alone the men, and they would all need supplies...so no water would have been a very serious problem. At Edington there are flowing streams, shelter from the Royal Lodge that had earlier been built there, ready access to supplies and a clear escape route back to Chippenham, fifteen miles away, should they need to get out fast, hunted by wildly excited Saxons on horseback! All points that Guthrum makes to Oscytel in the story.

Go there and see what you think. Then go to the 'Duke' at Bratton, or the 'Three Daggers' back along the road at Edington, and enjoy the food and atmosphere. Especially if you have exhausted yourself walking up to the top of the escarpment, round Bratton Camp's defences and peering down at the Westbury White Horse, imagining yourself to be very thirsty Danes running in a panic to escape your baying Saxon foes. Actually there is a good road and car park up there...but not in Alfred's day!

So, respecting the master story teller as I truly do, I have put the Danes across the road from Warminster to Chippenham along which Alfred would have had to march to reach the enemy in their fortress where he expected to have to beat them. Instead they marched out several days before to fight him to the death in one great bloody engagement which they expected to win.

Did Alfred really visit the enemy camp before the battle disguised as a gleeman? I doubt it very much. Alfred was no fool and the enemy surely would have recognised him. But it is part of the Alfred legend and so I have slipped it in for you to find, along with the equally famous story of the burned cakes which was first written down in the sixteenth century by Archbishop Parker, from a manuscript lost to a disastrous fire four centuries ago.

Distillation of alcohol was known by the Greeks in the 1st century AD, but true distillation came from Salerno in the 12th century so I don't really suppose that Gilbert could have given his special 'barley spirit' to Hugo while they were in the Rings. Neither could Heardred have sung the Song of Roland. That great hero died at the battle of Roncesvalles against the Moors in 778, when he blew his horn, but his tale wasn't written until the early Middle Ages, between 1040 and 1115. However, it seemed good to me to slip them both in. Just little touches!

The battle itself must have been a terrible affair, as I have done my best to depict, despite the paucity of contemporary detail. Hand to hand fighting always is; nothing has changed when you get close up and personal with a rabid enemy doing his best to slay you! Monks don't go much on description, and of course they were not there. So the ASC simply says: '…one day later {after the camp at Iley Oak} to Edington; and there he fought against the entire host, and put it to flight…' And that's it!

The good Bishop Asser says much more: '…When the next morning dawned he moved his forces to a place called Edington, and fighting fiercely with a compact shield-wall against the entire Viking army, he persevered resolutely for a long time; at length he gained the victory through God's will. He destroyed the Vikings with great slaughter, and pursued those who fled as far as the stronghold {Chippenham}, hacking them down; he seized everything he found outside the stronghold – men, whom he killed immediately, horses and cattle – and boldly made camp in front of the gates of the Viking stronghold with all his army…'

Please note that nowhere, neither in the ASC, nor in Asser's 'Life of Alfred' is the battle referred to as being anywhere other than at Edington!

The great Iron Age fortress at Battlesbury Rings near Warminster I have talked about in the other book, but it is a magnificent place to visit. With awesome ramparts, the whole site is just amazing. Thank god I never had to storm them as the Romans may have done, probably Vespasian's II Augusta Legion, known to have been in the area a year after Claudius's invasion in 43AD. Many shattered corpses of men, women and children were found when

8

the site was extensively excavated in 2008, prior to a major tank road being built at the bottom. From the top the view is magnificent and the wind always blows, as Leofric told Brioni long before they ever went there. The excavation also yielded a mass of social material, so the site was extensively occupied, but what they did for water is a mystery as, contrary to my tale, there were no cisterns or springs ever up there, so just a lot of fetching and carrying from below where there are springs and streams.

As for what happened afterwards, the events are exactly as they are stated in the story. Both the ASC and Bishop Asser confirm them if you choose to check them out, and I have taken them almost word for word from the original documents, but I shall leave you to find that all out for yourself if you wish to do so.

So, the real History of the day, and my story, begins and ends at Chippenham.

On 6th January 878, the Danes assaulted the fortress town in a surprise attack and drove Alfred and his family into the wilderness, and Wessex fell to Guthrum. On, or around, the 8th of May the same year Alfred led his army against the Danes at Edington and thrashed them, chased Guthrum back to Chippenham, where it had all started, and after a bitter two week siege Guthrum came and begged for peace, and so Alfred seized back the town and his kingdom. He was an amazing man…the only English king ever to be called Great!

And as for what happened to Heardred of the Somerseatas after Foxley? Or to Brioni after she was captured at Chippenham, and to Leofric, Brioni and all their friends on that bloody field? You will just have to read the book! Enjoy!

Richard de Methley

9

GLOSSARY

Aethling	Saxon prince
Aidan	One of the greatest of Saxon saints, who brought Christianity back to the North of England.
Cuthbert	Another great Saxon saint and much loved in his day.
Baldric	The leather belt, sometimes across the chest, or even the back, that carried sword and seaxe in often fleece-lined leather.
Bearded Axe	A special form of axe head, where the bottom edge is drawn down, and slightly back, so that, in profile, it looks like a beard…a sort of hook that can be used in battle for pulling down an enemy's shield, so that he can be speared or thrust through by another warrior standing closeby.
Bothy	A small house, often with a turf roof, like a ridge tent, made of wattle.
Byrnie	Chain mail jacket, often with short sleeves, riveted iron links, or scales, stitched on leather. Worn by both sides and very expensive.
Churl	Peasant farmer with village rights, and land to farm.
Devonseatas	The people of Devon.
Dooms	Judgements given before all the people, either at a village moot, a bishop's court or from the King himself.
Cruck House	A house with a wooden frame, like an upside down boat.
Ealdormen	The leaders of a county, from which the word 'Earl' comes.
Gebur	A farm labourer without land of his own, but rights of common.
Fyrd/Fyrdsmen	The Saxon peasant army of England. Brave as lions, but largely untrained and poorly equipped levies from the countryside. The Fyrd was raised from every county.
Halidom	The sacred relics, often in beautiful golden caskets, and the altar vessels and ornaments, held by a Saxon Lord.
Knarr	A Viking cargo ship, wider and slower than a warship.
Moot	A meeting to decide details of village, town or country.
Odin	The Viking king of the gods, closely associated with ravens, the Viking bird of war and death.
Pauldrons	Protective armour for the shoulders.
Ravens	The true bird of war of the Vikings. Odin had two, Huginn and Muminn, 'Thought' and 'Memory', his winged

	messengers, who brought him news from all over the Norse world. The raven absolutely defined the Vikings for everyone in those days.
Rhynes	Narrow waterways within the Somerset marshlands around Athelney
Runes	The extraordinary angular script of the Vikings said to be a gift from Odin himself.
Scramaseaxe	A long-bladed sword with a single cutting edge and runic inscriptions cut into the steel.
Seaxe	The long-bladed stabbing knife that defined the Saxon warrior, more like the old Roman gladius of the legions but with a finer blade.
Somerseatas	The people of Somerset.
Swithun/Swithin	St Swithun. Still remembered today. 15th July. If it rains on St Swithun's day it will rain for forty days!
Thane/Thegn	A lord. The Saxon equivalent of the Norman knight. Dedicated to giving his people justice and protection by the king's order. Made the front of the battle line.
Thrall	The meanest form of Saxon society…other than slaves.
Twelfth Night	Epiphany, January 6th; then and now.
Valkyrie	Maidens of war attached to Odin/Woden, who chose the living from the dead on the battlefield. Those going to Valhalla, the feast hall of the gods, and those going to Hel as shades. They may also appear as lovers of heroes and other mortals, where they are sometimes described as the daughters of royalty, sometimes accompanied by ravens and sometimes connected to swans or horses.
Wattle	Interwoven hazel sticks in large panels, then packed both sides with mud, animal hair and dung and allowed to dry.
Witan	The Council of wise men who advised the king…all the most important men in the land, including all leading churchmen.
Woden	Woden is the Anglo-Saxon equivalent of Odin in Norse mythology. He is the King of the Saxon gods, who married a mortal and thus became the forebear of Anglo-Saxon royalty, and anyone else who could prove a connection, like Brioni.
Wolfsheads	Outlaws
Yule	Originally the pagan equivalent of Christmas.

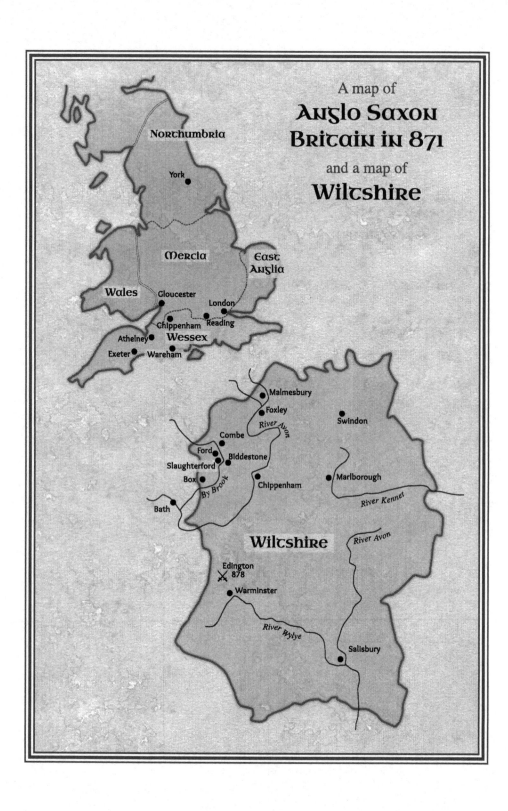

A map of
Anglo Saxon Britain in 871
and a map of
Wiltshire

Northumbria

York

Mercia

East Anglia

Wales

Gloucester

London

Chippenham

Reading

Athelney

Wessex

Exeter

Wareham

Wiltshire

Malmesbury

Foxley

River Avon

Swindon

Combe

Ford

Biddestone

Slaughterford

Box

By Brook

Chippenham

Marlborough

River Kennet

Bath

River Avon

Edington
878

Warminster

River Wylye

Salisbury

The Ravens Fall

Athelney, the Somerset marshes: March 878.

Chapter One

*A*thelney on a bitter wet day in March, thought Heardred, gazing morosely out across the dreich, windswept marshlands that surrounded him, was probably the gloomiest, loneliest, and most miserable place in all Wessex. God knows they were safe enough from prowling Danes, but the emptiness, the constant sighing swish and rustle of reeds, the rippling chuckle of water, and the endless keening bird calls were sometimes enough to make a man doubt his sanity.

Surrounded by the miry bog-lands, reeded waterways and rhynes of the River Tone and its fens, the high grounds of Athelney, and nearby Lyng, raised themselves out of the ooze and drowned wetlands like floating islands in a swampy sea. A vast watery desert made tidal by the rise and fall of the River Parrett where it flowed into the sea. The water extended for miles, almost as far as the eye could see, with the huge hill of Burrow Mump towering up in the distance behind it all. To those who knew its secrets there were many paths and hidden trackways that led to every 'island' heart, but to strangers it was an eery, misted place of imminent danger; an inland sea where the water lapped and furrowed everywhere. A fearful watery mire that could swallow men and horses without a trace, sucking them down to a desperate death, their last despairing cries echoed by the curlews across the waving reed beds.

Eight weeks or more since they had first arrived there, saddle sore and weary...and still he could not forget her, *Brioni*. She had become an even more important part of his life than he had realised. And now that he had lost her, he felt as though only a part of him still lived. Even her name still conjured a picture of such sweetness and flowering beauty that it made him want to cry out, a pain so deep it was embedded in his very soul.

He sighed, and turned to look around him at the dozen or so horses busily cropping at the tough sward left over from the winter, and at the remains of his battered command. Those who still rode with him after the constant warfare to which he had committed them all in defence of Alfred's lost kingdom. The desperate raids, the fierce cut and thrust with sword and spear at a brutal enemy, the howling rage and spitting fury of every fight, the blood and stench of close combat and the loss of good men who could not easily be replaced.

Dear God, but they were a sorry lot from those who had set out from his home at the cusp of the New Year, before Guthrum had burst out of Gloucester in January and raced across Wessex to seize Chippenham and destroy the king.

A dozen men less.

Some killed, some wounded and left behind in Athelney, the remainder now stood in little armoured groups quietly discussing the day's activities, their shields on their backs, swords by their sides and long spears grounded at their feet. Their armour, rust-free but no longer shining, was dulled with hard usage, helmets dented and tough leather hose scuffed and streaked with mud.

And how much he missed the companionship of his friends, of Edwin and Harold…and how he wished they could all have come south together instead of having to split up after the horrors of Foxley.

He coughed in the fire smoke and smacked his big hands together as he turned to crouch down over the flames that Baldred had finally managed to coax into sulky life after the heavy overnight rain, and warmed his hands. The man was a miracle worker. He knew of no-one who could get wet wood to burn the way he could. No matter how terrible the conditions he had never failed them yet, never setting out anywhere without his fire-pouch well stuffed with dry grasses and fine chippings, neatly chopped kindling and a fine pair of flints.

Now he looked at the flames flittering and sparkling around the crude pyramid of sticks that Baldred had built in the great hollow beneath a huge fallen tree, its twisted roots making a fine overhanging shelter, and shivered as he cracked his knuckles over the flames.

*

*T*he journey down to Athelney had been a nightmare.
Mercifully the days had been too crowded with the simple problems of staying alive and free from the Danes for his mind to dwell on the misery and shock of finding Brioni's body so brutally hacked and mangled.

For two days they had pushed south-west as hard as their beasts could carry them, and in some of the bitterest weather that anybody could remember. A real wolf-winter, when the stars were brittle-edged with diamonds and the frost-rime lay finger deep each frigid morning, the raw breath freezing on the beards and whiskers of man and beast alike. Nights when the grey brothers

14

howled to each other from the forests and deserted uplands, the *woo-ooo-ooo* of their calls making the hair stand on end of every man who stood guard…and days of hard riding, sometimes on proven trackways, sometimes across open country, and always with the threat of pursuit to spur them on.

Changing horses whenever possible, even at sword point on occasions, they had pressed on relentlessly. Occasionally they had found willing shelter in some loyal hall, or in some abandoned steading, but sometimes they had been forced to spend the night huddled round a great fire in some wretched clearing in the bleak woodlands that lay all round them. Wrapped in their thick cloaks and watching the hungry eyes of prowling beasts beyond the leaping firelight, flicker and blink out…only to reappear balefully somewhere else.

And all the time they had been aware the Danes would follow them hard, knowing that they must keep constantly on the move, even doubling back on their tracks to throw Guthrum's flying raiders off the scent of their desperate quarry. Truly all Wessex seemed in turmoil, whole villages fleeing into the woods at their approach, terrified they were heathen outriders of the Danish host that had burst like a steel wave across the land, carrying death and destruction beneath its raven wings.

Nor had they escaped unscathed.

Just past Chippenham, on the long road to Bath and Taunton, they had been forced to fight off a band of Guthrum's marauders. Mounted Vikings who had been driving hard to seize Bath, both sides coming together in a violent hell of blood and steel. Horses twisting and biting in a spray of snow and torn ground, the savage thrust and hack of spears and swords, the screech and spark of blades and the roar of men fighting for their lives; the screams of the wounded, blood spewing from heads and arms; hands lopped and the bang and smash of shields.

It had been a furious, pell-mell skirmish at the back-end of a long day as the sun had tilted in a scarlet ball towards the misted hills. A fierce struggle that had left eight of the enemy spread-eagled on the bloody ground along with three of his own men, with others wounded, bruised and battered by the fight; while the survivors of Guthrum's war-band had routed, their blood flying in scarlet splashes as they went, the horses of their dead racing away with them in snorting terror.

Finally at Glastonbury they had drawn breath, pausing at the old abbey church to take stock of their situation: to gather news of the King, for fresh food for man and beast, and a last night's rest in peace and comfort before the final stage of their long journey into the desolate wastelands that surrounded Athelney. And it had been there, amidst the quiet of the ancient church first built by King Ine nearly two hundred years before, with its pattering monks,

15

hushed chanting and deserted grounds, that he had at last come to terms with his bitter loss. There was something timeless and ethereal about the place that had drawn his heart and mind into more peaceful waters than at any time since he had left Foxley.

Though Brioni's memory would live with him always, there were others now to whom he was responsible, who looked to him for leadership and a safe passage through the harshly troubled times in which they found themselves. He would still grieve for her, for her beauty and her loving warmth and gentleness, her sparkling spirit and her laughter. His body would still yearn for her, and he would still hear her voice whispering to him on the wind, and turn and call her name.

But there, in the faded, winter emptiness of the abbot's garden into which he had wandered unawares, he had finally said goodbye to her, folding their love into his heart like a precious flower whose summer glory would never die.

For several moments he had stood there wrapped in thought amongst the tangled weeds that filled the abbot's herb beds, the silence broken only by the piercing sweetness of a robin's song. His heart suffused with longing and sadness as a myriad pictures of her ran through his mind, he stared into the chill, misted distance in the thin sunlight of that bleak January day his eyes seeing nothing. It all seemed so far away. Then, with a sigh, he smiled and kissed the wind. She was gone, and life must go on…and yet he felt her close, as if he only had to turn quickly round and she would be there smiling, arms outstretched to hold him, lips already parting for a kiss.

He shook his head at his foolishness.

It was only an illusion, and turning his back on the solitude he had so badly needed he had gathered his cloak around him and quietly walked away, committed to wreaking a terrible revenge upon his enemies that would not end until he had seen Guthrum cast down, Oscytel slain and Alfred returned to his rightful place as the true King of Wessex.

*

Since then he had filled his days with fighting and constant warfare. The Heathen had taken her from him, and they should pay full score in blood for his loss. No task that Alfred gave him was too difficult or dangerous for him and his men to attempt. They had become the shock troops of the royal warband, and wherever he led, his command always followed, stirrup to stirrup there was no separating them.

They killed the most Danes and took the most booty as a result, stripping the dead of armbands, coins and armour wherever they killed them, terrifying friends and foes alike with the ferocity of their attacks and their single-minded determination to wipe the Viking pirates from the face of God's earth. And it was in pursuit of just that need that they had left the King a few days since to follow up a loose report that had come in from one of the more remote villages on their northern flank.

A small group of outlanders had been spotted quartering the marshes in that area. It could have meant anything. In those parts the word 'outlander' covered anyone who wasn't a fen dweller. On the other hand it could have been a sign that the Danes were on the move against them. It had happened before – after all, they had been raiding and killing out of Athelney for nigh on two moons now – it couldn't just be left unexplored. So he and his men had left to enquire into it. But that had been days ago, since when they had found nothing. It was very frustrating…and the foul weather did not help!

He sighed, poked the fire with a stick, and huddled deeper into his cloak. If only it would stop raining and they could get a sight and feel of the sun. Then this bloody mist haze would lift clear of the drenched land and they might really see something worthwhile. If nothing else they would all feel a deal more cheerful. One more day of this and he would lead them back to Athelney, and good riddance!

"So, what's new in the world this bright and sunny morning?" a harsh voice broke in on him suddenly. "You're looking more clenched than a fist full of nails!"

"Oh, it's you, Siward," he replied, twisting round to look up at the tall warrior who now loomed over him. "I thought I recognised your dulcet tones. Come and warm your hands, this filthy weather is enough to make anyone's muscles creak…is there any further news of our missing quarry?" he continued as the well-armoured man he had been addressing chinked down beside him. "Dear God, but I wish these blasted peasants would get their information correct. Neither hide nor hair have we seen of any enemy since we arrived here. Whoever it was must be long gone by now!" And he poked the fire with sudden anger.

The man Siward was a hard-faced, rangy-looking warrior with a shambling gait that belied his speed. His grey eyes missed little and his thick wrists and powerful forearms proclaimed the well-practised swordsman that indeed he was. A dangerous opponent at any time, he was a fury on the battlefield - as many an incautious Danish carl had discovered as he breathed his last, his body shattered by the Saxon swordsman's brutal attack. He was a

17

loyal friend to those he took to, and after Foxley he had become Heardred's right-hand man.

"Nothing, lord, bar an old campsite or two, and they looked long abandoned. If there were Danes around here there can't have been many of them, or we must have come across their tracks by now. The Saints only know what those fools saw...but it certainly wasn't a war band of Guthrum's heroes."

"I agree. But you know what the King's like for information. So, we'll make one more sweep to the north-east, then call it a day and turn back.

"Aller and Stathe? Beyond Burrow Mump?"

"Why not? It may add a day to our journey, but it will be wonderful to ride dry ground once more before plunging back into that bloody mire around Athelney. And the people around there won't have seen any of the King's men for a moon's length. I could do with a good meal in my belly after the rubbish we have been eating. And a good night's rest under a proper roof would be a blessing."

"How long?"

"As soon as possible. We broke camp at dawn anyway, so it shouldn't take long, Tell the men to check all equipment and horses. Feet particularly. We cannot afford a lame beast today. And the sooner we are on our way the better. The weather's foul, and we have a long way to go."

*

*A*nd so it was done. Within a candle-bar's length they were all re-mounted and on their way again: peering through the cloying mists of rain, pleased to be on the move, but too collectively damp and low to make any but the briefest of conversations. Then, quite suddenly, not a mile from where they had set out, they came upon fresh tracks, three sets altogether, showing one man mounted and two on foot...and all making for Athelney.

Heardred, who was in the lead, flung up his hand and the whole troop came to a bouncing halt, their breath hanging in the chill, damp air, the steam rising in thin tendrils from the heaving flanks of their horses.

"So, there is strange life in these parts after all," he said briefly, turning to Siward as he did so. "'Though I doubt they are Danes. I thought you said this section had been checked out already?

"It was, Lord, at first light. These tracks are very fresh."

"How long since?"

"Half an hour, maybe more. These hoof prints are still quite clear…and two men in clogs. See, the rain has not had a chance to decay them yet. Trouble?"

"Most unlikely. Least of all not for us, and not a trap either. This pathway is obviously little used and no others have passed along it save those three and ourselves. If it were the enemy, they would be in far greater numbers."

"What now then, my Lord?" Baldred asked, coming up beside him.

"We'll take them; but no killing if we can avoid it. I doubt they'll show fight anyway, whoever they are. Well, would you when confronted by these ruffians?" he asked with a smile, looking round at his command, sitting fierce and glowering in the pouring rain. "I would sooner run than fight any day. So, come on. Let's find out who it is that dares brave the wrath of the King on such a lovely day as this!"

And, with that, they dug in their heels and flew along the narrow miry path, the shaggy hooves of their beasts lost in a welter of dark spray and far flung oozy filth.

It was a wild ride that made each man want to shout and shake his spear arm in the air, despite the rain; the sudden release after days of painful, sludging progress a swift tonic that forced the blood through their bodies in a surging torrent. The sheer exhilaration of the ride driving each man to be the first to spot their quarry, and reap the quiet praise of their leader.

Along the sodden track they went at breakneck speed, their horses' heads stretched out in their efforts, nostrils thrown wide and eyes staring, while the foam from their snorting mouths flecked their riders like the salt spume from a curling roller on a storm-wracked shore, and their tails streamed out behind them.

Careering round first one corner and then another, they covered a half hours' journey in just a few minutes, and burst upon their startled prey like eagles, with talons stretched and curved beaks ready to rip and tear.

There were three of them.

One was mounted on a powerful bay in riveted mail byrnie and mail-clad chausses, shield and spear across his back, and nut-shaped helm on his head with a silver crest, and incised face plates hanging open. Cloaked and spurred, he forced his horse backwards, making no move to draw his sword, while the two men with him on foot, with wooden staves and mud-stained cloaks, threw themselves face down on the muddy path with cries of terror.

Wrenching his mount's head up, Heardred brought his whole column to a plunging halt, then sat his steaming horse with hands crossed upon his pommel while Siward and two others leapt at the mounted warrior and dragged

19

him, unresisting, from his prancing steed, taking his helm from his head as they did so, and gripping him firmly by arm and shoulder so that he could in no way reach his weapons.

"And who are you to come so boldly into Saxon lands?" Heardred growled down at him, as his men held their captive motionless before him, hard eyes staring into hard eyes, with not a flicker of anxiety or fear to betray the stray warrior's thoughts. "A warrior by all you carry with you," he added, pointing to the man's sword and waving his helmet at him that Siward had handed over. "Come now, your name and whom you seek, and I warn you to be careful how you answer. We have learned not to be too particular with prisoners for whom we have no care."

"Tell your guards to leave me be," the man replied smoothly, shrugging his wide shoulders in their grip. "I am a freeborn Saxon, as you seem to be yourself. And who are you to lay hold of peaceful travellers? Is it forbidden for a man to ride through Wessex that he needs must be arrested and questioned by any who may seek to say him nay?"

"Release him, Siward," Heardred gestured as he spoke, leaning back in his saddle, his eyes still fixed on the armoured man before him. "But watch him like a hawk! Now, friend, see, my men have stood you clear. They have even left you your sword and seaxe in your belt..."

"Still I have not your name," the tall Saxon warrior interrupted grimly, gesturing with his hands. "Nor your business in these parts, where Danes ride free and many Saxon lords support them!"

"I am the Lord Heardred of the Somerseatas, and I ride for the King."

"Which king?" the man replied swiftly with a barking laugh. "There are two kings in Wessex now so I hear!"

"For the true King," Heardred snarled back, his hand flashing to his sword hilt. "For Alfred of the right line of Cerdic. Seize him, Siward!" he ordered sharply, waving his men back towards the big Saxon standing stiffly before him. "You are too bold and peremptory for my liking, Saxon. Watch your tongue or I may order it plucked out before it wearies me completely!"

"Call off your hounds, Heardred of the Somerseatas," the man replied, leaping back and drawing his sword. "You have no cause to fear me and I have no wish to test the mettle of my sword in the flesh of those I come to seek. My name is Aldhelm, and I am sent by Leofric Iron Hand, Lord of Wimborne, with a message for the King. I have it here against my chest with orders from my Lord to hand it only to the King himself. Now, for pity's sake, grant me safe conduct, that we can all end this charade and get out of the rain! My belly cleaves to my backbone, and I am as sapless as a pine in high summer!"

20

Heardred laughed and flung himself out of his saddle, tossing his reins to one of his men as he did so. Casting his arm across Aldhelm's shoulders he walked the big Saxon warrior across to where his own horse was standing, now quietly pulling at the drenched tussocks of grass that were growing nearby.

"So, you are from Leofric. And despite the rain are parched for a good clack of ale."

"Does it always rain here? I have never known it so wet."

"More often than many realise. And when it's not falling on you from above, you are soaking it up underfoot. In Athelney we are surrounded by meres and marsh water on every side. Here, have a stoup of this," he said, pulling a leather flask from his belt. "It is a fierce spirit the people make from barley in the autumn time. It will put fresh heart in you. Especially on so dreich a day as this," he added, looking round with a shrug of his shoulders. "I am sorry about our brisk welcome. We do not have open arms for strangers in these parts, as you may have guessed."

"You are wise to be careful, "Aldhelm replied, drinking from the flask that Heardred had handed him, gasping as he did so, while the Saxon war-leader grinned at him. "By Saint Cuthbert that *is* warming! Just the thing on so miserable a day. How far from here to the king?"

"Two days' journey at the least. The paths are difficult to follow even for those who know them, and after this rain many may have disappeared, forcing us to cast around for another way forward. Is your leader still being successful?" Heardred asked as they came up to his horse. "You are not the first of the Iron Hand's messengers to reach the King. We heard about Bath, that made good reading for Alfred. He needs to know that not all his people have deserted him."

"Bath was a triumph. We put down two crews, and took much silver. It is all in Leofric's report. We pulled a rare trick on them there."

"Ah, yes," Heardred agreed. "The traitor Gytha and her wretched husband; all that reached us too. Swindon instead of Bath…that must have made Oscytel really grind his teeth!" and they both laughed at the thought of the Jomsviking leader's rage at being so neatly duped. "No wonder Leofric had to move his base, and all his people. Did that go well?"

"Not smoothly, but efficient. The people's column was attacked by a notorious band of wolfsheads. But they had bitten off more than they could easily chew and we cut them to pieces."

"Many losses?"

"Not amongst the column. Some injuries, but we lost no-one, except a handful of goats! And since getting there everyone has worked hard to turn the

Rings into a proper fortress. The folk from the town as well. You would be amazed."

"And the Lord Leofric?"

"When I left him he was preparing to rough up the enemy some more. Just to keep them on their toes," he added with a deep chuckle. "We have been pressing the bastards fiercely. Especially the Jomsviking's king, the Lord Oscytel."

"The Black Jarl of Helsing?" Heardred queried, astonished. "He is a perilous man by all accounts, and his troops are the most brutal. But if you can hit him hard, that will put a real dent in those bastards' confidence...and in their king, Guthrum. And that is what Alfred needs the most. But I am sure he will tell you all that himself when you get to Athelney."

"Since January we have put down many of his best crews, burned their barracks and their toll houses, taken their silver, which Leofric is hoarding for the King, slain their messengers and generally made their lives as wretched and fearful as possible. In fact we made the area too hot to handle safely, just another reason Leofric has moved all his people up to Battlesbury Rings above Warminster."

"So, many crews and their captains. That is excellent, Aldhelm. Alfred will be delighted to learn all the details, especially of Leofric's move to Warminster. And what of the Skald, Grimnir Grimmersson?"

"He is safe. Or was when I left, and still keeping his eyes and ears open in the King's Hall in Chippenham. There is much to tell."

"I am sure there is, and a rare tale at that. But we must move on. What about these two poor devils here who have guided you? The people around are good friends to us. They give us warning when danger lurks, and have never failed to provide for us when we have needed it. The King has a fine tale to tell of that himself! In return we give them protection and fresh meat when we can get it. Truly there is more grit in them than in a duck's gizzard!" And both men laughed, the sound seeming thin in their surroundings, while the two hapless peasants whom Aldhelm had persuaded to guide him, stood close by looking fearful.

"Away with you, my friends," Aldhelm said then as he sat once more astride his horse. "You have served me well, and I am grateful. Here," he added, tossing each a coin, "a silver penny for your pains, and never say a Saxon warrior does not pay his dues!"

And with a final stricken glance over their shoulders they turned and fled away down the track as fast as their clogs would carry them, the raucous laughter of Heardred and his troopers following them. Such fierce men were beyond their understanding. They were just pleased to have escaped with their skins intact and real money in their pouches. Let others fight the heathen pirates. They were borel folk, happy to be left to their plodding oxen and their eel traps.

And so Heardred and his men left that place and turned their faces towards the crude earthen ramparts of Athelney. That simple gated enclosure surrounded by the endless waters and deeply sodden reed beds of the rivers Tone and Parrett, with its deep ditches, stout palisade of logs and brushwood that were all that stood between the last true King of Saxon England...and his Viking enemies.

Chapter Two

*T*wo days' hard travel it took them, though the actual distance was not great. The streams and rivers, swollen from the heavy rains that had fallen in the distant hills, made their passage difficult, and with so many horses they could not travel by punting barge or reed-raft, but must seek out the secret corded trackways that criss-crossed the mire, often just below the surface. But with the weather finally clearing from the west, and a stiff drying wind blustering in their weary faces, they finally reached firm ground again without mishap. Their tired beasts as anxious as they were themselves to reach the shelter and dry straw bedding that the royal outpost offered them, before the short spring day ended.

They were first spotted by hidden watchers along the reeded causeways that led onto the island itself, their chirping bird calls taken up and passed on before them. Thus by the time they approached the great ditches that guarded the entrance itself, the King was by the gateway to see them home, Queen Ealhswitha by his side, and some half dozen of his royal companions clustered round them.

Alfred had changed greatly since Aldhelm had seen him last at Wareham in '75, before his own steading had been burned down and his family slain, when he had thrown in his lot with Leofric, and gone north into Mercia to make his fortune. And it was seven years since the Saxon host had slaughtered the Danes at Ashdown, and the year of battles in '71.

At Ashdown Alfred had been a young warrior of twenty-four summers with few cares, the Aethling not born to rule; the youngest of four grown princes of the right line of Cerdic. A prince who had followed his royal brother, King Aethelred, with a true heart...and a mind full of strange thoughts and outlandish notions. A prince who had been consecrated by the Pope in Rome, when he had travelled there with his father as a small boy.

At Ashdown the King had been a slender young man with an interest in books and music and the laws of the ancients, and a determination to learn to read and write both Saxon and Latin so that he could study further and understand more. He had a love of learning that had been with him since he was very little, garnered from his mother, the saintly Queen Osburgh, who had promised a beautifully illuminated book to the first of her children who could recite its poems.

24

Now he was King and a proven warrior in his thirty-first year, his body thickened and filled out with hard riding and warlike exercise…and wracked with pains that griped in his bowels at times so badly he could hardly walk. A travail he had not had in his younger years. And though his neatly clipped beard and honey-coloured hair were still unmarked by the grey streaks that men of his age so often carried, the long years of constant warfare, struggle, disappointment and pain had left him with deep lines across his face that often made him look sterner and more forbidding than he really was.

Yet when he laughed and smiled his blue eyes sparkled with merriment and the years of toil would slough away. He loved the chase, and could wield both sword and axe with a vengeance. He was a man for whom warriors tramped miles to join his standard, and he venerated the church for its learning and its vision for which the bishops loved him and gave him their support. He was a true Christian prince, who cared for his people in every way; who fought his enemies with determination…and a complete conviction that, with God, he would triumph over them, and bring their leaders to Christian baptism.

It was good to be near Alfred, if unsettling, for his confidence in the face of awful danger was infectious, his knowledge and learning startling, and his observance of Christian ritual an intimate part of his life. But no man could be in his company long and not warm to him. Even the heathen pirates respected him, though they would not hesitate to slay him if they could, as he was the one thing that stood between them and total conquest of the rich, fertile island they had coveted so long.

"Welcome back, my Lord Heardred!" he called out, striding from amongst his hearth companions, his hands out in greeting. "You have been looked for all day. My lady was becoming fearful for your safety! And I see you have a stranger in your train," he continued, giving Aldhelm a piercing look, his eyes missing nothing of the big Saxon warrior's face and armour, and the quality of the horse he rode.

"Yes, my Lord King. It was he of whom that report spoke," Heardred replied, swinging down off his jaded mount to greet his King on bended knee, while the rest of his troop, bowing their heads, rode on through the open gateway into the wide enclosure beyond.

"We came upon him two mornings since, away on our northern flanks, a day's ride from Aller. His name is Aldhelm," he added, standing again and pointing to where the big Saxon was now off his horse and kneeling before his King. "He comes from Leofric Iron Hand, the Lord of Wimborne, with a closed message," he went on quickly in answer to Alfred's swiftly raised eyebrow at Leofric's title. "He will not say what is in it, but insists on presenting it to you personally."

25

"So," Alfred said heavily, indicating Aldhelm to rise, as the horses were led away, and his royal companions clustered round them both. "You come to me from Leofric. What manner of man are you who rides with a renegade wolfshead?"

"I am a Dorset man, my Lord King, from one of your late brother's estates near Shaftesbury, and a true Saxon. I fought in your brother's host at Ashdown in '71 when we broke the enemy's shield wall and chased the Heathen back to Reading. Then my home was burned and my family slain when Oscytel and his Jomsvikings sacked and brutalised Wareham in '75. That was when I joined Leofric. But he is no wolfshead, my Lord King," he added, looking straight into Alfred's eyes. "He is a man after your own heart. A loyal Saxon in all he does, and a fine leader of men. But after he had been betrayed and demonised by Aethelwold…and cast off by you, my Lord King," he went on without flinching. "We left Wessex for a while and went and fought your enemies in the north, in Danish Mercia, and gained much booty."

The men around them shuffled their feet at mention of Alfred's nephew, and the shaming of Leofric of Wimborne, and growled, as all knew Aethelwold to be venal and untrustworthy, lusting after his uncle's crown. They were frustrated that the King would do so little to bring the young man before his court and charge him with his many crimes.

Alfred stilled them with a gesture, and glancing at his wife, stepped back to look at Aldhelm again, standing straight and firm before him. His eyes running over the big Saxon warrior, noted the fine workmanship of his shield and body armour, and the Danish artistry about his long sword and nasal helmet with its incised cheek plates and silver boar's crest. These were fine weapons. He doubted whether he now owned any himself that were so finely wrought and decorated.

And he was intrigued.

He had heard much of Leofric Iron Hand since fleeing Chippenham, both from the messages that had reached him at Athelney from the renegade's own hand, and from those from the Norse Skald, Grimnir Grimmersson, his secret man within king Guthrum's court. A mightily skilled harper who knew Leofric well, and was the Saxon war-leader's eyes and ears around that area also…but he was Alfred's man first, before he threw in his lot with Leofric.

He paused then to look at the simple buildings within the palisaded enclosure that surrounded them, and away across the watery wastelands beyond towards the distant sea, and grunted.

Box, Bradford on Avon, Malmesbury, Melksham…Bath, all Danish outposts put to the sword by this same Iron Hand; their garrisons and messengers slain, their silver taken, their barracks burned, their confidence

26

shattered. Leofric's men had put the fear of the gods into the heathen around Chippenham, and beyond; encouraged the men of Wessex everywhere that the enemy could be made afraid...could be defeated. Leofric's activities had forced Guthrum to draft in more men from other parts of the Saxon lands he had seized to fill the places of those who had been slain. It thinned out the Danes' forces, and made Alfred's own activities in the land of the Somerseatas ever more successful.

Yes! Leofric Iron Hand, the former Lord of Wimborne before he was denounced, was living up to his name. Proclaimed 'Wolfshead' before the big Danish push into Wessex had forced himself and his family to flee to Athelney, Leofric had been named *Traitor* and *Nithing*. Details he should have questioned, if it hadn't been that Wulfhere, the Ealdorman of Wiltshire, had supported them...and look what a traitorous bastard he had turned out to be!

Alfred grunted again at the remembrance of Wulfhere's treachery that winter, and shook his shoulders, making his long cloak ripple. Leofric, a seeming brutish renegade, so he had been told, who usually fought as a mercenary for plundered money...now strove for a King whom many people had deserted. Some paying tribute to the enemy, some fled abroad and others, like Wulfhere, convinced the Saxon cause was lost, had shamefully joined with Guthrum to increase their lands and titles at the expense of others.

But Leofric Iron Hand fought the Heathen wherever they could be found, and fought them with more dash and cunning than many who had served in the Royal warband before that fatal Christmas. And none was the act of a traitor, or a dishonoured war chief. Rather they were acts of daring and high courage that should be well regarded.

He was intrigued, and smiled, while Aldhelm stood his ground beneath his King's hard scrutiny, and Alfred's royal companions stood back and talked softly amongst themselves and with the queen, all used to their Lord King's thoughtful pauses.

Alfred's face twisted as his bowels griped him, then smiled as only he could.

This Leofric must be a remarkable man indeed who could inspire such loyalty amongst his followers. And Danes fought beside him too, against their own people...Christian and pagan Danes together, so it was said. It was a strange story, but one to which he felt warmly drawn. The thought of this unsung war-leader, with his motley crew of Saxon and Danish warriors hunting down their enemies like rats in a grain store filled him with glee, his face suddenly flushed by the risks they were taking for him, a King whom they must earlier have learned to avoid like marsh fever!

He smiled again, and beckoned Aldhelm to him.

"Come. You have nothing to fear from me. We need every man we can find, especially one who comes so well appointed, and mounted," he added, looking to where Aldhelm's and Heardred's horses were now being led away. "You have a message for me, I understand," he continued, holding out his hand. "I am impressed that your Lord can read and write. There are many of my companions who do not have those skills," he added, waving his arms about him. "Tell me," he went on, taking the rolled parchment that Aldhelm handed over to him, and breaking its seals, "what manner of man is this Leofric of whom we hear such tantalising news? Look at you. You could take your place at the fore point of the royal war band itself. You carry enough valuable war gear to make yourself a thegn…yet you choose to serve a wolfshead," he said pausing briefly, "rather than your own true King!"

"My Lord King, we are all wolfsheads in England this day," Heardred gently interrupted him. "The true King lives like a bog-wight skulking in the marshes, his kingdom an island in a reeded sea, and his loyal subjects a small handful of lunatics who refuse to give up the flame of freedom for the iron chains of Danish servitude!"

Alfred stopped in his tracks, and throwing back his head he laughed.

"Well said, my friend! A royal rebuke indeed, and you are right of course. We *are* all wolfsheads, right down to the queen herself and the children. Well, Heardred, it is time the wolves banded together and showed their teeth, and more fiercely than we have ever done before. Our attacks against the Heathen, and those of others across Wessex, like Leofric, and your friends Edwin and Harold, have shown that the enemy can be beaten. They give heart to everyone.

"Come, Aldhelm; we will talk this matter out over a hot meal and some fresh ale. Cooked by the Lady Ealhswitha's own fair hand no less, with the help of those handmaids who have come in to her since we fled Chippenham, she has surpassed herself.

"I will read this before I join you at the table," he went on, waving the open parchment in his hand, clapping Heardred on the back as he spoke. "It is real pot luck for us these days," he added over his shoulder with a chuckle as he strode away. "I only hope you enjoy fish as much as we have come to do," he ended with a mock grimace. "But it is Lent now, and a Friday, and if anyone must keep the Christian traditions going it has to be the King!"

As Alfred turned away, followed by a handful of his closest advisors, Heardred and Aldhelm continued forward to where a crude hall had been thrown up around a series of great timbers, hauled with enormous effort from the distant forests, and thatched with thick bundles of reeds and deep cut turves. Together with a collection of smaller buildings for kitchens, brew house, stables and storage, it was the centre piece of Athelney. Here the Queen waited to welcome her husband's guests with a gilded bowl of spiced ale, and a brilliant smile that quite took Aldhelm's breath away.

She may well have been dressed in a thick woollen dress of russet brown, with a greasy leather apron that would not have disgraced a butcher, but her wimple was of spotless white linen, held with a circlet of gold, her cloak was of supple wolfskin, and she carried herself with the easy grace and assurance that came with the noble station to which she had been born, and he was captivated.

Taking the silver bowl in two hands each man drank, bowed their heads to their queen and went inside, all blinking like owls in bright sunlight to accustom themselves to the dimly lit, smoke-filled interior, of the King's hall on Athelney.

Outside the sky was clearing fast, the rich after-glow from the vanished sun painting the darkening heavens with broad swatches of brilliant red and gold, edging the fat clouds that sailed there with deep imperial purple. Along the ramparts, where armed guardians paced with spear and shield, the dying light cast stark silhouettes against the glowing background, while skeins of duck and goose flighted with a rush and whistle onto the waters that surrounded them. Then horns blew, the gates were closed...and Athelney was secured for another night.

Chapter Three

Within the long building itself the fire smoked abysmally, billowing down from the draught-hole in the roof so that there was almost as much of it within the great room as there was escaping. Here there were servants to fetch and carry, garnered from the villages of East Lyng and Athelney, but not many, for this was a fighting outpost where those not on guard or seeing to the horses and assorted war-gear, shared out the menial duties amongst themselves. Not even the presence of the King and the royal family of Wessex made much difference, for there could be no ceremony under such Spartan conditions, only mutual co-operation and understanding.

So, after the King's grace had been spoken by Father Conan, Alfred's mass priest, the meal all had been waiting for began. While some companions, seated on crude stools and benches at rickety trestles, filled their beakers from leather jacks, brimming with ale, from the great barrels that had come in that day, others scooped up their food from their wooden platters with coarse bread and greasy fingers. The King alone was served his fish stew, thick with barley grains and simple herbs and leeks, by hand from an old cook-pot that hung leerily on chains from an iron tripod above the fire, and ate with a simple wooden spoon.

Finally, when the serving women had cleared away and retired with the royal children, the queen remaining by her husband's side, and those whose good opinion the King most desired had also eaten and drunk their fill, Alfred brought the discussion to a head.

"This message you have brought me, Aldhelm, is vital news," he said, bringing out the rolled parchment Leofric had sent him. "Three hundred pounds' weight of silver from Bath alone, and an army building around him at Battlesbury. He says more men are coming in to him every day and they are running out of iron pigs to make more weapons."

"And I have this from Grimnir, who is still safely embedded with the Danes," he went on, producing another short roll of parchment. "He says that Guthrum is preparing for a new push into Wessex this spring; that he has Oscytel's men under his hand as well, and that all Leofric's attacks have made the Danes wonder whether their god, Odin, is losing his power.

"Certainly they have renewed their attacks on our churches and our priests. And while that is bad for our people, it shows that the Danes are afraid of the message the Church teaches. This message is one more thread in the tapestry I have been stitching since my own campaign against the enemy began. One thing is certain, your leader believes in killing Danes, no matter whom he may have in his warband!"

"Leofric believes in a free Wessex, as you do, my Lord King," the big Saxon warrior replied firmly, his eyes fixed on the King's. "He believes in always fighting the enemy and never giving in. The Lord Oscytel particularly," he added through gritted teeth. "He is committed to that man's overthrow and death, for all his wickedness and brutal murdering ways!"

"The blood eagle?" Alfred queried heavily.

"Yes, my Lord King. That which Guthrum banned after Wareham, and which the Black Jarl has continued to use with impunity. Truly he is an evil monster who needs to be put down like a foaming dog. It is his men, his Jomsvikings, whom we have harried with all ferocity and cunning. Cut them down without mercy; sent them howling in fear from the battlefield."

"Many crews?"

"Yes, my Lord King. Many crews. And much silver has been gathered, and gold, that my Lord, Leofric, is holding for you in his treasury," and all the men there gasped or shuffled their feet, for this was news of the utmost importance as many had not been paid since Chippenham.

"So," Alfred said, looking around him and then back to Aldhelm, "your Lord stands for me and for Wessex."

"Yes, he does, my Lord King. And in the hopes that his efforts may persuade you to grant him a free pardon for the shame your nephew, and Ealdorman Wulfhere, have placed on him!"

"Aethelwold the 'Loyal'!" Heardred broke in bitterly, while those around the tables drew in their breath at Aldhelm's words. "Aethelwold and Wulfhere. Together they have brought nothing but grief. Whatever that young man touches, he turns to ashes. And Wulfhere? Guthrum would never have reached you at Chippenham, my Lord King, if that snake had not turned a blind eye to what Guthrum was up to.

"The Danes never would have reached you from Gloucester that dawn without his help, Alfred. He knew what was planned. He could have raised the Fyrd against the Heathen," he went on, almost shouting. "Instead he did *nothing!* Rode away with his household and abandoned his king to the Viking's battle-fury. I declare him Nithing! *Nithing!*" And he banged his hand on the trestle top, making everything jump.

"That young man burns with resentment that the Witan did not name him king when his father died," Ealhswitha said quietly from her stool beside her husband, putting her hand on his arm. "And ever since he has made every effort to blacken your name, my Lord. He will dabble in any lies if by so doing he can bring you harm."

"Yet he is my brother's son, my Lady," Alfred said quietly. "And I feel some guilt in the matter of my kingship."

"You were the only choice, my Lord," Ealhswitha replied firmly. "Aethelwold was only a small boy when Aethelred died. And the Danes were pressing hard."

"All men remembered how you fought at Ashdown, Lord King," Siward chipped in in his deep voice. "How your charge broke the Danish shield wall and forced them to flee the field. Like Aldhelm, I too was there, when they fled and we cut them down in their droves. Like hay beneath the scythes, their bodies lay in heaps! Your people needed a proven war-leader in those desperate days, not a boy in short coats. So the Witan chose you, and we all shouted your name and punched the air. You owe your brother's whelp nothing, and nothing he has done since has made me change my mind."

Alfred sat back at that and looked around him in the smoky air, at his wife seated beside him, her hands in her lap; at the intent faces around the table, their eyes glittering in the twisting firelight like brooding hawks in moult, waiting for his reply…and he sighed.

"I have tried to do what I can for the boy. Given him his own household and advisors to help him. Money and lands to rule over - and supported his decrees. Yet he hates me for it. Promises faithfulness on the cross and the knuckle bones of Saint Cuthbert…and yet I have sure knowledge that behind my back he plotted with that devil's hound Wulfhere, and consorts with the enemy!"

Then turning to Aldhelm, holding out his gold-rimmed horn for a refill, he asked: "What exactly was Leofric's crime, my friend? No-one has found the time to make that situation clear to me before, and with so much in turmoil within Wessex the problems of one man did not seem that important. Besides," he added with a smile, "other messengers were not so close to him as you seem to be. Come. Tell us your tale thoroughly. It seems I endorsed the Lord of Wimborne's banishment on the false word of others. Now I need to know the truth."

"Perhaps I am the best man to do that, Lord King," Siward broke in at that.

"You, Siward?" Alfred replied astonished.

"Yes, my Lord. I was in the Aethling's service at the time, and it was the reason I left him to serve the Lord Heardred."

"So?"

32

"So, a greedy noble of Lord Aethelwold's entourage coveted Leofric's father's land around Wimborne, where your late brother, King Aethelred, is buried. And in a sudden night attack this Lord and his hirelings, and some Danish mercenaries in Aethelwold's employment, slew the old man and his household, and seized the lands. When Leofric heard of this he sought redress from Aethelwold, but was jeered at, arrested and rebuffed. Furious, and black with rage and sadness, once freed, Leofric hunted down all those who had destroyed his home and family and killed them all, and seeking out Aethelwold once more, he cast all the heads he had taken across the young man's floor where he was sat at meat with his entourage."

"And for that he was proclaimed traitor, and *Nithing!"* Alfred exclaimed, appalled, his face flushed with anger. "By Saint Michael but that boy will have some answering to do when all this bloody nonsense is over. That noble who coveted the lands? Who was that?"

"One of Ealdorman Wulfhere's followers, subsequently slain in the wars. Wulfhere holds those lands now."

"No wonder he was so keen to press me for Leofric's outlawry! What a monstrous injustice has been done here, Aldhelm," the king continued, turning to where the big Saxon warrior was quietly sitting and listening. "Your Lord is just such a one as a good king needs by him. He shall have his pardon, aye and full compensation for his losses."

"The Iron Hand will be hugely pleased, my Lord King," Aldhelm replied, holding up his own drinking horn and bowing to Alfred across the table. "But that is not all that I was sent for..."

"No, indeed," the King interrupted him urgently, "for his letter also tells me what I have been waiting for, and is confirmed by an added note from Grimnir Grimmersson, that the tide is turning in our favour at last.

"The people are tired of paying unlawful tribute: of having their lands taken by Danes despite agreements made with Guthrum; of having their businesses raided and despoiled; their families torn apart on a whim; their women taken into slavery to be whored at the unbridled demand of their Danish overlords. Our people are groaning under Guthrum's yoke. They know that their King lives, and fights their enemies wherever he can find them.

"It is time to send out my summons to the muster. To call out the Fyrd from all my lands; my thegns from across Wessex and all those Saxon war-lords who have held firm to my cause since Chippenham fell to treachery and Danish steel. We will try one more throw at our enemies...and this time we shall not fail!"

It was the kind of fighting statement that they had been waiting for since first they had been forced to flee into the wilderness of the Somerseatas, and they roared their approval like the faithful hounds they were. Stamping their feet on the hard earth floor, and hammering on the tables, their raucous baying rolling round the darkened compound and even startling the horses into snorting life.

"How is it to be done, Lord?" a harsh voice shouted out from further down the board as the noise subsided. "For there are more forces poised against us than just those of Guthrum. There is Ubbi, come from Ireland into Wales with his own forces. I fear the Great Army is gathering once more against us."

"We do things with great care, Hereward the Strong!" The King replied, throwing his head back and laughing. "With great care, my Sword Guardian...and I promise to leave plenty of Danes for you to whack down with that sword you love to talk to!" he added with a smile for one of his most loyal and trusted companions. Then, after the laughter in which all had joined died away, he went on quietly: "Now, come close, my friends, and I will tell you what has to be done. What the Lord Heardred and I have planned, and what, with God's aid, will happen in the end. The sons of Ragnar Lodbrok will not defeat us again, of that I promise you!"

*

*F*or ever after that evening in the King's hall on Athelney, remained in Heardred's memory like a shining beacon. The air thick with blue wood smoke, the twisting flames from the long central fire-pit casting a ruddy glow across shadowed faces...and the tense concentration of all as the King outlined the moves he meant to make in the tricky game of cat-and-mouse he meant to play with Guthrum's and Ubbi's forces.

The eyes of all those gathered there gleamed with excitement at the prospect of fighting in the open at last. No more ambushes and skulking; no more wild hit-and-run raids and the burning of isolated outposts. This was to be war as all men understood it: the clash of sword on shield from thousands lined up to front the enemy; the stamping and neighing of war horses; the waving banners; the shouted challenges; the jeering insults and wild boasting...and the stench of fear, of loosened bowels and vomit that made up being in the shield wall, without having served in which no man could call himself a warrior.

That night the heavy rumble of male voices rose and fell in the sweated air, while the sharp tang of wood smoke was ever in their faces as the big leather jacks were passed up and down the tables, ale was quaffed and the men's armour twinkled in the firelight. Until finally Alfred sat back and grinned boyishly, his face glowing in the close atmosphere, his arms stretched out expansively as though to embrace them all.

"So, there you are. All my informants tell me the same thing, from Southampton to royal Chippenham, from Thames River to the sea: the people are ready to rise. For weeks now I have been receiving messages that resistance is growing. Ealdorman Odda of the Devonseatas will raise his forces to oppose Ubbi...and I will raise the Fyrds of Hampshire, Somerset and Wiltshire, even from Dorset if I can, though their Ealdorman lies beneath the Danish yoke...and with any others who come to join us from across Wessex, from Berkshire, Surrey, Kent and Cornwall, I will lead our men against Guthrum.

"Now is the time to act! Before their courage fades again. You all know what fyrdsmen are like, brave as lions for an hour...then, like rabbits beneath the eagle's glare, ready to run for the safety of their burrows!

"It is now the first week of March.

"Easter is on the 23rd and Whitsun seven weeks later, on the 4th of May. I will call the muster at Ecberht's stone for the Tuesday following our celebration of Whitsunday, when God gave his Holy Spirit to the apostles...the 6th of May. That should please both our Christian supporters and those who still follow the ancient gods of our people, for Tiw was ever the Saxon god of war and battle, and what could be a more appropriate day to muster against our enemies than the day given over to remember the ancient god of war?" But while all the men gathered there growled their agreement, Father Conan leapt to his feet to complain bitterly of the King's decision to mix Christian belief with that of pagan imagery.

"You insult God, with such idolatry," he said loudly, his eyes blazing. "That is not what the bishops will want to hear. They will abhor such a statement as wickedness."

"Enough!" Alfred said then, bringing his hand hard down on the table top with a resounding bang. "*Enough!* I mean no insult to God, Father," he said holding up his hand in the face of Father Conan who was forced into gobbling silence. "But my people are still struggling with which god they should worship, and I need us all to be together in this. So choosing Tiw's day for our muster against the Danish pagans seems to be small beer when judged against all the damage and fury the Heathen have brought to these lands. Yes?"

"Yes, my Lord King." The cleric replied, abashed.

"*Good!*" the King exclaimed loudly, banging his hand once more on the table top. "For you and your brethren have a long night ahead of you. I will dictate to you all that I need to say to Leofric, Lord of Wimborne, and then I want parchments prepared to send out all across Wessex, to all Ealdormen, King's reeves, shire reeves and thegns who have remained loyal to the throne. I want my words to carry all across Wessex that their King is alive and moving in the west to destroy the Viking army that has done such scathe to his people.

"Heardred, take half your men and find Leofric; Aldhelm can guide you. Warminster, and the old fortress walls of Battlesbury Rings, are not so far from here and are in our direct line of march towards Chippenham where Guthrum lurks. We must lure him out of that fortress he sits in, into the open where we can destroy him once and for all…and I have a plan for that.

"The rest of your command split up and send to Harold and Edwin in the south and order them to join with you and Leofric. You others all know to whom you are being sent. Hereward, you will stay by my side and guard my standards, the Fighting Man and the Dragon of Wessex, and where I go, go you also my friend."

"What about the queen and the children?" Siward asked him then.

"They will go under escort to the abbey at Glastonbury, and await news of our success."

"Are you so certain, my Lord King?" Father Conan asked him, quietly. "Is it not tempting fate to be so bold in the face of such enemies as the Vikings of the Great Army?"

"Yes, Father!" Alfred almost snarled at his mass priest, exasperated. "It is bold! But God brought us safely out of Chippenham, and has prospered us here mightily. Everywhere the Danes are in disarray, all my messengers say so. Guthrum bit off more than he could chew when he struck at Wessex; he doesn't have the resources to be everywhere. Had I not listened to so many smooth words from you and the bishops, and that snake Wulfhere, and kept more of my army in the field last winter, then maybe none of this might have happened," he admonished the holy Father, wagging his fingers at him as he spoke.

"But I learned a bitter lesson from that disaster last Christmas. To trust my own judgement, and believe that God *will* be with us! That we *will* triumph over His enemies, and that together we will free Wessex of the Danish ravens who flew here from Frankland thirteen years ago!"

And taking hold of his drinking horn he stood up, while the men around the table leapt up also, stools and benches flying in all directions.

"I pledge you our freedom. *Victory under God! Death to Guthrum and the Danes!*"

"Death! *Death to Guthrum and the Danes!*" came back the thunderous, roared reply. "*Victory under God!!*" feet pounding the hard earth floor, fists

36

punching the air in a wild acclamation of their King's appeal to their loyalty, and their fierce Saxon, fighting spirit.

And one by one they left for their own quarters, streaming out into the blustery night, with the north star dazzling overhead, and Orion striding across the distant black horizon, his sword hanging down by his side, his great hunting dog at his feet.

The king was indeed stirring in the west, and soon all Guthrum's host would know it.

Chapter Four

*T*hat night Heardred slept badly, tossing on his straw pallet within the confines of his narrow sleeping shelter in the King's Hall, alongside those others of Alfred's companions who were also quartered there. His mind raced though his body ached with weariness. His dreams were troubled, filled with haunted faces whose gaping mouths gibbered at him wildly, and whose pain-wracked figures twisted endlessly in space. And by the image of Brioni calling his name in screaming desperation, begging for him to save her; while all around dark figures in black armour advanced upon her with swords and axes.

He awoke drenched in sweat on the floor, shouting out "No! No!" His coarse blankets bunched about his feet, his wolfskin cloak cast awry, and sitting up he held his head between his hands and moaned her name. Despite all the months since she had died, still she called to him when things were difficult; when he felt lonely, tired and weary. If only he had left for Foxley earlier; if only the weather had not been so bad; the Danes not so determined or well led! *Oscytel!!* That black-hearted bastard!

He cursed and held his head.

He should never have drunk so much; it felt as if all the blacksmiths on Athelney were hammering iron in his head. Guthrum, Oscytel, the Danes…it seemed at times like these that there would be no escape from it all - ever! And rubbing his eyes with his palms and fingers to remove the sleep, he reached for the water jar that stood close by and drank deeply, before tipping the remainder over his head.

He and Alfred had stayed up into the small hours, marked by the King's famous candle clocks, long after all the others had left for their pallets, deep in deliberations for the coming campaign. Poring over the many messages that had flooded into Athelney from those loyal thegns who had remained on their estates, digesting the information sent in by Alfred's spies from all over Wessex and working out the moves necessary to bring the Danes to battle.

Nor was it only the problems of supply, weaponry, numbers and horses, for Guthrum also had been gathering his power. Some crews had come in to him from Frankland. Not many yet, but with the spring now upon them, soon the sea lanes would be open and hundreds of war boats would flood in to England's shores. And, as Hereward had said, there was now the problem of Ubbi Lodbroksson! Not only was the main Danish host poised in Chippenham, and growing, as more men marched in from every far flung outpost…but King Ubbi, the sole surviving son of the mighty Ragnar Sigurdsson, Ragnar Lodbrok, the 'Hairy breeks' of Viking legend whom King Aelle had murdered in a snake pit, had sailed to Wales from Ireland.

Twenty-three dragon boats he had brought with him, with more than fifty men in each. Twelve hundred men at least, all professionals and armed to the teeth - and they had the magic raven banner, Landravager, with them. The famous banner sewn in a single night by the daughters of the great Ragnar, and filled with Norse magic. When the banner fluttered the Vikings would win, when it drooped the Vikings would lose. It was their most potent symbol.

If those men landed on the north Devon coast, and Ubbi marched them inland towards Taunton, while Guthrum launched his attack from Chippenham, they could catch Alfred in a pincer movement and Wessex would be finished.

But there was Odda, the Ealdorman of the Devonseatas. If he, with all the Fyrd and thegns of the county could meet with Ubbi, and defeat him, and take Landravager, then that would deal a massive blow to Danish morale, and free Alfred to pounce on Guthrum's forces and wipe them out for all time.

So many 'ifs' it made his head hurt even more. No wonder Alfred had burned that poor peasant's bannocks!

*

*L*ost on a hunting expedition beyond the Burrow Mump, miles from Athelney, in filthy wet weather at the backend of January, tired, hungry and soaked through, the King had sought shelter in a woodman's little cruck house, and been taken in. Dirty and disreputable, it was a wonder the old woman living there had done so, with her man, a verderer, away in the woods minding the very deer the King and his companions were after.

And she had been baking.

Bannocks, with the last of her flour and oil, and a little salt, 'til her man could take her to the nearest market. So she had sat Alfred down by the fire to warm and dry off, and ordered him to watch the bannocks on her old griddle so they didn't burn, while she had gone out the back to do her business, and bring in some wild honey to have with the hot buns.

But Alfred, looking into the crackling fire with his mind full of Danes, Guthrum, Ubbi and Wessex, and his family in Athelney, and his hunting companions - and would anyone find him before the Danes did? Was not thinking of what he was supposed to be doing and the next thing he knew the bannocks were not just cooked…they were smoking ruins! And the old lady had come back and been furious with him: "You useless bliddy varmint! You raggle-taggle no good earsling! You just wait 'til my man gets home! He'll learn yer yer manners!" And she had taken her birch broom to his back as she drove him out of her house…and there Heardred and his men had found them both. Alfred cowering behind a small tree on the edge of the tiny garth, where the King's horse was doing its best to keep out of the way, while the old woman beat wildly at every part of him she could reach. The rain just tailing off, the bare trees round the clearing running black with water, and Heardred's men, horrified to see their King treated in so dastardly a manner, threatening to slay the old woman out of hand and burn down her cottage.

Into this her husband had walked, who recognised the King at once, having known him as a younger man, he being a verderer and guardian of the King's deer in that place. And then *he* had berated his wife, who by now was terrified, weeping and shaking as she knelt before her King and begged his forgiveness.

Alfred, of course, had smoothed everything.

Begging the old woman's forgiveness for her burned buns, he had lifted her off her knees, pressed some silver coins into her hands and kissed her cheeks. A royal kiss of peace. Told her husband to come and find him once he had been properly restored to his throne…and then mounted his horse and with a wave of his hand had ridden off with his companions, a fine deer strapped to a sturdy pack horse at the rear…the old verderer and his wife bowing them out of sight.

Heardred laughed at the memory.

Alfred had looked so stricken, and the old woman so angry, with her shouts of rage and her broomstick hitting the tree as many times as she managed to hit the King…and the wretched horse dancing around both of them. It was a wonder the old biddy had not whacked the horse as well! It had been a light-hearted interlude amidst some truly desperate deeds.

*

Now Alfred had gauged that the time was ripe to make his move. That the current of resistance was flowing strongly through the land, and that his time had come. The Saxon wolf was rising from his lair and the call to the pack was going out.

He shook the water out of his head and groaned.

It had been a long and liquid night, and his brain felt crushed by the hammering pain that filled his skull. Yet the memories of the evening still burned hotly in his mind, despite the nightmares. Especially the King's dictated pardon that he had promised for Leofric, and the additions he had made to it that had made Father Conan's quill splutter everywhere, so incensed he had been. It was not often that Alfred rode so rough-shod over the advice of his priests, and Heardred smiled at the remembrance. But that was what was so amazing about his King. You never knew what surprise he would bounce on you.

And he loved him for it.

*

*T*hree hours later, with the sun newly risen in a cloudless sky of cornflower blue, and a light wind blowing warm out of the west that rippled the watery wastelands stretched out around them, fluttering the reed beds so they bowed and swung their heads to its bluster, they were all armed and ready to leave.

Freshly mounted on sturdy beasts taken from their enemies, and with sufficient supplies on pack animals for their first day's journey, one by one they all came together. Alfgar, Edric, Baldred, Aedgar, Cynric the Tracker and all the others who had survived the journey from Foxley, and all the fighting that had followed, looked what they were: a tough, professional troop of fighting men, all with their armour cleaned and shining, their shields on their backs above their wolfskin cloaks, long swords by their sides and spears in hand.

With Aldhelm and Siward by his side, Heardred went to take his leave of his King who had come out with Father Conan and Hereward the Strong to see them on their way, all well wrapped against the early morning chill.

"So, my friend, it begins at last," Alfred said, clasping Heardred at arm's length round his armoured shoulders, his blue eyes, ever intense, fixed on the tall warrior's face. "You have been the most loyal companion these past months, and my most successful war-leader. I shall miss you greatly. Both for your friendship and for your counsel."

"No warrior could want for a finer man to serve, my Lord King," Heardred replied with his steady gaze. "You have not failed Wessex despite all that has happened, and I shall not fail you now. Look for me at Ecberht's stone on that first Tuesday after Whitsun. And you will see a greater company of fighting men than even you could hope for!"

"It will be sufficient for my needs just to see you there, Heardred," Alfred answered him with that slow crinkly smile that all men looked for from their King. "The strength of your sword arm by my side is greater security for me than a dozen warriors with axe and shield."

41

Then, turning to Aldhelm, he drew a sealed tube of scarlet leather from a scrip on his shoulder and bid him kneel, before handing it to him.

"Here is the pardon for your Lord Leofric that I promised you last night. It restores to him all that my nephew, and that treacherous weasel, Wulfhere, stole from him. In addition, and against all that my priests could say to me on the matter," he added with a nod towards Father Conan standing closeby, glowering darkly, "this pardon also confers the title of 'Royal Companion' on all who follow in his train, Christian Saxon or Heathen Dane, with full forgiveness for any fault that may have been done them during the current emergency, together with a gift of silver as compensation. I will expect to greet all of the Lord of Wimborne's men with the kiss of peace when next we meet at Ecberht's stone. 6th of May. Be there!" And he smiled at Aldhelm's confusion, the burly warrior in his shining mail, helmet in his hand, able to do no more than nod his head and give his King a beaming smile, his face flushed with pleasure, his tongue unable to form a single word.

"Just so!" the King said, reaching out to draw the man off his knees. "So guard it well, my friend, and deliver it to the Iron Hand with all the thanks and honour of a grateful King. No other man is to break the seals it carries. Now, hasten to your mount, for you have a long ride ahead of you before we meet again."

Then turning to Siward, as Aldhelm walked amazed to where his horse was being held for him, Alfred addressed Heardred's big second-in-command, with his hand on his shoulder: "Siward, watch your master's back. There is a devil rides him when the scent of battle is in the air and the war horns blow. He has not been the same since the Lady Brioni was slain. He says little, I know, but the Queen and I are sensible of his distress, for we both miss that girl as well. She was a treasure that all men loved, and her loss has been keenly felt in the royal household.

"He is a man I value most highly and you are his guardian now. Deliver him safely to me at the muster, and you shall know just how a King of Wessex rewards all those who show him faithful service.

"My life on it, my Lord King," the big man replied, colouring, bowing his head. "Reckless he is at times, our Lord Heardred, but we who follow panting in his wake all love him for it. And were I, by some mischance, to fall, then there are a dozen warriors who would gladly take my place and guard his back as well as I," and he bowed his head again.

"It is enough," Alfred said with a laugh, giving the man's armoured back a sharp buffet as he spoke. "Now, go quickly. Your Lord is mounted and eager to be on his way, and I, for one, would not wish to hold him back!"

42

So it was they all left together, two score fighting men and ten, pair by pair in tight formation, their shields on top of their cloaks, armour sparkling in the bright sunlight, clattering over the wooden trestles that bridged the great ditch before the gated entrance. Then away towards the first of the narrow causeways that led by twisted secret routes off the island, and into the haunting, swirling mists that still cloaked the marshes.

*

*B*y midday they were finally clear of the wastelands that marched along the eastern edge of Athelney and were climbing up towards the higher ground around Somerton, making the first long push towards Warminster and Leofric's camp amidst the Battlesbury Rings that reared themselves so steeply above the little town. Here Heardred called a halt to rest their mounts, pegged out to crop, while his men lounged in the midday sunshine of that bright spring day, and looked out to where the vast, watery mire they had now left behind glinted in the distance.

Then, while his command chewed on the smoked meats they had brought with them, and drank from their wineskins, he called Edric the Axeman and Alfgar to his side.

"This is where we must part company, my friends. You, Edric, will journey with your sword brother south-east towards Southampton and find the Lords Harold and Edwin, and tell them of the muster. Travel swiftly and light for speed is of the essence, and take not more than two men with you each. That way you will draw less attention to yourselves, and more people will be willing to help you. And do your best to stay out of trouble. Any more armed men and the people may flee for fear you may intend them harm."

"Do we take what we need, as is the custom when on the King's business? Or do we pay?"

"You pay! The King needs all the friends he can get, and the people of Wessex have been robbed enough by their enemies. For loyal Saxons to be no better than the Danes who have scourged them so sorely will only damage Alfred's cause, so he has given me monies from his hoard to smooth your way. And be advised," he added, seeing the swift gleam in Edric's eyes," the King will expect a close account of every penny, and woe betide you if any word gets back to me of any wrong doing! Yes?"

"Yes, my Lord!" His man replied with a twisted smile and bob of his head. "All will be well, I assure you. What of you now, Lord?"

"We go to find the Lord Leofric Iron Hand above Warminster. In the ancient fortress of Battlesbury Rings. Aldhelm says he knows the way. But I expect we will get news of the man before then. So finding a guide should not be a problem."

"What if he is not there?" Alfgar asked him quietly.

"Then, Alfgar, we will just have to search for him. These are important times, and the King needs men like Leofric and his warband. Would you care to return to his hearth-place and tell Alfred you had failed for lack of resolution? No? No more would I! So, be warned, be sure you find those two friends of mine as well. I expect nothing but the best from you.

"Now come, God speed to you both. There is no time to linger here, nor would it be safe to do so either. Search out the men you wish to go with you, and may the saints aid you. We meet again at Ecberht's stone on the 6th May…and then, with God's Will, we shall give those heathen bastards who have lorded it over our people such a lesson in Saxon warcraft that they never shall forget!"

Thus it was done, and with the breeze beginning to back round to the north-east, and the sky now feather-flecked with goose-wing streamers of fine cloud, their company broke apart. Edric, Alfgar and four others of their war band, with a nod to their leader as they rode past, struck in their heels and at a fast canter rode off towards Yeovil, Blandford and the distant sea, their horses' tails stretched out behind them as they went.

Just once they paused, standing tall in their stirrups, stark against the sky, their spears brandished in their hands, the freshening wind in their faces…then they swiftly turned and vanished from their sight, the horizon suddenly more bleak and empty for their going.

With a raised hand of his own, Heardred, with Siward and Aldhelm beside him, Cynric out in front and Baldred bringing up the rear, signalled his company back onto the trackway they were following towards Somerton.

Beyond lay Bruton where they would seek shelter for the night, and then the Deverills, where King Ecberht was used to hold his moots by the ancient stones that bore his name. Where the King's muster would be held in eight weeks' time, and the armed might of all Wessex would assemble before marching out to do battle with Guthrum for the last time. And finally to the ancient fortress of Battlesbury Rings high above the town, and the tributaries of the Wylye river that run beneath the Rings and through the small settlement of Warminster itself.

Here Leofric Iron Hand, Lord of Wimborne, had made his encampment, and Heardred couldn't wait to get there, to meet this man of whom he had heard so much, and to share his pleasure of Alfred's pardon for him and all who served with him. It would be a joyous meeting, and looking round at Aldhelm, he smiled and dug in his heels with a shout, bringing his men to the canter, their horses pushing forward hard, ears pricked, nostrils wide and snorting, clods of earth flying from their hooves as they pummelled the soggy ground with their iron shoes. It was spring, the sky was blue and the sun was shining; he was doing what he loved, with men he knew and thought well of, and in the King's service, a true 'Hound of the King', and he exulted in it.

On such a day it was good to be alive, and he led his men forward with his heart high for the first time since Foxley.

February 878: Chippenham beyond the walls.

Chapter Five

*B*rioni finally came to her senses as the big mercenary who had been carrying her flung across his shoulders, unceremoniously dumped her on the beaten earth floor of the gated compound to which she had been rushed. Immediately she was dragged back on her feet and her wrists bound behind her with strong cord that bit cruelly into her flesh, so that struggle as she might she could not free herself.

Next moment, at dagger point, she was driven towards a deep doorway at the front of the large thatched building she had been carried to. Surrounded by a simple palisade in a distant corner of the town, close to the river, it was a secure holding and well-guarded, with several armoured figures close by who hooted in derision as she was forced past them. Splattered with blood from their brutal skirmish, her captors were not gentle; pushing and sharply kicking her so that several times she fell, only to be dragged up again. Determined she would find no easy balance for either body or mind, they harried her forwards without mercy, the darkness around her lightened by a handful of flaring torches that cast wild shadows everywhere.

Down a long corridor they hustled her, past several doorways and the startled faces of a handful of servants, and one half naked girl, whose bare breasts gleamed briefly in the torchlight before she slipped back out of sight.

The next moment a pair of doors before them were flung open and she burst, stumbling, into a small, torch-lit hall, her captors driving in behind her. At the end, on a broad dais, beside a long table with a rack of candles on either side, a man in black leather, with almond eyes of steel blue, sat upright and alert in a high-backed chair. A Viking war lord with his right arm supported in a sling, his great war shield, with a gold dagger rimmed with scarlet slashing its face, on the wall behind him. A man she knew. The Jomsviking leader she had humiliated at Malmesbury; Captain Ránnulfr!

"*You!*" she exclaimed, horrified by her recognition, giving a shout of pain as her captors kicked her feet from under her; then forced her to her knees before standing back with swords drawn, their faces pale in the flickering torch and candle light.

46

"Yes, me, you little *bitch!*" the tall man replied tersely, rising from his chair and coming to the edge of the raised dais to look down at her. "*Me!*" Then, turning to the nearest of his mercenaries, he said: "I sent five of you to capture this little Saxon whore, Bjarke. Where are the others?"

"Dead, my Lord!" the big Dane replied, dropping his eyes from his master's face. "Or too injured to be worth a bronze sceatta. We had clubs, she had a short sword and knew how to use it. You told us she was just a girl, but she fought like a Valkyrie. We could not lay a hand on her until the end."

"*Three dead?*" the Danish captain exclaimed, astonished. "It seems I underestimated you," he added, stepping down off the dais to come before Brioni, now swaying on her knees, her face wincing at the tightness of her bonds. "I should have had you killed, not captured," and with careless disdain he struck her face open-handed with his left hand, so that she fell sideways onto the rush-covered floor, her feet scrabbling for purchase as she struggled to right herself. "You have given me more trouble than you can possibly know!" And ordering his men to pick her up he hit her again, the force of the blow snapping her head round, bringing tears to her eyes and smearing her cheeks with blood.

"You humiliated me at Malmesbury, and my king made a mockery of me before all my fellow captains. Since when I have had my men search for you far and wide. But no sight of you until this afternoon at the camp of the *Circus Maximus*. You should not have had your hair cut," he sneered at her, cuffing the top of her head with sudden vigour. "It has made you distinctive. And when you cast back the hood of your cape by the bear wagon, two of my men spotted you. The rest was easy."

"Not so easy, you heathen pirate!" Brioni snarled at him then, spitting blood out of her mouth. "I was not taken without a fight. Three of your men are crow's bait. Spitted, gutted and ripped by Blood Drinker. And these two would have followed them if they had not got lucky. Five to one, *captain?*" she mocked him. "Five to one...and me just a simple country girl. I hope you are proud of yourself! The mighty Ránnulfr of the Great Army...and one small Saxon girl. No wonder your king mocked you," she added with a wicked smile. "*In our army you would be fit only to stand with boys!*"

And he suddenly stiffened, flushed with violent rage, wanting to kill her there and then. To batter her face into a bloody ruin; to strip her naked and flog the skin off her back in torn ribbons!

But he could not.

Guthrum had declared her 'his meat' before all in his Great Hall. Even the Black Jarl himself could not lay his hands on her. Guthrum would not

47

allow it, and he was the High King. Nevertheless, she would be the means of re-establishing himself in the eyes of all those who mattered most to him.

He alone had captured one of the leading members of the band of marauders who had been tormenting them for weeks. The Lady Brioni of Foxley, whose home the Black Jarl had so utterly destroyed. He would be delighted to get his hands on the last member of the family who had slain his only son.

But not before he had forced her before Guthrum.

Dragged her in on the end of a leash, dressed as the whore she was, humiliated, before the High King when he returned from his visit to Cricklade. Present her before the whole Viking Council so that they could force from her the place their enemies were hiding…and the real name of the Fox who had so tormented them for weeks. Then they could destroy the Wolfshead band that had slaughtered so many of their men, and put down their leader like the rabid dog he truly was.

He stared down into Brioni's face, her blue eyes filled with defiance, and smiled. "You have no idea of the pains my Lord Oscytel can inflict on a woman," he said quietly, the candles flickering wildly behind him making the shadows dance. "He is a stark leader, ruthless. Big men have been broken by his anger; the more so as your family slew his only son. He thought he had stamped out every last one of your foul line. He will be delighted that I have found you!

"And the High King of the Danes, my Lord King Guthrum, will be just as pleased that I have found the key to unlock the gate to his direst enemies. Those Saxon marauders, and their supreme leader, who have slain so many of his crews. You will tell him what he wants to know," he said into her face with complete conviction. "His methods never fail."

"Torture me as you will, you devil's breath," she spat back at him. "I will tell you *nothing!*"

"*Nothing?* When your flesh begins to bubble, and your feet are being crushed," he added with relish, "you will tell him everything! But until then you will bide here under my guard. I have just the place for one such as you, my fine Lady Brioni of Foxley…in a locked and guarded chamber with rats for company and a hole in the ground, and be grateful that it is not the lock-up by the river's edge, where every time it rains the water floods in to keep you company. That is your level now! Later I shall send my whores to you. They can wash and primp you, for you smell like pig shit," he added, wrinkling his nose in disgust. "Rank as a stag in rut! Then they can dress you like themselves...so all can see what you truly are. Guthrum likes his whores pretty. Who knows, he might take to you despite the smell!"

48

"He would not *dare* to treat me so!" she shouted at him. "I who am close to the King…"

"What king, you *doxy?*" he roared at her, seizing her face in his big hands and shaking it violently. "There is but one king in all Wessex today, and that is Guthrum, High King of the Danes. Alfred fled his command. He is only King of the Marshes…he is the *Nithing* here, not I. His writ runs here no longer! He cannot help you. You are my prisoner, and I will relish your downfall. Were it not that Guthrum has named you his meat before his Council, and his alone, I would have brought you to my master, the Lord Oscytel, and he would have had the skin off you in ribbons. As it is, even he must obey the leader of the Great Army."

Then turning to the men who had forced her in he said: "Bjarke, you and Hakon take this creature to the upper lock-up, then free her. Make sure there is no weapon to her hand, and guard that room well. Two men outside it at all times, and choose your best. And if she escapes, know that I will see the colour of your backbones before the day is out! Now go, for I have much to do. The king returns today, and I must have word with Grimnir Grimmersson the Skald before he does so!"

And without another word the tall Viking leader stood back and watched as his men roughly dragged their struggling prisoner away, still shouting defiance.

And she was amazed!

She had quite expected to be beaten and tortured straight away. At least to be thrown in some noxious lock-up alive, even though it be with the rats that lurked everywhere, was better than that. So it seemed that Guthrum's word really was law in Chippenham, and she was to be saved until brought before him. What would happen then was anyone's guess. Ránnulfr had made it clear that foul torture was still a possibility, and the thought terrified her, making her heart and body quail. But while there was life there was always hope…and her friends were not far away. Grimnir especially would know what to do.

Soon Leofric and Hugo would also learn what had happened, and much could be done in a day; though how a rescue could be mounted in the very heart of the Danes' best armed and guarded fortress she had no idea. But she had her wits, was not to remain tied and the girls might help. Brioni of Foxley might be caged…but she was not out, not yet!

*

*R*ánnulfr was ecstatic!

For weeks he'd had his men scouring the area north of Chippenham, right to the Thames and the Vale of the White Horse, and especially the markets, as Grimnir the Skald had suggested, in the hopes that they would spot the wolfsheads who were doing so much damage to the Black Jarl's reputation, and to the fighting morale of his men. Those foxhead badges, left behind after each successful attack, had enraged everyone. And always Oscytel's men, but until Malmesbury they had not been understood.

Malmesbury!

His whole body squirmed at the memory. That fight before the burning gates: flames shooting up everywhere, the bang and crack of the timbers; the storms of arrows, the shouts and screams as his men were cut down; the terror of the animal masks their enemies wore, and those two huge hounds bounding out of the smoke, teeth bared, great bodies bristling. And himself crossing swords with the small Saxon warrior on springs, every cut and swing met by another as they had made the dance of death around each other. Then, just as he was getting on top of his enemy at last, the numbing shock of that arrow through his right shoulder. Hurling him to the ground, the pain excruciating, disabling him completely…would have done so for anyone, no matter what Guthrum had said about it.

Then the total shock of the realisation he had been fighting a girl! Unheard of except in the myths of his people, and the pantheon of their gods. Blade for blade she was as good as many in the Danish host that he could name, but he could have taken her, he knew it, but for the arrow through his shoulder. At close range it had knocked him flying, and she had been so contemptuous, and forthright about the curse she had laid on the Lord Oscytel, with the very hounds of Ragnarok at his throat.

Even now, despite a bloodied face, and the threat of torture, she was no less defiant. She intrigued him…and she was so lovely. Were it not for the war, he would be pleased to have taken her for himself. Beornwyn and Merwenna were pretty enough, but they were common gulls to the Lady Brioni's falcon. A Gyr falcon from the frozen north, all white feathers and the fierce talons of an eagle.

He laughed.

If that were ever so he would need to watch her like a hawk, for she would stab him as soon as look at him for certain. And he wondered to whom she looked for love and comfort since her family had been destroyed by the Lord Oscytel. He had not been there on that day, but he had heard all about it. How her father, too, had cursed Oscytel even as his living body was being butchered.   And then had come the foxhead badges, the attacks on their outposts and the deaths of his crews. So that some now said the Black Jarl's days were numbered. That *Sica* was losing its power.

Sica, the Lord Oscytel's jade green knife in its golden handle.

He knew the stories that surrounded that stone blade, and the hairs on his arms and neck bristled. But such power was not for him. His gods were simpler. But then maybe Guthrum was right? Maybe the Christ god was more powerful than Odin? Despite the priests they had killed and the churches they had burned, somehow they had not yet managed to stamp out the people's beliefs. Nor would they as long as their King was still alive, and still fighting! As long as the wolfsheads were still being successful. As long as people like the Lady Brioni and the Fox who led them all were able to defy their enemies, Saxon resistance to the Danes would carry on.

He ground his teeth and snorted.

Well, he had her trapped and disarmed, and would parade her before his king this very night. One of the wolfshead's leaders. He would show Guthrum that he was a fit warrior to lead a royal Danish battle group. When the horns blew at the feast's end, and after the entertainment that the *Circus Maximus* always performed, he would drag in his captive and surprise the king. Then Guthrum could determine her end. He might take her amongst his own whores, to be whipped and branded as he pleased…or even give her to him as a slave, as a fit reward for his diligence and determination. But not until they had wrung the knowledge from her they so wanted. After which she might be worth no more than a slashed throat!

He hoped not, for the capture of the Lady Brioni of Foxley, wolfshead leader and enemy of the Danes, was an event to be savoured. A dish to make the mouth water, and he intended to enjoy every mouthful of her defeat!

*

*O*nce out of the hall, Brioni was marched once more at dagger point back down the passage-way she had been driven up before, past where she had seen the half-naked woman, and down a narrow flight of wooden stairs to a wide holding area lit with resin torches in iron sconces around which there were a series of storage rooms, one of which was used as a lock-up.

With a grunt the big mercenary, Bjarke, who had carried her away from the skirmish, sliced through the cord binding her wrists, and opened a heavy door with an iron grille in it. And while Hakon placed a candle stub that he had been carrying in a tin holder on a low shelf just inside, Bjarke flung Brioni into the lock-up.

"That's it, you stinking bitch!" he growled, looking down at her as she rubbed her wrists where the cords had bitten her. "And after what you did to my mates," he added, giving her a swift kick, "this is better than you deserve. I wish we had pummelled you harder. But orders is orders. We were told not to break your bones, or your head. Just seize you and bring you here. And no-one breaks the captain's orders!" And bending down he dragged her up and threw her roughly onto a narrow wooden pallet that lay along one side of the lock-up.

"That's me done with you for the time being, my fine Lady," he sneered with a mocking bow. "Proper facilities too," he added pointing with a snort of laughter to a stinking hole in the ground at the back of the room full of flies. "A real croucher! Can't wait to see what those two bitch-whores of the captain do with you. You look as if you'd clean up pretty...and Guthrum likes his whores pretty!" and wracked with laughter, he and Hakon slammed the door shut and left.

*

*A*lone in the darkness, lit only by the candle stub Hakon had left her, and stray torch light through the grille in the door, Brioni sank down onto the edge of the pallet, with its thin straw mattress and soiled blanket, and looked around her with a sinking heart. The room was not big enough to swing a cat in. Beaten earth floor with that noxious hole in one corner, a crude pitcher of stale water, the narrow pallet on which she was seated and the shelf on which Hakon had placed the candle, that also held a simple horn beaker. Nothing else, and putting her hands over her face she rocked herself and cried.

Outside, two men were placed on guard who grunted, farted and moaned as soldiers do, while inside Brioni dried her tears and did her best to wash her face and wrists with some of the water from the stone pitcher, having first removed the cobwebs she found around it and that festooned the corners of the room.

What had the captain said?

That he would send his whores in to wash and prepare her for appearing before the Danish king, Guthrum...and that nothing would be done to her until Guthrum had decided. Especially not by Oscytel! And she thanked all the saints for that. For if the Black Jarl ever got his hands on her she would be dog's meat! What he had started at Foxley would be finished in Chippenham, of that she had no doubt.

So, she was safe for the time being. No time to enjoy the luxury of any more tears. She must prepare herself for the next ordeal, which would be her presentation before the Viking king and his council...dressed as a whore, her body open to their view! How humiliating that would be, especially with her short hair that all would think was an abomination. No pure woman cut her hair short. Long hair was a sign of virtue; short hair a sign of vice. Her mother would have been appalled. She was damned before she ever set foot inside the king's hall.

And what of Leofric? What would he say? What would he be doing now? And despite herself, the tears welled up in her blue eyes and she choked. If ever she needed his strong arms around her it was now. But he was preparing to leave that morning for the attack on Bath...just as she was supposed to be leaving with both villages for the ancient earth fortress of Battlesbury Rings.

How could things have gone so wrong?

She thought about Hugo and Grimnir...and Godric and the message about Swindon, and Ford. Surely someone would do something to help her - but what, and how? So many thoughts raging through her head, and still no solutions. And could Ránnulfr's women, who were to prepare her for her entrance to Guthrum's Hall, be persuaded to help her? Could they get a message out to Hugo, or even to Grimnir, to let people know where she was and what was planned for her? And would there be time?

She sat on the edge of the mouldy straw mattress and buried her face in her hands. If anything this was worse than Foxley. There she had at least been in the open with weapons to her hands. Here she was trapped, entirely in the hands of others, with no form of defence, and she shouted her fear and frustration to the world, hammering the floor with her feet, until the men outside roared back at her and banged the door with sudden rage.

Chapter Six

*F*ord.

And Cadoc's stumbling arrival on Charlie from Biddestone, without the others, caused a wild upheaval in the crowded steading, with shouts of dismay, people running to support him and Trausti swiftly striding off to find Leofric and Beornred. Hannes, standing nearby, helped him off his horse, while Aelfrid and Osburgh led the little Welshman inside the house place, where they sat him down by the fire, with a beaker of mulled ale, and Alfweald's wife, Ethelinda, ran for a cold compress for his head, where Gytha had struck him with the skillet.

"What has happened, Cadoc?" Aelfrid, the tall Headman's wife, asked him anxiously. "And where are the others?" she pressed him moments later as the hall swiftly filled with people: Finnar, Raedwald, Arnwulf the farrier and Sigweald among many others. Indeed, most of Leofric's war band who were quartered in Ford, along with others from Slaughterford and along the valley, swiftly crowded in so that the Welsh bowman was soon surrounded.

"Where's Leofric, bach?" he asked Finnar urgently. "I must speak with him at once."

"I am here, Cadoc," came a deep voice as Leofric pushed through the crowd around the fire. "What has happened? Where are Brioni and Jaenberht?" And pointing to the bulging wound on the archer's head, now covered with a linen cloth dripping ice cold water: "Who attacked you?"

"Look you, my Lord," Cadoc said in his lilting voice, peering up into Leofric's face. "I would rather not say in this crowd. It is harsh news, Lord. News you might rather hear alone."

The big Saxon war-leader drew in his breath sharply and looked at his injured man in silence, his head slightly cocked to one side as he thought hard on what Cadoc had said. Then, with a sudden jerk, he straightened and said with quiet intensity: "*Gytha!*"

"Yes, Lord...Gytha!" Cadoc answered softly.

"Sweet Jesus, it would have to happen now. I had hoped to defer this until after Bath, at Warminster. Now is the very worst time of all. Beornred, bring me Cuthbert," he ordered sharply, over his shoulder. "Anyway you please, but bring him to me now!"

"Now, Leofric? Are you sure?" his big second queried, looking round at everyone.

"Yes, my friend. This boil has to be lanced tonight, and all the pus squeezed out. Ethelinda, bring me my big scrip from our room. Hurry now, girl," he called after her running figure, "there is no time to waste."

"What is this about Cuthbert?" Aelfrid asked urgently, standing up to face Leofric, her eyes wide with sudden fear. "And I heard you mention his wife, Gytha. What have they done, that you should order my son's immediate arrest. *Eadwine, come to me now!*" she called out wildly to her husband, as he entered the crowded room. "There is trouble, and I need you. Cuthbert needs you." And clutching at the rangy Headman's arm as he came up beside her, their eldest son, Alfweald, close behind, she waited for Leofric's response.

"I had hoped to spare you all this until we had all moved up to Battlesbury Rings," he said steadily, looking at both of them. "But what Cadoc has said now makes that impossible."

"But he has said nothing," she railed at him. "Just spoken Gytha's name."

"What has that got to do with Cuthbert?" Eadwine asked sharply, as Beornred returned with the young man, forcing him through the crowd into the space that Leofric had now created. "What has he done that you should treat him so harshly, and in his own home?"

Leofric looked at them both and sighed deeply. They were good people and had served him and his warband well, with courage and willing determination. The rotten apple in their barrel was the last thing anyone needed.

"There is no easy way to say this, Eadwine, but your son and his wife have been dealing secretly with the Danes to bring them down upon us all here. They are both traitors! He and his wife, Gytha. Both together!"

"*No!*"

"*Yes!* They have been dealing with the Danes behind our backs. Sending secret messages to Guthrum through Godric the Cobbler...or have tried to do so."

"The man she was to marry, before I arranged things for Cuthbert?" Eadwine asked fiercely.

"Yes. With whom she cuckolded Cuthbert underneath his nose every time she went up to Biddestone market. That's what they had such a fight about the other evening up by the cow byre."

"*No!*" Cuthbert shouted out then, struggling beneath Beornred's hands. "*No!* She swore that nothing had ever happened between them..."

"You knew about her and Godric?" Eadwine thundered, reaching out to shake his son.

"Yes, father. But she promised on her life that nothing happened."

55

"And you knew about messages for the Danes?"

"I...I..."

"*Answer me, boy!*" his father raged. "Did you know about the messages to the Danes? I cannot believe that you could be so..so..."

"Treacherous?" Leofric finished for him. "Cadoc," he then ordered crisply, turning to where the Welsh bowman was still seated by the fire holding a freshly dipped linen pad to his forehead, "tell us all you know. And you, Eadberht."

And while all around listened with eyes agog and breath hissing through their open mouths, Cadoc told all that had happened earlier that day, both by the privy in Slaughterford, and in Biddestone market: the meeting with Godric, being hit with the skillet and Gytha's escape to Chippenham...and of Brioni and Jaenberht's determination to pursue her to the Danish fortress.

All the while his parents, and all the people crowded there, listened with horror and the utmost dismay to all that Cadoc said, so that many cried out in anger, and fear, and others shook their fists in rage.

And when Cadoc had told them all he knew, Eadberht told of Brioni's earliest suspicions: of the meeting he and Brioni had had with Grimnir and Godric that first time at the market, before the attack on Malmesbury. Of the time when Gytha had wanted Godric to pass a message to Guthrum's guard commander, Bjorn Eriksson, and all the while Aelfrid and Eadwine stood by white-faced and stricken by the unfolding treachery of their youngest son.

"And what of Brioni and Jaenberht?"

"They were going to meet up with Hugo and Maritia at the circus encampment, and try and get word to Grimnir. They were desperate to find Gytha before she could tell the Danes about your attack being on Bath, not Swindon; about us all being here at Ford...and about someone close to the King being a traitor. About Grimnir. She was going to tell them everything!"

"But what has that to do with my son? With Cuthbert?" Aelfrid demanded fiercely. "All you have said so far is about Gytha."

"And she I have learned not to trust," Eadwine added, and would have said more if he had not been interrupted by Ethelinda returning, breathless, with Brioni's big leather scrip.

"Here, my Lord Leofric," she gasped, handing the bag over to the Saxon war-leader. "I had to search in your closet. It was behind the cloaks." And immediately everyone craned forward to try and have a better look.

"Back! *Back!*" Beornred ordered loudly, both hands gripping Cuthbert fiercely as he wriggled to break free, shouting out to his father all the time: "I am innocent! I know nothing of all this!" while Leofric swiftly went through the papers in his scrip, finally pulling out all the messages that Gytha had taken to Godric, signed with Cuthbert's name.

"See!" Leofric snarled, holding them up for all to see. "This is the real proof of their treachery. Look! Each of these has been signed in Cuthbert's name. "This is the first one, and he read it out: '*Beware. This comes to you from a Saxon well-wisher, happy to accept Guthrum as King of Wessex. Know that your enemies are at Ford, below Biddestone. Come quickly. Cuthbert of Ford.*' And all the others are similar. Every one signed '*Cuthbert of Ford*'. Your son and his wife planned to sell us all out to Guthrum and the Great Army."

"*No!* He would not do such a thing! Not my Cuthbert," his mother wailed, reaching out for her son's arm. "Not betray his own family."

"*Yes, I tell you!*" Leofric shouted at her, thrusting the letters into her hands. "He and Gytha had it all planned. They wanted the land for themselves. And I bet you that Gytha was ready to sell out her husband in order to inherit the lot. For be certain of this. If the Danes come here, they will slay everyone they find. *Everyone!* I have told you all this before. It is why we have all planned to be gone from here by the morning. Now even more so than before."

"*You earsling!*" Alfweald shouted at his brother, striding past his father, standing shocked beyond movement, and cuffing Cuthbert's head mightily. "You piece of absolute pig shit. Mother may be blinded by you, by your simpering and smiles and willingness to do anything to help her, her '*little soldier*'," he added bitingly. "But father and I know what you are really like, you earsling! Sly, underhand, lazy and afraid. You never work in the fields as we do alongside our men, never keep the wolf-guard at night, never work with the shepherds amongst the flocks. Too good for all that. You make me sick, Cuthbert. And now *this!*" and seizing his brother from Beornred by the open neck of his leather jerkin, he shook him violently, before throwing him to the ground in a shaking heap.

"*This is all that Gytha's doing!*" his mother shouted out, desperately. "She's the one, she's the one behind all this. My Cuthbert would never turn on his family. Never plan for us all to die. He is innocent!"

"This is all your fault, Leofric," Eadwine said heavily, seizing the letters from his wife and throwing them back at Leofric's feet. "You coming here with your men has changed everything. I knew Cuthbert was weak, and lazy, and what Alfweald says of him is true," he went on, looking across at his younger son, now back in Beornred's hands and drooping with terror. "But I hoped that having a wife might help him to change; to live up to his new responsibilities.

57

"Then you came, Alfweald and I joined with you, while Cuthbert held back and made excuses. And while we revelled in our successes against the Danes, everyone belittled him. Never much in our decisions before, he was now cast even further out."

"How can you know that?"

"Because he is my son! I have watched him; seen his weakness, listened to his excuses for staying safe here in Ford when we have gone with you against the enemy, and accepted his excuses…and I have watched Gytha. Watched her sneer at him, listened to her tongue flay him, felt his distress…seen him run to his mother for comfort.

"Before you came he was not a problem. Now he threatens our very lives with his treachery." And all those gathered there growled in fear and anger, and pushed forward towards the fire where Leofric stood in a wide space, while Ethelinda picked up the scattered papers, and Cuthbert was still held firmly by Beornred. With his parents closeby, and Leofric's warband now forming a circle of drawn swords and grounded spears, it was a theatre from which none could escape the drama that was about to be played out.

*

"**N**o Eadwine! *No!*" his wife cried out in torment. "You cannot believe he truly signed those letters, those messages. That is Gytha's hand," she added, stabbing her fingers at the big scrip that Ethelinda now had over her shoulder. "I know it well. It is she who lies behind all this, not Cuthbert!"

"There is one way to be certain of the truth," a voice said clearly from the back.

"And what is that?" Leofric called out, craning his head to see who had spoken.

"Put him to the Ordeal," and Osburgh walked into the circle, holding up her right hand and arm so that all could see the livid scars and shocking pink skin where it was wrinkled and shining in the fire light.

"I had to face the Ordeal when I was falsely accused of stealing from the church. No-one believed that I had not taken the money from the poor box. The priest and Thane Ormerod made me suffer Ordeal by Cauldron. A stone plucked out of a vat of boiling water.

"I suffered all the pains of hell. More terrible than I can begin to describe to you. Blessed by the priest, sprinkled with Holy Water, then given three days to show no poisoned wounds…or lose my hand to a woodman's axe. For him," she shouted, pointing at Cuthbert as he cowered in Beornred's grasp,

58

"Ordeal by Fire! A pound of red hot iron in his hands and walk three paces. I was judged innocent…maybe he will be too?" And with a withering glance at Cuthbert, and a flash of malice towards his mother for all the times she had been belittled since coming to Ford, she walked back to the edge of the circle.

"Ordeal! *Ordeal by Fire!*" came a ripple of sudden shouts from the packed hall, as many of the villagers responded harshly to her words.

Leofric looked around him and nodded, his face deadly, his eyes fixed on Eadwine as he spoke. The tall Headman standing rigid beside his wife, now leaning half-fainting against her husband's shoulder, his eyes fixed on his son whose own face was to the floor.

"Very well. Ordeal by Fire it shall be!" Leofric growled. "Arnwulf, bring me a bar of iron and your bellows. Finnar, mark me out three paces across this floor. Beornred, bring Cuthbert to me, and let us get this over, for we have much to do and I want this business settled tonight."

And while all the arrangements were swiftly made, and Arnwulf set up his bellows on the edge of the fire before the bar of iron he had brought with him, now cast in amongst the flames, Leofric and Eadwine had a furious discussion away from all the rest.

Chapter Seven

"*You cannot do this to my son,*" the tall headman shouted furiously, shaking Leofric's arm.

"Yes I can! He threatens all our safety. You know that he is guilty. His whole demeanour shows it. The letters prove it."

"*No!* They merely show that his name has been used. The letters are Gytha's doing, not Cuthbert's!"

"And Gytha writes letters to Guthrum, in Cuthbert's name, without his knowledge?" Leofric challenged him, incredulous. "Do you *really* believe such an impossible nonsense?"

"I don't know what to believe. But I do know you cannot do this. You have no priest!"

"No...and no Holy Water, and no three days to spare for so pointless a trial."

"So, what are you doing?"

"Forcing him to confess! We cannot move forward with this poison in our very midst. I cannot condemn him out of hand, though I am sorely tempted to do so. I believe him to be guilty as sin. He and Gytha are in this up to their precious necks! All that I have said about his treachery towards all of us - you, Alfweald and Ethelinda - I absolutely believe. His mother? Maybe not his mother, not from him. But Gytha? I believe she wanted you all dead so she could inherit everything."

"But why this Ordeal? *Why?*"

"You said it yourself. The boy is weak. He lacks courage. Faced with a glowing bar of metal and the frightening reality of it all, he will confess!"

"Then what?"

"So you believe it?"

"Yes..yes! Alfweald would take the three steps...but then Alfweald would never betray his people. *Never!* But Cuthbert? He has been coddled by his mother all his life. He is the youngest and she dotes on him. He will not accept the challenge. But if he confesses? What then?"

"You told me on the day that I arrived here, when I said I had heard that Cuthbert might not be trusted, that you were master in your own home. That if you found him to be without trust you would proclaim him *Nithing* and cast him out. And I said that if any action of Cuthbert's should threaten our security then my hand would fall upon him like a thunderbolt.

"I remember that."

60

"*Then see to it, Eadwine!*" he hissed fiercely, shaking the man's shoulders. "If the boy confesses - and I am sure he will, then you must deal with him. For if you do not, or cannot, then I will…and that will destroy your standing amongst your people for ever. Hundreds of my men and all the folk here are looking to us to save their lives and I will not stand by and see them all threatened, by anyone!"

And he turned then and stalked back to where everyone now stood waiting, a-buzz with comment and speculation, jostling for the best sight of all that was about to happen. Beornred with his prisoner facing the fire, his back to the wall of the house place; Arnwulf with his bellows and a great pair of pincers to hold the bar of metal, now glowing red hot in the flames shooting up around it, ready to be plucked out, a great bucket of water standing by.

"Beornred, bring the boy here," Leofric called out as Eadwine came across to join him. "Arnwulf, bring me that bar."

His legs barely able to carry him, and his face filled with terror, Cuthbert was dragged before Leofric. Standing before the central fire, his men holding back the homesteaders, his face was like stone, pitiless; while Aelfrid stood weeping near Finnar where the steps her son must soon take had been marked out.

"Cuthbert of Ford, you are accused of treachery of the basest kind: of messaging the Danes, with your wife, for the destruction of your family, of my men and of all those whom you have lived amongst all your life. You are called to the Ordeal. Admit your guilt, and be judged by your father, who is the Lord of your Life…or be judged by God through the Ordeal of Fire," and turning he called out: "Arnwulf, bring me the heated bar!"

Bending forward with his long tongs, Arnwulf stabbed amongst the flaring embers, clasped the bar of metal firmly, now glowing red hot and shimmering with heat, and rising carried it at arm's length to where Leofric was waiting. Around them the crowd gasped, while Aelfrid shrieked to her husband, and covering her face with her hands wept piteously.

Cuthbert, almost beyond standing upright, tottered in Beornred's tight grasp as he looked with horror at the glowing bar of red-hot metal held out towards him by Arnwulf the Farrier. Even though it was still several feet away from him he could feel its heat. His whole body trembled, his hands wet with fear as his mind grappled with the horror of what the fiercely glowing metal would do to his bare hands, to the soft pads of his fingers and his palms as the searing iron burned his flesh away and charred his very bones.

He looked up at his father, his mother's shrieks filling the room, his face wet with tears, and he shuddered with the sheer awfulness of what he had tried

61

to do. How could he have been reduced to this? And he cried out in his terror, his spirit groaning, his voice cracking as he tried to speak.

"Speak up, boy," Eadwine said as he confronted his son. "What is it to be? Guilt...or Ordeal by fire? Your doom to be proclaimed by me...or by God's own challenge?"

"Father! Please father!" Cuthbert appealed desperately, sinking to his knees. "Don't do this to me! Forgive me!"

"Stand him up, and hold out his hands, Beornred," Leofric ordered fiercely, his voice harsh, eyes of agate. "Raedwald, help him. Arnwulf bring the iron to his flesh...let him feel God's fire!"

And while Cuthbert struggled like a fly in a spider's web, Beornred cuffed him hard and forced him to hold out his hands, while Raedwald held him up and Arnwulf brought the glowing bar of iron closer and closer so that Cuthbert could feel the heat pulsing over his palms and fingers, making the hairs on his wrists shrivel and singe with the bitter smell of burning.

Suddenly squeezing his hands into fists away from the searing heat, Cuthbert shrieked out "Guilty! *Guilty!*" and sank to the ground on his knees, while Arnwulf tipped the glowing bar into the bucket of water by his side in a massive *hiss!* and great boiling clouds of steam.

"Why?" his horrified father demanded of his son, stepping past Leofric to confront Cuthbert, still grovelling on the fire-hardened earth of the hall place. "*Why?*"

"I thought Alfred was finished," the boy said weeping, his voice gulping. "That Guthrum must surely win, and that you and the Lord Leofric are fools to keep fighting. I wanted to be the one all men listened to, to be Thane in your place. You and Alfweald have always hated me, always belittled me," he whined pathetically, "never listened to my ideas. I wanted to be the leader, and Gytha showed me how. It was all her idea. She wrote the letters and signed with my name to encourage the Danes to believe us. It was Gytha. Gytha. Not me!"

"You pathetic *earsling!*" his brother shouted at him striding forward, and picking him off the ground drove him back against a great roof tree. "You pile of shit. What of the rest of us? Of mother and all the people. Of whom would you be a Lord after the Danes had destroyed everything, and slaughtered everyone? You misbegotten fool! You utter *mazeling!* The very touch of your breath soils me," he added, casting Cuthbert from him with a violent shove. "Such black treachery demands death. That is the only thing left to do with rancid scum like you, put you down like the frothing dog you have proved to be. Hang you from the rafters, and leave you here with a note pinned to your chest for Guthrum to find when he gets here!"

And kicking out at his brother, now on his hands and knees, the tall Saxon warrior-farmer turned and walked away to where his mother was slumped on a stool, weeping.

"Death! *Death!* Banish him, cast him out!" came the shouted responses from all around the house place, as the people from Ford who had now crammed within the hall, and many from Slaughterford who had joined them, appealed to Eadwine, and to Leofric, for judgement.

"You said you would deal with this, Eadwine," Leofric quietly reminded the man. "But if you won't, then be certain that I will. I told you, a thunderbolt will fall on this man's head if it is left to me to decide his fate."

Eadwine looked at his wretched son, now sat huddled on the floor with tear stained face, and then to his wife, whose reddened eyes and outstretched hands pleaded with him for their son's life, and then across the sea of faces packed in around him: angry, bemused, feral. People whom he had known and worked with all his life, who looked to him for justice and support, even though he was not their rightfully proclaimed Lord. He owed them everything. He could not fail them now, especially not on the eve of their all setting out together to Battlesbury Rings.

"Berhtulf, Thurwold, Brorda the Smith, come and take hold of Cuthbert. This is a thing that my men must do, my Lord Leofric," the tall headman said bitterly, turning to where the Saxon war-leader was standing by the fire, impassive, Beornred and Arnwulf beside him. "As you said, this is my responsibility," and he turned then to face his son, now pinioned between the two men whom he had called out of the crowd around him.

"Cuthbert, in more peaceful times you would have been taken to the Shire Reeve's court and tried for your wickedness before the Bishop and the King's Reeve. You deserve death for all you have done. To be taken to the hanging tree on the edge of the garth and there be hanged by the neck until you be dead!"

"No! *No, Eadwine!*" Aelfrid shrieked at him, her voice breaking in its intensity as she interrupted him. "This is your son. You cannot hang him! *You cannot!*"

"But that is a course not open to me now," the rangy headman continued undeterred, his voice growling as he spoke. "The Danes have broken everything, and I am not proclaimed Thane of Ford by the King, so I do not have the right to take your life - though as God is my witness I am sorely tempted to do so. Now, stand up straight you earsling, and hear what doom I proclaim upon you for your treachery. Brorda, Thurwold, bring this traitorous bastard before me, for he is no flesh and blood of mine!

63

"Cuthbert, I proclaim you *Nithing* and *Wolfshead!* A coward, a man of no honour but of treachery and dastardly dealing, a man with no place to call his own, an outcast. You are to be banished from this place forthwith. Any man, or woman, of these villages who harbours you, or succours you in any way, will similarly be banished and cut off.

"You will be driven off these lands with sticks and drums at first light, no matter what else may be going on around you. And you will go on foot with no more to sustain you than you can carry on your back, and all men shall know of your going and the hand of all men shall be against you.

"Cuthbert of Ford, I declare that you are no son of mine. Your name will be expunged from all records as I shall lay before the King and the Bishop when time and chance allow. The King likes all records to be kept, and notice of your banishment shall be sent to every village in the land. Now, take him away and put him in the lock-up. Let his mother go to him. But no-one else is to come within ten paces of him. His doom is pronounced and this moot is finished!"

And staring Leofric in the eye, without a flicker, he turned and stalked away, following the small bearer party who had Cuthbert firmly by each arm, past his weeping wife and appalled elder son who fell in behind them, and then all their people who flowed out of the hall into the gathering dusk, as the sun sank in a ball of fire below the shoulder of the hill.

*

*B*ehind them Leofric's men clustered round their leader, while Beornred raised the question all of them were thinking.

"What about the Lady Brioni, Leofric? If she has chased after that Gytha as Cadoc has said she intended to, then surely she is in deadly danger. Especially after Malmesbury!"

"Deadly danger indeed, which is why I told her not to go into Chippenham for any but the direst reason, which chasing after Gytha would have been. I cannot put off the attack on Bath tomorrow, nor can we fail to move from here as planned. Either would be impossible. Nor can we leave the Lady Brioni without support, even if all *is* well."

"What's to do then, Lord?" Beornred asked in his deep voice.

"We must send an armed party immediately to Hugo, for he is in almost daily contact with the Danes in Chippenham. If anyone can get Brioni out it will be him. But he will need professional armed help to do it! The *Circus Maximus* has proven to be every bit as successful as we had hoped it would be,

64

and if anything has happened he will be sure to know of it. He is also in touch with Grimnir, and he knows everything."

"Who goes, Lord?" Trausti asked him urgently.

"Not you, my friend. Whether the Lady Brioni returns tonight, or not, you, Trausti, must lead the villagers tomorrow with your war group, as planned, but in command."

"Yes, Lord. But before first light. I want to be on the way before the cock crows. We do not know what the Danes will do. Whether Gytha was captured or not, and I do not want to be caught by them on the hop."

"Good! See to that, and make sure everyone understands what is happening. Now," he went on briskly, turning to his Danish sword-master. "Finnar, you are to take Raedwald, Hannes, Aggi, Gunnar and Ricberht our best tracker and leave immediately, with Orn the archer, Aelric and Caewlin..."

"...And me, Lord, look you," came Cadoc's lilting voice from the corner. "My Rhonwen works in the King's Hall, see. She is the one who has been passing our messages to Eriksson. She knows the Hall like the back of her hand, and that might be helpful."

"Are you fit for this, Cadoc? That was a bad knock you took this afternoon."

"My head is as hard as your English oak. There may be a lump there still, but that will not stop me from doing my duty."

"I am reluctant to commit you, Cadoc the Archer," Leofric replied uncertainly. "I need every man of this detail to be on top form, or he could endanger the whole operation."

"Don't worry, bach," the little man replied. "My head is as good as any Saxon's. It was muzzy before, but this compress and a beaker of mulled ale have done wonders. And anyway, I owe it to the Lady Brioni to be by her side if she is in need. So, I am going, Lord. Just you try and stop me!"

"Very well," Leofric replied with a laugh. "You too then. Go armoured up and ready for anything, all of you. Most of you are Danes anyway, that is why you have been chosen. Swagger, and wear your Thor's hammers where all can see them, and with so many troops moving around you should not be noticed. You archers go with full quivers and a further bundle each for spares, and stick close to the others. You also speak a little Danish, I know, so you should get by, but do not get separated...and don't forget that Alfred is an earsling and not fit to lace up Guthrum's shoes, let alone be King of Wessex!"

"That's hard, Lord," Gunnar snorted, "When we have been shedding blood these many months for Wessex's King..."

"And for your mates," Finnar chipped in. "So a little bit of play-acting will do no-one any harm."

"And watch the drinking, all of you," Leofric admonished them most sternly. "If you get to Hugo you will find his hospitality can be overwhelming. So be careful. A drunken huscarle will be a dead one. Either from a Danish sword, or my seaxe. So be warned," he said, as they clustered round him.

"Maybe you will meet with Brioni and Jaenberht on their way back, and all will be well. If not, then go with care and go with God and the Valkyries.

"And take Foxhead with you as a saddle horse, with her armour, helmet, shield and her long sword packed on his back. I do not want her to be without them for a minute longer than necessary, and Foxhead has been superbly trained. It is a shame you cannot take Bran and Utha as well," he added, patting both giant hounds as he spoke, "but they would give the game away at once!

"Here's money from my hoard," he added, tossing Finnar a small leather bag as he spoke. "Now, off with you and God willing I will see you all at Battlesbury Rings!"

And with a chime of mail and clatter of heavy feet they all surged out into the sharp, moonlit darkness of a fresh spring night.

Chapter Eight

Chippenham.

And Jaenberht was with Hugo and Maritia in the big circus tent, with others of the Bearmaster's troupe, appalled by all that had happened earlier.

*

For some moments after he had heard Brioni's shouts he had searched desperately for her in the darkness but apart from her cape and her sword, of his battle commander there was no sign. Nor could he hear her voice calling out for him as moments before she had been. And as he searched with ever growing despair, Maritia came running back to join him, so together they quartered the ground again and found the three men whom Brioni had killed and wounded.

One dead in the open with his entrails around him; one who had crawled away to die, his severed hand like a discarded glove on the bloodied ground; and one still just alive, his leg ripped from crotch to ankle.

"Now, you *bastard!*" Jaenberht swore at the man fiercely as he knelt by his side. "Before I put a sword in your hand and send you to Valhalla, whose man are you? Who sent you out tonight to seize the girl? Come, tell me, swiftly, while you still have the life to do so."

"And you will send me to the Hall of the gods?" the injured man gasped, stretching his face up towards the big Saxon warrior.

"Yes!" he said, dragging the man's sword out and placing it near his hands, thick with the blood that still coursed down his shattered leg. "*Yes! Now tell me!*"

"We are of Captain Ránnulfr's command," the man panted, his eyes white in the moonlight. "He has been searching for this girl since Malmesbury. Since Guthrum humiliated him before the Council...oh, Odin, *it hurts!*" he cried out clutching at his ruined leg.

"Maritia, give him of your flask before we lose him."

And while the dark-haired circus girl lifted the dying man's head into her lap, and held her flask to his lips, Jaenberht continued to question him.

"How did you know about her?"

"She was spotted this afternoon," the man said through gritted teeth, the sweat pouring off him. "By the circus, near the bear. The captain sent us out to watch and capture. No blades, just cudgels. We thought she would be easy meat, but she fought like a tiger," he said further, his body trembling, his voice almost shrunk to a husky whisper. "Bjarke disarmed her and seized her, carried her off to the compound. By the river...Lord, I cannot give you more. I am faint, and hear bells in my head. Give me my sword," he cried out then, his hand scrabbling in the grass, "and send me on my way."

"Here is your blade, soldier," Jaenberht said quietly, pressing the man's right hand around the hilt of his sword to a long sigh, as the life rushed out of him. "But you need no sword of mine to send you to Odin's kingdom," he added, as with a final gush of blood the man's head flopped to one side and his eyes lost their spirit. "My Lady has done that for you already!" And reaching down his hand, he closed his eyes and pulled Maritia to her feet.

"This bastard is finished," he growled nudging the body with his foot, Blood Drinker in his right hand, her long cape over his left shoulder. "But at least we know what has happened. Now what?

"We go to my father's encampment, and send a message to Leofric immediately. He must be told that Gytha is dead, killed before she could betray them all; that his message is safe with Godric, who will deliver it today; that Grimnir is still by Guthrum's side...and that Brioni has been captured by Ránnulfr."

"Who will take it?"

"Angel. He is Julio's young brother. Julio would be missed, but Angel is still just a boy. He can slip away from camp on Brouha the mule before first light, and get to Ford in no time."

"Very well. Now let's get to your father with all speed, there is much to do. Do you know where Ránnulfr's compound is?"

"No, but we will find it. He said by the river, so it will not be within the walls. Father may know, but if not, we all know someone who will."

"Grimnir!"

"Yes...and he must be told also. Come on, Jaenberht, there is no time to lose!" And taking a deep breath they both loped off together, Maritia leading, slipping through the moonbeams and along the empty ginnels of Chippenham beyond the walls, as they made their way back to the *Circus Maximus* and to Hugo the Bearmaster.

*

"So, our little lady has been captured," the big man said, shuffling his shoulders beneath his bearskin cape, and shouting to Gilbert for mulled wine and sweet cakes, while Julio, Hugo's lithe horse-master, and Marcus his troupe-arranger swiftly joined them.

"That is bad…and by Ránnulfr too! That is worse. The man was humiliated by Guthrum in front of the whole Viking Council and his fellow captains, when the news of his defeat by Brioni came through. Mocked before everyone. 'You are no man for me!' the king said, so Grimnir told me. And now he has her under his hand. And it will not be a gentle hand either, for he will be out for revenge in any way he can achieve it. The mercy is that Guthrum has made her his 'meat' should she ever be captured. His alone to do with as he pleases. So not even Oscytel can get his hands on her himself and Ránnulfr will not dare to do her any real harm either.

"He won't…force her?" Maritia asked urgently, skating round the reality of it all.

"Oh, he may knock her about a bit. That is to be expected. But he will not torture, nor mutilate her. Nor rape her, which is common for Saxon wenches taken in battle. There is much to be thankful for."

"Do you know this compound, father?" Maritia then questioned eagerly. "It is near the river I think."

"Yes, Maritia. A palisaded area close to the water on the southern side below the ramparts, this side of the bridge. But not well, you understand," he added quickly, reaching for his great gilded horn of steaming wine that Gilbert had that moment poured for him, "but enough to know that we cannot take it. It is his command post, and thick with Jomsvikings. Inside, I am told, is a maze of tunnels, corridors and storage rooms. She could be anywhere. And we have no real fighting men to hand."

"You have all of us!" Marcus said firmly. "My lads are keen and would do their best. They have some skill with weapons."

"But against professional warriors, who have spent years with their harness on their backs?" he replied, quaffing deeply. "They would be dead in minutes."

"Do we know anyone who works there, Hugo?" Julio asked him a moment later. "Someone who could get a message in to the Lady Brioni. Let her know that she has not been abandoned."

"No, but Rhonwen might," Jaenberht chipped in brightly. "She is Cadoc's girl and works in the King's Hall. She is their brew-mistress, and well thought of."

"She might know one of Ránnulfr's whores, Beornwyn or Merwenna," Maritia added, reaching for her goblet of mulled wine. "They are always in and out of the Hall for the titbits their master likes; though not so often since Guthrum almost threw him out of the army."

"You know them?" Julio asked, sharply.

"No, only in passing. By reputation only."

"But Rhonwen might know them to speak with," Jaenberht chipped in eagerly.

"She may also be able to speak with Grimnir," Maritia added. "That would be even better, as he has great influence with both Guthrum and the Black Jarl. He can go everywhere, I know, and is often in the King's Hall, especially when there is a fresh brew of heather beer coming in. It is a weakness of his."

"Then we must have speech with her urgently," Jaenberht replied, banging his hand on the table.

"That is better news," Hugo said, stroking his massive beard, "for we need to get a message through to Brioni somehow. You know," the big man added, after a pause, bringing his attention back to the group seated around him, "Ránnulfr's capture of Brioni could yet be the best way of getting her out. Maybe the only way!"

"How?" Jaenberht demanded, his head thrust forward, his big hands drumming on the table top.

"Of course, it would be very risky. Very dangerous…and would require well-armed men, whom we do not have. And archers."

"You mean an assault on the King's Hall?" Maritia quizzed her father, incredulous. "That would be madness. We would all be killed!"

"No! Not so. Not if it was done with skill and great guile, and by a small number of desperate men. And if we could persuade Brioni to fight."

"*Brioni?*" Jaenberht gasped. "What can she do?"

"Challenge a Viking to face-to-face combat…"

"*What?*" Maritia exclaimed, appalled. "Fight one of their best? She wouldn't last five minutes. Not without shield and armour, even if she had a long sword, and not just Blood Drinker!"

"Why not? She defeated Ránnulfr, well almost, and the Vikings love a good fighter. Let her prove how good she is against one of theirs."

"To what end, father?" Maritia asked, stunned.

"For her freedom!"

"*For her freedom?* Are you mad, Papa? They would never grant her freedom. She is the Lady Brioni of Foxley, a leader of marauders who have been killing Vikings for months. They would never let her go! They would lie, and lie and lie again, before releasing her."

"Of course they will lie," her father boomed at her, with a huge grin. "But she will be armed! That's the thing. I could not see how to get a weapon to her, and armour. She will need both if we are really to fight our way out of the place."

70

"You mean an ambuscade, from within the King's Hall?" Jaenberht queried in an audible gasp, sinking down onto a bench as he spoke.

"Of course! What else?" Hugo replied fiercely. "Get some archers up into that gallery above the Hall, where Alfred had his chapel," he said, raising his great horn like a pointer. "That which the Heathen do not use any more; then get some good men into the main body of the place, and with all our troupe, and Oswald, bless him, what a wild rumpus we could make...with a little fire to go with it, I should think."

"You mean set the whole place on fire for good measure?" Marcus questioned, appalled.

"Why not? Alfred won't care, it can always be rebuilt, and it would create a massive diversion."

"And in the smoke, flames and wild confusion...we get out."

"Yes! Out the back of the town as Alfred did in January...and bar the doors of the Hall for good measure as we go," Jaenberht growled, thumping the table with his fist. "They have done that enough times to our own people, the bastards. So now it would be our turn to burn them out!"

"Well, whatever we do, we have just one day in which to do it..."

"One day?" Jaenberht queried aghast. "To arrange all this?"

"Yes! Guthrum has been out of Chippenham this past week. He returns today."

"I remember; Godric told us before we came here," Jaenberht agreed. "Gone to Cricklade to see some ships."

"Well, he returns today. And there is always a feast to celebrate his return, and he will expect the *Circus Maximus* to entertain him. We have made quite an impression on him, as I always expected we could do; he will insist on our being there. But, tonight, as well as the usual tumbling, and Oswald's tricks, which they all love, we could stage a sort of gladiatorial masque."

"Gladiators?" Jaenberht gasped, amazed. "As in *Roman* Gladiators?" he continued, so astonished he could only goggle at him, his eyes on stalks.

Julio, beside him, was not so stunned and looked at the Bearmaster with sudden realisation. *"Yes!"* he exclaimed, with excitement, catching on to Hugo's idea. "Why not? We can dress up. We have the helmets and weapons we need in one of the wagons. We did that in Neustria before we came to Wessex. Got the idea from ancient mosaics we saw on a visit to Libya a few years ago, do you remember, Maritia? Before your dear mama died? At Lepcis Magna, a famous ancient city of the Romans, on the coast. The city was in ruins; mostly covered in sand, but there was one villa there still standing, whose mosaics were magnificent, just as we had been told. Every sort of gladiator was shown there with all their weapons and armour."

"You're so right!" Marcus exclaimed, jumping up excitedly. "That is a sparkling idea. I remember those mosaics well. We modelled those helmets, and the greaves we have, on what we saw there. That will put us all right in the centre of Guthrum's hall, with weapons not allowed to any but his personal guard. They will all laugh at the sight of us…"

"…Without realising the danger they are all in," Hugo finished for him.

"And they will be intrigued," Julio chipped in. Marcus and I can practise some moves beforehand, with some of the others. But how does this help the Lady Brioni?"

"We can provide her with the armour she will need to make good her challenge."

"You are very sure of all this, my Lord Hugo," Jaenberht said, puzzled by the Bearmaster's confidence. "You seem to know what the Heathen will do, before they do."

"I have been amongst them for some time now. I know how they think. Confronted with Brioni's challenge, us clad in ancient, outlandish armour, and her looking lovely and vulnerable in her silks, Guthrum will call for me to arm her, especially as Maritia will be similarly dressed for war.

"Oh, not that awful Amazon outfit you had made for me, Papa, with bare breasts and feathers?

"No, my darling girl. That was only when you were very little, before your darling mother died. No…you can wear her shaped cuirass and Greek helmet with the tall horsehair crest, and painted shield. You and she are very similar in shape and size now. It will fit you like a glove…you will give those bastards heart failure! And you can carry her shield and spear, wear her short pleated skirt, loin protectors, pauldrons and greaves. You will look magnificent. You will stun those pirates, trust me. They will never have seen such a warrior maid. You will remind them of Freyja, their goddess of war. They will gasp at you, sweetheart, and want to see Brioni in something similar."

"It is a shame we don't have some cheetahs for me to stroll in with on leashes to complete the picture!" she added, laughter spilling out of her. "They would really see me as Freyja then!"

"No, not cheetahs, but you will have Oswald. He will be huge beside you, but Wuffa's Greek armour will make their eyes pop out, and we must get Brioni armed and armoured somehow. Can you think of anything better?"

"No, Papa," she said, putting her hand on her father's arm. "I will do all I can to help you in this, of course. Brioni is my dearest friend, and I cannot bear to think of her cooped up in some noisome hole without hope," she said, squaring her shoulders and standing up with her goblet. "But there is a major flaw in your plan, dearest. From where do we get archers and proven warriors who can mingle with the enemy and lull them?"

"From Leofric," her father answered her confidently, holding his gilded horn out for a refill.

"*From the Lord Leofric?*" Jaenberht gasped. "But he is leaving for Bath at cock crow, and all the rest not with him towards Battlesbury. He needs all the men he can lay his hands on. It's impossible!"

"No! Not if someone leaves immediately. It is still the dark of the night, and the moon is high. The Danes have no idea how close to them their enemies are. But we do. We could have a fast messenger at Ford in no time."

"Send Angel on Brouha," Maritia responded at once. "I was going to send him with a message anyway. He is little and won't be missed. Who is going to stop a boy on an old mule?"

"Don't send a boy to do a man's job!" Julio said then, sharply, putting his arm across her shoulders. "And not because he is my baby brother, but because he may fall in with murderers. There are bad people out there, Maritia. Look what has happened already tonight. Let Rufus Stabwell go, and live up to his name!" he said with a grin. "He knows the way, and can wield a sword as well as me. He could fight his way out of difficulty if he had to, and he can go on Caesar, my own bay stallion. He needs a run and he is as brave as a lion."

"Very well, Julio," Hugo responded, leaning forward to look at his Horse-Master closely. "Rufus can go…but not on Caesar. You will need him yourself, and Rufus will not be coming back. He will go with the villagers to Battlesbury! Agreed?"

"Agreed, Bearmaster," Julio replied after a moment's thought. "Then he can go on Swallow. She is fast and nimble, and he has ridden her before."

"That is good. On Swallow let it be," Hugo replied with a nod of his head and a bang on the table with his hand. "Now…we must get organised. Maritia, go with Jaenberht to the 'Stag' and sort out Gytha's horse, Gemma. She is far too valuable to be left in their stables, and Paega is as untrustworthy a weasel as any ostler I have come across in years. Pay Beorhtwulf what he is due, with my thanks, and make sure that nothing was left behind in Gytha's room while you are at it. In fact stay the night under his roof, Beorhtwulf and Thelflaeda are fine hosts and you need the rest. In the morning, before the world is stirring too much, slip out and find Rhonwen and see what she knows about those whores, and if Grimnir would be a better choice. You know where her house and brew-house are, behind the 'Stag'…and Jaenberht, you go with her. I will not have her beyond my walls without protection; but lay a hand on her and I'll have your balls in white wine and garlic!" and they all laughed.

"Marcus," he said briskly, "find Anton, Russell and Magnus and roust out that gladiator equipment we had made. I have my Wuffa's armour with me, and have carefully maintained it all these years. That is what love does," he added with a deep sigh. "The rest will need working on and shining up, so give everyone a good shake about. And every blade is to be sharpened. I know that we can all look the part, but we need to be able to play the part tonight as well. And if I am to fight Vikings I want to be certain that I can cut them in bloody pieces!

"Right!" the huge Bearmaster said, standing up, his great black bearskin cape flowing from his shoulders. "I will go and see to Oswald presently and prepare his armour. He will be our secret weapon tonight. The Danes have only seen him dancing to pipes and tabor with a muzzle on; they have never seen him roused, with mouth agape and dressed for war. He loves Brioni as much as Maritia, and when the girls call him he will come running, teeth and claws bared, and roaring his head off. He will be unstoppable!

"Now, as you Saxons say," the giant man roared out in his enormous voice, raising his great goblet refilled by Gilbert with steaming ale: *"Wassail!* and *Death to our Enemies!"*

Chapter Nine

*L*eaving Ford that night beneath a brilliant moon, a faint mist rising off the By Brook, Finnar, on his big gelding, Storm Crow, splashed his men through the water and away up the steep track that led directly to Biddestone, high on the ridge above them. All rode in single file, three days' rations packed round them and full aleskins by their side, with Foxhead bringing up the rear on a long leading rein, Brioni's armour and fighting equipment packed on his back. Every man was alert for the slightest noise that might herald an attack, their eyes straining to penetrate the blackness around them, where the trees and bushes pressed in upon the track.

Behind in the steading was all the excitement of thrusting Cuthbert into the lock-up, with shouts, jeers and thumping blows; and the continued turmoil of everyone getting ready to leave: wagons being packed, tilt carts piled high with what treasures the people had been allowed to take with them: chickens, ducks and geese in crates, piglets in high-sided waggons, goats and hounds at foot, cats and kittens in boxes, and all a shimmer of constant movement as the families of both steadings readied themselves for the move to Battlesbury Rings...and Leofric's war-band prepared for their assault on Bath.

Up ahead of Finnar rode their finest tracker, Ricberht, the sharpest eyed amongst them, to point the way, and it was after they had crested the steepest part of the trackway, and were on the long lead-in to the very edges of Biddestone, that the sound of a horse being ridden fast came clearly to him in the stillness of the night. Instantly he threw up his hand and called out, urging his horse off the track, ready to rush out and attack anyone who might offer them danger.

At his signal all the others behind him followed suit except Finnar, who drew his sword and pulled his great war-shield off his back to cover his left side from chin to thigh with coarse leather, iron and lime wood, the painted wolfshead on its surface leaping out with teeth bared to face the enemy.

So Rufus, on Swallow, was brought to a plunging halt, the mare skittering nervously across the track as she was swiftly surrounded by the rest of Finnar's command. All bristling with weapons, they looked terrifying as the moon's bright light fell on them in thick bars of black and white, and the trees creaked and sighed around them in the breathy darkness.

"Who are you who rides so swiftly at dead of night?" Finnar demanded sharply, pushing Storm Crow right up against Stabwell's mount, sandwiching

75

the rider between his sword and that of Raedwald, who had plunged up the track to join him.

"But I know you!" the man exclaimed with a shout, as he backed Swallow against Raedwald's big chestnut. "By your shield, you are Finnar Olafsson, one of Leofric Iron Hand's closest hearth companions. It is the Iron Hand I seek. I am Rufus Stabwell, come from Hugo the Bearmaster on a most urgent mission. I beg you, let me pass!"

"So you say," Finnar replied, staring into the other man's face and finally recognising him. "Master Rufus, indeed," he added, sheathing his sword. "You have been this way to us before. I too am on a mission; to the Bearmaster, with armed men at my back. The Iron Hand has sent us forward, anxious for the safety of the Lady Brioni, hoping for the best but fearing the worst. Cadoc the Archer has told us she went in to Chippenham after the woman Gytha. Quickly now; what do you know that we do not?"

"The Lord Leofric is right to be concerned. Gytha is dead! Slain by Jaenberht as she tried to escape. But the Lady Brioni is taken!" And while all who could clustered round them both, Rufus told them all that had happened, about Ránnulfr, and about Hugo's plans for Brioni's escape.

"So, I was on my way to find the Iron Hand and beg for his immediate assistance…only to find that he has already sent you forward to help us. What should I do now?"

"Push on hard down this trackway, it will lead you directly to the Lord Leofric's command. Tell him that you have met with us just below Biddestone, and tell him all you know. He leaves to assault Bath before first light, so you must be as swift as you dare, for the hill is steep and treacherous.

"And tell him to look for us at Battlesbury Rings in three days' time. God willing, we will all be there together. Now, Rufus, kick on!" he said jagging Storm Crow away from the mare as he spoke. "Already the moon is setting, and we must reach Chippenham before first light ourselves."

Clasping his arm in a brief farewell, he stabbed in his spurs and took off along the track for Biddestone, his whole command swiftly following with a jingle of steel, their hooves digging into the rutted surface in a spray of stones and scattered turf, while Rufus urged Swallow towards the steep hill that led down to Ford, from where Leofric and his men were readying themselves to leave.

*

*I*n her foul lock-up Brioni waited and waited in the candlelit darkness, while the guard outside was changed, and the stench of her cell ate into her very being. No food was brought to her, and the water in her pitcher was stale and laced with cobwebs. She was cold, alone and frightened; the straw palliasse filthy with age and gnawed by rats, the blanket soiled, stiff with dried blood, while the candle stub that Hakon had left her slowly burned down to a puddle of grease.

As the hours passed, with nothing to sustain her, her imagination worked overtime, and despite her determination to remain hopeful, her very isolation worked on her mind and dulled her spirit. She began to feel abandoned. That the very fact of her being so deep within Ránnulfr's command, and surrounded by his Jomsvikings, would make any kind of rescue impossible.

Shortly she would be called for, she knew that.

Shortly she would be brought out to face Guthrum; out of this foul, noxious hole and into the starlight. She must not give in to her growing despair, and she breathed deeply and dug her nails sharply into the palms of her hands. By then, God willing, Godric would have delivered her message and Oscytel would no longer be in Chippenham, he and his Jomsvikings would be fiercely riding for Swindon. But so would Leofric also be gone, racing off to Bath. Pray God the enemy would believe their trick and rush in the opposite direction. Even that Guthrum might be preparing to assault Ford, and empty Chippenham of Danes. Then, perhaps, a rescue might be possible.

Pray God they did not torture or rape her as had been the fate of so many Saxon girls. That her birth might protect her. That her beauty might shield her and make her more valuable to the Heathen?

She sat on the edge of her pallet and covered her face with her hands. It was suddenly all so dreadful! So hopeless!

Not even Grimnir would be able to help her without revealing his position in Guthrum's Court...and that secret was infinitely more important to the Saxon High Command than the fate of a single Saxon maiden trapped by the enemy in their most powerful fortress in all Wessex.

Dear God, that it should come to this!

And, at that moment of real horror, the door of her prison was suddenly flung open and Bjarke stooped in and dragged her, blinking, into the torch light.

"You are to come with me," he snarled, Hakon lurking beside him. "The captain wants you prepared for your presentation before the king. I would as soon leave you to rot, you foul bitch," he swore at her, giving her a violent shake, "but as it is, you are to be brought to the captain's chamber where his women will prepare you. I would have you flogged for your wickedness. But the captain wants you primped and dressed like the stinking whore you are!" And with his knife once more in her back he forced her to walk before him, back up the stairs to the corridor above, into the afternoon sunlight and along the same corridor to where she had glimpsed the half–naked woman when she had first been brought to Ránnulfr's command post.

Stopping by a broad arched doorway, Hakon reached round her and flung open the door.

"You have your orders," Bjarke snarled at the women inside. "Here is the slut that Captain Ránnulfr took prisoner earlier. Do what you can. If the captain is not pleased with your efforts, you know what will happen!" And with a great shove of his hand he thrust Brioni into the room, while Hakon slammed the door closed behind her.

*

*A*cross Chippenham, behind the 'Stag' inn, Jaenberht and Maritia were standing on the edge of a small compound, near a neat cruck house with a roof of wooden shingles and a long, low building behind it, tiled in slate and surrounded by a tall fence of lapped larchwood. From this building smoke rose in soft clouds, and the unmistakeable yeasty smell of brewing billowed in the stiff wind that eddied around them. Above them the sky was lightening from the east, the wind still brisk, the clouds overheard brightening with every minute, while all around them the town shivered into life, men already leaving for work, and smoke spiralling up into the morning as fires were stoked into life and ovens lit.

"Well, this is the right place without doubt," Jaenberht said, sniffing the yeasty air. "And that is a fine brew I am smelling…heather beer, if I am a judge," he added appreciatively. "The Vikings' favourite. No wonder Rhonwen is so well thought of! But there's no point in knocking on her house door," he said with a smile. "She'll be in the brew-house over there," and he led the way into the compound, passed massed ranks of great oak barrels that were stacked against the long fence line beneath a thatched lean-to shelter. Just beyond them was a set of stables, with two great wains close by, onto one of which a crew of men were loading full casks of beer ready for the feasting that would follow the King's return from Cricklade later that day.

"I am astonished!" exclaimed Maritia, looking wide-eyed around her. "This is some operation. I had no idea that Rhonwen was running such a thriving business. There must be a dozen working for her," she said, waving her hands at the men striving with ropes and pulleys over a triangle frame of great timbers as they struggled to load the wagon, with its team of four horses, drivers and ostlers standing nearby. "And there she is!" she shouted out, with a wave of her hands to the young woman, with a rough leather apron round her waist, who now came out to see what was happening with her beer.

"Rhonwen! Well met," Maritia called out with a smile, running up to give her a swift hug and kiss on her cheek, Jaenberht following close behind. "We must have speech with you. Urgently and softly," she added looking round. "Where none can hear us."

"*Cadoc!* Dear God, say he is not harmed!" the girl queried, stopping dead in her tracks, her hand to her face.

"No! Not Cadoc, sweetheart. Worse, if anything. The Lady Brioni. She has been taken, and we need your help."

"Come with me to the house," the Welsh girl said swiftly, with a gasp. "I will just have word with these men, see, before they ruin my latest brew, and then I will join you. Go now. I will be close behind you!" And leaving them to walk to the cruck house that stood beside her brewery, she strode over to the men on the wagon and after a few sharp words and fierce gestures, she swiftly turned and ran back to join them.

Moments later, they were inside and seated on low benches before a central hearth which Rhonwen coaxed into sparkling life with flint, knife and kindling, so that in a very short time there was a cheerful blaze with spiced ale in a copper pannikin on a metal grill over it, the redolent scent of cinnamon making their nostrils quiver.

"Now, tell me all. What can I do to help?"

And Maritia and Jaenberht told the Welsh brew-mistress all that had happened, and what they needed her to try and do.

Chapter Ten

"Yes, I know Ránnulfr's women, Beornwyn and Merwenna," Rhonwen said after Maritia had finished explaining all that had been discussed with her father. "But of the two of them, Beornwyn is the one we would want. Merwenna is Cornish, and has no love for Wessex. I would hesitate to trust her. But Grimnir would be even better."

"What about Grimnir?" Jaenberht asked, urgently. "Is there any chance you can have word with him? He must be told all we know. He alone is in a position to help the Lady Brioni the most," he added, putting more wood on the fire. "He has the ear of both the Danish king and of the Black Jarl. He is one of the most subtle men in the kingdom, and will know just what to say when Brioni is dragged before the king - which she will be as sure as eggs are eggs!"

And they all sat there in silence for several moments, taking in the implications of what had happened, staring into the fire, watching the flames leap and flicker amongst the logs, lost in their thoughts: of Alfred driven into the wilderness; of Leofric getting ready to assault Bath; of Trausti leading the villagers to Battlesbury...and of Brioni locked in a vile hole, desperate for freedom and surrounded by mortal enemies.

Then Rhonwen sighed, and stirred the spiced ale with a large wooden spoon, while the others sat up and looked at her.

"That wagon you saw being loaded up," she said carefully, sitting back onto her stool and looking at them both, "is due into the fortress this morning, as soon as the horns blow and the gates are opened. It is for the feast tonight to celebrate the return of the king. It is the first of two. The second will go up after noon. That is when Godric will come in; when he will leave Brioni's message to be found.

"By that time Grimnir will be in the hall, where I will be setting up these barrels, and I will have speech with him then. It would not be unusual for me to do so, for he always takes the first pull of every cask I bring in. It is a ritual with him. Indeed it would be thought odd if I did not have speech with him.

"I can then tell him all, and make sure he goes to Eriksson about Godric's message, and then to see Ránnulfr to discuss Brioni's presentation. He may even get to see her, as the captain is sure to boast of her capture, and our little Skald is not known as Guthrum's advisor for nothing! A single word from him could put the captain right back in favour with Guthrum, and Ránnulfr will know it.

80

"And if Grimnir can get to see Brioni," Jaenberht said, pouring the spiced ale Rhonwen had now warmed into deep bowls for them to drink from, "then he will find some way of letting her know she is not alone, even that a plan is being hatched," he added.

"Well, I am not the king's brew-mistress for nothing," Rhonwen said proudly, "despite those bastards slaying my parents when they seized the town," she added, through gritted teeth. "But all men know that I brew the finest heather beer for miles, which is why Guthrum has continued to employ me, and Grimnir loves it so, reminds him of his own Norse family…just as all men will know now that the captain has a rare prisoner under his hand. And If I know anything of the Lady Brioni of Foxley," she added with a grin, "that will be the only part of him that she will ever be under!"

And they all laughed, standing up to leave as they did so, pleased that the bare bones of Hugo's plan were already having flesh put on them.

If only Leofric could be reached in time to release some of his men for their venture, there might yet be a real chance of success, and it was with high hearts that Maritia and Jaenberht left the brew-house to return to Hugo's encampment.

*

*T*here, Finnar and his men had already arrived, slipping into the giant Bearmaster's encampment like the shadows of the night, their hooves muffled by the turf on which they trod. And just in time, for already the light was strengthening in the east as the night faded into the new day, a fine mist subtly veiling all that was going on from the Danish watchers on the ramparts that ringed the town.

Nevertheless, these were dangerous moments, so his men were swiftly drawn under cover, and their horses led away to mingle with those of the *Circus Maximus* under their sheltered horse lines. Meanwhile the whole encampment had been stirred into action by Hugo as the gladiator-style armour was retrieved and cleaned, blades were sharpened, and the whole business of daily maintenance and feeding got under way, with Oswald calling from his night wagon for the attention he craved.

Below them in the town horns were blowing and the great gates dragged open for the new day, while a stream of men and horses, wagons, tilt carts and even sheep and cattle were driven in, including a great wain stacked with huge barrels, and pulled by four horses, that scattered everyone as they hauled their burden through the gates.

Today the king would return with all his guards and retinue, so the whole town was a-buzz with comment and activity as it prepared to receive him, and got ready for the famous horse-fair that would take place in the week following. Extra stabling was already being erected, booths thrown up and tents raised while a host of extra workers mobbed round the well in front of the bridge that led into the town, all seeking work, with their tools on their shoulders or in stout canvas bags at their feet.

Amongst them strode the Viking guards and soldiers of the fortress, some clad from head to toe in bright mail and scale armour, helmeted, with weapons in hand and shields on their backs, checking passes. Others were more softly dressed in wool and leather in vibrant colours, cross-gartered hose and fine half boots on their feet, swords at their hips and many with girls on their arms in bright dresses, tripping cheerfully by their sides.

For several minutes Finnar watched the whole shifting scene from the edge of Hugo's vast striped tent and smiled.

It was a kaleidoscope of changing colours and movement, the more so as the women of the town, and of Chippenham beyond the walls, came out to join the throng, clogs on their feet, children in hand and baskets on the arms. Many had hounds at foot, or on the leash, and all were come to see what bargains they could get from the booths being set up, and from the many pedlars who had been drawn to the coming fair, their poles on their shoulders, from which every trinket imaginable hung in glittering festoons.

The horse fair was coming, a wild distraction that he had forgotten about, and he was delighted.

With so many people in and around the town, slipping his men in amongst them all would be far easier than he had feared, and banging his hands together with a snort of laughter, he turned and went inside to find the Bearmaster.

*

"*F̀innar!*" the huge man roared, the moment he clapped eyes on him, rolling forward to throw his arms around his shoulders. "Never was I more pleased to see you, and you have brought a fine collection of warriors with you, and archers too! It could not have been better. That man, Leofric, is a magician. A wizard. It is as if he had looked into my own heart, and answered all my prayers! How come you have got here so soon? It is almost a miracle!"

"The moment Cadoc returned to us with his tale of what Gytha had been up to, and that the Lady Brioni had rushed after her, Leofric prepared for the

82

worst, and sent us all off immediately to find you. And then we met Rufus on the way, and rode like the wind to get here before the darkness gave way to the new day. Where's Jaenberht?" he asked urgently, looking around him.

"Don't worry, he is safe. I have sent him with Maritia to speak with Rhonwen, the Viking's brew-mistress, to get word to Grimnir and also to Brioni…"

"You know where she is?" he demanded instantly, his eyes lighting up.

"Yes! And who holds her. No, Finnar! It cannot be assaulted," he added quickly, before the tall Dane could speak. "She is in a palisaded compound, stiff with Jomsvikings all armed to the teeth, and just below the main ramparts close to the river.

"She is the prisoner of Ránnulfr, the Jomsviking captain she humiliated at Malmesbury. But Rhonwen is Guthrum's brew-mistress. She is in and out of the King's Hall all the time and maybe can get word to Grimnir. Maritia has gone with Jaenberht to speak with her and see what may be done through him to get word to Brioni of what I have planned for her rescue. It is a risky strategy, Finnar, and would be impossible without your men. But you are here, and four of Leofric's best archers, who are vital for my plan's success. It could not be better.

"Now, come, sit by me, and bring your men up to the table, and I will tell you what I have in mind," and calling to Gilbert for mulled ale and fresh bannocks with butter and honey, hard boiled eggs and smoked meat, Hugo the Bearmaster hauled his bulk into his great armed chair, and bade all Finnar's men to come and join them.

*

"So, that is your plan?" the big Danish huscarle said after Hugo had finished speaking, sitting back with his gold-rimmed horn of steaming ale between both hands.

"Yes, my friend. That is the best that we could all come up with."

"Well, you are right, my Lord Hugo, it is very risky. But with all that is going on around the town today, it is not without merit. I had forgotten about the horse-fair, and getting my men into place may not be as difficult as it might have been. Like all these things however, getting in is less of a problem than getting out again. We will need a brilliant exit strategy to pull this off. And we need the Lady Brioni to be fully in the picture.

"To challenge the Vikings to a fight will take exceptional courage, and determination. She is as likely to be stripped, whipped and branded as to be given weapons and armour, despite Maritia standing by like an Amazon of old.

83

Nevertheless, we have brought her fitted byrnie with us, and her helmet, sword and shield, and her stallion, Foxhead. Leofric tried to think of everything. But what about Oscytel?"

Hugo sighed and shuffled in his chair. "That is an impenetrable question, Finnar!" he exclaimed at length, quaffing from his great ox horn, with its gilded rim and golden feet. "Godric will come in later today, and will get Brioni's latest message to Eriksson, who will surely take it to Oscytel, as Guthrum will be absent until the evening. With good fortune, after what happened at Malmesbury and Melksham, that black-hearted bastard will be so inflamed that he will lose all sense and rush off with his men to trap Leofric at Swindon and destroy him once and for all. Leaving Guthrum to deal with Brioni and the traitors at Ford."

"But what will he do about Brioni?" Finnar questioned him urgently. "He must know about her by now. And Ránnulfr is one of his chosen men."

"Ránnulfr has been mocked and humiliated by Guthrum, and the king has declared Brioni to be his 'meat'. Grimnir tells me that because of all the losses of his crews at Leofric's hands, Oscytel's standing with the Viking Council is not what it was! He will not reach out a hand to touch Brioni while she is seen to be under Guthrum's protection, such as it is, and as such he will not move to help Ránnulfr either."

"So Brioni is safe?"

"For the moment. But that moment is brief, and we cannot wait for a better time."

"And you really believe this plan will work?" Finnar asked of Hugo, looking straight into the huge man's periwinkle eyes, one eyebrow raised. "That those bastards down there will be sufficiently intrigued about having the Lady Brioni under their hands, that they will sanction her being armed and allowed to fight?"

"Yes!"

"*And I agree!*" the big Dane said with a grin and a swift bellow of laughter. "That is *exactly* what they will do. They will be so taken by her beauty, and her defiance, and so stunned by her presentation as a common whore that they will want to see her in action. Maybe against Ránnulfr himself; after all she nearly defeated him before, and he has something to prove. Or maybe against another of their men, and they will have plenty from whom to choose, as everyone will want to go up against so unlikely a Saxon champion. When do we strike?"

"At the cry of '*First Blood!*' And hope to God it is not hers!"

"By Odin that is a fearful strategy," the big Danish leader said sternly, looking first at Hugo, and then around the table at his men. "No matter, that is a clear signal," he added, with a sharp nod of his head. "They will surely all shout that out, that is for certain. No matter, I will shout it out myself! And, you archers, when you hear my voice, that is when you will let all hell loose in that hall. Drench those bastards down there with arrows...but not the king. Guthrum is Alfred's meat, and I will not have him struck down like that. But the rest are all fair game. Out swords and at them. What about your troupe of heroes?"

"We will guard your back. I will be with Oswald as our spear point. When he is fully roused he is a terrifying enemy, and remember, apart from the king's guard, the enemy will not be armed. So, you archers, mark down your targets carefully. Take the time to spot every one of Guthrum's armed men before you are called upon to fight."

"And how do we get out, Lord?" Raedwald asked.

"After we have set the place on fire!" Hugo replied blandly.

"*On fire?*" Ricberht gasped, appalled.

"Yes...on fire. Blazing, rampant fire!" the great Bearmaster exclaimed, tipping the last of his ale down his throat. "I want the whole building to go up around us like a huge bonfire at Beltane, and in the smoke and confusion we will escape! You archers from the gallery, down the stairs to the outside.

"All the rest through the double doors we came through at the start, with Brioni and Maritia. Oswald and me from the back. I have discovered there is a door there, behind that huge tapestry. That is where they will get Guthrum out, and I will plan to be fast behind him. Then swiftly through the ginnels to the main gate at the back of the town. You archers get there fast, for you may need to clear the gate towers, and the gateway, of the enemy.

"What about the gates themselves? Surely they will be closed against all comers?" Raedwald said anxiously.

"Tonight they will not be a problem. The Danes are confident in their hold on this area, and because of the Horse-Fair, and the king's return, the curfew bell has been suspended, so the town will be open tonight. It could not be better for us. Just beyond there is a dingle shielded by a ring of trees and thick laurel where we will find all our horses, many with packs on their backs for we will be leaving everything behind...and a large tilt cart for Oswald, which Signet and Beauty will pull."

"A cart for Oswald? How will you get that there?" Finnar asked, astonished.

"You are forgetting the Horse Fair," Hugo responded swiftly. "There will be carts and horses everywhere, and stray camps as well. There always are; with traders, horse copers, pedlars and quacks all over the place, we will be lost amongst them...and Oswald cannot make the journey to Battlesbury on foot alone. It is too far and we will be travelling too swiftly. He would get left behind and that is just not an option; he is far too valuable to all of us."

"Won't that slow us down, Bearmaster?" Raedwald asked, leaning forward over the table.

"No. The tilt cart has been specially designed with large spoked wheels and a strong bed. We often use it. Oswald can get in and out easily and it is ideal for display as it has bars around it that he can hold onto when he stands so all can see him. We will be using it tonight for our parade. Trust me, it is all arranged, including my hoard and Wulfstan's halidom and treasure. Then, God willing, we will all escape into the wilderness beyond, as Alfred did after Christmas."

"And with all in absolute turmoil in Chippenham," Finnar said slowly. "With no-one knowing who is doing what, or to whom, nor where the king is amongst the flames, smoke and towering sparks...we should all get clean away!"

"Sweet Jesus, we must all be mad!" Ricberht gasped. "Gladiators, Amazons, arrow storms, raging fires, furious Vikings! Thank God all I have to do is obey orders," and he buried his face into his drinking bowl while everyone laughed.

*

"So this is what happens the moment my back is turned?" came a bright female voice a few minutes later, and Maritia came bounding up onto the dais and flung her arms around her father's neck. Behind her came Jaenberht, his face wreathed in smiles at the sight of Finnar's command lounging round the table, drinking bowls in hand, and shouts of welcome on every lip.

"*By saint Cuthbert!*" her father shouted, pulling his daughter onto his knees. "But you are a sight for sore eyes, my bird. How is it with you? Did you and Jaenberht find Rhonwen...?

"My Rhonwen?" Cadoc asked swiftly. "My cariad girl; the light of my life?"

"Yes, Cadoc the Archer," Maritia replied with a broad smile. "Your cariad girl, and she is in fine form and still loves you dearly, though God knows why, for you test her heart every step of the way. Now, listen up, for there is little time and I have much to say."

"And we have much to tell you too," Hugo said, giving his daughter a big squeeze. "And much more that Grimnir needs to know also," he added, giving her a smacking kiss, "so you will need to go back and find Rhonwen again. No matter, sweetheart," he went on with a grin as she gave a long groan of annoyance. "Sit by me now, and tell us all you know."

And slipping onto a stool beside her father's great armed chair, and close to where Julio was also seated, she told them all that she had managed to arrange with the young brew-mistress, while Gilbert brought more drinking bowls and fresh food from his kitchen.

Chapter Eleven

*F*or a moment after Bjarke had slammed the door shut Brioni lay on the floor, half stunned by her fall, but was on the balls of her feet in moments, ready to fight for her life if necessary, while the two women amongst whom she had been so violently cast, were amazed.

"Who are you?" Brioni snarled her hands clenched into proper fists, as Finnar had shown her long ago, with her thumbs tightly round her forefinger, and her arms drawn back to cover her chest as she faced them, her back to the door.

"Dear God, it is a wolf come amongst us, Beornwyn," the nearest girl said with disdain, brushing her long black hair out of eyes so dark as to be almost black. Her skin white, her accent strongly Cornish, her body sheathed in green silk, her naked thighs thrusting through long slits that ran up to her waist, itself cinched in with a wide belt of white suede dotted with seed pearls. "At least she looks like a wolf with her teeth bared and her hair shorn like a criminal's! What on earth are we to do with her in the time we have before the king returns?"

"She is the Lady Brioni of Foxley, Merwenna," the other girl said, sitting down half naked on the great box bed that dominated the room, her russet hair draped over her bare breasts, her blue eyes wide with astonishment as Brioni turned to face her. "She is Ránnulfr's latest capture. The woman he has been madly searching for since he was wounded at Malmesbury. The woman who nearly defeated him!"

"*You!*" Merwenna shouted out, stabbing her fingers at Brioni. "You are the one responsible for all the beatings we have had, the curses, the shortened rations, the unusual cruelties," she added, showing a livid bruise on her right arm. "It is a wonder you are still alive!"

"Calm down, Merwenna," Beornwyn said gently, as the tall, black-haired girl hissed her anger across the room. "You cannot blame this girl for striving to defeat Tostig…"

"Tostig?" Brioni interrupted, astonished.

"Yes. Tostig Ránnulfr. He is our very Lord and Master," the russet haired girl said then, elegantly turning her shoulder to show Brioni the branded letters 'TR' that had been burned into her flesh with fine wire. "We are his to command until he tires of us. And we are commanded to prepare you for your presentation before Guthrum, the High King of the Danes."

"And who are you?" Brioni demanded, lowering her fists, and stepping forward into the centre of the wood panelled room, a large iron brazier on tall legs a mass of low flames in one corner.

"I am Beornwyn of Mercia, and that over there in green silk and a white waist band, is Merwenna from Cornwall. She is proud and spiky. I am soft and compliant, and we are his women. Tostig's whores," she added matter-of-factly, with a shrug and a certain smile. "The Vikings reward us for our services as long as we please them. The priests would shave us and burn us as heretics if they could. We would rather be good whores, than crisped maidens. What are you doing here, dressed like that, and all your hair cut off?"

"My family were destroyed by Oscytel just after Christmas. Now I am a fighter; my long hair was in the way so I cut it off," Brioni replied, sitting down on the edge of the bed, running her hands through her hair. "I was taken prisoner this morning after a fierce skirmish. I killed two of the bastards and sliced up a third before I was overpowered and brought here by Bjarke and thrown into a foul lock-up. Now I am here for you to prepare me for my presentation before Guthrum, whatever that means. I expected to be tortured and made to tell all I know. Now I am to be brought before the king, or that animal Oscytel, for their pleasure," she added appalled.

"The Black Jarl?" Beornwyn said in hushed tones. "He is the captain's commander. He makes my whole body shudder."

"He is a monster! He carved the Blood Eagle in my father's living body, while I was forced to watch from my hiding place."

"You were lucky he did not see you," Merwenna said sharply, her eyes sliding across Brioni as she spoke. "Where did you hide?"

"In the family midden, buried up to my neck!" Brioni exclaimed sharply, rubbing her hands over her eyes. "It was all so dreadful...and afterwards I swore a binding oath to be avenged on that *butcher*, cursed him with every pagan god I knew. I have been fighting his men ever since."

"Certainly you are like no other girl the captain has captured, Beornwyn said, running her hands over Brioni's arms and shoulders. "You have hard muscles where we just have softness. Your belly also, I can tell, and your thighs. You are truly unusual. You will fetch a high price."

"A high price?" Brioni asked, shocked. "Is that all you can think of? What about escape and freedom? Alfred and Wessex?"

"Alfred and Wessex?" Merwenna queried bitterly. "Are you mad? The King is finished, and Wessex is no friend to me. Wessex took over Cornwall, when my father was a young man. He was a prince of my people, of King Dungarth's family, who fought with the Vikings against your King Ecberht forty years ago at Hingston Down and were defeated...thrashed! My family lost everything, and my mother, then a child, was left destitute, despite her birth.

"Then the Vikings came again when I was grown and took me," Merwenna snarled bitterly. "So don't talk to me about Alfred and Wessex. Now the Vikings are everywhere and Alfred has fled. Here we are sheltered, well fed and cared for. Protected. Out there is a bear pit! The last girl who tried to escape was captured and raped to death....so don't talk to me of escape and freedom either!" And she turned away to lift a tall silver goblet of wine, obviously a former chalice, from a nearby chest beside the door.

"You asked the wrong questions," Beornwyn said, with a shrug. "I told you. She is proud and spiky!"

"So what happens next?" Brioni asked then, not willing to engage in a furious argument with those whom she needed most to assist her.

"We have you washed, cleansed and then dressed in such a way that all men can admire your undoubted charms," Merwenna drawled, coming up to the blonde girl and lifting her face to look into her eyes.

"You mean naked?"

"Almost. Your loins covered, your tits bare, your nipples painted, like Beornwyn's," she said pointing to Beornwyn's breasts with each sharp crest and broad aureole painted blue. "And like mine," she added pulling her dress open to reveal her own body, her thick tips and aureoles painted black, "so all men will know you for what you are. A whore like us!"

"*No!*" Brioni responded violently, covering her chest with her hands.

"*Yes!*" Merwenna hissed at her, squatting down so that her firm breasts pressed out towards her. "A whore like us, my fine Lady of Foxley," she sneered, snatching her hands apart, with a twisted smile. "And if you refuse to co-operate we will have Bjarke, or Hakon, in here to force you to comply. And they will not be gentle. Especially after you have been responsible for the deaths of three of their comrades!"

"You would not do that to me," Brioni replied, horrified, her eyes flashing with anger. "You might as well stand by and see me raped!"

"Wake up, girl," Merwenna replied fiercely, standing up again. "You are not free. You are a prisoner of Captain Tostig Ránnulfr. It is remarkable that he has not already had you! Ploughed you on your hands and knees while his men applauded his efforts. That's what happened to *me*, my fancy Lady Brioni of Foxley, and I was a princess!" the tall black-haired girl snarled at her. "The more I screamed and shouted the more he pounded into me, until I met him thrust for thrust, rode him to exhaustion and made *him* cry out for a change. That brought me applause from his men, and that pleased him, made him laugh, and he bought me off the king, branded me and kept me."

90

"Bought you from the king?" Brioni asked, bemused.

"Yes!" Beornwyn chipped in. "All captured girls that are brought in are the king's property first. Most just get raped where they are captured, their throats cut and left to bleed out. That's what happened in my village when the heathen came there. But the prettiest are brought in and presented.

"It is a cattle market," she said, kneeling up on the bed, her long hair parting over her bare breasts. "Usually the king's whores dress and present each girl to her best advantage. Whoever buys pays the whores for having done such a good job. Sometimes the girls are presented by the captains who have taken them, as you will be. But the king always has first choice. If he does not want the girl, then the Black Jarl gets second choice, the Lord Oscytel, Tostig's leader...or the capturer can buy her, and she will join those who already serve him!

"And if no one buys?" Brioni asked, appalled.

"Then they are handed out as gifts to whoever wants one," Beornwyn replied with a casual shrug.

"Then they are whored, forced to service anyone who is willing to pay for it until they are fit only for death," Merwenna added, covering herself with the green silk of her dress. "I am a happy pagan, but many nuns have ended up being whored. The Vikings love to boast of having had a bride of Christ! The more they scream the more the men like it. It is a brutal world that you have fallen into," she added, as Beornwyn lay back against a small mountain of pillows, her blue nipples matching her eyes.

"Like Merwenna, I also managed to please Tostig," she said, with a smile. "I had the trick of it right from the start, and I have a good body, like you I think," she added, sitting up to put her hands around Brioni's full breasts. "They like them firm and well rounded," she added, as Brioni pulled sharply away from her, her face a picture of distaste.

"Do I have any choice?" she asked of them, her eyes stormy, her voice clipped.

"None!" Merwenna answered her with malice. "But be sure we will prepare you the very best way we can. After all, we wish to please Tostig...and you are worth fistfuls of silver to us.

"Are the king's whores branded as well?"

"Yes. With a delicate crown," Beornwyn said, feeling her own brand as she spoke. "But they get better food and treatment, and do not get sold on, as may happen to us. Looks do not last, Brioni, and with hard work and much saving it is possible to buy one's freedom."

"That's what we are both trying to do," Merwenna drawled, reaching for a fine gilt-lined silver jug of wine, to refill her goblet. "Vikings like money.

They need silver for fine weapons, for clothes, for jewellery…and for slaves. Think of those poor wretches who work in the mines, on the salt pans and on the land. Most are worked until death."

"At least we are kept in luxury and warmth by comparison," the russet-haired girl added with another smile. "It is not all bad, and if you really please your lord it is not unknown for him to marry you!"

"Enough!" Merwenna exclaimed briskly, clapping her hands. "We have a job to do, so get those clothes off you, and let's see what you've got. Beornwyn, send for hot water from one of those oafs outside, and the half barrel we use for our bath, and I want fresh towels from Heidi, the house keeper. Swiftly, mind, or I will have her beaten before the sun sets. We have little time and much to do!

"You are very peremptory with your instructions" Brioni said, astonished, as Beornwyn covered herself with a blue shawl and went to the door, while Brioni pulled her bloodied tunic over her head.

"I am Merwenna the Black," the dark haired girl answered proudly, tossing her hair. "That is my colour, hair and tits as I showed you, and a black damask cloak. I am Tostig's favourite. Those fools out there know I can have them flogged if they do not please me. Just as I know he will flog me if I do not please him…or even if I do," she hissed at Brioni with a smile, and a shake of her shoulders, as the Lady of Foxley pulled off the last of her soiled clothes, which Beornwyn swiftly gathered and threw into a corner.

"My," Merwenna said, standing back to look Brioni over from top to toe. "You are lovely: such fine skin, such large eyes and elegant cheek-bones. Those tits are as firm as mine, but fuller, and your arse is beautifully rounded. When we have cleansed you and washed your hair, I have just the dress in mind that will set you off to perfection.

"Red silk, split from your tits to your navel, and bright scarlet crests to match. You will be a sensation, worth many pounds of silver. We should do well out of you, my brave Saxon fighter. Tostig will be overjoyed as he leads you in."

"Leads me in?" Brioni queried, stepping sharply back

"Yes. Like the prize bitch you are, my fancy Wessex Lady," Merwenna sneered at her. "Half naked and with a scarlet leash around your waist! Now, get over here behind this screen," she ordered crisply, as there was a knock on the door. "That will be the men with the bath and water. We cannot have the common soldiery seeing you like this - and Beornwyn, put a jacket on to cover your tits. We may be the captain's whores, but we are *his* whores…not just anyone's!"

Chapter Twelve

Some hours later, with the sun tilted to the west on a late spring afternoon of surpassing beauty, Brioni stood in Tostig Ránnulfr's large chamber as ready for her coming ordeal as it was possible for her to be so.

Her body washed, painted, and naked beneath a fine dress of scarlet silk, split to the waist to leave her legs free, with narrow straps that left her breasts bare, she looked stunning. Around her waist was a wide belt of white linen stitched over with blue beads to match her eyes, a brass ring in its centre, and on her feet were half boots of white suede with firm leather soles...and she felt appalled and humiliated.

Not even with Leofric had she ever dressed herself to look so brazen, nor painted her face and body as Beornwyn and Merwenna had done to her. Dark kohl around her eyes, lips rouged with red amaranth from India that had even been rubbed into her cheeks to give her more colour, and thickly onto the aureoles that crowned her breasts, and the long, pointed tips they supported.

She looked what she was supposed to be, a painted harlot. Like those who plied their trade around the docks and brothels of any port, or major town, in the land, and for almost the first time since leaving Leofric's side, tears sprang to her eyes, and she stamped her feet with anger and frustration.

"No! *No!*" she shouted, outraged. "I cannot go out like this...not like a common whore, for everyone to ridicule and step away from."

"*You stupid bitch!*" Merwenna shouted back at her. "Common whore? I could hit you! That dress would cost you *fistfuls* of silver, let alone the boots and belt. The kohl for your eyes comes from Egypt, and the rouge with which I have painted your tits, and lips, comes from India, a place of dreams! Tostig bought it for us from a merchant in Byzantium, and it cost a fortune, as does the musk perfume I have yet to daub you with! I told you, we would do the best for you. And we have done.

"You talked of freedom, yes? Well, you ungrateful *doxy*," she raged, "I told you that we get paid by our Lord and Master if we present you well and that money goes towards our freedom. It is all we can do, my fine Lady of Foxley," she sneered at Brioni, shocked by her violence.

"We carry no crown on our shoulders!" she exclaimed, outraged. "When our looks go, or the captain tires of us, we will be thrown out. So, unless your precious Alfred can rise up from his stinking bogs and beat the Great Army in battle - and fat chance there is of that, I am thinking - then what little silver we can cobble together, Beornwyn and I, will be all that will stand between us and a terrible end.

"We have dressed you and primped you to please the king, so that he will choose you for himself. So, don't you *dare* sniff and pout and weep pathetic tears before us anymore. You are a slave, and a whore, and of no value to anyone unless you can convince them otherwise with your posture, your body and your willingness to serve. You make me sick!" And she turned and swung away, almost shaking with the violent force of her feelings, while Beornwyn sat on the edge of the great bed and looked at Brioni with an apologetic shrug of her shoulders.

And then there was a knock on their door.

Not hesitant, nor peremptory, just a firm *rat-at-at* on the door, that Beornwyn rose to answer, her blue shawl round her shoulders to cover her body, while Merwenna turned to see who it was who could be visiting them, pulling the green silk of her dress closed across her chest. This left Brioni standing by the bed in all her scarlet finery and semi-nakedness, her face flushed with sudden embarrassment.

At the door, with two armed men of the king's personal guard behind him, stood a small man with silver hair and neatly trimmed beard, in red boots and blue suede tunic, a plaid cloak and a green harp bag across his back. It was Grimnir Grimmersson the Skald, glee man and advisor to the king, a broad smile on his face, who pushed his way into the chamber and greeted the two girls standing there like old friends.

"So, Beornwyn, Merwenna, how goes it with you?" he said in his precise voice, allowing the guards to close the door behind him. "I have not seen you in the King's Hall for many weeks. I have missed your smiles," he added, coming forward to kiss each girl on her painted cheek, patting shoulders in welcome and kindness as he did so…much to Brioni's stunned surprise, who had to do all she could not to shout out his name and fling her arms around him, even as her heart leapt in her breast at sight and sound of him.

"I am just come from Tostig's hall to see this rare capture the whole town is talking of," he went on in his clipped style, turning to Brioni and looking her over much as a man might who had come to view a horse, his face bland, his eyes steady. "It is said she is the Lady Brioni of Foxley, one of the leaders of the marauding band of wolfsheads who have been giving the Lord King Oscytel so much grief. She looks like a whore, not a fighting vixen. I am astonished. Does she speak?"

"Too much, if we let her," Merwenna said harshly. "She has been trying to teach us about Alfred."

"Oh, the bog-wight King of the Marshes," the little harper snorted with laughter, ignoring Brioni as if she were not there, and turning to accept a goblet of wine from Merwenna. "Guthrum and Oscytel will soon have him to rights. A message has just come in," he added, moving to look into Brioni's face with one eyebrow slightly raised. "It is said that the wolfshead leader known as the 'Fox' is going to assault Swindon in two days' time. His name is Leofric Iron Hand and the Black Jarl is almost purple with rage. He has called out all his men. Listen, there go the horns," he added as a deep *Hoom! Hoom! Hoom!* bulled out from the fortress town behind them.

"He will leave with his whole command shortly, all armed to the extreme, even before the king returns from Cricklade. Tostig, however, is forbidden to go, much to his fury, so step around him carefully, girls," he said with a chuckle. "He has to present this little beauty here to the king, who will be astonished at sight of her. Guthrum will be expecting a fighting Valkyrie…not a simpering, painted harlot. I commend you, my dears," he said, drinking deeply from his goblet and bowing towards them with a smile. "No-one could have done a more spectacular job, particularly on one whose hair has been almost shaved off as if she were a criminal! Simply disgraceful," he said with deep disdain. "But, with all of this on view," he added, sweeping his hands casually over Brioni's painted breasts, "he may want her to challenge one of his own for his amusement…or his protection," he added, laughing, his eyes fixed on Brioni's face as he spoke.

"*What?*" Beornwyn said, appalled. "After all we have done to please Tostig and the king? We need a silver reward, not the bloodied remains of Merwenna's best silk dress!"

"Never fear, girls," the little man said, turning towards them. "If the king accepts the Lady Brioni's challenge, which I am sure she will make with stamping style," he said with a caricature posture, "then be certain he will pay you what silver he thinks you deserve. Though Guthrum may be many things he is at least fair. He is sure to have her armed and armoured before any blow is struck."

"A challenge? From this painted harlot?" Merwenna queried, disgusted. "He would do better to have her humped by any challenger, than armoured-up with a weapon in her hand. Hasn't she done enough damage without her doing more?"

"Oh, the Vikings love a good challenge," the little man riposted swiftly, turning to look at Brioni again. "And, besides, they may want to see what a woman can do with a sword rather than a broomstick!" And he laughed, offering the half-naked woman a derisive toast that made her squirm.

"She might escape!" Beornwyn said, appalled. "Then where would we be?"

"Escape?" the silver-haired harper queried, throwing back his head and laughing again, raising his goblet into the air. "With the *Circus Maximus* right behind her, dressed up in Roman Gladiators' armour..."

"Gladiators' armour?" Merwenna interrupted, astonished.

"Yes! A whim of the Bearmaster's. He thought some form of masque might amuse the king this evening on his return from Cricklade. Mock combat by the famous acrobats of the *Circus Maximus*. It should have the Vikings rocking in their seats.

"And then there's the massive Oswald, sweet-stepping on his toes in the way also. So I don't think escape is likely, do you? You'd need armed men and archers in the old musician's gallery above the hall for that to happen," he went on, turning back to look again into Brioni's eyes, with one half lifted eyebrow. "And how could that be? With Guthrum's armed guards everywhere, and deep within the Dane's most well-defended fortress in all Wessex, they must surely be as safe as houses!"

"*Faux!*" Merwenna snorted, disgusted. "I don't believe one half of what we have heard of this little tart. It is said that she nearly defeated Ránnulfr single-handed at Malmesbury. But I know that Tostig was struck down by an arrow from behind.

"And as for killing three of his men last night before she was captured? How do we know she did not have help from someone in the town? No, she is too meek. Look at her, standing there almost goggle-eyed at your talk, all scarlet tits and painted face," she said with mocking laughter. "You just wait until she walks in there tonight after the feasting. The men will be hot for her. They will rave, and roar and roust for her. Fight for her honour? She has no honour, and if the king rejects her, she will go to the highest bidder, and her price will be enormous!"

"You don't like her very much, Merwenna, do you?" The little harper said.

"No, she challenges my sense of pride, and my well-being."

"But she has said nothing," Beornwyn replied swiftly.

"No! And that's why I don't like her," the tall dark-haired girl spat back. "She shows no spirit, no sense of value. Oh, she has airs, but no defiance...and she is a maid of Wessex, and that just enflames me more. The men in there tonight will eat her alive!"

"Well," Grimnir said, with a half grin, "you may be right. But you have done a great job on her, and I will reward you for that," he said brightly, handing over two pieces of silver to each girl. "If she fights tonight, and there is a shout of '*First Blood*' from the crowd," he said, turning back to Brioni with ultimate disdain, "and it is not hers, then there will be a riot, and her price will go through the roof like dragon-fire!"

And turning away from her with a final stare, he gave the girls a smile and a sweeping gesture of approval and left the room, leaving both women laughing at all he had said, and Brioni stunned into silence.

*

*T*he moment she had seen who it was at the door, she had been filled with such a fierce surge of hope that it was a wonder she had not shouted out her joy and danced round the room! Next moment she had taken a deep breath and forced herself to stay calm and detached. Knowing that Grimnir would not have come to the girls' room just to view Ránnulfr's prisoner, and threaten his own safety so dangerously, there had to be a real purpose behind it all.

And the moment he had talked about the message coming in, and about Swindon, she knew what he had come to do, and that she was no longer alone. That somehow her friends were mustering. And she had listened and looked with a studied calm and intense silence, no matter how much she had felt goaded by all that Merwenna had said.

Grimnir looking at her, his raised eyebrow, his pointed stares when he had talked about Oswald - and when he had mentioned about archers in the gallery, and armed men, she had almost shouted out again. Her eyes bulging with the effort to remain still, as she knew then that Leofric had been told of her plight and had sent men to Hugo for her rescue.

So, there was a plan, but it would require her to challenge the Vikings to let her fight for her freedom. Freedom from whoredom - freedom to choose what should happen to her - to be protected by Guthrum and not handed over to Oscytel? She was not sure, but it was clear that she was to make her challenge to fight with defiance and bravado, and she could do that in style, even more so dressed as she would be that night. Then there was all that talk about '*First Blood*,' a riot and dragon's fire. Were those signals for an attack? She supposed they must be. Every word that Grimnir had said needed to be considered for whatever truth might lay hidden behind them.

And not a word to either girl.

Beornwyn was one she felt she could have trusted, but Merwenna was as bitter about her life as gall, and would bring her down if she could...as much to do down Wessex as for the money and position that such an action might give her. She was a pagan and already half a Viking. That was the problem with

97

the Corn-Welsh, they were stuck between two cultures: the Saxons of Wessex and the Christian Britons of Wales, with the Viking Danes in the middle, and Merwenna seemed to have decided that her future really lay with Tostig Ránnulfr, Guthrum and the Danes, and not Alfred of Wessex.

She would need to be careful, very careful.

And turning back from the door through which Grimnir had just left she turned round to find Merwenna looking at her, her eyes a-squint in concentration and her eyebrows raised.

Chapter Thirteen

*T*he rest of the day passed slowly, despite the furious activity outside as Oscytel, the Lord King of the Jomsvikings, rushed out with his men for the Danish fort at Swindon beneath wide open skies of blue and a tilting sun, its long rays bathing the burgeoning countryside in shafts of golden light. Not his whole army, but all those who were garrisoned in the town, hundreds of them, in galloping pairs, hooves flashing and armour shining brightly as they barrelled out of the town, shields on their backs and helmets burnished so they shimmered in the sunshine.

Then, in the late afternoon, with the sun sinking in a ball of crimson fire, the horns bellowed out again, this time from the towers beside the gates, *Hoom! Hoom! Hoom!* as Guthrum, High King of the Danes, with flags and banners and his armed guards around him, swept back into the town from distant Cricklade.

With shouts and cries the vanguard rode with tempestuous style, stirrup to stirrup before their king, their raven flags fluttering bravely, black and yellow, as they came. Behind them, his great bear cape flying from his shoulders, his arms glistening with gold, a heavy golden torque round his neck and his head bare, Guthrum rode tall in his saddle, itself thick with silver, upright and looking every inch a great king. And then came the rest of his royal guard, streaming in behind him, their arms and armour shimmering in the late sunshine, the people ruthlessly pushed back as with helmets closed up, they pounded across the great trestle bridge in a thunder of iron hooves and up the hill to the King's Hall at the top.

There, ostlers and varlets ran out to gather in the horses while his women in silk, wool and furs rushed forwards to welcome their Lord King home, and his people standing round roared out their approval. And as he leapt off his horse and swept into his Hall, the jewels on his fingers and in the hilt of his sword flashing in the sunlight...so his armour bearer followed with his great war-shield, a fierce raven with wings spread and feet filled with blood, boldly painted on its leather surface.

Clustered around their king was his royal guard, spears in hand and swords by their side, their scale and mail armour burnished with sand and vinegar until it shone like fine silver, their shields gripped firmly in their left hands, each metal boss a weapon in its own right, and crested helmets on their heads.

With one great shout they turned and stamped inside, three men alone left to guard the doorway into the royal hall and the old wooden staircase, with its thatched lean-to roof, that ran up the side of the building. This led to a small covered platform at the top, and so through a recessed doorway into the old chapel gallery that Alfred's priests had used, and that the Danes had long abandoned. Three armed guards to check passes and keep order, who would have to be moved for Cadoc and his men to take up their positions above the main body of the hall before Guthrum's great welcome feast got started.

"They are confident," Finnar said quietly to Raedwald and Jaenberht as they watched the bustle going on before them from a sheltered doorway. "Only three men to do the work of six. Their Guard Commander needs his balls kicking! I wouldn't want to be in his shoes when this is all over. Only three men! I can think of half a dozen ways to shift those three for long enough for Cadoc and his crew to get up there and disappear inside."

"What if the door up there is locked, or barred?" Jaenberht asked, looking up the ancient covered staircase to where the hidden doorway led inside the King's Hall.

"Then they will have to break it down. With all the rumpus I have in mind that would go unnoticed."

"Angel and the mule cart?" Raedwald queried, his hand on his big leader's shoulder.

"Yes...or a wild fight and sudden upheaval right outside the entrance," he added as an after-thought. "But I think the mule cart is best; with a load of sticks and faggots on it for the royal hearth. The boy is young, looks as sweet and innocent as a maid and can bounce like a rubber ball. He can drive up under escort, our men all armed with passes, Cadoc's archers in the crowd that is bound to be there. All waiting for the *Circus Maximus* to make their entrance to the hall for the entertainment."

"After dark?"

"No, dusk, when the light is most difficult, confusing; then an accident and a tumble. Later there should be a fine night, with a full moon, but there will still be the usual beacons on either side of the gateway. They will be useful to us. Now, come away," he said, slipping back into the crowds that thronged the roadway up to the King's Hall, the others following. "We have some planning to do. Every man needs to be briefed, especially Angel. It is a good thing he is a bright lad, for his part in our play will be crucial. Julio should be proud."

And, with Raedwald and Jaenberht by his side, Finnar made his way back down the hill to the bridge gate, blue passes at hand, and to the guards who watched over it. But with so many coming and going the men stationed there were overwhelmed, and allowed most just to push past them with a shout and a smile. This was the strongest Viking fortress town in all Wessex, and filled with armed men. Who would dare to risk their lives in an attempt on such a powerful symbol of Danish might, especially when the king himself was in residence?

So, when Finnar and the others laughed and joked with them, 'by Odin' and 'Not 'til Ragnarok!' in their own tongue, just flashing their passes, they were happy to let them by, secure in the knowledge that no Christian warriors would wear a Thor's hammer round their necks with such obvious display, nor invoke the Viking god with such fervour either.

*

*I*n Hugo's great striped tent, and throughout his encampment, all was a scene of immense activity as his entire entourage readied themselves for the evening's excitement. This would be their last performance, and everyone knew it, for after that night there would be no going back to their tents and shelters. Everything that could not be packed into a bag or pannier would have to be left behind. Wagons and tilt carts would also all have to be abandoned, and all the furniture and fittings of Hugo's great tent, even his great chair. Only the horses could go, and while Hugo and his troupe of acrobats, musicians and artists readied themselves to entertain Guthrum and his Danes for one more time, every other person who worked for him got ready to move out, especial care being given to the Bearmaster's hoard, Wulfstan's Halidom and treasure, and Maritia's little casket of priceless perfumes, sponges, cures and ointments.

By evening the whole encampment had been stripped of all that could easily be moved and Julio, Hugo's horse-master, had arranged for all their mounts, including Foxhead, to be moved with care to the sheltered dingle beyond the Queen's Gate at the very back of the town...the same dingle that Alfred had used to spirit his family away when Chippenham had fallen that dreadful January morning.

Horse by horse, and sometimes in small groups, they had been led across the bridge, up through the town and out of the gates at the back. Foxhead the last to go, when the light was seriously fading into a chilly dusk, and before the great flambeaux before the gates, and on the battlements above them, had been lit. He was clearly an animal of great value, as was Starburst, Hugo's great chestnut gelding, and both had been disguised from being such with mounds of bags and packages which Foxhead had hated, snorting and stamping his feet so that twice Julio, who was leading him, was sure the guards would haul him in

101

for questioning. But with so many horses being led through and about the town for the Horse-Fair, the few extra that passed by laden with panniers were not exceptional.

With the darkness pressing down on the town, and people beginning to cluster round the King's Hall in preparation for the arrival of the *Circus Maximus*, always an occasion, with pie sellers, jongleurs, pedlars, pickpockets and prostitutes all jumbled in amongst them, it was time for Angel, Cadoc and his men to do their bit. Because of the king's arrival and the presence of so many casual traders and horse copers, the taverns in and around the town were packed with jostling drinkers and revellers, so many that the usual curfew bell had been suspended. The Danes so confident in their might that the town was open, and the great gates unbarred, just a doubling of the guard instead.

*

*B*rouha the mule was not happy.

He did not like the darkness gathering around him, it was late and he wanted his warm stable, even if that was only a set of sheep hurdles and a pile of straw. And he did not like the tilt cart to which he had been harnessed with much stamping of feet and snorting, despite it being Angel who was to drive him. He liked the boy. Liked the smell of him and the feel of his hands on his bridle, and the sound of his voice. But the cart was difficult, heavy laden, and its wheels rumbled and wobbled unusually. They were uneven and there were crowds of people through which he was having to wend his way. The hill up which he was being driven was steep and the four men on either side of him, fully armoured up, helmets closed and shields on their left arms to keep the crowds away, were roaring out 'King's men! King's men!' in harsh Danish as they marched beside him…and he didn't like that either!

In the back was a great mixed load of split logs, and bundles of sticks amongst which the great war-bows of Cadoc and his archers had been carefully hidden, along with closed bundles of arrows, two for each man. They, in long drab cloaks that covered their armour and personal weapons, were all in the crowds opposite the King's Hall which was guarded by three armed men. Each in chain-mail byrnie with simple nut shaped helmet, long sword by his side, and shield to hand, lounged at ease. Long spears propped up against the stone walls of the entrance, they cheerfully exchanged laughs and banter with the crowds that swirled and chattered round them like a great swarm of starlings.

Men, women and children, many dressed in their best finery, in brightly dyed garments of wool and linen, hoods and wimples, cloaks, tunics and leather breeks; hounds at foot and on the leash, even a stray pig that had

102

escaped from its sty and was being chased by a pair of small boys, much to the amusement of those all standing there.

And into this maelstrom of activity, the shouts, jeers and laughter, Angel drove Brouha and the tilt cart, with Raedwald, Gunnar, Aggi and Ricberht striding beside him shouting their heads off.

Right up to the entrance into the King's Hall they went, where two great flambeaux flared and smoked in the dusky darkness, Raedwald and his men fencing off the crowds with their shields, Angel standing up as they came nearer and nearer…when suddenly he seemed to slip and fall against the wicker sides of the cart. They smashed against the tall left wheel, and with a sudden lurch and bang, it fell off and spun away, scattering the crowd in all directions, and the whole equipage crashed onto the ground spilling its load of split logs and stick bundles out across the roadway.

Consternation, shouting, screams; Brouha *hawwwwing* his head off in wild terror, rearing and stamping in his twisted reins and harness, with people, children and dogs running everywhere…while the three guards lounging outside the entrance to the King's hall were suddenly catapulted into violent action.

Dropping their shields, they rushed to help; to manage the bucking, kicking mule and lead it out of its tangled traces; to pick up the boy who had tumbled off the cart and to gather up the stricken load of timber before the crowd went off with it, already pressing in around the shattered tilt cart.

So busy were they with all that was going on that they did not notice the four men who slipped out of the crowd and without hesitation drew each a long stick from amongst the scattered bundles that had fallen onto the roadway, and two long boxes each, and having gathered them ran nimbly up the old outside staircase with its lean-to cover, and in the swiftly gathering darkness disappeared under its ancient thatching.

A moment later there was a single *crash!* from above, lost to all but the most keen-eared and observant amidst the pandemonium and shouting going on below and all across the square outside the King's Hall.

"What the bloody hell is going on here?" demanded an angry voice, as Raedwald and his men struggled to collect the fallen timber, scattered across the ground. "And who are you?"

"I am Raedwald, a captain of Olaf Thorhollur's command. I am ordered to bring this wood up to the King's Hall for the feasting tonight."

"I know of no such order," replied the guard-captain firmly, a man of medium height, and stocky build, with a neat grey beard; his armour dinted in places and his helmet without face plates or crest. A tough professional, but not of Oscytel's command, the shield on his back not marked with the gold zigzag markings that all his Jomsvikings carried, nor was he wearing their black armour.

"Well, I have my orders here," Raedwald growled, reaching for a small pouch at his waist. "They came from Eriksson himself," he said, dragging out a small square of parchment that Grimnir had long ago given to Leofric if ever it should be needed. "See," he went on, pushing the message under the flaring light of the flambeaux beside the doorway. "'One load of split logs and bean sticks to be delivered to the King's Hall for the feasting.' Now, captain, you may question Guthrum's guard commander if you wish to. Personally I would not want to go near him. I hear he is not an easy man!"

"Bjorn Eriksson is a real bastard," the older man replied sharply, "and hard as iron! But I didn't know that Olaf's command had come in?" he queried, looking into Raedwald's face as he spoke.

"So...what is your name, captain?" Raedwald asked in broad Danish while his men continued to re-load the cart, chatting and laughing with the crowd in the same language as they did so, its big wheel having been rescued and hammered back onto its iron axle with a new pin to hold it firmly in place, while Angel dealt with Brouha, now calmed and ready to be backed onto the tilt cart once more.

"My name? Daag Andersson," the stocky man said then, taking off his helmet and scratching his head.

"Well, Daag Andersson," Finnar's big second laughed, tossing an armful of billets onto the cart. "Olaf's command has been all over the place since we seized this town in January. Back to Gloucester and across to Marlborough. Odin knows where he is now, but I am here under orders. So, what is it to be? We get on with this stinking job and deliver this bloody wood...or you go to Bjorn and ask him what to do?"

"Nobody tells me anything!" The guard captain groaned with vigour. "I didn't even know that any of Olaf's command were here. As for this?" he added, stretching his arms out across the mess of sticks and fallen logs that still lay scattered about, "I don't need that bastard's say so! Finish up here, and take your load round to the back of the hall, and get the camp varlets to unload it all. Then, if you're lucky the cooks will give you and your men something to eat.

"Arn Stollen is the man in charge round there. He is a good Viking, and owes me some favours. Mention my name and he will see you right. Now, for Odin's sake get this sodding cart and that bloody mule out of here!"

And while he stumped off to sort out his command, and clear the crowd out of the way, Angel clicked on Brouha, still trembling from his fright, his eyes rolling, while Raedwald and his men marched along beside him once more, delighted with the way their trick had worked.

104

Cadoc and his men were in...and so were they!

All that was needed now was for the cart to be unloaded and Angel to drive it safely back to Hugo's encampment, ready to return later with Finnar and the *Circus Maximus*, their props and equipment for the masque, and Brioni's helmet, shield, sword and armour.

Chapter Fourteen

*I*n the old chapel, Cadoc and his men made themselves as comfortable as possible, hugely relieved not to have been spotted by anyone as they had scampered up the narrow staircase, nor been heard when they had kicked in the old door at the top, the sudden crash seeming appallingly loud, despite the amazing rumpus going on below them.

Once in, there was a short passageway with several rooms off it, filled with discarded benches, chairs and tables, altar cloths and the black robes worn by Alfred's priests, before they came to the old chapel itself. This was a basic room with the remains of an altar, now hacked in pieces at one end, and a pile of shattered benches and other lumber. At the other was a long barrier of fluted wood, just over waist height, below which stretched the King's Hall itself.

Above their heads the great roof trees arched across the building, the massive timbers that supported it standing tall along both sides, the walls on either side pierced with small arched windows. And at the far end was the broad dais on which the king's great table was placed, lamps and candles in gold and silver arrayed along it, and behind it his great armed chair, once used only by the Saxon king, the chairs of his Council on either side. And everywhere there were trestle tables and benches for his warriors. Down the centre was a broad path of beaten earth and a long hearth in which a fire was already cheerfully burning, the blue smoke winding its way up to the wide smoke hole that was right above it.

Nearest the corner where the wooden barrier butted up against the side wall, was another door, already barred from their side of the chapel, from where Cadoc knew a staircase led down to the passage behind the great doors.

It did not seem possible that they had managed to break into the King's Hall with such a simple trick, yet as they stood hard against the very corners of the simple chapel room, their faces smeared with dirt, and peered carefully below, the whole hall was clear to their astonished view.

Painted shields hung along both walls, everywhere lit by resin torches in iron sconces, with fine weapons displayed amongst them that glinted in the flaring light; a vast embroidery of *Yggdrasil*, the Viking tree of life, and the gigantic dragon, *Nidhoggr,* that gnawed its roots, was stretched across one end above the dais in vivid colours shot through with gold and silver thread. And high in the rafters, pinned there with fat oak pegs, hung the great dragon head from Guthrum's war ship. The fighting longboat that had carried him across the sea from Denmark, when the Great Army of the Ragnar brothers had first come to shore thirteen years before.

And while Orn and Caewlin went back to the outer door and barricaded them all firmly in, Aelric and Cadoc relieved themselves in an old wooden bucket they found amongst the lumber in one of the abandoned rooms, before laying out their arrows, stuck point down in the worn timbers of the floor.

*

*O*utside, the darkness gathered in all the corners of the town, while lights flickered on in cruck house and bothy alike. Everywhere night took over from the day, and a cool wind hustled through the town as a full moon began to rise over the trees and ramparts all around them. The inns were packed with revellers and traders, while families all settled round their home fires for food and idle chatter until it should be time to sally out and enjoy the parade the *Circus Maximus* would make up to the King's Hall. With music, horns and spinning acrobats they would come drumming up from the old bridge, amongst them Oswald the enormous dancing bear, whom all so longed to see. And tonight there was to be a special spectacle. Gladiators from ancient Rome they said! No-one knew what that could mean, but all would be there to see and be amazed.

Upstairs in the old chapel, the men silently ate and drank from their aleskins, sitting crouched up against the outer walls of the hall. Then, apart from one man who remained on watch, each one curled himself into as comfortable a position as was possible and did his best to rest until it was his turn to be roused and take over the watcher's post.

Below them in the great hall torches and lamps were lit and a small army of servants moved round to ready the building for the king's arrival. Small groups of warriors moved in and out with laughter and cheerful banter, and all speculated on the evening's entertainment: on the food and drink that soon would fill the tables; on the acrobats and artists of the *Circus Maximus*; and on the extraordinary tale of Tostig Ránnulfr's capture of the Saxon leader who had almost bested him at Malmesbury. A woman, a Valkyrie, an Amazon of rare beauty it was said, the Lady Brioni of Foxley, who was to be presented that night before the king.

And while their enemies slept above their heads, and dreamed of a victory that would echo down the ages...the Viking Danes gathered below to boast of their battle skills, of the thousands they would slay, and of the Saxon king's defeat

*

*A*s the darkness pressed down all around the town Brioni also waited in growing tension for her ordeal to begin, flexing her body from side to side as Finnar and Eadberht had taught her, and jumping up and down on the balls of her feet.

She missed the weight of her armour and the drag of her weapons on either side. The very lightness of her dress, its exposure of her breasts, and her nakedness beneath on which Merwenna had insisted, made her feel incredibly vulnerable. She recognised that both Beornwyn and Merwenna were used to such dress, and were proud of their exposed bodies, but she felt stripped bare. Open to every ogling pair of eyes, ribald comment and lewd gesture that might be thrown her way. And she was grateful for the long green woollen cloak, edged with fur, that Beornwyn, herself dressed in blue, had given her to wear for her presentation.

They were used to being the pampered whores of a noted Viking captain.

She was not, and hated every moment of her situation...as Tostig Ránnulfr had known she would, as he too waited for the horns to blow for the start of the evening's entertainment.

Dressed in his finest clothes of gold and white silken chemise, short sleeved to display his many gold and silver arm rings, and belted into long chausses in scarlet suede, he looked every inch the Viking war-lord he believed himself to be. And it was with a broad smile that he pulled on knee length boots of blue leather and donned a soft leather jerkin studded with silver stars to match them, while a body slave pinned his long cloak of black bearskin to his shoulders with great ouches of burnished gold, and strapped on his sword and long dagger round his waist.

Tonight he would dazzle in all his finery and humiliate the bitch who had fought against him at Malmesbury by presenting her to the King as the whore she was, and he handled the broad belt and long scarlet leash with which he would lead her in to the King's Hall with deep relish.

Tonight would be a night to reclaim his place amongst his fellow captains, a night to regain his king's respect, a night to remember.

*

*M*erwenna, drinking wine from her gilded silver goblet beside the glowing brazier in Ránnulfr's great chamber, watched Brioni through slitted eyes and snorted at her exercises with derision. She may be the Lady Brioni of Foxley...but to her she was no better than a common doxy. And a Wessex doxy at that!

Alfred was a gurt fool, she thought.

A dangerous, deluded fool! Guthrum would win, and she would be revenged for all the indignities of her life since her father had been slain at Hingston Down, and her happy family life had ended. Deep down she hated all Saxons, especially this one who had supposedly humiliated her Lord to whom she was now deeply attached…and watching the blonde girl move her body, she was reminded of the visit they'd had that afternoon from Grimnir Grimmersson the King's Norse Skald.

And she was intrigued.

Was it possible that he had come to give that bitch some kind of message? Were the stares he had given her really any more than looks of interest? The sort of looks the girl's naked breasts, and lissom figure, might get from any man looking her over? She was certainly very lovely, and she shrugged her shoulders in angry acceptance. But why the quirked eyebrow? Twice? And the pointed comments about armed men, archers and shouts of 'First Blood'?

She emptied her goblet, taken from a plundered Mercian church a year ago, and smiled in pagan malice at the thought of all those murdered monks, and looked at Brioni again, her mind a twisting kaleidoscope of thoughts.

If the little bitch was so great a fighter, then why was she so meek? Why had she looked so stunned when Grimnir had entered their room, and been so determined to say nothing?

Could it all be some kind of trick? Could the Norwegian glee man, so close to both Danish kings, really be a traitor? It was surely ridiculous to think so! Yet the puzzle of all the little harper had said remained, and she was deeply bothered by it. Should she say something to Tostig, or wait until they had entered the hall and look for herself? Tostig would be far too busy with the coming presentation to listen to anything she might say, and she could not share it all with Beornwyn; she was far too enamoured of the Wessex girl already to want to listen. And she was a secret Alfred supporter!

No…she would bide her time, and see what developed while watching the Saxon girl like a hawk. After all, if everything went as planned, the little bitch still represented several fistfuls of silver!

*

*A*cross the river, in the field where Hugo's great tent was still pitched, Angel had taken Brouha out of his traces to be replaced by Gemma, Aelfrid's handsome dappled mare, rescued by Jaenberht and Maritia from Paega's tender mercies. Surrounded by men with flaring torches, the broken wicker sides of the old tilt cart, specially fixed to fall apart, were swiftly replaced, and the mended wheel checked again. Meanwhile Gilbert and his helpers piled in the props that might be needed that evening, the remainder of their belongings, dark grey capes for all in baskets and Brioni's fighting equipment, before leaving to join the throng streaming into the great tent for the last time.

Any moment now the horns would blow from above the gates that led into the town, and they would be off. Every man and woman of the *Circus Maximus* knew what was expected of them, and even now were gathering around the huge Bearmaster's wide dais, the benches all about it packed with his people, many of whom had resin torches in their hands, packs on their backs, or musical instruments: great drums, pipes, flutes, a harp, even a pair of buccinas, the great curved trumpets that the Romans had used to scream orders out across a battlefield.

And on the platform itself Finnar, Hannes and Jaenberht, their armour shining like polished silver in the lamplight, sat beside all those who were to portray the gladiatorial games of ancient Rome.

Julio, the Retiarius, the Fisherman, bare-headed with trident, weighted net and dagger, his left arm with armoured shoulder protector and tough sandals on his feet; Marcus, the Secutor, the Pursuer, to fight him, with smooth helmet that covered his face and two eye-holes to protect him from the fisherman's trident. He wore an armguard, loincloth and wide leather belt, great rectangular shield and gladius, and carried the short sword with which the Roman legions had always fought.

Beside them stood Magnus playing the Murmillo, with great fish-crested helmet, metal-covered right arm, loin cloth and belt, greave and gaiter on his left leg, tall auxiliary style oblong shield and short gladius. Opposite, in closed helmet pierced for breathing and adorned with feathers on top and either side, stood Anton the Thracian, with long greaves, square shield and twelve inches of vicious curved sword. And, finally, in quilted leg wrappings under long shin guards, with segmented metal along his sword arm, a broad-brimmed helmet with feathers like the Murmillo, stood Russel as the Hoplomachus, the Hoplite, Roman gladius in one hand and long spear behind a small round shield in the other.

All the rest of Hugo's people who were to perform that night were dressed in short tumblers' tunics beneath long flowing robes in a variety of colours, with soft leather shoes on their feet, and carrying wands in their hands with long ribbons of scarlet, blue and emerald green. Only Hugo himself was differently dressed, with a huge cuirass of hammered iron that appeared moulded to his body, tied round with wide straps of scarlet leather, beneath his

110

great bearskin cape that flowed from his shoulders almost to the ground. On his feet were great thigh-length boots of scarlet leather, iron studs in thick leather soles, and on his head he wore a crested helmet of Imperial pattern…and in his hand he grasped a gold painted stick with a curious basket handle of cunningly wrought iron enriched with gold and silver.

Beside him, one elegant booted foot resting on a rough bench closeby, stood Maritia, with a very short quilted tunic that hung in thick pleats from her waist that hung just below her loins, her body encased in her mother's Greek armour that barely covered her breasts, pushing them up in firm mounds that glinted in the lamp light around her, and flared out over her hips. Moulded greaves were on her legs over white leather boots, and her shoulders were protected with segmented metal pauldrons that were strapped to a moulded iron collar that ran round her throat on a thick white fleece.

On her head was her mother's magnificent crested helmet of purple horse hair that stood up nearly ten inches in its gilded holder and flowed down her back. At her side was a great round shield with no boss to mar its surface, its scarlet leather painted with the white figure of a leaping horse with feathered wings, Pegasus himself, and at her waist hung her long sword with shaped Greek blade and steel hilt incised with gold and silver.

To say she looked stunning was to fail in expression. She looked simply amazing, everyone's vision of a female warrior. And as she had walked in from her own tented area, wearing a long cloak of purple damask to match her helmet, lined with white silk, flowing from her shoulders, everyone had gasped. Even her father had started in his great chair she looked so like her mother, and there had been a sudden burst of wild cheering and clapping as everyone leapt up to greet her which made her smile and cock her head in acceptance of their homage.

Oswald, seated close to Hugo's chair, a scarlet jacket across his massive shoulders, and a vast metal breastplate in two pieces strapped round his upper body, stood up and roared at his mistress's appearance, waving his huge front paws in the air, his head mowing from side to side as he did so.

"*Right!*" the great Bearmaster shouted, as the noise died down. "It is full dark outside, the flambeaux flare before the gates and any minute now the horns will blow for our parade to begin. Drums, pipes and flutes in the front, with tumblers on either side. Then our Roman pageant, with the buccinas to herald their arrival. I will follow with Oswald in the cart, Maritia beside us on the ground with Finnar Olafsson and his men. We must do our best to keep our good old bear as calm as possible," he said, reaching across to ruffle the huge beast's shoulders, "so he will need his own pipes and tabor close by to keep him happy.

111

"Right at the back will be Angel with Gemma and the small tilt cart, and everyone else who is leaving with us today.

"We will be the first up for this entertainment. Acrobats and tumblers first, all the really clever stuff," he added, to great laughter. "Then our gladiators. The Heathen will have seen nothing like us tonight, I tell you, so the noise will be immense. The buccinas will announce you, and they won't have heard their like either! Julio and Marcus with net, trident, sword and shield...run about and make it look good, before the bastards start calling for your blood! Then Magnus and Anton, with your great helmet and curved sword. Stand and thrash each other with all the vigour and skill you can, before I send in Russel to join you. He will throw his spear first, and then join in the fighting. Two on one. Anton falls first then you and Magnus fight it out until Magnus falls. I have seen you all do this, and those bastards will be astonished, not least by the surprise you have prepared for them. But don't go down too soon, or you will lose their interest, and they will start to boo instead of cheer.

"Then the captain will bring the Lady Brioni in, along with his own women. She will be dressed and painted like a common whore, so it is vital that you do not call out to her. What happens after that is very much in the lap of the gods. We know what is supposed to happen. That she will challenge the king to allow her to fight, but not what the basis of that fight will be.

"It is expected that Guthrum will agree...but we don't know the conditions that may be laid down, except that he will call on me to arm her and arrange the fighters. After that is anyone's guess! But when Finnar shouts *'First Blood!'*, then all hell will break lose in there and we will all be fighting for our lives. There will be absolute pandemonium. Tumblers and acrobats out immediately. You all know where to go, and get Angel and the tilt cart away as soon as possible.

"We will not be far behind. Then, God willing, we will all set out along the road to Battlesbury Rings, which Leofric Iron Hand has shown me how to find.

"Do you all understand?" he bellowed at the end, standing up, as from the distant town the great horns blew at last.

"Yes, Lord! We all understand!" came the roared reply as everyone leapt up and began to move, lighting their torches as they went in strict procession, holding them high and shouting as they strode boldly towards the bridge, drums beating, flutes and pipes playing and great curved trumpets blowing.

The *Circus Maximus* was coming to town.

112

Chapter Fifteen

Within the town, the *Hoom! Hoom! Hoom!* from the walls brought the crowds spilling out from the taverns with wild delight, everyone desperate for the best view. Especially from the 'Stag' right before the bridge, where they poured out around the well to shout and cry out as Hugo's parade stamped and drummed its way over the bridge and up the hill. Horns blowing and trumpets braying as they came, strings of tumblers spinning, cartwheeling and back-flicking their way along in a swirling display of coloured tunics and bright ribbons.

And right behind the great buccinas that screamed out their challenge strode the five gladiators everyone had heard so much about: Julio twirling his net, his handsome face bare for all to see, his body gleaming with oil; Marcus beside him, his closed helmet under his arm, threatening the crowd with his sword; while the heavily armed Murmillo, Thracian and Hoplite, also carrying their helmets, all bravely plumed, stamped and bulled their way up the hill in fine style.

Behind them, in open helmets, with shields on their backs and armour burnished to a gleaming shine that glittered red and orange in the flaring torchlight strode Finnar, Jaenberht and Hannes, their faces wreathed in smiles as they looked to left and right, the giant figure of Hugo the Bearmaster, cuirassed and helmeted, closely following them with Oswald in his special cart. Signet and Beauty, in shining harness, and stepping bravely out, white fetlocks frothing at their feet, coats gleaming and great nodding plumes of white and scarlet feathers on their heads, looked magnificent.

Towering over everyone as he reared up to the sound of pipes and tabor, his chain attached to a great ringbolt in the cart bed, came Oswald in his red jacket and half armour, swaying on his huge furry feet to all his favourite tunes. And the crowd loved him, tossing apples gently for him to catch in his mouth which he crunched with enormous gusto as he clung to the bars around him, nodding his head and giving little coughs of pleasure to show his delight.

Beside the slow moving cart strode Maritia in her Greek armour, her helmet with its great purple crest on her head and carrying a light spear in her hand behind her shield with the leaping Pegasus, wings open, emblazoned on it. No-one had ever seen her in such an amazing outfit, more used to her black leathers and scarlet boots, and soon every young man who could was stepping out beside her, calling out and begging for a kiss. While she, disdaining all, marched on with stern face and eyes fixed as she strained not to smile at their antics.

*

*U*p the hill they made their way, through thickening crowds, the tumblers now walking as the hill got steeper, Signet and Beauty taking the strain as they hauled Oswald's cart up the hill to the King's Square at the top, plumes nodding, bits and harness chains glinting in the torchlight.

Then they were there at last opposite the entrance to the King's Hall, torches flaring, drums beating, horns and trumpets blaring, while the tumblers and acrobats danced, spun and flung themselves around for the enjoyment of the crowd who had gathered from every corner of the town to see the show, and admire the giant bear who stood in his cart and roared his pleasure to everyone. Grouped in the centre were the gladiators, who now put on their great helmets and briefly sparred with each other, while the crowd shouted their approval and howled for one or another of them.

Dashing in with sword and dagger, Hugo's men showed their skill, parrying blows on their shields or turning them on their blades with a flash of sparks...or dodging the fisherman's net whenever Julio whirled it round his head and let it go, giving a great roar of excitement when he tangled Marcus so brilliantly that he fell to the ground completely enmeshed.

And when it was all over, brief as it had been, the packed crowd gave the *Circus Maximus* a huge roll of applause with shouts and cries of great joy, as Hugo led Oswald out of his cart to rear up and clap his great fore paws together with a coughing roar of his own, while one of his men clicked on the horses and drove the cart away.

Then, with a final blast of horns and trumpets they all disappeared inside the King's Hall, itself in a ferment as news filtered in of all that had been seen in the town: gladiators, girls in Greek armour and Oswald the bear. They could not wait, and Guthrum's men were already standing in packed rows when the dancers, tumblers and acrobats came running in, leaping and twisting as they ran, the noise of music, horns and trumpets, and the wild shouts of the Vikings a huge cacophony that no-one could sleep through.

*

*A*bove them in the old chapel, Cadoc and his men were alert to every move. Their swords drawn but lying flat on the floor beside their

114

great war bows, their strings ready to knock in a moment, each man with his leather bracer on his left arm, helmets clamped to their heads and sitting tight against the side walls. Two men to each side. One man, Cadoc the Welshman, helmet off, face streaked with dirt, was stood to one side of the staircase that led down to the hall below. He alone would make the signal to stand and loose, as he searched the shifting throng below for those men of the Royal Guard who were armed...for they would be the first to die!

*

*B*elow them Hugo and Oswald had arrived to tumultuous applause, shouts and stamping feet, especially when the men gathered there in their finery saw Maritia dressed as a Greek warrior. They halloed and whistled her, while she, with Pegasus on her arm, a toss of her horse hair helmet and a swirl of her long purple cape, threatened them with her spear.

They loved the spice of her show: the way her armour flared over her hips and thrust out her breasts, and her athleticism, her moulded thighs and arms, oiled and gleaming, and her flashing eyes beneath the shining metal of her helmet. They knew her as a tumbler and acrobat, spinning and leaping in coloured tunic and light shoes...to see her dressed in armour and carrying weapons was something new and they responded with vibrant enthusiasm. Some of the younger warriors, carried away with the occasion, rushed out to offer their naked chests to her spear which she, with laughter, was quick to thrust out at them before knocking them sideways with her shield, or spurning them with her booted feet to the jeers and laughter of their friends.

After the giant bear had performed his tricks to tabor, pipes and drum, with laughter and applause all round, the great Bearmaster called for silence as his acrobats and tumblers cartwheeled and back-flicked their way out of the hall, followed by his dancers with their long sticks and bright ribbons. While Maritia led Oswald by his chain to the back of the hall, beside the big double doors, where he sat in his armour and scarlet jacket and drank ale from the bucket that always travelled with him.

"*My Lord King!*" Hugo then bellowed in his huge voice, arms raised, as he stood on the hard earth floor below the dais on which Guthrum was seated, his Council around him, Grimnir by his side, the little harper's eyes fixed on his with an unwavering stare. "It is my pleasure to present to you this evening, for the first time since leaving Neustria, a Roman masque. A gladiatorial pageant with skill and real weapons, as it was in the days of Ancient Rome.

"My Lord King, Rome may long have passed away, but if you will be our Emperor for the night," he added, giving Guthrum a deep bow, to roars of

115

acclaim, "we of the *Circus Maximus* will do our best to give you an evening you will not forget." And the hall erupted in a wild burst of sound as all the men there bellowed their approval and stamped their feet, both for Guthrum being named 'Emperor' as well as at the prospect of something new and exciting to see.

And while the varlets and house thralls went round with great jugs of ale and Rhonwen's heather beer to fill the horns, bowls and beakers of the drinkers, so, amid raucous shouts and boasts, with buccinas braying, the five gladiators, dressed for the fight, with their helmets under their arms, came out and stood in a line before Guthrum, High King of the Danes, with Hugo the Bearmaster immediately behind them.

Raising their right arms stiffly in front of them, weapons in hand, they all shouted the words that every gladiator had roared out in every arena in the empire: *"Ave, Imperator, morituri te salutant!"*…'Hail, Caesar, we who are about to die salute you!'

And with the Vikings literally rocking in their seats, shouting out curses, calling to their friends and making wild bets, Anton, Russel and Magnus made a stamping turn and marched behind Hugo, while Julio, the Retiarius, the Fisherman, bareheaded, with his lead-weighted net and trident and Marcus, the Secutor, the Pursuer, with his smooth closed helmet, shield and sword ran out and the Guthrum Games began.

And what 'Games' they were.

Julio running to escape Marcus's sword and shield, whirling his net as he ran, only to turn and spin it out towards his pursuer who brushed it aside with his legionary shield to lunge with his sword at Julio's neck who took the blow on his wide shoulder guard while stabbing at Marcus with his trident, the sharp spikes scoring his shield and scraping off his steel helmet in a shower of sparks.

Back and forth they went, jumping over the fire pit in the centre, and even among the closest rows of trestles. Once the net slipped off Marcus's smooth helmet to shouted groans from all those who were supporting his opponent, and once Marcus almost trapped the slippery Fisherman with his sword and shield only to have him slide away again, until finally, with a practised flick of his hands, Julio cast his net so cleverly that Marcus was once more enveloped in it, its weighted folds trapping him completely, so that he crashed to the ground and was instantly threatened with violent death.

But this was not the Roman Arena, and despite wild cries of '*Kill him! Kill him!*' from some in the hall, both men were adjudged to have fought well and were rewarded by Guthrum with small purses of silver.

116

And so it went on, while the drink flowed in ever increasing amounts, and the Danes got more and more drunk and more and more excited. And when Anton, playing the Thracian, was finally cut down and 'slain' by Magnus's Murmillo after a brilliant spell of sword-work in a violent spray of blood, there were gasps of shock from everyone, and howls of rage from those who had bet on him, two Vikings being physically dragged off the floor .

But that was nothing to the wild shouts when Russel the Hoplite cast his spear into a table of raucous Vikings, scattering drinking bowls and drunken warriors everywhere, followed by a desperate sword fight between him and Magnus. A fierce struggle that looked as if both men were really trying to kill each other: sword thrusts to helmet and shield that scored metal and shaved wood, and blade striking blade in fierce showers of sparks, until finally, with a great overhead smash to the head, Russel left his sword stuck in his enemy's helmet to a great spurt of blood, and wild, stamping shouts of acclaim as his enemy fell to the ground and thrashed his feet in death.

At first, Cadoc, watching from above, thought the Murmillo was truly dead, so violent had been Russel's overhead cut into Magnus's head, and there had been so much blood…and there was a concerted gasp and a momentary silence as many in the crowded hall thought so too.

But it was all a trick.

A block of wood had stopped the Hoplite's blade, and hares' bladders filled with pigs' blood had provided the spurting gore, so when he and the 'dead' Thracian both got up, their faces stained with blood, there was a further gasp of astonishment and a great roar of laughter and approval from the crowded benches, while Guthrum hammered his fists on the table and shouted out his praise.

And while Cadoc sank to the ground, exhausted just from watching the fighting, Guthrum demanded that Hugo bring his men out for a further bow and a welcome draught of ale, while more pouches of silver were distributed amongst them, with a larger bag for the Bearmaster himself.

"Bearmaster, you have surpassed yourself, and given my Council and my men a wild evening of excitement and rare skill. There are warriors amongst my host who cannot wield a sword as well as those I have watched tonight. And though I know many of those moves will have been practised and worked out, it has still been a magnificent entertainment, and I applaud you. *Wassail, Bearmaster!*" he roared, raising a deep golden chalice to Hugo and his men. "*Drink hael!*"

"Thank you, my Lord King," the huge man replied, raising his own horn that was always with him, in return. "You have been a most generous Emperor, and I salute you!" and he bowed to the High King of the Danes with steel in his heart as he moved away, his eyes searching everywhere for the armed men of the Royal Guard.

He might be delighted with the way his evening had gone so far; he might, in different times, even have liked Guthrum for himself, he had a reputation for being fair. But this was the Great Army he was amongst and he was under no illusions that until they were defeated there could be no peace in Wessex. Anyway, they were there to rescue the Lady Brioni from the violent clutches of Oscytel, and though the Black Jarl was not there that night he would soon be returning from yet another disaster, and Hugo smiled.

Another failed attempt to slay Leofric and wipe out his command. And when that happened, nothing would save Brioni from awful torture and a dreadful death.

It was then the horns blew again from the passageway behind, a violent blast of sound that shocked everyone as the great double doors were thrust open and Captain Ránnulfr strode in, his two women behind him and a stiff guard of armoured men.

In his hands he held a long scarlet leash with a beautiful blonde girl with luminous blue eyes at the end of it in a scarlet dress split to the waist, with painted face and body open to all who wished to stare, her breasts tipped with scarlet like the silk she wore, and scarlet boots on her feet. Dressed like a court whore in her fur trimmed cape of green wool, she felt like a stripped side of beef on a butcher's hook, and all who saw her howled and shouted, waved their drinking horns and roared out the price that each would pay to own her.

Behind her in green and blue walked Merwenna and Beornwyn, their painted breasts as prominent as hers, cloaks flowing behind them in russet and shimmering black damask, tipped with white wolf fur, their heads held high as Captain Tostig Ránnulfr led Brioni in before them all and bowed before his king.

Surrounded by a sea of faces baying and jeering, with the dais before her on which the High King of the Danes was now standing, his arms raised for silence; the Lady Brioni of Foxley had arrived at last.

Chapter Sixteen

"So, you have come to my order, Captain Ránnulfr," the big Viking king boomed at him, after the hall had stilled. "I hear you have a prisoner for me!"

His hair flowing silver and gold over the collar of his quilted tunic of orange silk, a full beard flowing down his face, his arms ringed with gold, gold at his throat, and his magnificent bearskin cloak falling from his shoulders in shining swathes of black fur, Guthrum looked every inch the mighty pagan warrior king that he was. Black leather chausses, adorned with tiger fur, a heavy gold Thor's hammer hanging on a thick golden chain from the great torque round his neck, two great brooches of intricately patterned whorls of gold and emeralds pinning his cape to his tunic, he was a huge, dominant figure on whom the torches on the walls, and the lamps on the table, flared and flickered red and yellow light.

He was the supreme leader of the Heathen Host that had smashed its way across Saxon England. The Great Army that had come from Denmark thirteen years before under the sons of Ragnar Lodbrok: Ivar the Boneless, Halfdan and Ubbi.

The great Viking host that had carved the Blood Eagle in the living body of King Aelle of Northumbria in retribution for the murder of their father, the great Ragnar Sigurdsson, in a snake pit, and taken his kingdom for themselves; foully slain King Edmund of the East Angles and seized his shattered kingdom...and driven the hapless Burghred of Mercia from his lands and taken them for their own.

Now only Wessex remained largely free in all England, its true King, Alfred, still alive, but forced to flee into the wilderness of Athelney, his kingdom raped by the Danes, his fortress town of Chippenham in their hands, his own hall and even his favourite chair occupied by his Viking enemies.

Guthrum was the most powerful Viking leader in all the land, and Brioni's spirit almost quailed before his magnificence, and that of his Council sitting beside him in all their finery. The slight figure of Grimnir Grimmersson was almost dwarfed by the men around him, his eyes fixed on hers, as she waited for Ránnulfr's response to his king's words.

"That is true, my king," the tall Jomsviking leader said boldly, jerking Brioni forward on her leash. "A prisoner of rare wickedness and beauty, through whom I am come to reclaim my place in the army, that you took from

119

me some weeks ago. You said I was not for you; that I was no longer your man. But I stand before you tonight, with the key to all your troubles."

"And how is that?" demanded the king fiercely. "What have you done that I should restore your honour and take you back into the ranks of my personal command?"

"As you see, my Lord King, I have taken a prisoner. A leader of those wolfsheads who have so plagued us with their bold attacks," he went on, turning to speak to the whole hall, now silent. "The wolfshead who led the attack on Malmesbury some weeks ago, whose men slew my command, who fought me, and would have been slain by me had I not been shot down from behind. A prisoner who can lead us to the nest of vipers that has so bitten us with their poison, my Lord King...and to their leader whom I believe is her consort!" he added, as the room erupted around him.

"Moreover, my Lord, a woman whose family the Lord King Oscytel believed he had utterly destroyed after the death of his son, Tarben," he continued, turning back to face his King. "One whom I have searched after for many weeks, and whom my men seized last night after a desperate skirmish!" And jerking Brioni forward, his men closing up around him as he did so, he forced her to her knees, her face lifted to Guthrum's with eyes filled with scorn.

"My Lord King, I present to you the painted whore, the Lady Brioni of Foxley!" And the hall erupted once more in a great roar of noise and stamping feet.

Again, Guthrum held up his arms for silence.

"So, this is she whom I know you have long sought for," he said, looking at the Viking warlord in all his finery. "Who fought you almost to a standstill?" he demanded fiercely.

"Yes, my Lord King," the man replied boldly.

"Who slew three of your mercenaries last night...Oh yes, I know about that," Guthrum added, seeing the look of surprise that flashed across Ránnulfr's face.

"Yes, my Lord King," the Jomsviking captain replied defiantly. "I sent five men with clubs to seize her."

"Clubs, Ránnulfr?" Guthrum asked astonished. "When last time she almost killed you?"

"I did not want her badly injured. I wanted her fit to be questioned."

"And have you questioned her, Tostig?" the King queried, using his captain's name for the first time.

"No, my Lord, she is your meat. So I am come to present her to you this night as a court whore, as is the custom in the army, for you to examine as you so please."

120

"Have you had her, Tostig?" Guthrum snarled, as a fierce buzz of interest went round the crowded room. "She is very lovely."

"No, my Lord King!" he exclaimed, shocked. "She has not been touched in that way by myself, nor by the men who took her and have guarded her. She was brought unharmed to my quarters, where my women have dressed and painted her for your pleasure. She is a whore, my Lord King," he said with complete disdain. "Uncommon, maybe; but still a whore who consorts with wolfsheads and murderers. She is no fighter. She was lucky at Malmesbury," he sneered dismissively. "Another moment and I would have killed her!"

"You say she is not a fighter, yet she slew three of your men, last night, Tostig," the king said, holding his arms out. "You sent five men to take one unarmoured girl, and she slew three of them! Gutted, handless and a leg ripped from crotch to ankle."

"Luck, my Lord," the Jomsviking leader said with conviction. "She had a short sword. My men had clubs and were under instruction not to do her bodily harm."

"Nevertheless, I am astonished, Tostig," Guthrum said then, pointing down at Brioni as she knelt on the hard earth floor, back lit by the fire that blazed up behind her, her painted breasts thrusting out from her silken dress, her green cloak draped around her, her short hair moulding her face, striking in its beauty, enhanced by the rouge that Merwenna had applied with such skill, her eyes enlarged by the kohl that ringed them, her neck slender.

"She does not look hard enough to have slain so many warriors, nor skilled enough either. Such good luck indeed, Tostig," he said, his tone full of disbelief. "It does not seem possible!" he added, looking back at the captain with disdain. "I can see her in my bed," he laughed. "Or in one of yours," he said mockingly, looking round at his Council, "if you have the silver - or the courage!" he added, as a wave of laughter went round the great room. "But not on a battlefield!"

Then, turning once more to Brioni, still on her knees before him, her eyes stormy despite her best efforts to remain unmoved, he ordered: "Stand up, girl! And show me what you are made of. This man," he went on, staring down at her and pointing to the captain standing with her leash in his hand, "says you are no fighter. That what you have achieved has been through luck, not skill. He says you are no better than a whore!"

"*The man lies!*" Brioni shouted, leaping to her feet, and with a fierce jerk on the long leash attached to her waist she unbalanced the Danish captain so badly that, with a flick of her left foot, and a rapid twist of her hands, she tripped and felled him to the floor. So swift was her action that it took a

121

moment for everyone to respond, the king with a shout of astonishment and a roar of laughter, the crowd leaping to its feet and shouting.

"Not a fighter, Ránnulfr?" Guthrum mocked his war-captain, while the crowded hall laughed and jeered him. "There's no whore in my bed could do that!"

"A trick, my Lord King! *A common trick!*" the Jomsviking replied furiously, dusting himself down, whilst one of his men grabbed Brioni's leash which had been dropped in the scuffle, and others leapt to pinion her arms behind her back.

"Of course it was a trick, Tostig," his king laughed at him, looking down with a grin. "And deftly carried out. You must get her to show you how it is done!" he said to the furious war-leader. "The Lord Oscytel will be impressed," and he gave the man a mocking bow that made him grind his teeth.

"So, what of you, Wolfshead?" he boomed at Brioni, as she stood with her arms pinned behind her back, her naked breasts pushed out of her dress.

"What should I do with you? Who humiliate my warriors and lead your men against them? Dead men today, I think," he added, staring grimly into her face, cool grey eyes into hot blue ones. "Because you have a traitor in your midst I think," he said with a cruel smile, waving her message in his meaty hands. "Cuthbert of Ford. A traitor who has betrayed your leader, Leofric Iron Hand to the Black Jarl of Helsing's vengeance...*Yes!* I know his name now," he shouted as she gasped and leapt against the hands that held her. "And the village he has been hiding in, on which I shall descend at dawn like a thunderbolt," he added as she dropped her head in her hands to hide her sudden smile. "By tomorrow's noon, Ford and all within it will have been destroyed," he added, while Grimnir leapt to his feet and led the roars of approval.

"Your cause is lost! Alfred's cause is lost! When the Lord Oscytel returns he will want you under his hand. Your family slew his only son. He thought when he destroyed Foxley that he had stamped out your line. When he finds I have you, he will demand I hand you to him for his pleasure. And, wolfshead," he said with relish, bending towards her, "he takes his pleasures hard!" And many in the hall stood and bayed for her blood, shaking their fists and stamping their feet.

"Right now you are my prisoner. My meat. To whom will you be called to answer in the morning?"

"*To you, Lord King!*" she shouted out, suddenly breaking free from those who held her, to stand boldly before Guthrum and his Council, the king signalling Ránnulfr's men to leave her be.

"I am no wolfshead, Guthrum, High King of the Danes. I am a freeborn Saxon of Woden's line and loyal to King Alfred. I am the Lady Brioni of

Foxley, and no man has taken my rights from me. *And I am no whore!* No man pays me for my favours! The captain lies again. I am a fighter," she declared with vigour, springing sideways on the balls of her feet. "Trained in battle to wear harness and wield a sword, and I have killed my man many times.

"Now I am your prisoner, Lord King, and cannot fight for my freedom, you would not grant it. But I can fight for the right to remain under your protection...and not that of the Lord Oscytel whose life is forfeit to me for the murder of my family," she shouted out, turning to speak to all who were assembled there.

"He carved the Blood Eagle in my father's body before my eyes. I witnessed all that was done on that awful day, and have cursed the Black Jarl by the old gods of my people. By Tiw, by Thunor and by Woden, and by the Christ child's Father, the God into whose care I was baptised. Oscytel is my meat, Lord King, and I would fight for the right to preserve that oath against any man of your army you may choose to name!"

And she stood foursquare before the Viking king, her body open to his gaze, her eyes blazing in their fierceness and held out her hands in urgent appeal for justice, and the hall rocked with noise. Some shouting, *'No!'* and baying for her blood for the deaths of those she had already slain. Others shouting, *'Yes! Let her fight! Let her prove herself in blood!'* Yet others calling for her to be auctioned as was the custom, some even for her to be whored by all who chose to pay to have her, and then cut down for her crimes against the Great Army.

The noise was fearsome, seemingly unending, until Guthrum raised his arms and stilled it again, before turning to his Council, his face blank, his eyes hard, unyielding, yet his mouth quirked in humour.

"You have heard the plea of the Lady Brioni of Foxley," he said slowly, acknowledging her name, and gesturing to where Brioni stood below the dais. "She asks for my protection. To remain my prisoner and not be handed to the Lord Oscytel, King of the Jomsvikings of whom her captor is a war-captain. She claims right of battle, and challenges me to name a champion on whom she can prove her warcraft. What say you to this?"

The men of Guthrum's Council were hard, experienced professionals, many of whom had fought beside their king since the keels of their dragon boats had first rushed ashore on the coast of the East Angles. Grey-bearded and silver haired, they were the very core of the Great Army, and Guthrum relied on them. But they had chosen him as their king over all others and would follow his lead, and looking at him now they perceived that he wanted this girl to fight. To prove herself? To create more distance between himself and the war-lord, Oscytel? To mock the Jomsviking captain who had taken her prisoner? Even for his own amusement.

And the leader of his Council, Bjorn Gunborg, a gnarled and knotted Viking of more than twenty years' fighting in Frankia and in England, rose to his feet and all waited to hear what he would say. The whole hall hushed by the presence of this man who towered over many, and was nearly as large a man as the king himself.

"Guthrum, you want this girl to fight? To prove herself, before Odin, that she is a fighter, not a common whore? That she deserves your protection?" he questioned in a voice laced with gravel, his eyes as grey-blue as the foam-laced rollers he had sailed for so many years. "*Then so do I!*" he roared out, banging a huge fist on the table, making everything jump. "Let her fight. And let it be the man who faced her at Malmesbury, who says she is lucky! Who lost three men to her sword last night.

"Let her fight Tostig Ránnulfr for your protection, to the death! Swords only, no shields or armour. Let us truly see what skills these two have, like the men of Ancient Rome we saw earlier." And the hall rose to its feet, along with the remainder of the King's Council, and roared their approval.

Clearly the gladiatorial skills they had so enjoyed earlier had whetted their appetites. But those fights had been staged; this was different. This was not even to '*First Blood!*'…this was to the death and everywhere the men shouted and called out their bets, casting their silver into wooden bowls, stamping their feet and calling for more ale, so that the hall varlets were rushed off their feet.

In all this, Guthrum, still on his feet as Bjorn Gunborg had sat down again to talk with the king's Skald, who had been looking round the room at the many weapons hanging from the walls, once more shouted out above the uproar: "Bearmaster! *Bearmaster!* Take charge of this woman. She cannot fight without weapons, nor in that dress and cloak. Your daughter has tunic and sword. Can she prepare the Lady Brioni for her ordeal?"

"*My Lord King!*" Hugo roared back now standing, the huge figure of Oswald beside him, Maritia already jumping forward to receive Brioni from two of Ránnulfr's men who were bringing her forward. "I will do what I can. Be advised that it will take a little while to prepare her properly. But it will be done within as short a time as possible."

"You have until the horns blow again. Then bring her forwards and let the fight begin. Tostig Ránnulfr, arm yourself, and put your men to guard the doorway. I do not intend our Saxon Valkyrie to leave this hall unless she is dragged out as dead meat on which the wolves can feast!

124

Chapter Seventeen

*U*p in the old chapel Cadoc had watched from the very corner of the room, while his men had heard everything, and now, on their hands and knees they crawled out dragging their bows with them, to stand in the narrow passageway beyond. There, out of all sight of those in the King's Hall below, they knocked their bows and greased their bow strings; relieved themselves in the derelict lumber room and washed the dust out of their throats with hearty swigs from their aleskins.

The promise of immediate action had dried their mouths, and filled them with nervous energy. Some bent and twisted their bodies to exercise muscles that had become stiff from waiting; others jumped up and down on their toes, and flexed their bows to test their strings, or rubbed their bracers to be certain they were not too firmly fixed across their forearms.

The challenge had been made, and been accepted. When the horns blew again, they must be ready to rush forward and open fire, their lives and those of their friends below depended on it.

*

*B*ehind the hall, amongst the kitchens and the hall varlets, Raedwald and his men had also heard the roars and shouts from within. Since unloading the wood from the tilt cart, and being fed by Arn Stollen, they had waited in a small ante-room nearby quietly out of sight and mind of those answering the shouts and yells from the main hall. Calls for bread and ale, and meats of every sort, rang through the rooms and passages with which the back of the hall was riddled, and no-one questioned the presence of four strange armoured men whom the many hall servants brushed up against as they rushed to carry out their orders. After all, by dress and language they were clearly Danes. What was there to be concerned about?

Two by two, Raedwald and his men had quietly explored the area, found the rear door behind the huge embroidery through which they would have to try and make their escape into the yard behind the hall, and so into the fortress town beyond. And they found their way right to the edge of the great hall itself from where they had watched all that was going on. Saw the gladiatorial fights, Brioni's entrance with Ránnulfr and her appeal to Guthrum from the floor of the hall in front of the long fire pit...and watched her being led away by Hugo to be armed and made ready for her fight.

The gladiators themselves; Finnar, Jaenberht and Hannes were all armed and ready, even Oswald with his half body armour and massive jaws and claws was ready beside Maritia, herself armed...while above them Cadoc and his men would also be in a state of supressed excitement.

It all now depended on Brioni!

*

*M*erwenna, on the floor of the hall, her black cloak around her, stood shocked beyond belief that Guthrum had agreed to Brioni's desperate appeal, and the manner of the fight that had been ordained between her and Tostig Ránnulfr.

She had stalked in behind the two of them with joy in her dark heart convinced that, at the worst, she and Beornwyn would be rewarded in silver for all they had done for Brioni's presentation - either by the captain, if Guthrum awarded the girl to his care, or by the king himself if he took Brioni into his own bed. She relished the prospect of the Wessex girl's branding, and of her humiliation. Of her being reduced to the status of a court whore.

She didn't mind being ogled by the common herd. They had nothing anyway. But clearly the Lady Brioni of Foxley hated it: the jeering, the pointing, the hands reaching out for her body, the wounding comments from those who knew no better, as Ránnulfr had led them from his compound, across the bridge and through the town to the King's Hall.

And she had laughed.

But now? As the little trollop was led away to be armed for her ordeal? She was infused with rage, and looked around the hall again to see whether her earlier suspicions had any basis to them at all. Whether Grimnir Grimmersson had influenced Guthrum, or old Bjorn Gunborg, to agree to Brioni's fight with Tostig. She had seen him lean over to both of them, and then watched as the little Skald had looked around the hall, but could not see why he should be so interested in the walls of the old building.

And she remembered his comment about armed men and archers, and looked to see what she could find. There were armed men in the hall. She could see them standing around with spears and shields and busy eyes...but all were known to her, of Guthrum's Royal Guard. The only ones allowed there with weapons.

Yet there were others.

Two who had appeared beside the huge embroidery that covered the end wall, and three others near the back doors with shields on their backs, who had

126

briefly appeared when the Bearmaster had come in with his troupe, when those great trumpets had blown and the gladiators had stamped in.

She had not known any of them, and what were they doing armed in the King's Hall?

But then there were so many strange faces about just now it was hard to be certain of anything. And as for the gallery above the far end of the hall, where the great double doors stood closed? In the flaring torch and lamp light, there was nothing she could see; the darkness beyond seemed impenetrable and there was no flicker of movement.

No matter how hard she tried, she could see nothing up there!

*

*R*ight at the back of the hall, where a space had been left for the Bearmaster's troupe beneath the gallery, there was now a mad flurry of activity as Julio and Magnus held up a great stretch of old embroidery as a screen, while Maritia leapt to help Brioni, and Jaenberht rummaged amongst their baskets.

"Quickly now, Maritia," she urged. "Bind my breasts and grease my arms and shoulders if you can…and do you have your black trousers? I will fight him as I fought Velda, in laced tunic and trousers. And your soft acrobat's shoes. This time I have no long hair to get in my way, and months of Finnar and Eadberht's hard work have toughened me. Now I know what I am doing. And I have fought this man before."

"That's right, my Lady," Finnar's dark voice growled in her ear, as Maritia got to work on her. "We have all your armour with us outside. Leofric sent it. But your way will be better, if more dangerous. You will be quicker and lighter than he is, more athletic in a way for which he will not be prepared. Besides, Jaenberht has an old friend for you to fight with!"

And with a broad smile the big huscarle handed her the great scramaseaxe she had found at Foxley after the battle; the sword with which she had fought Velda and that had been by her side ever since. It was an old friend indeed, and she felt a surge of confidence rush through her.

"*It is Blood Drinker!*" she exclaimed, delighted, while Maritia worked on her and Julio found her the trousers and shoes she needed. "I thought I had lost him forever."

"I found him in the grass where you dropped him," Jaenberht said quietly. "I have had him oiled and sharpened, enough to cut silk. He is perfect for your needs today. He fits your hand perfectly, and will help you balance when you leap around." And while Maritia laced up her leather tunic over the

127

wide cotton strips she had wound round her chest, Finnar came and squatted down beside her.

"Now, listen my Lady," the big Dane said, tying towelling strips around her wrists. "The space out there is narrow, the tables press in all round, and a long sword will be more of a hindrance than a help, he will not have thought of that. So keep on your toes and keep spinning and wheeling, use your speed and tumbling to confuse him, as Eadberht and I have taught you. But do not be fooled. He is a bold fighter, Ránnulfr, and has a good reputation; I have been listening to the shouts and betting round the hall, they all favour him.

"But I know these Jomsvikings. Puffed up with their own brilliance...so he will be confident of an easy victory, and will be burning to prove himself, and do it quickly."

"And remember," Jaenberht butted in. "Cadoc put an arrow through that bastard's right shoulder not that long ago. He will not be properly healed. Work on that, my Lady. You only need '*First Blood!*' to be roared out and all hell will break loose!"

"And you are not alone," Finnar added. "We all stand with you, and Foxhead awaits you in a clearing not four hundred paces from here. Do your business and we will all get out together. Now, stand, and show me you are ready!"

And with a laugh she clapped the big Dane on his shoulder and leapt to her feet, dancing from one foot to the other and twisting her sword in her hand as she did so, tossing it swiftly from one hand to the other in a sparkle of shining steel. Then, turning, she flung herself into Hugo's and Maritia's arms, before running across to Oswald and giving him a great hug also, while the Bearmaster and his troupe stood around and clapped her.

At that very moment the horns blew their summons and Brioni, with Hugo's great bulk beside her, stepped from behind the screen that had been held up for her, and holding her sword in her right hand, she strode down the hall to stand once more before Guthrum, the High King of the Danes and beside Tostig Ránnulfr, the man she must now fight to the death.

*

Tostig Ránnulfr, in his scarlet suede chausses, gold and white silk chemise and blue boots looked across at Brioni, at her oiled shoulders, light dress and footwear and short sword and grunted.

He would eat her alive!

His sword, Wolfsbane, with its long blade of multi strands of white hot steel and twisted iron, hammered and proved in swift flowing water, would cut her to pieces. She wouldn't last five minutes of close order fighting, and he flexed his shoulders so that his muscles rippled and his arm rings flashed in the flaring light around them from the resin torches along the walls. She might have met him blow for blow at Malmesbury, but here, in the King's Hall of Chippenham, with his friends around him and before the High King of the Danes, he would be invincible, and he looked at the slight figure beside him and laughed.

Brioni, with Hugo at her shoulder, staring up at Guthrum's cloaked bulk above her, his Council seated, heard Ránnulfr's laughter and shook Blood Drinker in her hand. Perhaps Finnar was right, and he was hugely over-confident. He was certainly big enough to fall with a mighty crash if she could achieve it.

He was big, she was quick and nimble.

If it went to a long contest then she would lose. He was stronger than she was, and wielded the bigger sword, no matter what Finnar said. If she was to get '*First Blood!*', then it would have to be quickly done, before the big Jomsviking war leader got into his stride.

She looked up at Guthrum's face and as he stared down he nodded his head at her in approval, and surprised, she bowed her head in response, while all around them the people gathered there waited for the contest to begin, calling out names, banging on the wooden trestles and thundering their feet on the floor.

On the dais, Guthrum raised his arms and the great room stilled.

"You are met here to challenge for the right to choose under whose protection this Saxon shall be held. Mine or the Earl Oscytel's. But not to the death," he said, listening to the sigh that went round the room. "I am persuaded that the rules of Ancient Rome do not need to apply here," he said, nodding towards Grimnir, where he sat next to Bjorn Gunborg the leader of his Council, now looking astonished. "She is too lovely to waste in such a brutal manner, and his life is not mine to hazard in such a contest. So they will fight to '*First Blood!*' only. I would rather have her in my bed than spread across my hall!" And a gale of laughter swept the tables.

"Are you ready?" he demanded of the two challengers a moment later.

"*Yes, my Lord King!*" they both replied in ringing tones, raising their swords above their heads.

"Then, Bearmaster, let them begin!" And all waited as both Ránnulfr and Brioni were taken by Hugo and placed opposite each other between the dais and the long hearth, four paces apart with the trestles pressed in behind them. Balanced on their feet, their eyes fixed on one another, their swords held low.

129

There Hugo left them, taking Beornwyn and Merwenna with him to the right corner of the dais away from the fighting that was about to start, both Brioni and Tostig Ránnulfr staring one another down, both looking for the right moment to begin.

*

*A*bove them Cadoc's men were now crowded at either end of the fluted wooden barrier, their faces streaked with dirt to break their outline, their eyes seeking out the armed Vikings of the royal guard who were placed around the hall...and looking for Raedwald, Aggi, Gunnar and Ricberht at the far end of the long building beyond the dais.

Right beneath them, Maritia, still in her Greek armour with sword and spear to hand, checked Oswald's armoured chest and brought him forward, along with Julio and the rest of the gladiators who had performed in Guthrum's Games. Beside them Finnar, Jaenberht and Hannes subtly shifted their shields onto their arms, and drew the swords that had come in with the remainder of Hugo's troupe, who had now left the hall taking Brioni's unwanted armour with them; running out into the night amidst the laughter and good humour of the guards still stood outside in the street.

There they scampered off to the rear gateway, still standing open beneath the moon's bright light, past the gate guards who hallooed them on their way, to where their horses and the tilt carts waited for them in the sheltered dingle just beyond.

*

*I*n the hall, varlets, tapsters and warriors with their doxies stood and sat in almost breathless silence, as Brioni and Ránnulfr, eyes intent, crabbed round each other, swords gently swinging, until with a great shout the Viking captain suddenly moved, bounding forward with his sword sweeping in from left to right, a violent scything blow that should have taken Brioni off at the knees, and led to a gasp of excitement from all around and an explosion of noise.

But she had seen the flicker in his eyes just before he moved, and as he leapt, she cartwheeled away from him, spinning out of his reach in an instant, a wild move that brought shouts of amazement as she then attacked him from the side with a vicious uppercut that he just blocked with a screech of steel, followed by two swift cuts *left, right* that she met with Blood Drinker in ringing blocks, and a fierce *lunge* at her throat that she ducked to come at him

130

with a swift flurry of her own blows. *Stab! Stab! Cut!* and *Block!* Both straining, eyes inches apart, panting, hearts hammering until she allowed him to push her backwards into a series of rapid back-flicks that astonished everyone as she bounded out of them onto spread feet with the fire pit now between them, while all around them the hall rose to their feet and roared their encouragement.

Her chest heaving, she watched Ránnulfr through slitted eyes as he swung his weight from one foot to the other, his long sword reaching out for her, his eyes blazing with fury. The next instant she leapt across the fire and cut down at him from above, a smashing overhead blow that beat him to his knees in a shower of sparks, while the Council on the dais jumped to their feet, even Guthrum shouting out in surprise, as Brioni danced out of the way again before her heavier opponent could move against her.

Shaking his head in disgust, Ránnulfr stalked after her round the fire-pit, his shoulders hunched, his head thrust forward in his determination, his sword gripped in his right hand, while Brioni backed away on her toes and laughed.

It was such an extraordinary sound, in that crowded, baying hall, that for a moment everyone paused while Brioni taunted him: "Is that the best you can do, *Jomsviking?*" she jeered. "We have boys in our battle line who can do better than that!" and she leaned back and pumped her sword at him so that he was griped in his belly with sudden rage.

Rushing at her with his sword held out like a metal tusk, his face contorted with feral anger, she mocked him: "Lucky am I, Tostig Ránnulfr? Not a fighter? I could beat you with one hand tied behind my back, you *earsling!*" And tossing her sword from one hand to the other she laughed again, offering him her chest to stab at, before cartwheeling again out of his reach, while the crowded hall stamped their feet and shouted. She needed to keep on the move, using her greater agility to keep him unbalanced, and not allow him time to settle into a routine that would overwhelm her.

Twice round the fire pit he chased her until suddenly she changed direction, making a jumping turn that brought her blade to blade with him once more: *Stab! Stab! Stab!* with Blood Drinker's point. Crowding in close where his longer blade was a hamper not an asset, as her thrusting scramaseaxe flickered around his chest and neck, forcing him to block each strike with the edge of Wolfsbane held upright against her attack without being able to use its greater length to reach out and strike her.

Then, as he drew back to swing at her she was gone in one great spring across the firepit, like a giant grasshopper, that left him looking to see where she had gone before suddenly she was back again, her sword flashing down overhead, screeching along the whole length of Wolfsbane in a shower of sparks that bent the Jomsviking war captain once more to his knees.

But in that instant a woman rose shrieking from the back of the hall, fighting off restraining hands and gobbling with rage as she did so, all the time pointing furiously at Finnar as he shifted his shield to get a better view.

"*Wolfshead!* That man is a wolfshead! *A wolfshead!* I know him! Finnar Olafsson, one of Leofric's fiercest men! Enemy! *Enemy!*"

It was Velda Gaerwulf!

Cast out after her fight with Brioni; helped by the silver that the Lady of Foxley had arranged with Maritia to give her; stitched and mended by old Anna; given a horse and food by Almaric the Smith, she had made her way to Chippenham, where she had swiftly established herself as a whore-mistress.

Welcomed by many in the King's Hall who relished the girls she provided, she had been brought in that evening by a hulking brute of a man who enjoyed her coarse ways, and thought nothing of the livid scar that ran across her breasts. Seeing Brioni once more dressed as she had been when they had fought, she had already been seething with anger; but the sight of Finnar, with his wolf shield on his arm, here in the King's Hall, was a final trigger.

Screaming out as violently as she was stabbing her fingers at Finnar, startled like everyone else into immobility, she struggled to get down to where Brioni was standing, astounded by so sudden an interruption, herself frozen to the spot as the big woman fought off all hands who tried to stop her, and forced her way to the floor, her heavy breasts swinging, her wild hair flying.

"*You fucking bitch!* You doxy! Now I will have you! Now I will see you dead! You ruined me…now I will see your blood. Kill her! *Kill her!*"

And in leather trousers and open tunic, she flung herself towards Brioni, with her hands stretched out towards her like claws, eyes filled with madness, spittle on her lips, while everyone goggled in astonishment.

Momentarily stunned by Velda's wild attack, Brioni waited until she was almost upon her before twisting sideways and knocking the big woman almost senseless. A swingeing blow to her head with the heavy butt of her sword; a masterly stroke that flung Velda to the hard floor, groaning on her hands and knees. And it was as Brioni was turned away from him that Ránnulfr chose that moment to attack her, lifting his sword high to bring it down on her shoulder. A vicious blow that would have ended their bout with Brioni brutally injured without hope of recovery.

But even as he brought Wolfsbane up over his shoulder, she caught the flicker of its movement and spun sideways so that it whistled down to crash into the floor, jarring his whole body. And even while Guthrum shouted out to his guards to seize Finnar, now standing with his shield on his arm and his

132

sword in his hand, Brioni pirouetted on the balls of her feet and drove the point of Blood Drinker into Ránnulfr's wounded right shoulder with a shout of triumph and a fierce spray of blood.

Finnar, already on his feet, let out a bellow of 'First Blood! *First Blood!*' that had the warriors in the hall, stamping and applauding Brioni's skill, even as Ránnulfr sank to the floor, his sword falling nerveless from his hand.

With Guthrum on his feet, roaring for his men to seize Finnar, and the hall still shouting to acknowledge Brioni's victory, no-one had noticed Merwenna as she leapt up onto the dais, her arm pointing fiercely up to the gallery. And as Velda staggered to her feet, blood pouring down her neck from where Brioni had hit her, the black-haired Cornish woman shrieked out: "Armed men! *Armed men!* Archers in the gallery! *Archers in the gallery!*"

And turning sideways she opened her mouth to shout out that Grimnir was a traitor, her black eyes filled with rage, her magnificent body rigid with determination.

Chapter Eighteen

*A*ll that time beside Hugo she had continued to search the room. Even during Brioni's fight with the Jomsviking captain she had kept her eyes busy, especially after Guthrum had announced his change of rules, and indicated that his mind had been changed by Grimnir Grimmersson.

She had seen his nod to the little harper, and to the Saxon girl on the floor. Why should he do that? He had all the whores he needed. Why add another to his bed? Why change the rules, when he had already declared a fight to the death? Even old Bjorn Gunborg had been surprised.

And she remembered again what the Skald had said earlier that day: *'You'd need armed men and archers in the old musicians' gallery for that to happen.'* And there were armed men she did not know in the hall. She had seen them. But what of the gallery? And she looked again up into the darkness, putting her hand up over her eyes to shield them from the glare of all the torches as she strove to see more clearly.

Then had come that woman's screeching about 'wolfsheads', and pointing at one of the men near where the bear was seated with the girl in the extraordinary helmet, and at that moment she had seen a flicker of movement up there in the darkness, a face. And not just one...but another! There *were* men up there after all. *She had been right!* Standing up she had shouted out her warning, tilting her head and pointing to the gallery, before anyone had noticed anything was wrong.

*

*I*t was Orn, shifting his position so he could see better, with Aelric close beside him at his shoulder. A subtle movement that had allowed the light to spill across them, and before Cadoc could order them back into the shadows they had been spotted.

With Merwenna's wild screaming coming so quickly after Finnar had shouted, it was several seconds before any of them could react, and by then the eyes of all were on the gallery, distracting them and causing their first arrows to go astray, leaving many of Guthrum's royal guard free to raise their shields and protect themselves, instead of being struck down where they stood.

But the sturdy Welsh bowman did not make any mistakes!

Drawing his string to his ear he fired down at the screeching woman, even as she turned to point her hand at Grimnir. A magnificent shot that burst through her head in a violent spray of blood and brains that showered everyone nearby, and hurled her, dead, to the ground before she could say another word; slaying her as she had lived, spiky and determined as ever and mired in malice.

So Merwenna the Black was the first to die that evening as Cadoc took her out...and with her death the air was suddenly filled with flying barbs that caused a wild panic in the hall.

Screams and shouts of rage and fear as those gathered there suddenly realised they were under attack: some rushing to get out through the big doors at the front to call for reinforcements, others scrambling to the back where Guthrum and his Council were already trying to find the escape door behind the huge embroidery that covered the end wall. But others reached for the many weapons and shields that hung from the walls, and were mercilessly shot down wherever Cadoc and his men could spot them.

"*Loose! Loose!*" the Welshman shouted, his great war bow bending and loosing, bending and loosing, as swiftly as he was able to pluck another arrow from the row he had placed for himself to draw on. And beside him the others were equally fast and accurate, doing fearful execution on the enemy in the great hall below.

It was a vicious sleet of death that Leofric's men unleashed upon the Danes that night; a barrage of arrows that slammed into the royal guard as they stood around the walls, stunned by the sudden ferocity of it all. One moment they were all watching the fight between the Saxon girl and the Viking war lord unfold before them...the next they were pinned to the walls, riddled with barbs that felled them in a burst of blood and torn sinews amongst the benches and tables in the hall.

But not all could be reached by Cadoc's archers, and while those who could rushed screaming from the hall, the men whom Guthrum had ordered to guard the big double doors at the front now pounded through them, and up the narrow staircase that led to the old chapel above. There they battered on the door at the top, shouting for axes and sledge hammers to break it down. And as they streamed out, so Finnar, Jaenberht and Hannes raced after them and attacked them from behind so that a vicious skirmish broke out in the flaring darkness.

With them went Hugo's gladiators, all armed and armoured as they had been since their bouts in the great hall, to face up to those guards at the main entrance who had also stormed in with Daag Andersson at their head, as soon as the first of the people inside had run out. Now the Murmillo, the Thracian and the Hoplite fought them for real, shield to shield and sword to sword, supported by the Secutor with his big rectangular shield and gladius, stabbing, cutting and thrusting, the Hoplite's spear taking out one man with a fierce

135

throw that took him in the throat, bursting it open so that all were caught in a violent shower of blood.

In the light of the great flambeaux that lit the entrance, the shadows cast by their outlandish helmets and armour so terrified one of the guards that he just dropped his weapons and fled, while the other was overwhelmed by the giant Murmillo whose legionary gladius and great bossed shield soon hammered him to the ground, where a swift thrust pierced his chest and left him flopped, arms wide, in a wide pool of blood that glistened blackly in the moonlight with which the whole area was bathed.

But the stocky captain of the guard was made of sterner stuff.

Covering himself with his shield and his sword like the professional he was, Daag Andersson fought the Secutor and the Thracian together with solid sword work that struck sparks from both his enemies. Fighting in grunting rushes, he drove Hugo's men back through the entrance of the hall his soldiers had been guarding, until the Retiarius cast his weighted net over him, tumbling him into a cursing heap, and struck him in the shoulder with his trident, the vicious tines piercing his armour in a spray of blood making the man cry out in sudden agony and flop backwards on the ground.

*

*A*round the staircase it was a wild confusing struggle as Dane fought Dane, that only ended when Cadoc lifted the bar that had kept the door above them closed, and fiercely attacked the men he found there.

Lunging and cutting with his sword, he gutted the first man and hacked through the shoulder of the next, blood and intestines spilling out over the wooden stairs so that they became slicked with gore and entrails, forcing the men behind to recoil with shouts and cries of terror, only to be mercilessly slaughtered from behind by Finnar, Jaenberht and Hannes, so that in moments the stairs were blocked by the dead and mortally injured.

"Get out!" Finnar roared up the blood spattered staircase. "You have done enough up there. Now, get out and fire the rooms as you go!"

"What of the Lady?"

"Hugo has her! No time for more, Cadoc. Fire the place, then make for the rear gates. We will be close behind. Now, move, you Welsh whoreson! *Move!*" And turning, he and the others raced to the main entrance which

136

Hugo's men had just cleared, Julio securing his net after dragging the wounded guard captain to the sheltered entrance of a nearby bothy.

*

*I*nside the King's Hall, even as Cadoc and his men rushed to gather their weapons and fire the lumber in the old chapel with flint and tinder…all was raging pandemonium.

There were dead and dying all around the walls from the arrows with which Cadoc and his men had drenched the great room, dropping the enemy amongst the trestles, benches and on the floor. Singly, men struck through staggered and cried out, and in heaps, some still twitching, the enemy lay everywhere, blood in broad streaks and pools lay all across the hall and up the walls, and arrows stuck up on every surface. A sudden foul crop of death standing up in the bodies that lay sprawled in every possible posture, as well as in the tables and benches on which Guthrum's men had been seated.

They also quivered in the great table on the dais itself, with its lamps and candles; in three of Guthrum's War Council who lay collapsed back in their chairs, and in the huge embroidery behind it. And where the lamps had been struck the table ran with oil, already alight in many places, flowing in fiery streams and runnels across the table and the floor.

There the fighting raged most fiercely, as those guards whom Cadoc's archers had not struck, protected by their shields in the first moments of the attack, now fought to overwhelm Raedwald and his men who had run out from behind to secure Brioni's escape.

Backwards and forwards the four men reeled, their shields locked together as they fought the men of the Great Army who had rallied round Bjorn Eriksson, the captain of the Royal Guard, the dead and dying trampled on as the vicious struggle reeled from side to side.

A huge man with a craggy, weather-beaten face and clad in shining mail armour, his helmet closed up on his head, and his great war axe in both hands, Eriksson was a daunting opponent. And though dozens of his troops had been struck down, there were still many who had clustered round him, and now hacked and battered at Raedwald and his men as they strove to cut their way to where Brioni was standing beside Ránnulfr, still crouched on the floor clutching his ruined shoulder, and near Velda now staggering back to her feet.

In front of her Hugo joined his enormous strength to that of Leofric's men, the long stick he had held in his hand all night turning into a sword stick, with a triangular blade of specially forged steel that flicked out between the shields like an adder's tongue. Lancing through scale and mail armour like a

137

knife through butter, it was a terrifying weapon, every vicious strike matched with a great bellow of rage as Hugo fought with all his skill and energy. Vanquishing the enemy who howled and fell beneath his steel, he pushed the four men he was supporting forwards with every stride he took, his breastplate running with blood, his imperial helmet splashed with it.

But despite all their efforts Gunnar and Aggi were both slain; Bjorn Eriksson breaking through their defence with massive strikes of his axe, whirling it round to take Gunnar's head in a fountain of blood as if it were a ripe marrow, and hacking through Aggi's shield to split his chest open in a single act of battle fury.

But he had no spearman and shield bearer to give him protection, and in launching himself at Raedwald's small command, Eriksson laid himself open to a vicious counter stroke that Raedwald delivered with all his strength. Driving his sword deep into the Viking's body as he stood bent over the dying Aggi, Raedwald burst the Viking Guard Commander's mail apart as he thrust deep into the big warrior's side, shattering his ribs and slicing his heart apart felling him in a violent burst of blood that utterly dismayed his men and made them fearful.

Behind her, in her Greek armour with shield and sword, came Maritia, her magnificent helmet fixed tightly to her head, with Oswald beside her, his head thrusting forward, his mouth gaping open, his enormous fangs bared as he roared his hatred of all that was happening around him.

For now the whole building was on fire.

Many of the torches on the walls had been knocked from their sconces, their resinous strands spilling everywhere so that fire had raced up the huge pillars that supported the building. Clouds of smoke swirled within and roiled out of the windows high up in the walls in spiralling plumes that were filled with dancing sparks.

Hearing Oswald's roar, Brioni turned and saw him, and leaping up called to him with her arms open so that he surged to his feet, towering above all who were fighting and struggling around him, his massive forepaws held out as if to greet her, each massive paw armed with its own collection of huge black claws.

Behind her, face streaked with blood, eyes screwed up in fury and armed with Wolfsbane that she had swept up from the ground where Ránnulfr had dropped it, Velda screamed out her rage, the long sword raised to hack down on Brioni's head from behind when Oswald saw her. Dropping on all fours, the giant bear galloped towards her, pushing Brioni out of the way as he barrelled past, and falling on Velda like a vast avalanche of fur and muscle, he simply tore her in pieces.

Crunching her skull with his enormous fangs, he split her carcase open with his claws, eviscerating her and spreading her body around him like human confetti, legs in one direction, arms in another, her entrails hanging from his mouth as he shook her body like a terrier with a rat, roaring and coughing in rage as only a great bear can.

Seeing him coming, Hugo urged Raedwald to disengage from Eriksson's forces and swing Ricberht backwards like a gate opening so that Oswald, now back on his hind feet, could surge through and fall on the Vikings whom they had been fighting just as he had fallen on Velda. Seeing Oswald soaked in gore and with bits of human flesh hanging from his mouth, they were terrified and tried to flee with wild cries of fear, but were trapped against the dais behind them and so fell to the bear's fury, hallooed on by Hugo and Maritia, as Beowulf's men had fallen to the monster Grendel!

By then the last of their enemies who had not fallen had fled and the whole hall was a mass of flames, the gallery burning fiercely where Cadoc's men had fired it before leaving, the flames reaching out across the roof in raging streamers of red and orange that twisted, turned and leapt from roof spar to roof spar, the debris cascading to the floor in flaring bundles.

"We must get out," Hugo shouted above the roar of the flames. "Before the fire meets across the middle, or we will all be trapped. Brioni go that way," he ordered, pointing to where the great double doors stood open at the far end of the hall, where Finnar and Jaenberht were now shouting and beckoning urgently to them.

"Raedwald, come with me. You know the way behind this great screen," he said pointing to the huge embroidery, now beginning to steam and smoke. "Ricberht, you go with the others, Leofric will need you. You are his best tracker. Don't mind me. Oswald and I are old friends," he said pointing to where the giant bear was lumbering back towards them. "Go now! We will meet you in the clearing."

"Father, let me come with you!" Maritia pleaded with him. "We have never been apart."

"No, my darling. Go with the others as we planned. As Leofric has ordered, and I will catch up with you. Now, go! And take this child with you," he said pointing to where Beornwyn was sitting splattered with blood on the edge of the dais, arrows all around her, appalled by all that had happened. "And that bastard you skewered. Even I cannot leave him to burn. Now go! Before this place collapses around our ears!" Pausing only to wrap his arms around his daughter in one final huge embrace, he drove the others from him, while he and Raedwald turned to plunge through the smoke into the back of the burning building, taking Oswald with them.

Turning, Brioni and Maritia rushed the others away, Ricberht doing his best to shield Beornwyn from the fiery debris falling from the roof with his shield, the girl still only dressed in the fine blue silk dress in which she had entered the hall at the start. Beside them staggered Tostig Ránnulfr, his gold and white chemise thick with blood from his wound, his bearskin cape abandoned where he had left it before the fight, along with his blue leather jerkin, its silver stars winking at him as he stumbled past.

*

*S*traight down the centre of the King's Hall they ran, through billowing clouds of smoke that made them cough and their eyes water, while all around them the flames roared up in red and yellow pillars arching overhead as the fire took complete hold of the ancient building. Everywhere shards of burning timber fell from the roof, and from the great trees that supported it, so that they had to jump and twist as they ran, fragments falling and scorching through their clothes as they went, Brioni crying out at each strike as she had no jacket on, her only protection the grease that Maritia had found to rub on her shoulders before her fight, and her Pegasus shield with which she did her best to protect her friend as they ran.

Then, at last, they were there; hurtling through the open doors beneath the burning gallery to where Jaenberht and Finnar had been desperately beckoning them.

Shouting and bellowing at them as if they were completing a marathon, they scooped them all out just as a massive timber crashed from the roof behind them to block off the rear of the great hall completely with a vast wall of seething flame that burst through the roof and sent a towering mass of sparks spiralling up into the night, dominated by a huge full moon that hung in the sky like a massive silver disc.

*

*O*utside, a great crowd had gathered to watch the fire, now roaring out of control like some ferocious beast, as wreathed in smoke they burst from the burning building, now wrapped in flame and smoke that funnelled down from the roof in billowing waves, driven by the wind that blew in gusts and hid them from any who might have been waiting for them to break free.

Immediately they were surrounded by the remainder of Hugo's troupe, now having covered their ancient armour with thick cloaks of dark wool that had been in the baskets that had come in with them.

"Where's the Bearmaster?" Finnar asked urgently.

"Gone out the back with Oswald and Raedwald," Maritia answered him, tears in her eyes. "I don't know whether they made it before that huge beam fell."

"Don't worry," Julio said, coming and putting his arms around her. "The Bearmaster was born under a lucky star. I am sure we will see him again soon, and that rascal Oswald. He will be back looking for apples before you can snap your fingers."

"What were his orders?" Finnar asked urgently.

"To comply with all Leofric's instructions and leave at once through the back gates."

"What do we do with him?" Ricberht asked, pointing to Ránnulfr in a far corner still clutching his shoulder and white with pain.

"Put him out of his misery!" Finnar said grimly, drawing his seaxe and stepping towards him.

"No!" Brioni replied sharply, holding up her hand and walking towards where Ránnulfr was groaning on the rutted ground. "We do that and we are no better than they are. We are Christians not pagans. I have fought him twice and claim the right to give him life a second time. Drag him over there," she ordered pointing to a doorway close by, "and leave him to his friends."

"Why do you do this?" the wounded man gasped out.

"Because it is the right thing to do," she snapped back at him. "The Christ child tells us to show mercy. So that's what I am doing. Let your friends patch you up again if they can, and see if they show you the same mercy as I have done! Now, God speed. I am done with you!"

Turning then, she ran off after the others, determined this time not to become separated from those she needed most, as she heard Finnar shout out: "Come on, we have yet to break free of this town, and Guthrum will not pause to lick his wounds for long!"

With that they made their way swiftly through the crowds that swirled around the blazing building, which opened and closed like a giant mouth as the smoke jetted out from all the doors and windows, masking them completely, while somewhere behind them a great bell was tolling.

In minutes they were joined by Cadoc and his archers, who had escaped from the hall and made their way to the back gates where the guards were clustered along their parapet, shouting and pointing to the flames they could clearly see now leaping and twisting above the rooftops, silhouetting the town, and at the vast pillars of sparks that were spiralling up into the night sky.

"*You there,*" Finnar shouted up to them fiercely in his rough Danish, stepping out into the open, Hannes and Jaenberht beside him, Cadoc's men close by, their bows over their shoulders.

"I am Captain Finnar Olafsson of Thorhollur's command. The King's Hall is on fire and Captain Eriksson has sent us to relieve you."

"He's dead!" Brioni hissed at him.

"They don't know that," he replied swiftly. Then, shouting up to the men once more he ordered: "Go quickly. You are to escort the king and his council to Captain Ránnulfr's compound. Two silver pieces a man. See, he has already paid us to take your places," he went on, waving a clinking bag in his hands. "*Go now!*" he ordered again sharply, giving them no time to think or disagree. "And we will see you in the Stag later!" and he stood, with his hands on his hips, like a rock in a storm, and laughed.

He knew soldiers...and he knew of Guthrum's Royal Guard Commander.

Captain Bjorn Eriksson was a hard bastard who would give any man hell who did not comply at once with his orders. No-one disobeyed the Captain of the High King's Royal Guard...and anyway, a fistful of silver would go a long way to making their lives merry.

Chatting excitedly, they rattled down the ladders that led up to the gates, and the ramparts beside them, saluted Finnar as they went by, and marching swiftly down the hill they disappeared into the smoke.

*

*M*inutes later Julio and Marcus led them all through the gates and down to the edges of the dell where their horses and the tilt carts awaited them. There most rushed to where the horses were standing pegged in long lines and mounted up, Brioni fussing Foxhead who was delighted to see her, struggling with Anton's help to put on her armour, while Maritia, Julio and the others ran back towards the open gates to wait for Oswald and the others, with Cadoc and his archers unslinging their bows to stand with arrows knocked and waiting, the rest stuck barb downwards in the soft earth.

*

*I*nside the burning hall, fighting their way along the narrow pathway between the huge embroidery, already bursting into flame, and the rear wall of the King's Hall, Raedwald led Hugo and Oswald to the broad

142

doorway that led to the outside yard. Pushing it open, they all fell out in great rush of smoke into the open, coughing and spluttering with their eyes full of tears.

But they only had moments to refresh themselves before breaking into a stumbling run that took them past the huge covered log pile that Raedwald had found earlier that day, through the cobbled yard beyond, and so to the maze of ginnels that lay behind the building now burning fiercely, Raedwald leading, with Hugo close behind holding Oswald's long chain in his left hand.

Round one corner, and then another they raced, Oswald bounding behind them, grunting as he ran, Raedwald always working towards the great ramparts that would lead them to the gates, beyond which lay safety and freedom.

And so they ran straight into a Viking patrol off the walls, running towards the flames with single-minded effort and concentration. Half a dozen fully-armed men with shields and spears who were almost as startled as Raedwald, who gave a great shout and piled into them before they had time to think. In moments he had killed two of them, his longsword cutting the first man down in a spray of blood, even as he drove his shield boss into the face of another who slumped unconscious to the ground, blood pouring from his shattered face.

Hugo, right behind him, whisked up the fallen man's spear and lunged it straight into a third man's bowels before he could protect himself with his shield. A vicious two-handed thrust and twist, that tore the wretched man's belly open with a whoosh of foetid air as he fell with a howl of agony onto the bloody ground, his entrails spilling out in a slush of blood and offal..

Then it became a swift and bitter skirmish as the remaining Danes locked their shields and drove forward with fierce energy, blocking the way through the narrow ginnel completely and calling on any friends who might be nearby to help them, their spears thrusting out at Raedwald and Hugo as they advanced, their heads tucked in behind their shields. So they did not see Oswald until they were almost upon him, only aware that something bulky was behind the two men who had attacked them. So when the giant bear gave a great coughing roar and rose up on his hind feet to tower over them they were appalled, stopped in their tracks and huddled together, doing all they could to protect themselves with their shields from the hideous monster who was about to fall on them.

At that moment Hugo leapt to attack them, thrusting with his spear into their terrified faces, while Raedwald hammered them from the side where their movement had created a small gap, cutting one spear in two pieces and driving his sword into the side of the man holding it so he dropped his shield to the ground with a great cry, just as Oswald burst past Hugo with a shattering roar to fall on his enemies.

He was truly a force from hell.

Lit from behind by the flames that were now boiling up into the night as the fire spread to other buildings close by, his shadow was enormous, his huge fangs glinting in the reddish light around him, and his great forepaws simply swept the two men aside. Tearing the face off one, they sent the other spinning into the fence of a nearby house that broke open as he crashed in to it, scattering a litter of pigs into the passageway that ran squealing into the fiery darkness.

But the sound of Oswald's coughing roars and the screams from the wounded Danes had attracted attention and soon more Vikings were running towards the skirmish, as reinforcements were rushed towards the burning hall from the houses and bothies closeby where Guthrum's men had been billeted. And still Hugo and Raedwald had not reached the gates where Maritia and the others were desperately waiting for them.

*

*T*hey, too, had heard Oswald's roar, and while Finnar ordered Cadoc and his men to move forward to the gates and give them covering fire if it were needed, he led the remainder of his men, including Ricberht and Maritia, towards the sounds of battle, calling out as he did so to encourage his friends.

And not a moment too soon.

For even as the smoke from the fire raging in the hall, and from other buildings nearby, whirled and thickened, so the enemy's forces were building up behind Hugo and his small command, now running towards the gates at last, Oswald galloping in their rear and Raedwald limping from a stray sword cut to his upper leg.

"Come on! *Come on!*" Finnar bellowed at them, beckoning fiercely with his sword, as the nearest Dane checked at sight of him, and the others rushing up to join him. "They are almost upon you! Maritia, see to Oswald!" he shouted as the three of them lurched past them. "Now, you whoresons, close up! *Close up!* And let's show these earslings some good Saxon steel!"

Linking their shields together, the four men paced backwards even as Brioni ran up behind to join them, Blood Drinker in her hands, just as the nearest Danes rushed on their swords.

But Finnar and his men were implacable, striking and cutting as one as they steadily retreated to where Cadoc's men could cover them, until there was

144

a slew of bodies in front of them, for their Danish foes lacked a leader, and cohesion. Singly, and in ones and twos, they flung themselves forward to do battle and were brutally slain as Finnar, Jaenberht, Hannes and Ricberht, with Brioni behind them, thrust them through, or hacked them down with their swords. Urine and sudden faeces, the true stench of battle, spilled from them as they fell, while Hugo helped Raedwald to stagger through the open gates behind them, and Maritia ran with Oswald past Cadoc and his archers still waiting to open fire.

Their great bows strung, their bracers firmly on their wrists and their arrows sticking up in rows in the ground before them, they were ready to play their part. There might not be many of them, but they would pack a mighty punch.

And surely that moment had been reached, for their enemy now held back, dismayed by the battle-fury of the Saxons who faced them and had bunched themselves together for greater protection. Hugo, Oswald and Raedwald were through their lines; and backlit by the raging fire the Danes, now pressing slowly forwards, made perfect targets. Gauging the distance perfectly Cadoc shouted "*Loose! Loose!*" and bending and firing, bending and firing, his men went into the routine they had practised so many times, and the enemy never really knew what hit them.

From a hundred paces, obscured by smoke and darkness, Cadoc's men could not be seen as their arrows leapt from their bows in a deadly stream. The Danes, standing out in bold silhouette with the raging fire behind them, were cut down where they stood, falling like hay before the mowers' scythes. With mortal screams and cries of terror the arrows plunged down on them out of the night sky, piercing faces, arms and bodies in a barbed rain of death there was no stopping.

One moment there was a bunch of heavily armed men steadily advancing with shield and gavelock intent on battle…the next their formation was torn apart and they were falling in heaps, staggering around shot to death, or fleeing, those left behind riddled with arrows that had fallen as if from nowhere.

*

*A*nd so they all left together after all, just as Hugo had planned.
Oswald in his cart, driven by the Murmillo, the Thracian beside him with Raedwald, his leg now firmly bandaged, his horse running at the tail; Hugo on his great chestnut gelding, and all streaming into the spring night beneath a brilliant moon. Ricberht ahead to point the way, Foxhead with Brioni now safely astride his broad back, beside Maritia with her cloak flowing

145

behind her, her mother's magnificent helmet still on her head; Finnar, Cadoc, then all the rest, with Angel, Gilbert and Beornwyn on the old tilt cart with Gemma, and Brouha the mule tethered to its tailboard.

Behind them the King's Hall at Chippenham went up in spectacular style, taking half the town with it: towering flames, exploding stones and timbers as the roof fell in with a huge crash, flames leaping high into the air and vast plumes of smoke that could be seen for miles, gushing into the night sky that hid the moon behind a vast cloak as they billowed upwards.

And as the Lord Oscytel rode back in a black fury from his useless strike at Leofric in Swindon two days later…so Brioni rode with Finnar, Hugo and Maritia to join that very Saxon war-lord at Battlesbury Rings above Warminster, having left Bath a smoking ruin behind him.

She was free!

And with a wild hoot of joy she dug in her heels and raced Foxhead towards the dawn to meet the man she loved above all others.

March 878, Somerset, towards King's Bruton.

Chapter Nineteen

Spring in the west, and Heardred, firmly mounted on Swiftfire, had left Athelney at first light with his command. Under orders from the King of the West Saxons to find Leofric Iron Hand, and tell him of the muster to be held at Ecberht's Stone on May 6th, there was no time to waste. With him rode Aldhelm, Leofric's messenger to the King, carrying Alfred's pardon for Leofric, and all those who fought with the renegade Saxon war-leader, now an essential part of Alfred's plans for the defeat of Guthrum and the Great Army.

They had left the great mire around Athelney as the sun had climbed into the heavens to give them all a brilliant start, early daffodils shaking their golden heads in a south-west breeze and lapwings calling overhead; pressing on until he deemed it time to halt and rest their mounts, lounge in the sunshine and eat a frugal meal.

Then it was time for a handful of his chosen men, led by Edric the Axeman and Alfgar, to leave for Southampton and find his greatest friends, Edwin and Harold, and tell them of the muster.

To give them Alfred's message to come with all their forces to Ecberht's stone in Kingston Deverill two days after Whitsunday, the seventh week after Easter. A vibrant message that was to ring round all Wessex like the great Easter bells of the resurrection. Now is the time! Rise up and be counted, for the defeat of the Danes is at hand. Yesterday was too early, tomorrow will be too late. Today's the day...come to the muster!

As Heardred watched the last of his men disappear over the far horizon he suddenly shivered in the breeze, now backed right into the north-east. Leofric and the Battlesbury Rings! By Saint Cuthbert, he hoped Aldhelm really did know the way, otherwise they would have to find some guides local to his area, and that was never easy!

He laughed, and drawing his cloak around him, jagged in his heels to send his mount skittering across the track, before cantering off with a puffing snort, his command following in a jingle of steel and spray of mud as their iron hooves dug in to the rich loam of the trackway.

*A*ll that day they pushed further north, the sharp uphill slopes of the Mendip Hills to the west of them growing slowly ever closer, while the sky steadily darkened overhead, the bright sunshine of the early morning giving way to great banks of cloud that thickened by the hour as they were hurried south before a rising wind from the north-east.

Just after midday they passed through Somerton, a prosperous small town of several hundred souls, with a busy market where the presence of so many armed men made the townsfolk nervous. Women hurried their children off the market square, dogs barked and men eyed them askance as they pushed through. Eyes hard, weapons free, they rode with brutal purpose and with rain threatening they did not linger, swiftly taking the trackway for Bruton, fifteen miles away, where they hoped to pass the night.

Bunched tight and travelling fast they made good time, meeting no travellers on the way, for these were wild times and the roads were unsafe. The predatory Danes made it certain that merchants would not dare to travel unescorted by armed men, and the rapidly darkening sky ensured that most others would stay close to their fires. Not even the borel folk were stirring in the fields, left bleak and empty after the autumn ploughing. For this was the quiet time of the year, life only just beginning to return after the coldest winter for years, and the long early rains holding everything back, so the few fields they passed were barren expanses of sodden earth and windswept trees, not even a cow wandering amongst the empty furrows.

Finally, with the thatched roofs and turf bothies of the Charltons behind them - tiny hamlets in those days without a church between them, where a handful of families eked out a living off the land with their pigs and poultry, goats and a few scrawny cows - they entered the dense oak and beech woods that cloaked the valleys and low foothills as they pushed on towards Bruton. And with that the sleety rain that had been threatening them since late afternoon began to hiss about their frozen ears, battering their faces and making the horses drop their heads to shield their eyes from its sudden fierceness. All about them the bare trees swayed and clattered, their trunks dark with running water, their knotted hands rattling to the soughing wind that hustled through their branches.

Already their progress had slowed as they had begun to thread their way towards the Brue valley, with its steep sides and rushing waters, not just because of the terrain, but because they were now in an area where the Danes were known to be active, several raiding parties having been reported to Alfred in Athelney, and Heardred had no wish to be surprised.

148

Now, as they crested a slight rise, his caution paid off, for of the two men whom he had ordered on ahead of the main party following half a mile behind, one now came flying back, driving his horse along the miry track as though the Devil himself was on his heels.

Instantly Heardred threw up his hand and his men came to a halt, their horses shaking their heads and snorting through their bridles, their hot breath pluming in the frigid air, the cold metal jingling as they did so, the heavy sleety rain almost turning into snow.

"What is it, Bridger?" Heardred asked sharply, as the man brought his plunging horse to a stamping standstill.

"Strangers, my Lord," he replied breathlessly. "Some ten or twelve of them, maybe more, armed and dangerous; camped in a shielded hollow below this narrow trackway, just below this ridge, with a large barred cart and mules. And they have women with them too...in chains!"

"*Danes?*"

"I think not, Lord. Clun and I watched and listened for some little while before I decided they could not just be left. They speak no Norse amongst themselves, only rough Saxon, and their weapons and armour have no pattern to them. One or two mailed byrnies, and more wooden helmets strengthened with iron than nut-shaped metal with nasals. More fyrdsmen than Great Army."

"Wolfsheads!" Siward growled in his stony voice, banging his hands together. "As if Wessex did not have enough troubles with the bloody pirates, without the need for her own people to prey on her ravaged carcase!"

"Slavers!" Baldred snarled, disgusted.

"Leofric's men?" Heardred questioned, as his troopers drew in around him, shrugging their heads deeper into their cloaks to escape the weather.

"Never!" Aldhelm answered fiercely, jabbing his horse forward. "*Never!* For one thing the Iron Hand does not make war on women, and for another this place is far beyond our raiding parties, even from the Rings. No, my Lord Heardred, these will be slavers who travel in the wake of Danish raiders and take what women they can find for future profit. They are animals! Vermin to be exterminated! You dishonour my Lord Leofric by even suggesting such foulness!"

"Easy, Aldhelm, easy," Heardred answered him calmly, pulling his hood forward against the sleet, eyeing the big Saxon warrior carefully, reaching to touch his arm as he did so. "I did not intend any such dishonour. Forgive me, it was a careless question."

And there was a brief pause after that as Aldhelm nodded his acceptance of Heardred's words, the sleet turning to a bitter drizzle as he did so. But even

149

as they watched, the big Saxon's face changed, becoming intent with concentration.

"What is it, Aldhelm?" Siward asked him moments later.

"Do you know something of these men after all?" Heardred questioned him urgently, pulling the hood of his cloak further over his head.

"Tell me, Bridger," Aldhelm demanded suddenly of the man who had brought in the report. "How long did you watch for?"

"Long enough!" he answered sharply. "Why?"

"Did you see a smallish man amongst them? About the height of a well-grown boy…slim, with a helmet bearing an eastern spike on its top?"

"Yes! Yes, I did," the man replied, astonished. "Like a young sapling in an oak grove!"

"Sapling indeed!" Aldhelm replied bitterly. "The man is full of gall. He is poisoned ivy, henbane and deadly nightshade all rolled into one, and the oak grove is one of yew and laurel, committed to death!"

"Do you know this man, then?" Heardred asked him, surprised.

"Yes, my Lord, I am afraid I do. He is Medraut the Slaver, that helmet is a landmark. He is the most unprincipled devil you would not wish to meet! I have seen his handiwork, and it is not pleasant! He was a scourge when we were in the north, but we never managed to catch up with him; we only ever found his leavings. He needs to be put down once and for all, skewered to the ground like the rabid dog he is!"

"Very well," Heardred said after a pause. "The hour is late, the weather foul and I am hungry. We shall not make Bruton tonight, we need a camp and they need killing so we'll do it now. Quick, sudden and no fuss. No prisoners, but I want those women alive and unharmed…so be careful!"

"How do we do this, Lord?" a voice called out

"Swiftly!" called another, with a burst of laughter.

"From two sides, Hathored," Heardred replied calmly, his hands moving decisively as he spoke. "You go back with Bridger to Clun and wait to cut off any who may try and make a break for the uplands. Cenwald, you take six men and drop back down this road a pace. About half a mile or so, I'd say. You should find a narrow trackway there that leads off it. I noticed it on the way up. It is the only way they could have reached the spot that Bridger has told us of. You, Siward," he said, turning to his big second, "come with me along with all the rest, and we'll find a spot beyond their site where we can drop down onto the track and take them from the rear."

"What about the pack animals?" Cenwald asked looking down the line.

"We'll leave them here with Osbert," Siward growled at one of Heardred's men sitting beside him.

150

"Why me?"

"Because you're the youngest," he said with a broad grin, giving the burly warrior a sharp rap on his helmet. "And your mother asked me to look after you!" And everyone laughed.

"Right!" Heardred said as the humour swiftly died down. "Let's get this done before we get any wetter. With this vile sleety rain, no guard will be watching as closely as he should. No signal, just the clash of arms to guide all who may come second to this party, and God aid us for our cause is just!"

And without another word they all moved off towards their allotted places, walking their horses carefully between the glooming trees, their hooves deadened by the thick leaf mould that carpeted the muddy ground.

*

*D*rawing level with the three men he had sent ahead, Heardred halted his small column and, signalling silence, slipped off his horse and went across to join them, Siward following closely.

"See, my Lord," Bridger said softly, pointing with his spear towards a small, well-screened clearing some forty paces below them. "A real nest of vipers. Men on watch-guard at each vantage point, cloaked and well-armed, the rest gathered near the fire, beyond that travelling cart and those mules and horses…this side of that stream."

"Bring Aldhelm," Heardred ordered quietly over his shoulder. "He knows what manner of men these are."

"Where are the women?" Siward asked, as Clun ran back to carry out his leader's order.

"There, Lord!" Hathored answered, stabbing downwards with his forefinger. "Beneath that shelter of laurel and rough canvas. Some five or six of them huddled together. They are chained and hobbled in pairs so they cannot hope to escape."

There was a brief rustle behind them then and Aldhelm was suddenly there.

"You called me, Lord."

"What do you think?" Heardred asked, pulling the big man down beside him and pointing with his hand, waiting patiently while Aldhelm scanned the scene below.

"Yes! There he is, the bastard," he grunted. "See? The man with the pointed helmet, sitting with the fire behind him? That is Medraut, and he is getting careless," he added, peering through the bushes at the clearing below them. "He must be feeling secure to have posted so few men about his

151

encampment. They will drop like pine needle pins before an autumn gale when you attack. Most are scrub fighters, not warriors; bandits and marauders who prey on those weaker than themselves. Though some are good, so do not take any chances with any of them. Strike hard and show no mercy, not one down there deserves it!"

A wild burst of raucous laughter came up to them just then, making their eyes glisten with anger as Aldhelm added: "And judging by their drunken laughter, they have had more sport with their wretched captives than most men have stomach for!"

"I have seen and heard enough," Heardred snarled, easing back from the edge. "Cenwald should have reached that track by now. It is time for us to play our part."

Without more ado they remounted and pushed further along the narrow ridge, before attempting the slope that fell sharply away to the spot below them where Heardred judged the hidden track that led to the slavers' camp should lie.

Slipping and sliding, lying well back in their saddles, they slithered their way downwards, hard branches whipping at their wet faces and tangled briars sliding over their mailed chausses, until they reached the narrow pathway, severely shaken but intact. And shaking their shields round to cover their sides, they thrust in their heels to drive their horses forward, reins held loosely to give their mounts full play, thighs gripping tightly as they thundered towards Medraut's encampment.

Round one corner, then the next, and suddenly they were there, the flickering firelight leaping up towards them as they burst upon the scene like swooping eagles. Swords and spears in hand, and shouting wildly, they brought terror in their wings, and pandemonium broke out on every hand: women screaming in sudden fear, tethered horses bucking and stamping, mules *haaawwwing* in terror, and men scattering in all directions to grab discarded weapons and rush to defend their camp.

Shield grasped firmly in his left hand as he bored in, Heardred hewed down at the hapless guard whom Medraut had placed upon the eastern approaches to the clearing. Splitting the crude wooden helmet he wore and cleaving through his skull in a single monstrous blow, he exploded the man's whole face apart, bloodied brains and shards of bone spraying up across his hands and face. Then it was onwards to the next, his dripping sword waving above his head as the man fell, with a single piercing shriek, beneath the trampling hooves of those who followed.

No sooner had Heardred and his men arrived, than Cenwald came crashing down upon their flanks with wild cries and a bitter struggle took place, lit only by the leaping flames from the fire in its sheltered hearth, spitting and hizzling as the rain landed amongst its red hot timbers.

They may not have been true warriors, those men of Medraut's who followed the stolen flesh trade, but with nothing to lose but their miserable lives, they fought back hard to keep them, striving as fiercely to pull Heardred's men off their horses as they fought to cut and thrust their way into the heart of the encampment.

But their enemies were all mounted, and between a running man and a mounted trooper armed with spear and swinging sword there is little contest, and Medraut's men were swiftly hacked down or lanced in great spurts of blood and shattered bodies as his men panicked, and rushed everywhere in a desperate effort to escape their nemesis as it hurtled in upon them from the soaking darkness.

But some fought back.

A handful of those better armed and equipped banded together, and shield to shield they resisted strongly, rushing beneath one horse to gut it and bring it down, pouncing on the man whose beast had fallen kicking and screaming and hacked him in pieces, while all around them the noise and fighting was intense.

But such a final stand could not last, and in the end it was Aldhelm who broke the enemy's resistance.

Drawing back his horse he launched it at the steel wall that was still holding them at bay, clearing the startled heads of those fighting below to engage in personal combat with their hardy leader, his spiked helmet marking him out from all the others.

Leaping off Blazer, Aldhelm flung himself at the man with tigerish ferocity, raining blows at him from his greater height and smashing him to the ground with merciless fury until he lay spread-eagled and helpless on the sodden turf. Finally the big Saxon stood over him, and with eyes of stone, he plunged his sword into the slaver's throat in a great gush and gurgle of blood, and wrenching its great blade downwards through scale armour and leather he ripped Medraut's body open from chin to navel, his steaming entrails, liver, lungs and heart bursting from his butchered corpse to lie in bloodied heaps beside his eviscerated carcase.

And with that it was over, for within moments those who had survived him also fell as Heardred's men, many now on foot, hacked and cut them to the ground, or speared them through from the back of their horses, until their blood-boltered remains dotted the little hollow like shattered puppets. Not one escaped to carry a warning to their Danish masters, and before long peace descended once again apart from the sobbing, moaning women who clung to

153

one another in terror, uncertain whether the men who now gathered before them, with bloody hands and faces, and weapons encrusted with blood and hair, were their new conquerors or their friends.

"Don't be afraid!" Heardred called out as he strode through his men, towards the terrified women huddled at the back of their ramshackle shelter, their arms round each other, many with their faces hidden in the shoulders of those around them. "We mean you no harm. I am the Lord Heardred of Taunton, one of the King's companions. We are Alfred's men, good Saxons sent by him to raise the country against his enemies. We are your friends and will do all we can to help you!"

"Leave them awhile, my Lord," Siward said to him quickly in his deep voice when he received no answer, the women only huddling closer together. "They have not had kind treatment and you are not a pretty sight either. None of us are! Wait until the rest of the men have arrived and this bloody refuse has been removed," he added, waving his arms around at the shattered bodies that lay all about them. "Let them see that we mean what we say, and maybe things will be different."

"Very well, Siward, but I want their chains struck off as soon as possible, the fire built up and hot food handed round. Has Osbert come down yet from the ridge with the others?"

"No, Heardred, though he will be here shortly, I have no doubt."

"Alright, the chains and food will have to wait," he said, banging his hands together and looking round him. "But in the meantime we can deal with the fire and rebuild the shelters that were knocked flying in the fight," and he issued a string of terse orders: "Cenwald, detail some of your section to round up the horses and mules that have broken free. I want no advertisement of our presence in this area; Baldred, deal with that fire, and get some water on the boil. We need to clean ourselves up; Siward, post guards, double strength. The rest of you tether up your horses and let's sort out this pigsty. God knows we have been doing that for long enough!"

And turning away, he left the women to their own devices, now wide eyed and beginning to hope, while he and his command got down to the task of setting things to rights.

*

*E*ventually it was all done to his satisfaction: the bodies searched and dragged together in a disgusting pile at the farthest end of the clearing, the fire rebuilt, water boiled, men and weapons cleansed, fresh shelters thrown up, loose animals gathered and the horse lines organised. By then

154

Osbert had arrived with their precious pack horses which were swiftly unloaded, the rations for the night handed over to Hatherod for preparation, and Wiglaf's field anvil set up on a convenient broad tree stump.

"Right, Siward," Heardred said, turning to look at the women in their shelter as he shook reddened water from his hands. "We have waited long enough. Bring those women forward and Wiglaf can strike off their chains. Then perhaps we can find out who they are and where they have come from!"

Chapter Twenty

*B*y that time most of Medraut's captives had recovered their spirits, shuffling forward eagerly, their eyes darting over their rescuers while they chattered and giggled behind their hands, those braver than the rest casting flashing smiles and bold glances at those of Heardred's men who had caught their eyes.

Two, however, held back slightly from the rest. Their garments, though badly torn and soiled, were of finer quality. Smooth wool and linen, and their faces were more refined, lacking the brassy coarseness of the other girls whom they had rescued. The taller of the two was a handsome blonde: eyes set well apart and a startling emerald green, like a great cat's, high cheek bones, small nose and soft generous mouth. Her firm breasts pressed tautly against the clinging wetness of the blue linen dress she wore beneath a blue serge cloak edged with tattered fur.

Beside her, and leaning on her shoulder, was a younger girl, dark-haired and slighter than her companion. Her clothes, though of good material, were not so finely worked and she had a simple woollen cloak around her shoulders, once fine, but now soiled and torn, and she lacked the natural grace of the woman she clung to. Also she was more fearful and trembled violently every time she caught sight of one of Heardred's men gazing at her.

He was intrigued, and watched them both closely; observed how the other women tended to avoid them, almost as if they were not the same in some way. And the two did their best to help one another, especially the blonde girl who made every effort to shield her young companion from the obvious interest his men were beginning to show towards them.

Finally they, too, were struck free by Wiglaf with lump hammer and cold chisel, and while Siward went off to deal with the others, now visibly relaxing and mixing freely with his command who had gathered round the fire despite the drizzly rain, he ordered Aldhelm to escort the other two to his own shelter out of the weather, and for food and drink to be brought to them there, himself following later.

*

*O*nce seated on a couple of sack bundles, with wooden bowls of thick potage in their hands, the blonde girl was at last ready to talk, her earlier reluctance and fear now conquered by the warm food and kindness that he and his men had gone out of their way to show them. But not so the dark-haired girl. She still almost cowered way from him, and watched him intensely over the rim of her bowl, looking round her almost like a small wild animal fearful that its food might at any moment be snatched away from it.

But her blonde companion, with her green almond-shaped eyes and generous mouth was really quite lovely, despite the grime that now marred her face and arms. And Heardred felt the first stirring of real interest, and warmth, towards a woman that he had not experienced since that awful moment when he had discovered Brioni's shattered remains in their shallow grave at Foxley.

Of course, there had been others who had tried to attach his interest since then. After all, he was quite a catch, close to the King and wealthy in his own right, and there were other women at Athelney...but he had been too wrapped up in killing Danes to be aware of any of them.

But this one was quite different.

Vulnerable, and yet determined; needing help, yet unwilling to seek it. Besides which, there was something vaguely familiar about her. He thought he ought to know her from somewhere, but could not say remotely why.

"Tell me," he said quietly, putting down his eating bowl and wiping his mouth with the edge of his cloak. "Who are you? You are not like the others out there mixing with my men. And I know this may sound ridiculous, here in these damp, empty woodlands, but I have the strangest feeling that I know you. Or have met you some time in the past. Tell me, please, who you are and where you have come from."

For a moment he thought she had not heard, for her eyes were lost to him, staring out beyond the fire, with its flickering flames and everyone clustered round it, cloaked against the rain...out to some distant, unknown corner of the world. But then she sighed, placed her wooden bowl on the ground and turned towards him with a smile.

"I am the Lady Judith, daughter of Thane Ecbert of Bishops Waltham, near Southampton," she said quietly, "the son of Earl Brihtnoth of the Somerseatas. And this poor flower," she added gently, putting her arm round the dark-haired girl snuggled close beside her, "is Aelflaeda, my maid."

*

157

*F*or several moments Heardred just sat there in stunned amazement. It was as if someone had hit him in his lower belly and knocked all the stuffing out of him. No wonder she and her companion had been so unwilling to speak out at first. Heardred and his men could have been anyone. And no wonder that the other captives had treated them so differently; for this was no mere thane's wife, or daughter, as had been his first thought from her appearance. She was a member of one of the most powerful and respected families in all Wessex. Her grandfather, Earl Brihtnoth, was one of Alfred's most loyal and most trusted advisors, and her mother had royal connections.

"I see you are surprised," she said, smiling softly.

"Surprised is hardly the word I would use," he replied slowly. "Stupefied would be far nearer the mark. My Lady, what in the name of the gods are you doing here? Whatever possessed your father to allow you beyond his boundaries when everything is so dangerous and uncertain?"

"He didn't!" she answered him firmly, shifting her body slightly to face him. "I left home without either his knowledge or his permission. And what I am doing here is quite plain for anyone to see."

"But your mother…"

"My beautiful mother is dead. Died of the fever last summer, and I have no brother to turn to."

"You mean you left without an armed escort? Alone with only your maid for company? You must have been out of your mind!" he remonstrated with her, appalled.

"I was, nearly," she replied in a simple, matter-of-fact tone, giving the girl beside her a caring squeeze. "Aelflaeda and I thought it all out between us. And you are wrong when you suggest we left alone. We didn't, only those who with us were either killed or fled when Medraut attacked our party."

"But where were you trying to get to, with just a parcel of servants as escort? This place is miles from your home! And, more to the point," he continued, pulling his mantle further round his shoulders, "why did you leave home in the first place? There are Danish raiding parties everywhere. There are few things you could have chosen to do that are more dangerous!"

She put her head on one side and looked at him consideringly.

He was the first good thing that had happened to her since setting out. A kind man certainly, and one who felt others' distress, despite his fighting ability and background. Most men would have sought to turn the situation to their own advantage. After all she was worth a lot of money. In fact there had only been one other in her life whom she would have trusted in such a case, and for all she knew he was dead! Yet there was a gentle quality about this man that she felt drawn to. She felt she could trust him with all she knew.

"Well?" Heardred prompted her after a while. "Do you like what you see? Do you feel you can trust me?"

"Yes, strange as it may seem, my Lord Heardred, I do!"

"Then perhaps you would care to answer my question," he replied, smiling. "For I, like you, need to be sure I do not have a renegade in our midst!"

"*Renegade?*" she exclaimed bitterly, tears springing to her eyes. "If you only knew the bitter irony of that!"

"Then tell me," he said quickly, shocked by her reaction, and reaching for her hand in the flickering darkness, he added gently, "for unless you can tell me what it is that has so distressed you, then I cannot help. I will not harm you. I think you know that. But I do want to aid you, and at the moment my lack of understanding makes me powerless to do so."

Judith sighed deeply, and dropping his hand she released her hold on her friend and put her arms round her knees, hugging them closely to her chest, her long blonde hair falling forward in two great plaits.

"It is difficult to know quite where to begin," she said at last, gazing emptily across the little clearing to where his men were leading the girls to their own shelter before settling for the night, guards being replaced, the horses being checked, more wood being flung onto the fire, still sizzling from the rain, that must be kept burning all night. "So much has happened since Christmas. But if I don't share my problems with someone then I feel I shall lose my reason," and she turned to him again and took his hand. "You have no idea how terrible these last few days and weeks have been!"

"Ah, you wrong me, Judith," Heardred replied softly, rubbing his thumb over the back of her hand, moving closer to her as he spoke. "These are dark times that we are living through. The iron hand of war has touched many people, I promise you. I also have felt its brutal touch! But that can wait. It is you I am concerned about."

She looked at him and paused, her heart suddenly moved by his open gentleness. It was not what she expected of a Saxon fighting man. One of the King's 'hounds'.

When she had first seen him, with blood running down his face and off his hands, surrounded by his command all as bloody as himself, her heart had quailed. After Medraut she had not believed that anything could be so dreadful. But in the flaring darkness, with the freezing rain running off his armour, his face half in shadow and the litter of the slain lying in bloody profusion all around him, she had not been so sure.

So she had remained silent.

159

After all, in these troubled times, the habit of taking ransoms was strong in even the most honourable Saxon. It had become a way of life for many whose families and estates had been ravaged by the Danes; their only source of money when everything else had been destroyed. The fact that he claimed to be one of Alfred's hearth companions meant absolutely nothing. She and her maid were rich enough prizes to keep him and his men in good health and comfort for many years.

Since then his actions had proved his words.

But more than that, there was some deep-lying hurt in the man that drew on her compassion. She could read it in his eyes when they were unguarded. She sensed an emptiness in him that she had an unreasoning desire to fill, an unbidden feeling that made her want to pour out her troubles and forge a new bond with this strange Saxon warlord.

She smiled and touched his arm lightly, and with her voice gaining strength she began to talk.

*

"You may be right when you say you have seen me before," she said, her green eyes glittering in the firelight, "because I came with my grandfather to the King's Hall at Chippenham two years ago or more, but it was not you who caught a young maid's eye that bright sunny afternoon," she added, taking his hand again and turning it over. "It was a different young warrior, who was as tall and strong as an oak; an axeman, with corded muscles, hair as yellow as a cornfield, eyes like the sky in high summer, with a bright wit and a merry smile.

"The court ladies fawned on him and he loved it. He was always off with some girl or other. There must have been half a dozen who felt themselves in love with him. And he had no time then for a shy, young girl still gawky and unformed. I cried for a week when he left with his father for his family lands until my mother, still alive then poor love, boxed my ears and sent me to the Queen's sewing bower for the rest of the visit!

"Even my grandfather's patience was strained, and he has always had a great fondness for me," and she laughed lightly at the memory. "I must have been a sore trial for everyone. A real watering pot!"

"And who was that heartless Saxon axeman who was so blind?" he asked her with bravado, making her smile wistfully. "I cannot believe that anyone could be so cruel as to deny such a beauty a safe place by his side."

160

"Oh, I was no beauty then, just a raw country girl on her first visit to court, knocked sideways by all the grand ladies, and misty-eyed over a warrior with blond hair and big muscles."

"So, no-one really special then?" he asked quietly, still holding her hand.

"No, that came much later; last spring, after we had met properly; when the King came to Southampton. You might have seen me there, I suppose. Then he showed me real kindness and sought my company above that of others. He was gallant, generous and more gentle than I had expected. We fell in love. I mean completely in love, like Helen for Paris, and were to have been betrothed this year."

"And who is this paragon of all the virtues?" he asked, a hint of disdain in his voice that surprised him as, dropping his hand, she turned away, her eyes filling with tears that made him feel guilty.

"His name is Gyrth. Is, was? I don't know any more. The only son of Thaegn Wulfstan of Foxley, near Malmesbury; one of the King's advisors, like my grandfather. He went home at Christmas to tell his father of his decision. And then…then," and she stopped speaking, unable to finish her sentence, covering her face with her hands, her throat blocked with emotion.

Gently Heardred pulled her to him and held her close, wrapping his arms around her slender frame, the hot prickle of tears behind his own eyes, blurring his vision.

"And then," he whispered hoarsely, "the Danish army broke into Wessex. Alfred was driven out of Chippenham and Foxley was destroyed in their advance by Oscytel, Guthrum's right hand man. He put everyone to the sword. No-one was spared!"

She raised her face then and looked into his eyes as dark with pain as her own, incomprehension giving way to awful certainty as the full terrible meaning of his words struck home.

"Oh God! *Oh no!*" and burying her face in his shoulder she wept, her spirit suddenly crushed with tears, her body shaking to the bitter grief of her loss. She had prayed so hard and hoped so long that he might still be alive, that the realisation of his death was almost a relief. Now she could weep for him, and in her tears find some measure of peace from the awful uncertainty that had slowly been tearing her apart.

Wracked by his own pain, Heardred held her close and rocked her as a mother would a child, his face buried in her hair.

Eventually she stopped and pushed herself away from him, while he reached across a strip of cotton bandage to her from his carrying pouch and dipped it in a pan of water, so she could wash her face and ease the stinging soreness of her eyes.

161

"How is it that you know so much, my Lord?" she asked quietly a moment later, dabbing her eyes and sniffing. "How can you be so certain?"

Heardred swallowed hard and looked away briefly, his eyes flitting over the campsite: the men on guard, the horses in their lines, someone throwing more wood onto the fire, his body silhouetted against the flames.

"Because I went there, my Lady," he said at last, turning back towards her, his voice slow and heavy. "I arrived there with my men the day after. I saw the carnage for myself, and found the bodies of Gyrth and all his family in shallow graves within the shattered compound. Everything was smashed and burned. We should have been there the night before, but the weather was awful and we were delayed. We got there too late to help," and there was a long pause then, while he looked away again, and she squeezed his hand.

"Why you, my Lord?" she asked softly, putting her other hand on his shoulder. "What took you to Foxley? Why are you so distressed?"

"Because I was to be betrothed to his sister, the Lady Brioni!"

"Oh no, Heardred!" she gasped appalled, putting her hands to her face in shock. "Oh, no! Not you too, not Brioni!"

"Did you know her, Judith?"

"No, not really. I had met her, she was one of the Queen's favourite ladies; but Gyrth spoke of her often. He adored her, and she loved him greatly in return. He said she was to be betrothed this year, but did not say to whom," and she dropped her head to his chest. "We were too wrapped up in each other to give much thought to anyone else. Oh, Heardred, I am so sorry!" she said lifting her head to look into his eyes. "So very sorry! And to have found her yourself, too.

"My grief has sprung from words carried by another from afar. I at least did not see the manner of Gyrth's death. I have a picture of him in my mind that shows him as he was when last we parted. But you?" she went on, instinctively opening her arms to him. "You have to live every day with the awfulness of what you found there and my heart goes out to you."

And without hesitation she put her arms around him and drew his head onto her shoulder as a mother would a small child, shocked by the storm of emotion that wracked his body, his tears falling like oceans as he wept for Brioni as he had not been able to since he had found her.

The agony of months flowing out of him in one great burst of grief.

And all the while Aelflaeda sat silently beside them and rocked herself backwards and forwards, her eyes seeming blank holes in her white strained face that took in nothing of what she saw, nor did there seem to be anything behind them either.

*

*F*inally they slept, cuddled into each other as if they had known one another for years, exhausted by their spent emotion, while the rain died away and the camp settled quietly for the night under Siward's careful guidance.

Just once he approached his leader's shelter, but stopped short when he saw how close the strange blonde woman they had rescued had become to him. Only the young girl seemed to be awake, but she stared silent and unseeingly through his whispered questions, so he left as quietly as he had arrived, disturbed that one so young should be so far removed from all around her.

Yet he was also glad that his young Lord should have found someone with whom to share the grief the Lady Brioni's death had brought on him. Perhaps the girl, Judith, would be able to do for him what all the months of killing and desperate struggle had so far failed to do?...make him forget the lass who had been slain so brutally, in the joy of finding someone else to love.

And with a lighter heart than he had carried for many moons, he went on to complete his rounds before returning to the fire, now burning fiercely in the middle of the little clearing, and boot the next watchman into bleary life!

Chapter Twenty One

*D*awn came creeping in amongst the trees with a fine grey cloak to hide her face, the light pale and thin, the sky still heavily overcast, and the air both chill and dank, though the sleety rain of yesterday had cleared overnight. A cold wind hustled across the clearing, the smoke from the fire blowing over the wet ground in choking streamers.

Beneath his wolfskin cloak Heardred stirred and wiped his face, his arm deadened by the weight of the girl lying across it. He brushed a heavy plait away from his eyes and smiled ruefully. A fine warrior he was to behave in such a fashion, weeping like a maiden after her first kiss. His men would think they had a milksop for a leader...yet he felt better than he had done since Foxley. Ready to face the world single-handed and defeat it!

He looked down at her and shook his head.

She really was very lovely: soft skin, long lashes, a gentle mouth and those amazing emerald eyes. His own, travelling over the rich curves of her body, noted the firmness of her breasts and the tautness of her cold-pinched nipples as they pushed against the blue fabric of her dress...and he felt the faint warming of desire run through his loins.

He was startled by his body's response, and turning his head he found her watching him, left eyebrow raised, a smile on her lips, her hand firmly on his thigh. Hesitating briefly he bent and kissed her forehead to a small gasp of pleasure that surprised them both. But this was neither the time nor place for warmer work. It was enough that they had learned to trust each other. Anything further must be left to develop in its own way, or not at all.

The mood was right, the timing wasn't.

"So, you are awake as well," he said, smiling. "Aelflaeda, too, has found some rest at last," he added, looking across to where her young maid lay curled up on a bed of hay beneath a coarse blanket he had found earlier, her dark head resting on a saddle, a rolled up sack behind her neck as a bolster.

"Yes, we seem to be very much in your debt this day, my Lord," she said. struggling up into a sitting position, dragging her own cloak around her in the chilly dawn.

"That is my pleasure, my Lady. But please call me 'Heardred'. 'My Lord' is far too formal for our situation today."

"And you must call me 'Judith', too," she said, putting her hand on his arm with a smile. "After yesterday, anything less would be ungrateful."

"My men will be stirring shortly, and then we must be on our way. We have some distance to travel, so there will not be the time to talk later," he added, sitting down beside her and taking her small hand in his large one. "So tell me, Judith…why did you decide to leave your father's hall in such troubled times, with just your maid and a pack of servants? It seems like madness!"

She leaned back against him then, slowly rubbing her shoulders as she did so, her face turned towards the camp site where Heardred's command were rising: going to the stream to wash their faces, relieve themselves, check the animals, refresh the fire and hang their big cauldron on its iron tripod over it, Hathored throwing a handful of herbs into the water, while Siward rousted them all out and life generally returned around them…and she sighed.

"When the news of Alfred's flight reached us at Bishop's Waltham, I became certain that something must have happened to Gyrth as we had no news of him. But with no information coming to us from that area it was impossible to be sure of anything. All I could do was sit and wait, while the whole world turned upside down around me."

He took her hands and kissed them softly.

"Not knowing is always hard," he said, rubbing the back of her hand with his thumbs as he spoke. "But not knowing about a special loved one must be the very worst."

"It is! Oh God, Heardred, it is! Weeks went by, with everything going up in smoke and flames around us, quite literally. And then the Danes came to see us. To talk with my father, 'though no damage was done to us directly, which was strange. It was a very hard winter, as you know, with the enemy raiding far and wide for supplies…"

"So it was not long before they began to demand food tributes," Heardred interrupted her. "And rather than see their land and villages destroyed many people paid up, including your father. Even I can see that. But that is not the reason you left home is it?" he questioned her softly.

"No, it isn't," she said breathing deeply, and looking away from Aelflaeda, now beginning to stir into wakefulness. "If it had only been that, then I wouldn't have minded. It was better to pay them something than have the lives of all our people torn apart. No, my problems really started when Spring came in and Alfred and his warriors became active…your men I suppose?

"Yes, my men amongst others."

"After that the enemy became more demanding and more vicious. If they'd had men killed in the area then they came and put whole families to the torch. Destroyed everything as a warning to others. A potent threat of what could happen if the people didn't co-operate."

165

"Co-operate?"

"Yes, Heardred. Pass on information as to where you were operating, where your hide-outs were, who was giving you intelligence, or supplying you with food and shelter…but it never happened on our lands! The enemy seemed to pass us by."

He could see it all so clearly: a brutal Danish raiding party, the terrified peasants sullen yet determined, then the threats, the vicious killings, rapes and burnings that would follow and finally their capitulation. Only if their lords resisted would the peasants do the same. All it took was for one locally powerful thegn to break, and probably all the countryside around would follow his example.

He sighed deeply.

Their life in the marshes had been dangerous, but at least they had been in control of their destinies. For those who'd had to endure the results of their attacks it must have been terrible.

"Sometimes, Judith, the price of freedom comes very high. There was no other way to make our presence felt. The only way to defeat the enemy is to fight them wherever they may be found. That is Alfred's way. It is what he believes in. What we all believe in."

"I know that, Heardred. The people understand that too. God knows many have paid with their lives for their King to keep in the field. But greed and fear are powerful enemies, and those who had most to lose were the most severely threatened. And not everyone shares the King's belief, nor has his courage," she added, looking into his eyes, her green ones suddenly flooding with tears. "I know now why the enemy passed us by. Why our lands were not burned and our people slain."

And suddenly he grasped what she was hinting at, his face reflecting his amazement and sorrow for her shame.

"Your father! That's who you mean, isn't it?"

"Yes, Heardred," she replied slowly, dropping his hand and covering her face with her own. "He did a wicked deal with the Danes. He couldn't bear to see everything he and his family had built up over the years destroyed for something he didn't believe in."

"How could he have been so blind?" Heardred broke in angrily. "How could he have lost his faith in his King so easily? Dear God, his father is one of Alfred's closest advisors. The knowledge of his son's weakness would break the old man's heart! Does he know his son has paid tribute willingly?"

"I don't know. But father is not the only one. There are others."

"I know that," he replied calmly.

"Doesn't that bother you?" she queried sharply, her head on one side.

166

"Don't jump to conclusions, Judith," he said quietly, looking into her eyes. "Some of those nearest the King have been ordered to do just that,"

"*What?*" she exclaimed appalled, sitting upright. "Pay tribute to the enemy? I cannot believe that!"

"Don't be so hasty. It is a ploy, designed to lull the enemy into a false sense of wellbeing," he said, taking her hand in his again. "Tribute is paid to keep the Danes off guard, while the land is used by Alfred's warriors as they need. My men and I have saved our skins on more than one occasion hiding out on tribute lands.

"In some cases war groups have been led on secret raids by tribute payers, far from their estates, whom the Danes think are safe. Two of my best friends from around Southampton, near your father's lands, have been doing just that for months. The Lords Edwin and Harold. Maybe you know them?"

"No, Heardred," she said after a pause for thought. "They are not names I know, but then my father has never been one to court the welcome of others. Nor is he one to join the King's battle line."

"No matter, but I have known them all my life. We have fought together many times. Theirs is dangerous work, Judith, and takes real courage. Maybe I have been too hasty in my judgement of your father."

"I would it were so," she replied bitterly. "But in truth he has betrayed many who fought for the King. Remember, last night, when we talked about renegades? My father is one! Our lands are no haven for those who fight against the Great Army. On the contrary, the enemy have been made truly welcome, and my father has denounced those neighbours who support Alfred...and has benefited from it with their lands."

"But that is treason!" Heardred replied, deeply shocked.

"My father is a fool. He cannot see the damage he has done to our family. He believes that Alfred's days are numbered, that it is only a question of time before Guthrum's host destroys him and all Wessex is secure under Danish rule. After all, they rule everywhere else: East Anglia, Northumbria, Mercia! So he has thrown his lot in with Guthrum in the hopes that he will be rewarded by the enemy when the war is over. He is *Nithing!*" she exclaimed fiercely, her eyes spitting green fire.

"So, that's why you left."

"*Yes!*" she replied hotly, taking back her hand and turning away from him again. "I could not bear the shame. I loved my father once...but he has dishonoured all of us. Now I despise him. Even my grandfather may not be able to hold up his head again when this is all over. Nevertheless, I resolved to make my way to him here in the land of the Somerseatas, where he lives, near Yeovil."

"But that is miles from here!"

"Of course it is. I am not here because I want to be. I am here because Medraut dragged me here in his foul cart! I would have flung myself on the King's mercy if I could have penetrated the marshes that have held the Danes at bay all these months. Besides, there was always the chance I might come across news of Gyrth and his family from my grandfather. If anyone knew anything, he would."

"So you and Aelflaeda vanished from your home, together with a small party of loyal servants and what you could carry on your horses."

"Yes. And we made good ground at first, and might well have succeeded had not Rufus cast a shoe. We made our way to the nearest village, Stourton Caundle; a tiny place some miles from Sherborne, in the middle of nowhere that you would have thought was safe as the abbey itself...but in our ignorance we did not think to check it first. It was getting dark, the weather was not good, we were tired and hungry, and the few lights we could see looked so inviting.

"But?" he said, putting his arm round her.

"But the place was in Medraut's hands," she said bitterly, dashing tears from her face. "I thought the smith seemed nervous, but by then it was too late. Suddenly we were surrounded. Oh, God, Heardred, it was just terrible. The shouts, the screams, the blood, the sheer merciless slaughter and brutality of it all. The men with us stood no chance. Those who tried to fight were butchered where they stood. The rest abandoned us, dropped their weapons and fled away into the darkness. And then Medraut took us prisoner.

"Me they left untouched. He felt I would be worth more as unspoiled goods. But poor Aelflaeda," she said, looking round at the dark-haired girl as she got up to walk out to the stream, her face like stone. "Her he gave to his men for sport...and forced me to watch while his men raped her. She wept and screamed and begged for mercy, holding her hands out to me to help her, wailing piteously while his chief men brutalised her. They were animals! *Animals!* Dear God, it was awful!" And covering her ears with her hands she flung herself against him, burying her head in his arms to block out the ghastly sounds and images that had risen up to torture her.

"So that's why the poor child is so strange and detached from everything," he said a few moments later when she had recovered her composure. "It is a miracle she has survived at all. Not just in body but in mind as well."

"Poor, poor little thing. I am the only one she will speak to now. The only one whom she will allow to touch her. If you had not rescued us I am sure that Medraut would have killed her, cut her throat and left her to bleed out as he has done to others amongst the girls he has taken who are no good to him," and she shuddered, her whole body suddenly shivering as if she had the ague.

"I feel so helpless, so guilty," she sighed moments later, looking across to where the girl was washing her face in the stream. "She would not be here, but for me. She was such a bright cheerful soul. To see her like this tears my heart."

"At least she is alive," he said then, moving to hold her more securely. "Many others faced with the same horror die as a result of their treatment. And she has had you to care for her. What happened after Stourton Caundle?"

"Medraut added us to his bunch of wilting flowers. And a sorrier bouquet you could not hope to find. Those over there still have some spirit in them, as your men will quickly discover," she said, watching the girls mingling with his men as they were all rousted out by Siward. "But mostly they have learned to keep it cowed. No man wants an over lively slave girl! And Medraut was swift to deliver a sound thrashing to any he thought were too forward, or unco-operative. He has dragged us in that beastly cart from Danish settlement to settlement over the past few weeks or more. Stripped naked, soused with rain water and thrown up onto a table or upturned stool, and forced to show off their wares before beginning the sale.

"Those you have amongst you now are the pick of the bunch; he was keeping those for the Danish host at Chippenham. All the rest he has sold along the way, as I said, or killed. There is no profit in keeping merchandise for whom no buyer can be found! Me he meant to present to Guthrum himself. A royal gift-offering to ensure the Danish king's continuing support for his activities," she ended bitterly, dragging her soiled cape around her, while he put his arms around her shoulders and drew her gently towards him.

*

*T*hey had been together for only a short time, yet already he felt he had known this extraordinary girl for years. Bonded in grief, it seemed incredible that they should both have been about to be betrothed into the same family without either knowing of the other's existence! It was as if some invisible thread had inexorably drawn them together. Some would call it fate. The priests would call it God's will. He simply felt that it was part of their destiny, and he gloried in it.

*

169

"What are you thinking?" she asked him, nestling into his warmth, while beyond their shelter the whole camp was now thoroughly stirred into action.

"About you and me!" he exclaimed softly. "About how strange that we should meet like this, across the bodies of a bunch of slavers, the scum of the earth! Both looking for a fresh start yet not knowing how, or where, to achieve it. And how suddenly I feel changed inside, in a way I had never expected to feel again. I can't help thinking that this was all meant to happen."

She turned then in his arms and kissed him softly on the cheek.

"Me too, Heardred; I only wish we didn't have to break the spell."

"Unfortunately, my beauty," he replied with a sigh, "there is no escaping it. There is a war on, and I have my men to see to, and if I am not mistaken we are about to be officially roused from our slumbers. My second, that big man over there beasting that idiot, Osbert, is Siward. You met him yesterday. He will be calling the muster shortly, and I must be there cloaked and armed to check the men through with him. You go with Aelflaeda and refresh yourself by the stream...and do your business," he added shyly. "And I will come for you when all is ready. We have a long and difficult ride ahead of us, and I cannot allow things to slip now, however much I might be tempted.

"I will send one of my men with hot food and some mulled ale against the journey. Now, let me kiss you briefly," he said standing up, "and then I will be on my way. Wessex and the Danes await my arrival, my Lady Judith," he continued with a mock bow, laughing brightly as he did so, "and they will not be denied."

With a grand gesture she held out her hand for his lips before rising to greet Aelflaeda as she came back into their shelter, while Heardred strode stiffly across to where Siward was standing by the fire, Hathored stirring a rich broth in the old cauldron, while Baldred tended the fire and the rest of his command busied themselves about the campsite: watering the animals, checking the cart and generally making ready to move, with the half-a-dozen girls whom they had rescued the day before doing what they could to help.

*

"So, how did you fare last night, my Lord?" his big second asked him slyly, as he came up to him by the fire.

"Better than of late, you old ruffian," he replied with a grin. "But nothing like that at which you are hinting with such subtlety," he said drily to Siward's raised eyebrow. "She's not that kind of girl!"

"Well, that's more than can be said of that lot," the big Saxon grunted heavily, pointing to where the other women were making ready. "Given half a chance and those precious warriors of ours would have turned this clearing into a whore's paradise!"

"As bad as that, eh?"

"Very nearly, my Lord, and it's no laughing matter," he said, as Heardred snorted with amusement. "If we are not careful those jades will turn your command into a jealous rabble. The men have been away from normal creature comforts far too long, and there are not enough girls to go round."

"Good God, Siward, you make it sound like a gift-offering at Christmas!"

"Well, my Lord," his second replied succinctly, throwing another piece of wood onto the fire, "there are some precious pieces amongst Medraut's former captives, I can tell you! Some very passable wenches indeed, and now that there is no obvious threat to their safety they are beginning to flight their feathers, encouraging the men to vie for their favours. If I had my way I'd put the whole lot of them back in that bloody cart and leave them there," he growled, pointing at the barred cart standing in the far corner. "The sooner we can get on with our proper work the better. One thing's for certain, my Lord," he ended caustically, "I am damn glad no pretty hussy ever got her claws into me!"

And Heardred threw back his head and laughed uproariously.

"Don't worry, my friend. Help is at hand, I promise you. I will put them all under Lady Judith's control. It'll give her something to think about other than her own problems, and her maid can assist. The Lady Judith is well used to dealing with her father's servants and estate people since her mother died, so she should have no problems."

"That is sweet news, my Lord," the big man said, with a grin. "Heathen pirates, wild berserkers, murderers, thieves and bandits I can cope with. Silly women who giggle and make cow's eyes at me from between their fingers, and run shrieking from me when I growl at them, are quite beyond my understanding! I must say, you seem to have all the answers this morning. This Lady Judith who has come so suddenly amongst us, must be a rare and special jewel indeed to have made our dour commander all sweetness and light on such a grey and dismal morning."

He paused then, and looked around at his command as they made ready to come forward to the muster, before bringing their bowls to the fire for their morning meal: armour brushed down and correctly worn across their bodies, weapons present, belongings rolled and ready to be strapped to their saddles,

171

horses groomed and fed, the whole camp effectively struck and ready to be abandoned.

"In truth, Siward, I barely know her. But there is that about her that draws a man from the heart. She has a loving gentleness that I had not looked for beyond the grave," and he paused again to admire the way his men had readied themselves under their officers; checking each other's war gear, making themselves as smart as possible; at the women now straggling forward from their shelter and from the stream where they had gone to wash themselves; and at the clouded sky above them, heavy streamers of dark cloud moving swiftly against the paler overcast.

"She was to have been betrothed to my Lady Brioni's brother, Gyrth. It seems almost too strange to believe. She is a very special link with the past, my friend. I do not mean to let her slip through my fingers."

Siward drew in his breath sharply at that, and looked at his commander, then he banged him on the back.

"Perhaps it is an omen?"

"Perhaps it is. One thing I do know, Siward," he said smiling.

"My Lord?"

"She is the prettiest omen I ever saw! Now, come on, we have wasted enough of the morning as it is. Let's get the men fed, and those doxies who have come among us," he added, pointing to the half-a-dozen women also waiting to be fed, their eyes all over the men now standing waiting for Hathored to feed them.

"Send Wiglaf across to my shelter with food and ale as soon as it is ready. I want Osbert and Alfgar to check the mules and horses for loose nails and shoes, and that damned cart for its wheels and shaft. Those women can travel in it as before. The Lady Judith and her maid on their own horses that Medraut kept; we'll call the muster within the hour, and then we must be away."

"Aldhelm reckons it will be a good day's ride to Leofric's new base."

"Provided we don't get lost and don't run into trouble," Heardred responded firmly. "Through Bruton, and on through the Deverills to Warminster. That is what Alfred has advised for a small party like ours. We are approaching the edge of Guthrum's heartlands, remember. We will be in bandit country and must expect to find the enemy more numerous and alert than elsewhere."

"Bush and boulder country, eh?"

"Just so, my friend. An enemy behind every bush and boulder! I want four men ahead of us, not two. Cart mules and pack horses in the centre...I know, that will slow us down, but rather that than lose the lot to a sudden ambush. So, the sooner we get started the better."

"Very well, my Lord. And I for one," he added darkly as the sound of giggling and snorting laughter broke out amongst the men, "could not be more pleased! It's time and enough that these so noble troopers of ours remembered what they have been trained and paid for. Warriors?" he snorted derisively as he turned away. "Gurt lummox fyrdsmen more like! As feather-brained as those foolish doxies they are so taken with. God help me, my Lord, but there are times when I wish that I had gone into a monastery!"

Chapter Twenty Two

*T*hey left the clearing with the wind in their faces beneath a louring sky, and headed for the uplands around Bruton, which they had failed to reach the previous day. This was the first leg of their journey to Warminster and Battlesbury Rings where Leofric had established his new base, and before long they crossed the old Fosse Way at Lydford, where long ago the eagles of the Second Augusta had marched into the west. Here the air was fresh and clean, and though the sky was heavy overhead, they rode with high hearts, the girls in the big mule cart calling out to the men who rode by their side.

By mid-morning they had crossed the Brue and marched through the small town named for its river, with its water mills and busy market, Hathored and Osbert pausing to buy fresh supplies of bread and meat with the money that Alfred had given them on Athelney. The men, upright in their saddles, rode through with pride, their faces wreathed in smiles; while Heardred, with laughter and good cheer, ordered the people to clear their way, the girls in the old mule cart making a real exhibition of themselves that shocked the matrons of the little town. Pressing their bodies up against the bars that surrounded them, they shouted out and made lewd gestures, until Siward spurred up and roared at them, when they collapsed onto the cart bed and dissolved in giggles that embarrassed him hugely.

Once past Bruton they climbed into the hills and through the upland woods that cloaked them. Overhead the clouds broke up before a sharp wind from the north-east, occasional shafts of bright sunlight breaking through to warm the countryside, in which the men and horses revelled.

*

*I*n many places through which they passed the villages and steadings were working normally, the scent from the wood-fires heavy on the wind blowing across their faces. There were people, and animals, moving about their strips in the great fields that surrounded the houses and bothies they passed by, and there were herd beasts quietly grazing on the common land that lay around them. Some lords had even placed mounted watchers at vantage points on the edges of their hide lands to give warning of the approach of armed raiders. Watchers who spurred up and demanded to know what they were doing, and who were pleased to note that Heardred and his command came directly from the king, and promised to pass Alfred's summons on to their lords and all those who stood for Alfred and not Guthrum.

But elsewhere the lands were empty, only the charred mitres of burned out crofts and lofty halls to show that once the country had been fat and prosperous. Here the fields were already rank with weeds and grasses, the tumbled wattle ruins returning to the soil that had given them birth. There were dead cattle and their young everywhere, and the few animals that had escaped the heathen raiders wandered aimlessly in the wastelands, or rooted hopefully amidst the rotting shambles of fallen byres and abandoned woodlands gone completely wild.

Occasionally they came upon small groups who had escaped the slaughter, foraging desolately amongst the shattered jumble of their fallen homes. But always they fled away as they approached, back to their brushwood shelters and turf huts in the dense woods and brakes that dressed the landscape.

But all was not completely barren, for spring was on the move at last, the blustery wildness of March giving way to April's softer weather, despite the stinging sleet and rain of yesterday. Already the shrubs and bushes were touched with a fine green fuzz that heralded the warmer months to come. Daffodils clustered in golden clumps in nooks and hollows, while stitchwort and primroses rioted along the wooded slopes and by the muddy trackside, and bugle, the carpenters' herb, rioted in blue and purple spires everywhere. Soon the swallows and martins would return to their ancient haunts and skyways, and the cuckoo would call again across the fields and valleys to assure the world that winter now had truly passed away.

Pushing hard along the ancient trackway that led from Bruton to Maiden Bradley and Crockerton, they made steady time, coming by stealth and great care to the wider plough-lands around Longbridge Deverill. This stood on the edge of the River Wylye which flowed from there in a great loop beyond Sutton Veny, the next tiny village to where they were sitting, and the safety of the huge earthworks of Battlesbury Rings beyond. And it was at Longbridge that Heardred ordered a halt, while he called up Aldhelm to help him plan the next part of their passage to Leofric's encampment.

*

*F*rom where they were stopped by the long trestle bridge that crossed the river, the ground was more open and less secure with rising uplands, heavily wooded on either side through which the track they were following wound its way. Here, where churls and geburs had laboured for generations, the thick woods and coppices were more broken up.

So far they'd not had any real problems.

No horse had cast a shoe and the cart had not broken a wheel or cracked its shaft. But the presence of the women had already strained the rations with which they had set out, it was getting late in the day, and horses and men were tired. The tiny hamlets through which they had passed could not support so many sudden strangers amongst them, yet camping out here in the open would be asking for trouble. They couldn't split up, that was far too dangerous, and besides they only had one reliable guide, Aldhelm, who knew every inch of the land ahead of them.

Heardred did not.

*

"So, what do you think?" the russet-haired war-leader asked him after they had sat and looked out across the empty countryside, resting their arms along the top of their saddles.

"We must press on, my Lord. The Wylye here makes a great loop which we have to cross to reach the next village, Sutton Veny. Just beyond that we cross the river again from where it is only a short hop to the Rings, where Leofric and his people will be delighted to greet you."

"So, we cut across that loop, cross the river again beyond Sutton Veny and then we will be there…yes?"

"Yes, my Lord."

"Then I agree; we press on. We have no choice, and the weather has closed in again, those clouds do not look good," he said, looking up at a darkening sky, "though a big storm right now might help to keep any Danish raiding party off our backs. How are the women taking it, Siward?" he asked as the big man pushed his horse up beside him.

"Well enough, my Lord. But they are tired, hungry and fractious. They may not be riding, but that cart is a jolting, numbing experience, and such hard travelling as we have been doing is foreign to them."

"It cannot be helped. We cross here, and I dare not let up the pace until we have crossed the river again," he said to his big second, pointing across the bridge to the countryside beyond.

"Again, my Lord?"

"Yes, again! The river makes a big loop here to the north. We must cut across that to the next village, two miles or so, then over the river once more. After that Aldhelm assures me we will be within a stone's throw of safety. The thick woodlands and broken country that border the river will help us. We have not seen hide nor hair of the enemy all day, and surely we are not like to see them now. Especially if we are so close to Leofric's base. Nevertheless we will take no chances," he said, looking all round him.

"Siward I want you to lead our scouts yourself. You have a quicker eye for danger than any man I know in this command. Take Aldhelm with you, and push forward immediately. And this time we will be close behind you; it doesn't pay to take too many chances!"

And so they moved out: Siward, Aldhelm, Clun and Aetheridge leading, with Heardred, the mule cart and all the rest of his command, pack horses, and those from Medraut's camp following behind them, with Baldred, Osbert and Wiglaf as a final rear guard.

*

*L*ess than three miles, but they took them slowly.

From wood to coppice to spinney they went, each time the main party remaining in cover until cleared to move forward again by the scouts whom Heardred had sent on ahead as, pair by pair, Siward worked them steadily as they advanced towards Sutton Veny and their final river crossing just beyond.

His eyes constantly alert for any sudden unnatural movement that might presage an enemy assault, Siward missed nothing. Nor did his ears fail him either, for he was able to detect no alarm call from blackbird, jay or pheasant that might have warned him of others than themselves who might be moving in the empty countryside around them.

Ahead the village was tiny, no more than a collection of sturdy buildings, cruck houses and barns that had grown up where two roads crossed over, and a couple of water mills built by the Saxon lords who farmed the estates. And it was here, at the crossroads, that Siward threw up his hand and brought the long column to a bouncing halt. While holding Swiftfire to a steady walk, Heardred threaded his way through the vanguard to where Siward and Aldhelm were in discussion.

"Which way do we go?" he asked, sitting back in his saddle to stretch his back.

"Straight ahead leads to the closest crossing of the Wylye," Aldhelm explained, which is what Siward would like to get over as soon as possible. And you can get to the Rings if you do that. But if you take the left-hand road here, although it is further to the river, and you will have to cross it twice in quick succession…"

177

"Why?" Heardred asked quickly.

"Because there is a kind of island in the stream that must first be crossed. But, my Lord," Aldhelm said with a rush, before Heardred could complain, "the left-hand road will get us to the Rings much more quickly. The other way is a dogleg. The island way is much more direct."

"How far to the Rings now?"

"Close, my Lord. Not much more than a couple of leagues. Look, from here you can see the escarpment on which the Rings are built."

"Very well. We will take the more direct route. The weather is closing in on us," he added, looking up at the sky, now deeply black and threatening. "God willing we will find help as well as shelter. My Lady," he went on, turning to Judith who had edged closer to him as he had been speaking, "how are the girls in your charge…and can they ride?"

"Flagging, Heardred. But not so bad they cannot hang on. And, yes, they can ride," she said surprised. "They are all country girls, and all country girls know which end of a horse you kick to make it go. Why?"

"Because now is the time to abandon the cart," he said, looking round at everyone. "I am uneasy. It has been too quiet for too long and I do not trust the Heathen any further than I can see them…and that I cannot do!" he added grimly. "So, Judith, Osbert, Wiglaf, get them all mounted. It is in my mind that we may need to put on some real speed, and that is not possible dragging that wretched cart with us, and it can always be recovered later. Put those mules on long leading reins, same as the other spare mounts we took from Medraut, and let's make some real progress to Battlesbury. I don't expect a fight, but if we have to we cannot do it weighed down with a parcel of doxies in a cart! Siward, stay be me now. Aldhelm, you take the lead with Aetheridge. You know this area better than any of us. Our lives are in your hands now!"

"You honour me, my Lord," Leofric's messenger replied with a bow of his head.

"Nonsense, my friend," Heardred threw back at him with a broad smile. "I am just saving myself for later! Now, let's be gone, we have jawed enough. Time not the heathen pirates is our true enemy today!"

*

*T*wenty minutes later, with Aldhelm and Aetheridge in the lead with a strong vanguard, all the women now mounted in the centre, they took the left-hand track out of the village and spurred away down the rutted track. Siward and Heardred rode just ahead of the women, and the remainder followed as a rear-guard, with all the spare mounts and packhorses on long leading reins at the back, their pounding hooves sending up fat chunks of turf in earthy clusters spinning through the chill air.

*

*A*bove them the sky stretched away to the horizon in unbroken ranks of rolling cloud, their curved edges black with menace that now loomed over the land as they were hurried on before a keening wind. And as they rode a tumbling flock of crows flew caarking dismally overhead, their faces to the west, for the day was already fading and an early darkness was beginning to gather in the north-east, the horizon rapidly disappearing as the deep blackness of a gathering storm leapt out upon them.

For over a mile they moved forward briskly, the trackway straight, but full of ruts and potholes, so that at times it was better to leave it and ride across virgin land along its verges, save where clumps of trees and thick shrubs and bushes forced them back onto it.

Then, with the river in sight at last, less than a mile away, just as Aldhelm and Aetheridge were turning in their saddles to check that the rest of Heardred's war-group were still in view, the way ahead of them, some few hundred yards short of the bridge, was suddenly filled with silent armoured figures. Well mounted and heavily equipped, their black iron byrnies and shields matching the ever darkening sky, the gold zig-zags rimmed with scarlet painted across them just catching a stray shaft of light as the storm clouds thickened overhead.

*

*A*ldhelm dragged his horse to a rearing halt and his face was grim. "God aid us now," he murmured between clenched teeth, "for there will be no escape from those men!"

"Who are they?" Aetheridge asked. "Why do they not attack? They seem different from the Heathen whom we have come across elsewhere."

"Those are Jomsvikings, my friend. The elite of the Danish host, some of the Earl Oscytel's personal army. Only they wear black armour, and see, they carry his symbol of the ragged knife on their shields. Dear God, but it is an evil mischance that has brought them across our path this day!"

"What are they waiting for, and why are they so still? Such silence in heathen pirates is unnatural. They make me afraid!"

179

"That is their intention," Aldhelm replied, backing his horse away as he spoke. "It unnerves the ill-trained and frightens the faint-hearted. Don't let them get to you! They bleed as well as we do and get cut down just as messily, and they fight on foot as we do. But when they do charge they do it all together, as one, and whether mounted as those are, or not, they are always formidable!" And wheeling his horse, he stabbed in his heels and thundered back to where Heardred and Siward were already cantering up to join them, their horses snorting with excitement and tossing their heads from side to side.

"So, Jomsvikings!" Heardred exclaimed as he brought Swiftfire to a stamping halt beside Aetheridge. "The Lord Oscytel's men," he added darkly. "I have heard much of that black-hearted bastard and his chosen warriors, and have seen their handiwork!"

"How many do you reckon, Siward?"

"Hard to tell, my Lord," the big man said, shading his eyes. "The way is narrow and it grows darker by the minute. But more than we have with us here."

"Is there a way round, Aldhelm?"

"No, my Lord. The river bounds us on the right, and to go left across open country would be fatal. They would be on us like leash hounds after a deer, and who knows whether there aren't more of them out there to hem us in. We have women and pack animals in our rear, we would never get away.

"Well, they stand between us and the bridge," Heardred said, "and plainly they are expecting us to fight. But I wonder if they know the area as well as you do, Aldhelm," he added slowly, looking at the big scout. "For there is another way, isn't there?"

"Yes, my Lord. For a small party, back the way we have just come; yes there is. And over the other bridge across the Wylie and on to the Rings from there. The way Siward wanted to go in the first place."

"Well, clearly there is going to be a storm, and soon," Heardred said looking up as a rumble of distant thunder rolled across the sky, gentling his horse with his hands as he spoke. "Even the horses can feel it. Under the cover of that, and if we can keep those bastards occupied for long enough, a small party might just make it away from here to safety, as long as they had a fearless guide," he ended, looking at Aldhelm.

Silence followed as Heardred sat still, and looked round at his small command, at the sky overhead, at the set faces of his men, the anxious, fearful ones of the women they were guarding…and the distant enemy, black and formidable in their silence.

Clearly they must fight.

There was no way of avoiding it; but though he might fall, and all his men with him, there was now a chance that Judith and those with her might be saved.

"Me, Lord?" Aldhelm asked quietly, while Heardred looked again down the track to where the enemy had assembled, horses and men in one long line across it.

"Yes," he said at last. "You are the only one who really knows his way around here. You must take Aetheridge, Osbert, Wiglaf and the women with you, and the packhorses. Leave the rest to run free, I am sure they will follow you. They are herd beasts and will run with the herd. Meanwhile we will go up against those men and engage their interest," he said drily, with a grim smile. "While you take the road behind us back to Sutton Veny. Whatever happens you must find the Lord Leofric and give him Alfred's news, and the pardon he has entrusted to you. No, there can be no argument, soldier," he cut in on Aldhelm's instant move to object. "It is the only way. You know it to be true!"

"I won't let you do this, Heardred," Judith said desperately, pushing her horse up beside Swiftfire. "Osbert, Wiglaf and the others must go with Aldhelm certainly. But Aelflaeda and I will stay with you. Please Heardred, let me stay."

"He looked at her stricken face, and the tears that had sprung into her eyes and his face softened.

"Judith," he said, drawing her to one side. "I cannot leave you and Aelflaeda to fall into Danish hands without a struggle. Not after everything you have already suffered. My honour will not allow it, and anyway, you mean too much to me for that."

Then bending towards her across her horse, he kissed her on the cheek. "Quickly now, my little lady, be brave. There is so little time left, and the others look to you for a lead. They need you, Judith. And I, and my command, need to know that you are all being led to safety for us to do our part."

She looked into his eyes and loved him.

And leaning across his horse, she took his face in her hands and kissed him on the mouth, her tears running down her cheeks as she did so. She wanted to cling to him and hold him close, to tell him that she cared, that she understood him, that he only had to ask and she would be his.

But this was not the place and there was no more time.

With infinite care and softness he pushed her away from him and wheeled swiftly back towards his waiting men.

"Aldhelm, Osbert, Aetheridge, Wiglaf, to the rear! Take the women with you and wait until you see us ride to meet with the enemy. Then withdraw as fast as your beasts will carry you and make for the river beyond Sutton Veny. The storm will soon be upon us," he shouted above the rising wind as the first flickers of lightning jagged across the sky, "and we will hold them for as long as we can. By that time you should be clear away. Siward come to my right, Cenwald hold the left. Everyone else packed in behind. We'll use the flying wedge with me at the point, as we have done before, and may God and His saints be with us.

"Now, we have waited long enough. Spears first, then swords and axes. Everyone keep together and we may yet win through to see another day!" And slipping his great war shield round to cover his left flank, he dug in his heels and pulled Swiftfire into a rearing stand.

"*For God and King Alfred!*" he roared out, shaking his spear wildly at the silent ranks of their foe.

"*For God and King Alfred!*" came the fierce reply. "*Death to the Danes! Death! Death!*"

And with that final shout they drove in their heels and rushed furiously towards their enemies, while the thunder growled and menaced overhead and lightning lit up the great escarpment on which the ancients had built Battlesbury Rings beyond the river.

Chapter Twenty Three

Closer and closer they came to the steady line of Danish horsemen in their black armour who blocked their way to the bridge, and still they did not move; until it looked to Heardred as if the enemy commander intended to use his horses as a living wall to soak up their attack.

Then, when they were almost within a spear's length, there was a single great shout, and suddenly the whole Danish line peeled open to reveal a double rank of Danish archers, with spearmen and axe-bearing warriors clustered in behind them.

Heardred had barely time to take in what was happening before the first arrows were swooping down on them, whistling like iron sleet about their ears as they struck at horse and rider alike. He heard the screams of wounded men and horses, felt the crashing fall of those who had been brought down, and then they were upon them.

Hurling his spear ahead of him into the now roaring mass of Danes who had leapt forward to meet him, he drew his sword and hacked down at the enemy, flensing left and right across Swiftfire's withers as he fought his way amongst them. Glittering eyes and thrusting spear points, black shields and shining axes seemed all about him. Twisting and turning in his saddle, gripping and driving onwards with his thighs and heels, forcing his horse sideways and backwards, he fought to clear their path, Siward still on his right side and Cenwald on his left.

But already their desperate charge was slowing as their foe closed in around them. Yet, even though the Danish arrows had claimed a number of his troop and their horses, the power of their formation had driven a sharp wedge into the enemy line, bowling over the archers who had not managed to get out of their way, and all around him his men were fighting fiercely. If they could but drive, hack and cut their way further forward, before the mounted warriors on either flank could press in on them, they might yet break through the enemy line completely, and reach the open road that lay beyond the river.

Cut, thrust, hack and block! The struggle was as vicious and bloody as any that Heardred could remember.

A spearman running in upon him. Thrust with his heels, twist and hack down in one slicing movement. A piercing scream, the man's face opening like a flower, blood and teeth spraying up over his sword arm as the man fell beneath the trampling hooves...a wild axe blow sweeping up towards his horse's neck. *Turn! Turn!* the great blade hissing past, the Danish warrior

183

shouting and roaring as he swung his weapon back and round in a powerful reverse sweep. Turn again and cut down, blade meeting blade in a crash of steel and flying sparks, both men shouting and yelling in their battle-fury, locked together by fear and hatred.

And all around was the terrible detritus of battle: the entrails of horse and rider besmirching the ground, blood puddling the rutted track, the stench of urine, faeces and vomit filling the air...and the bodies of horses and riders, of enemy archers, spear, axe and sword-Danes, and Saxon warriors, scattered in bloody heaps all across the trackway.

Then, suddenly, the Danish foe broke and ran back dragging their wounded with them, only to turn some fifty paces further on, clear of all the battle debris, shields locked together, spears thrust out, eyes and helmets glittering above their rims.

It was a feint to clear the way. The Danish horse were coming in at last.

"*Back! Back!*" Heardred shouted wildly above the rising wind, and the growing rage of the storm. "Face left and right! *Move! Move!*"

With what seemed agonising slowness those of his men still mounted responded to his desperate cry. Wheeling and pulling their horses round to face the new threat, dragging back on their reins to force their trembling mounts into some kind of order, while they waited beneath a ravening sky for the heathen Northmen to attack, the remainder of his command, wounded and whole, whose horses had been slain, also struggled into line, their own shields locked and spears thrust out amongst them.

It was a brief respite, for moments later the enemy horsemen who had drawn aside at the outset now hurled themselves at the remains of Heardred's troop, just as the heavens opened and the rain roared down upon them in icy torrents, and the thunder hammered overhead.

Now, as never before, they were fighting for their very lives, as hemmed in on every side they were steadily forced in against one another, the rain falling so fiercely they were almost blinded.

Sword to sword and shield to shield they hewed at each other in mortal desperation, while the ebony sky above their heads was riven by great jagged flashes of blue-white fire. Each sizzling bolt lighting up their faces and casting the whole broiling scene into terrifying stark relief, each falling blow or waterfall of drops momentarily stopped in the flashing glare, the stunning detonations that followed making the horses rear and stumble, the whites of their eyes shining in terror as they splashed and struggled in a foul morass of bloodied mire that the violence of the flash storm had created.

Even as Heardred at last picked out the Jomsviking leader of the men who were trying so hard to destroy him, he felt Swiftfire shudder violently,

184

saw his head rear up and heard his scream of pain as the spear that had struck him burst his chest apart. He just had time to fling himself clear before his brave charger crumpled beneath him and crashed lifeless to the ground, blood gushing from his mouth, eyes wide and staring.

Landing heavily on all fours, Heardred did not have the time to mourn his friend, but leapt swiftly to his feet, his armour running with water, his shield held high against the deluge of blows that fell on him from the enemies around him as he leapt and twisted violently from side to side, sword gripped tight as he rose to meet each furious attempt to cut him down.

"*Aid me, Siward!*" he roared above the tumult. "*Guard my back!*" And leaping forward he made a wild dash for the tall armoured figure who had led and organised the surprise attack on them with such skill and daring.

Astride a great bay horse with a white blaze and a Roman nose, he towered above Heardred, his black armour running with blood and water, his face masked by the steel cheek pieces, eye protectors and heavy nasal that made up his helmet. Only the glitter of his eyes in the violent flashes of lightning showed that he was human, and not some unknown god of war...and like demented smiths they hewed and cut at one another. Blade to blade, with scrape of steel and flare of spark, each struggling for an advantage, while the storm passed directly overhead, the rain cascading down their faces, the wind howling all about them.

Cut, thrust, parry. Block! An eldritch screech of steel, Heardred on his toes, slipping in the muddy wreckage of the trackway, with his sword two-handed against his enemy's downward slash. Arms locked, teeth gritted, then away again, Heardred dancing clear, the big Danish leader following him round on his curvetting steed, wild hooves skittering in the puddled water.

The man was strong and skilful and harried his grounded enemy without mercy. He knew, as Heardred did, that here was the very kernel of the whole affair. Without leadership the Saxon warriors would lose heart, might even try to break and flee, and so he pressed his advantage with ruthless power.

On the ground Heardred was struggling fiercely, hampered by his cloak and the sticky mud churned up by the rain, the screaming, fighting warriors and the trampling horses. He was tiring...and the enemy commander knew it.

Crash! Crash! The last blow taken on his shield split the leather-covered wood and gouged his arm deeply. He felt pain lance through him and cried out at the hot gush of blood that flooded down across his hand...and his shield dropped, he could no longer bear the weight.

Round went the big Dane's arm and down at Heardred's unprotected neck, the blade flashing in with lightning speed. *Clang!* As the Saxon war-lord brought his sword up to stop it. Up, over and back again in a wide reverse cut.

185

Block! The muscles in Heardred's sword arm and shoulder on fire, quivering, unable any longer to bear the strain, but with a final effort he turned his sword blade over and leapt back unscathed.

Stabbing his horse forward the Danish commander followed him hard in the pouring rain, knowing that his enemy was weakening fast from sheer exhaustion and loss of blood.

Up, down, up! his sword a thing of flame and sparking life as he hammered at Heardred with all the power at his command. Blind to everything but the need to kill this man, to see him fall and hear his screams as his body was trampled to a bloody pulp beneath his horse's iron hooves, he had eyes for nothing else.

Siward, fighting shoulder to shoulder with Cenwald and Hathored, heard his Lord's cry for help and with a sweeping axe blow that severed his opponent's shoulder in a violent spray of blood and shards of bone, he rushed to bring him aid.

But even as he turned his horse he was suddenly surrounded and pushed out of the way by a phalanx of bruising riders who crashed into the rear of the Danish lines across the bridge with wild shouts and cries, and fell upon the startled enemy in a welter of smashed water like screaming furies. Swords and axes raised high, they hewed at the heathen men with animal ferocity, brushing their defence aside and tumbling them in twisted agony upon the flooded ground.

Those who stayed to fight were brutally hacked down and slain. The rest fled howling into the storm now passing, their commander cursing them as he struggled to keep them under his control before leading them off the field; while the newcomers raced after them. Their horses splashed friend and foe alike as they plunged past, anxious to cut down any stragglers whom their comrades were forced to leave behind.

Heardred himself was knocked to the muddied ground by the armoured riders as they charged past him, and even he was amazed at their appearance, for every man was masked. Each mask was that of some wild beast of the forest: fox, wolf, boar and badger, with the leading warrior bearing a great bear's head on his shoulders that covered his steel helmet so that the bear's fangs framed his face leaving his eyes glittering in the darkness, lit up by the dying flashes from the storm.

Heardred had heard of these masked warriors, had indeed come a long way to find them, for these were the wolfsheads of Leofric Iron Hand's command, whom the King had sent him to seek out and bring back into the fold, with a royal pardon and the King of Wessex's true goodwill.

"Who are they, Lord?" Siward asked him astonished, as he leapt off his horse and ran to his leader's assistance as he sat slumped in the rain against poor Swiftfire's flank.

"They are Leofric's men, Siward," Heardred replied, wiping his face through gritted teeth, as his big second sought to staunch his wound. "Remember, we have heard of their masked raids from others. *Dear God, but my arm hurts!*" he gasped, clutching his wound fiercely to stem the pain. "I feel so weak! A moment longer and he would have had me knocking on St Peter's door! Quickly, find something to bind up this wound. I am still bleeding like a throat-cut hog at the autumn slaughter!"

"At least the storm is past now," Siward replied, as he wound a tight bandage from the wound-bag hanging off Heardred's saddle, and helped him onto his feet and out of the way. "We might even get a sight of some clear sky before nightfall," he added as the rain stopped almost as swiftly as it had started

"Sweet heavens, Judith! And the others!" Heardred exclaimed, coming to a sudden halt. "They won't know that we are safe. They may even run into the Danes whom those people have just driven off!"

"Don't worry, my Lord," Siward replied soothingly, helping him on again. "Aldhelm and our boys will see that they are all safe, never fear. And there is no way that those Jomsvikings will run into them either. They are well clear of this skirmish field by now. No doubt we will find Judith and all the others clustered round Leofric's fire in his hall warming their toes. They are the least of our problems."

Heardred groaned and sat down on the still warm carcass of one of the slain horses, shivering violently as the shock of his wound and the desperate struggle in the pouring rain overtook him.

"What a disaster, Siward," he said, looking about him at the appalling mayhem scattered round the bridgehead, drawing his sodden mantle round him as he did so. "I tell you this, old friend," he went on after a pause, "had it not been for those men coming to our assistance, we would all be dead by now. The Danes do not make prisoners of Saxon warriors any more than we do of theirs! Dear God, how many have we lost? And how many will not live out this night, I wonder?" he added with a sigh.

"I don't know yet, my Lord; Cenwald is doing that office for the both of us."

"So he lives?"

"Yes. Somewhat battered. It's his horse you are leaning on."

"Swiftfire also was slain. He took a spear in the chest, poor boy. I will miss him greatly."

"That is a great sadness, my Lord," his big second replied, sinking down beside him. "He was a lovely boy. And brave!"

"Yes! There was nowhere he would not go, and nothing he would not do. It will be hard to find another to match him," and both men paused in thought, their eyes going to where the horse lay stretched out in death, the blood from his dying puddled all round him with the rain now just fat drops as the storm moved away.

"Thank God for those masked raiders, my Lord." Siward said, breaking the silence. "They came out of nowhere; over that bridge and straight through those bastards like a knife through butter. I don't know who were more startled? Us or those Jomsvikings to whom they took their swords with such fury."

"Yes! They were a Godsend, my friend," Heardred replied with more animation. "I cannot wait to meet their commander. He must be a rare leader to have dashed so furiously at the enemy. They fled like girls from a rampant bull in the field," and both men laughed.

"Well, it looks as if you will get that chance, my Lord," the big Saxon growled, "for he has just returned with the rest of his command. Look, if you are more comfortable now, I will go and see to the men. I will send Baldred to deal properly with that arm of yours before you lose any more blood."

"Does he live then?"

"That one?" Siward answered him laughing. "He would survive the last trump!" And giving his commander a gentle pat he turned and walked away through the puddles, as the leader of the strange masked fighters who had rescued them swung off his horse and came and stood over where Heardred was resting.

Close to, he was much shorter and slimmer than he had first appeared. His mask, that of a great brown bear in raging fury, with its rounded ears and enormous fangs made him seem taller, and the linked steel pauldrons he wore over his shoulders seem broader, and his eyes glittered as he reached up and lifted off his extraordinary headgear, his right hand ruffling his blond hair, his mouth quirking as he did so.

"Hello Heardred. I had not expected to see you here like this!"

Chapter Twenty Four

*H*eardred looked, stared and was momentarily puzzled, then his heart turned over. If he had not been seated he might well have collapsed, for the shock of what he saw made his head reel and his whole body shake as with a raging fever. The short hair had confused him, but the slow, husky voice was unmistakeable.

"*Brioni?*" he whispered, awestruck, the blood suddenly draining from his face, already pale from his wound, so that his head spun and his vision wobbled. "*Brioni!*" he gasped, reaching out for her. "My life, I cannot believe it! Tell me it is really you. I found your body at Foxley. So badly hacked and mutilated, with my betrothal gift on your arm; I was sure it was you. Reburied you with tears and honour. I have mourned you dead these many months. Oh God...I cannot believe this is true!" And struggling to his feet he lurched towards her and took her in his arms, staggering against her armoured body: love, relief and tears all twisted together in one great well-spring of emotion that deadened the pain in his arm.

Brioni herself felt completely numb.

She realized, with a great sense of shock, that until she had seen his white face staring up at her as she had driven past him moments before, she had scarcely given him a thought since that dreadful day when her father had been so brutally slain.

And now he was holding her to his heart as if he would never let her go.

Certainly her vow to the Old Ones over Wulfstan's shattered corpse was partly responsible for that. But since then she had also met and fallen in love with Leofric; become his mate in every possible way. They were lovers and friends; shared complete trust, and their continued fight against the Danes had only served to bring them closer.

Whatever else happened in her life she knew, without question, that Heardred no longer had a close part to play in it. She would never be his bride now.

Dear Lord, but war made strange bedfellows.

She had always known that one day, when they rejoined the King, there was every chance that she would meet with Heardred again, but she had really given it very little thought. To do so now in this dramatic fashion, without Leofric by her side, and surrounded by the men of her command, was the very devil. She had never been so surprised in her life than when she had realised exactly whom it was that she and her men were risking all to rescue.

*

Steinar Olafsson was one of Oscytel's most experienced war leaders, and he had laid his ambush well. Right where it might catch an enemy unawares so close to the huge Saxon base that Leofric had built on top of the Rings. Where a returning troop of raiders, tired and relaxing so close to home, might be surprised and destroyed. In many ways it had been fortunate that Heardred had been the one to spring it, that it had been his warriors who had blunted Steinar's attack and not her own; otherwise he might well have succeeded in killing her and her men at last...including his brother. For Finnar and Steinar shared the same name, cousins. One for Alfred, one for Oscytel.

Life was so strange at times, you couldn't make it up!

Nevertheless, to see Heardred's white face staring up at her as she had swept past at the head of her command had been a terrible shock. Now she had to try and explain her feelings and desires to a man who had every reason to expect her to feel the same way about everything as he did. It would have been a difficult enough situation under ordinary circumstances, but now, with the knowledge that he had believed her killed at Foxley, it was a hundred times worse.

"Heardred, my friend," she said at last, sliding away from his grasp. "Come and sit down. Your arm is a bloody mess and you look as pale as a boggart. Hey, Trausti," she called out to a large warrior in a great boar mask, "take that thrice dammed thing off your head and bring me some of that spiced ale we always carry with us. This man is injured. And bring me my wound-scrip, and a flare, this bandage needs re-setting. Then have Rowan see to Foxhead. He could do with a quick rub down and a handful of oats before we have to move on."

Heardred, who had watched and listened in open-mouthed amazement, could not believe that this was the same girl he had left behind in Chippenham before Christmas. That girl had been gentle, quiet and loving. This one had a hard edge to her that he had never known before, and she was cool towards him in a way that she had never been before either.

Then she had just been one of Queen Ealhswitha's handmaidens, very beautiful, with an endearing reckless streak, who loved weapons and armour more than her stitchery. But now she was a war-leader, and as good a fighter as any man in his own command, if what he had witnessed was anything to go by. Proven warriors obeyed her orders without question.

190

It was all very strange, even frightening.

He would have begun to question her immediately, had not the warrior, Trausti, interrupted them at that moment with the medical bag she had asked for, carrying a resin-dipped flare in his other hand to light what she needed to do, near darkness having pressed down on them after the storm. And almost immediately came Baldred as well, with the salves and bandages that Siward had asked of him.

So, Heardred was forced to sit still while both Brioni and Baldred saw to his injury, slipping off his mail byrnie to reveal a deep gash in his lower arm where Steinar's blade had gouged him, while their patient gritted his teeth and groaned in his pain.

"That will need stitching, my Lord," Baldred said as soon as he saw the depth of the wound still oozing blood.

"Yes, and that's what I will do in a moment," Brioni replied, reaching for her instruments. "But we must wash it first with a solution of carpenter's herb, next the stitches and then bind it with woundwort and yarrow. Especially yarrow, which Achilles is said to have used to stop the bleeding of his soldiers wounded in battle."

"How do you know all that?" Heardred gasped, as Baldred poured a deep blue lotion into the exposed wound, which Brioni began expertly to stitch up with curved needle and sheep's gut in the wavering light of the torch that Trausti had stuck into the sodden ground.

"From my mother. She always saw to the injuries around Foxley. As I do for the men in Leofric's command. Have done for months," she added, searching in her big scrip for the salve she wanted. "Now, Baldred, while I hold his arm out, you put these herbs on it and bind it tightly to help keep the wound together. And I will see it again tomorrow morning, when we will need to redress it. It will throb horribly," she said, turning to where Heardred was now leaning back against Cenwald's dead horse, his face still pale, "but it should heal clean. Now on with your jacket again. But you must not ride for a day or two or your wound will burst open, you can travel in that cart we saw abandoned on the track, with the other wounded that your man, Siward, is busy organising. Where is Swiftfire?"

"Slain! With a spear in his chest."

"That is a great sadness. He was a fine charger, as I remember."

Baldred would have liked to have stayed and listened to what they now had to say to one another. The knowledge that the leader of the fierce masked warriors who had rescued them was a woman, a real shield maiden out of myth and legend, and not only that, but she was also the same girl they thought they had found and buried at Foxley, had gone round his comrades like wildfire! They were all eager for news.

But no sooner had he finished helping than Heardred dismissed him, sending him off to help Siward sort out the mess left after their bitter skirmish, for he was desperate to discover for himself just how his lost lady came to be there, and how it was she had escaped from Foxley after he had found it shattered and burned out.

*

"What are you doing here, Brioni, and where have all these men come from?" he questioned her slowly, after Baldred had finally dragged himself away. "I thought these were Leofric's warriors?"

"So they are, Heardred. But they make up my command, and have done so since I assaulted Malmesbury, nearly two months ago."

"*You assaulted Malmesbury?*" he asked, astonished. "Killed all those Vikings and took all that silver? We got the message in Athelney. How?"

"With guile and determination, hard courage and good fortune!"

"But I saw you dead at Foxley," he said disbelieving, his face shocked, his eyes glittering in the flaring torchlight. "However did you escape? What happened there, Brioni? When we got there the place was a charnel house, burned out, shattered. Nothing lived. Just piles of bodies and a string of crude graves."

"That was me."

"*You!*" he exclaimed, appalled.

And so she told him all: about Oscytel's attack, the midden, the butchery of her father, and the oath she had sworn in his blood with his ring she still wore on a gold chain around her neck; about the cairns she had built and about poor Agatha who had set out so bravely that morning in her mistress's cloak, and how she had put Heardred's betrothal gift on the child's arm; and about the wolves and finding Foxhead and Bran and Utha; how she had left that afternoon with the old tilt cart in the snow for the charcoal burner's bothy in Helm's Wood.

"So that *was* you we saw that day!" he said, horrified, breaking into her narrative, while their men mingled around them, cautiously at first and then more readily, as soldiers will, as more torches were lit and the living were sorted from the dead; the old mule cart was filled with the wounded, spare horses being found to pull it, and every bit of good armour was salvaged from all those who had been slain. "Cynric said there were tracks, and we could see someone moving in that white wilderness close up to the forest edge. We even discussed sending a party to find out who it was!"

"That was me," she said quietly, before going on to tell of her meeting with Maritia and Oswald...and about Leofric.

"*Leofric Iron Hand!*" he shouted, when she had completely finished. "*You?* Brioni of Foxley, are Leofric's woman? A wolfshead's doxy? *I won't have it!* By God and all the Saints I will not allow it to happen, not now that I have found you again. You are mine by right, and by Heaven I mean to claim you!"

"How dare you treat me so, Heardred!" she replied, leaping up furiously. "I am no man's chattel to be taken, or not, just as you please. Look around you. These are my men and they follow my commands. No, Heardred!" she snarled as he tried to restrain her with his good arm. "Let go of me this instant, before I have you seized. You have no formal claim on me. Our betrothal never took place, nor will it!"

Then, more softly, she went on, putting her hand on his shoulder: "I love another, Heardred; heart and soul, aye, and body too. Our time is past, my friend. Too much has happened now, too much death and killing. Things between us can never be the same."

"But, Brioni, I love you!" he protested desperately. "I have always loved you. I have not found another to take your place, not indeed have I ever sought one."

"*No, Heardred!*" she replied, forcefully. "You don't love me. You love the idea of me. The Brioni you knew before Chippenham, before Foxley was destroyed and my family were slaughtered...before I made my vow upon my father's butchered corpse, is dead. This Brioni," she ended sharply, "is different!"

She sighed and looked away, feeling his pain and distress in her heart, knowing that she had hurt him deeply, yet unable to do anything about it. Bad news was always the same, no matter when you broke it. There never was an easy way to break bad news, and trying to spare a person's feelings often did more harm than good.

Heardred hung his head and groaned.

He was tired, hungry and his arm hurt him. How could she be so hard? Certainly she had suffered greatly. The sight of her family being hacked in pieces must have crucified her. And what that heathen monster had done to her father, before her very eyes, was enough to turn most sane people mad. But to give herself willingly to a Wolfshead leader was inexplicable. Beyond his understanding. Even though the man had noble blood in him, and had been exonerated by the King, it was still deeply wounding. How could she have played him false so lightly?

"Brioni, I just don't understand," he railed at her. "What has happened to the gentle, loving lass I fell in love with? Don't you remember those long summer afternoons, the things we talked of, the promises we made, the plans we had? Was it all a dream?"

"Oscytel happened, Heardred!" she exclaimed bitterly. "The Danes came and destroyed everything that mattered to me. After Foxley I was committed to revenge. There was no other thought in me than that. You got lost along the way...and then I met Leofric!"

"Don't mention his name!" he burst out angrily, struggling to his feet. "The man doesn't deserve to live for what he has done! Oh, my Lady, forgive me," he snarled sarcastically, "I am forgetting how much you love him. How much you have given him also!" he ended bitterly

"Sit down, you fool," she shot back at him angrily. "You are making a ridiculous spectacle of yourself before your men and mine. Besides," she went on more softly, "that bandage Baldred and I have wrapped you in, and the stitches underneath, will come unseated if you are not careful, and then not only will you bleed more, but it will all have to be done again. Then where will you be when the horns blow and the muster is called?"

"Dead, most likely!" he snarled at her. "And none more pleased than yourself. Perhaps it would have suited you more if the Danes had finished me off?"

"How dare you speak like that! Grow up, Heardred. You sound more like a spoiled child than one of our King's most trusted war leaders."

"How else am I to feel, Brioni?" he questioned her furiously, continuing to pace up and down. "Here am I, your acknowledged mate, who has carried his love in his heart for you these many months, believing you foully slain, now being given to understand that all that time you have been lying warm and snug in another man's arms! How in the name of all the gods do you expect me to feel?" he shouted down at her. "*Overjoyed? Ecstatic?*"

"No, of course not, Heardred," she replied, no less angry than he was. "But neither did I expect this tirade of petulance and childish behaviour. For God's sake, Saxon," she went on, exasperated. "Please sit down! You are making me dizzy with your constant movement. What you need is warmth and food. It won't make my news any more palatable, but it might improve your temper!"

Heardred ground his teeth at that in impotent rage, knowing her to be probably correct. They'd not had a proper meal since leaving Athelney, so, with stiff reluctance, he ceased his pacing and came and sat down beside her.

194

"Look, my friend, my very dear friend," she said quietly, putting her hand up to turn his face towards her, "what else would you have me say except the truth? No, don't speak, I beg of you," she went on, putting her fingers up to his mouth. "I am sorry for what has happened. Truly I am. But that is fate, God's will even. The simple fact is that I am not in love with you anymore, Heardred. I do not have those special feelings that made my legs turn to water whenever I saw you.

"War and the months with Leofric have changed me. Look around you, Heardred, those are my men over there helping to put things straight. Pulling the horses in a pile, and the dead, ours and theirs. Then they will set fire to them all. Burn them. We have neither the time nor the energy to bury them all, but neither do we want the stench of death and rotting corpses to poison our air.

"I lead those men in battle, I make the decisions, I have killed many times and shall go on doing so until this war ends. Face the facts, Heardred; I am not the kind of girl with whom you would be comfortable. Not now, not anymore."

"Do you think that helps me, Brioni?" he questioned her urgently. "Or that I care? I love you still. It doesn't matter what you have become now," he said taking her hand in his. "When this war is over, and God willing it will be soon, then you will become what you were before. It is the way of things."

"Then you are blind and deaf as well, most probably," she snapped back at him, snatching her hand out of his grasp. "Have you understood nothing?" she seethed at him. "I am not yours anymore, nor ever shall be again. I don't know how else to convince you, you thick-headed Saxon oaf!" she added, her voice rising in frustrated anger. "Leofric and I are soul mates, and bed mates also. Your love is misplaced now. I have indeed changed, and I have no wish to change back again to the meek, mild innocent I was when you first met me.

"As I am now, you would hate me, and I you also. It would be an absolute disaster. For the love of Heaven, Heardred, go and find someone else to pine over. I have my own life to live, and a war to win also."

And leaping to her feet, she roared across to her giant second-in-command: "*Trausti, we are moving out!* We should reach the Rings within the hour, but take things gently. We do not wish to wrack the wounded in that wagon any more than we need to. That way we should get them all safely back. Send Eadberht and Finnar ahead with news of our arrival. Do you come with us, Heardred?" she asked quickly, turning back to him as she spoke, Baldred holding Foxhead for her by his bridle.

"Yes, my Lady of Foxley," the wounded Saxon war leader answered her with biting sarcasm, hauling himself once more to his feet. "We go with you, but don't believe for one moment that this business between us is ended.

Leofric may have gained the King's free pardon...aye, I forgot that bit didn't I? But he has not gained mine. My shield arm may be injured, but not so the one that holds my sword. There is a reckoning to be met, my Lady," he said bitterly, "and he it is shall pay it!"

And he turned away from her, stalking over to the mule cart to join the rest of the wounded, his heart full of gall.

Chapter Twenty Five

An hour later, with the sky clearing after the storm to reveal a star-dazed sky, a half-moon just rising to the north of east, they came to the edges of Warminster, now a ruin of broken mitres and scattered planks. All that had been left after Leofric and his men had plundered the entire village, before burning it out; taking everything they could to build shelters and defences up on the Rings, where everyone for miles around had clustered for fear of the Danes.

It had been an awkward journey, for they had many wounded and the track was rutted and uneven, so that the wagon lunged and jerked as it was pulled along, with flares on each top corner, and the leaders up ahead picking their way as carefully as they could. Now, with the onset of evening and a clearing sky, the wind had a cutting edge that made their wounds ache and their bodies tremble beneath the thick firs that covered them, and without warmth and hot food soon those more badly injured than the rest would soon begin to die.

"How much further, Brioni?" he questioned her from the cart, when she pushed her horse up beside it. "The night draws on, and many of my men are badly hurt. And I am deeply concerned about Aldhelm and the Lady Judith, and all the other women he has with him," he added in a rush.

"Not far now. You can see the Rings clearly from here, we just have a small tributary of the Wylye to cross and we will be at the foot of the long chariot slope that will lead us up to the south entrance. There you will find real shelter, a small hall, roaring fires and good food. But Leofric will not be there," she added sternly. "So you can save your bloody urges for another day. And don't worry about your men, or the women in Aldhelm's care, they will be in good hands, I promise you."

"But the Lady Judith? She is Earl Brihtnoth's grand-daughter!"

"Don't fret, my Lord Heardred. Noble blood or slave, she will be well cared for. The Iron Hand does not make war on women!" and she kicked on to join Trausti and Finnar at the head of their little cavalcade, where troopers with flares led the way.

Heardred watched her move away from him and gritted his teeth. So he was not to meet the man after all. He had so hoped to see this being who had so suborned his place in her dreams and her affection, and his whole body writhed in suppressed anger. No matter, his day would come, he could bide his time. Patience in the chase was something he had learned from his months with Alfred in Athelney.

He shook his head,

It was hard to believe that anyone could change so much, and not for the first time he wondered what had happened to Judith, Aldhelm and the others. They were his responsibility and he was deeply concerned for their safety. But when he had told Brioni about them, she had shown little emotion. Aldhelm was one of Leofric's most able warriors, he had been hand-picked for his mission, and knew the terrain they were crossing intimately. If anyone could bring a party through intact, he could. There was no point in worrying about three warriors and a parcel of women, no matter who they were.

But it had all been so cold, so unfeeling!

From a strictly military standpoint she was probably right. Quite apart from anything else she knew the man better than he did, his capabilities and the difficulties he would have to face in getting his little group safely away across the Wylye and up to the Rings. But he felt she could have shown more warmth, more concern, less ruthlessness. If anything happened to the Lady Judith - and the others of course - then he would hold her partly responsible. He knew he was being unreasonable, but that was how he felt.

And as for himself and the Lady Judith? Only time would tell. But the thought of such a gentle, pretty creature coming to harm in the wilderness that sighed and moaned around them made his blood boil. He grimaced in the darkness. Brioni had been like her, once...if ever he got his hands on Leofric Iron Hand he would cut his heart out! And with jealous anger spurting in him, adding fresh fire to his resentment, he slumped down onto the bumping base of the old mule cart, his eyes red-rimmed with fatigue as the massive fortress they had been making for now rose above them, ringed with flickering flares along its mighty ramparts.

*

*B*attlesbury Rings, was a series of massive earthworks that covered the whole hill top, and dominated the area for miles around. Its highest ramparts, now edged with huge timbers dragged up from the surrounding woods and forests, and dug and hammered into place, were awesome. Steep to almost precipitous in places, they were a stunning monument to the ancient people who had built them before the Romans came so many centuries before.

There were two entrances, one up a long slope that rose beside the southern rampart now towering up into the night sky, dwarfing the small cavalcade now toiling up it to the main entrance. This was enclosed by a pair of enormous gates, almost a foot thick, hung on huge pintles and lit on either side by great beacons in iron baskets. All round them there was a formidable guard of mail-clad warriors and archers, their armour winking in the flaring light as they moved along the parapet walk. This ran above the gates, and along the palisade that ringed the great earthen ramparts that defended the whole fortress.

The other entrance was opposite, but had been closed off with fresh banks of earth to shutter the wide hole left after centuries of neglect. From there triple rings of huge banks and ditches ran round the north-west of the fortress, the whole now defended with a new palisade of logs and hewn timber.

Inside was a vast empty area, constantly brushed by the wind, where sky larks spiralled upwards, and cattle, sheep and goats could safely roam guarded by small boys and a string of hounds. And there the trackway from the main entrance led past a mass of small huts and bothies, lean-to stables and shelters, storage and poultry sheds, piggeries, and makeshift barns. All were clustered round a central hall of cruck timbers and wattle that marked the centre of the whole defence, where there were two great stone cisterns, and towards which they now made their way.

All around them people came to see and be welcoming, helping with the horses and the old cart laden with the wounded from the skirmish field, clapping, cheering and walking beside them right to the wide entrance to the hall. There Hugo, Maritia and Gilbert and his own household stood to receive them, Aldhelm nearby with the Lady Judith and the other women whom he had rescued from below Sutton Veny.

It was a bustling scene as the cart jerked to a halt and everyone rushed to help the wounded out, some led by the hand, like Heardred, others carried in on hurdles or with arms draped over shoulders, until the cart was finally emptied and could be led away, the horses rubbed down, fed and stabled.

Inside the hall was a wide open space covered with rushes and filled with trestle tables, benches and stools, with a long fire pit lined with stone and a raised dais on which there was a great table made from several long planks of oak on sturdy trestles, itself ringed with tall-backed stools and two great armed chairs covered with white fleeces.

All along the sides were small alcoves and sleeping chambers, with one great room separate from the others with a large box bed and several simple chests. Shields and weapons hung from the walls, along with resin torches in iron holders; there were braziers in dark corners and oil-filled lamps on many of the tables and it was a joy to be out of the cold at last and into the warmth where a great fire blazed and mulled ale could be served in silver-rimmed horns and wide drinking bowls.

*

*B*rioni greeted Hugo and Maritia warmly before walking to Leofric's great chair on the dais and taking off her mail byrnie and seating herself with a deep horn of Gilbert's mulled ale. There she watched Heardred settle his men, seeing to their welfare, their wounds and their general comfort, while her own men gathered round the fire in the main body of the hall. Behind her, the Lady Judith and the other women whom they had rescued bustled round and did what they could to help, Judith doing her best to ensure that Heardred was properly cared for and his wound salved and re-dressed.

Clearly the girl was drawn to him, and she felt that there was more warmth of feeling in him towards her than he was willing to admit, even to himself. He had mentioned her with real interest on their journey up from the river, and his concern for her was clearly genuine. She pulled a face. Her own sudden appearance had obviously shaken him badly, which was not surprising given the circumstances surrounding her supposed death. And now he was feeling guilty about having warm thoughts towards another, trying to show indifference towards Judith in order to bolster his position with herself; despite her having made her feelings towards him as clear as possible.

Obviously he was still struggling with his emotions.

Brioni was the first girl he had ever really fallen in love with, now a completely different person from the one he had known so well, and openly living with another man. The Lady Judith, newly met, was one with whom he felt a great affinity, to whom he had been unexpectedly drawn and whom he clearly believed was everything that he had expected herself to be....and wasn't any longer!

She put her head on one side and grimaced.

She felt she knew to whom he was most drawn, despite his seeming indifference, only his experiences at Foxley, his male pride and his injured honour were all holding him back. Well, she would just have to see what she could do about things, even if that meant portraying herself in the worst possible light. What she could not afford was an open bloody feud between him and Leofric. That would ruin everything! Quite apart from the fact that the King loathed the blood-feud, Leofric would surely kill him, and she had sufficient feelings for the both of them not to want to see blood shed over her when it was all so unnecessary.

200

She turned in her chair to greet her tall second as he came up beside her, just as Gilbert came by and re-filled her horn. "How are things going, Trausti? The wounded seem settled and hot food is being brought round. That will cheer everybody."

"All as you see, my Lady," the big man growled softly, sitting down beside her at the long table. "Seems to be settling nicely. Much more to the point," he continued, looking at her closely, "how are things with the young Lord? I couldn't help noticing that the situation did not seem to be very friendly."

"To be perfectly honest he is spitting blood and splinters over Leofric," she sighed, adding after a pause: "He is the man with whom I was to be troth-plighted!"

"*The Lord Heardred?*" he questioned astounded. "By Thor and Woden, our meeting was ill-timed," he mumbled darkly. "Does Leofric know about him?"

"Yes, of course he does, Trausti. But it never crossed my mind that I should meet the man again in this fashion. In fact," she added ruefully, "he has not entered my mind at all since I met Leofric and became so involved with Alfred's resistance to the Heathen. Now he feels dishonoured and is intent on challenging the Iron Hand as soon as the opportunity presents itself!"

"That is very bad, my Lady," he replied heavily. "Very bad. Leofric will destroy him. I know of no man stronger or quicker in a fight than the Iron Hand."

"I know he will, Trausti! And the stupid thing is the wretched man is no longer really in love with me. He thinks he is, but in truth it is an illusion. His heart is drawn to another."

"The Lady Judith he rescued the other day?"

"Yes! Only he hasn't the sense to acknowledge it. Stupid man! And the worst of it is that the King has pardoned Leofric."

"*No!*" the big Dane gasped, suddenly overwhelmed. "A Royal Pardon? For all of us?"

"I think so, but I don't have all the details. Aldhelm only told me the bare bones a few minutes ago. Alfred gave him the sealed parchments himself, with orders not to give them to anyone except Leofric. But if they fight and Leofric kills him, a royal companion and one of Alfred's closest friends and advisors, then we will be condemned all over again. You know, my friend," she added with a heavy sigh, "I sometimes feel that someone up there is laughing at us. And very cruel laughter it is, I am thinking!"

He looked at her, and put his heavy arm about her shoulders: "You worry too much, little one. We who follow you have learned to trust your

201

judgement. Your problem is that you have yet to learn to trust it on your own accord. Come now. Cheer up. You will find an answer, I'm sure of it."

"You know," she answered slowly, looking across to where Judith was still talking with Heardred, "I think I already have. Only it isn't me that I have to convince, it is the young Lord. And if I can't do it, then by tomorrow's sunset everything we have fought and struggled to achieve may well have been wasted. The King abhors feuds, and no matter what the circumstances such a slaying as that fool contemplates," she went on, gesturing to where Heardred was moving amongst his men, Judith by his side, "would simply serve to convince the King that Leofric has been a wolfshead for too long, and can't be trusted to live a normal life.

"His pardon is the one thing, next to Oscytel's death, that I have needed to make my life complete and I have no intention of letting it all go wrong now. Not if I can possibly help it!" And standing, she turned on her heel and made her way towards the welcome glow of the fire that Aldhelm was busily attending.

*

*I*nside the hall, the centre of the long hearth was blazing, two great cauldrons on iron tripods hanging over either end of it where the embers were fiercest. A thick pottage of beef, onions and turnips, thickened with barley corns, and flavoured with herbs, seethed within them, filling the air with juicy savour. Already there was a goodly company crowded round as the women whom Heardred had rescued did what they could to aid those who had been injured, many of whom were still being brought in. Their stooping, rising bodies cast great flickering shadows on the walls of the building, the groans and whimpering cries of those who had been badly hurt by Steinar's warband only adding to the infernal picture they presented.

Brioni's sudden arrival brought a brief moment of silent stillness to the bustling tableau in which she and Judith caught each other's eye, both women seeming to stand alone amidst the clustering commotion going on around them. Then the spell was broken, Judith turning to address Aelflaeda who was standing close to her mistress...and Brioni moving with firm steps towards the fire.

*

*S*o that was the girl who had stolen her brother's heart? Brioni thought as she unbuckled her baldric and handed it to a passing servant to hang in her room, along with her shield. Well, she was certainly pretty enough! Even under the grime, and beneath the coarse mantle she was wearing, her natural grace and beauty were unmistakable. Blonde hair as golden as her own, a shapely body and those amazing green eyes. No wonder Gyrth had been bowled over.

She smiled to herself.

In other circumstances she might have felt a little jealous, though she knew her own figure to more than adequate! Yet there had been a hint of fear in those green eyes, a sense of deep anxiety in the way she had turned her head away to talk with her young companion.

Well, she had no cause to be afraid.

Once she might have done, for Gyrth had been her adored big brother, and no golden-haired beauty was ever going to be good enough for him. But that was long ago now. Now she was fighting for her lover and her Lord and nothing would be allowed to stand between them, and she crouched down and gazed into the flames that leaped and flared in the hearth, luxuriating in the waves of heat that washed over her tired, aching body.

*

*T*urning away from Baldred, who had come up to have a quiet word with her about the food, the Lady Judith stood and watched Brioni as she crouched down over the flames, her eyes taking in every line and curve of her body, from the slender arch of her neck to the rounded curves of her haunches.

So, that was the girl to whom Heardred was to have been betrothed?

She shivered.

Fierce of eyes and heart by all accounts, her breasts crushed in hard steel, her loins guarded by thick leather and stiff mail and armed with swords, she was the very epitome of the shield maidens the old sagas so often sang about. A true Valkyrie! Including her extraordinary short hair that made her wince every time she looked at her. Nevertheless she was just the kind of lady a warrior could glory in...so different from the picture that Gyrth had painted of the gentle, loving sister he had so adored.

Her heart shook.

She so wanted Heardred for herself. Needed him in her life. She had felt his heart and body stir beneath her hand that night in the clearing when she had laid her hand on his thigh, and had known, with only that blinding certainty that a woman has, that this man lay within her power. Then Brioni had been only a fading memory to cherish, a bright dream to be lifted out of the deep

203

recesses of the mind, polished, held up to the light and then carefully returned to the darkness from whence it had been drawn.

Now she was alive, the lost love miraculously returned from the dead. A still, armoured figure bent before the flames who seemed inviolable...yet somehow had to be overcome.

She shivered again.

Theirs was a meeting she did not relish, but it was one that could no longer be put off, she was not sprung from Woden's loins for nothing, and straightening her shoulders she brushed back her hair and walked towards the fire where Brioni was now stretching and flexing her weary muscles.

*

*H*earing a soft footfall, Brioni turned and found Judith standing just behind her, a look of quiet determination on her open face.

"So, you are Gyrth's sister, the Lady Brioni?" the girl asked her tensely after a brief pause. "I have to thank you and your men for saving Lord Heardred's life, and those of us who were with Aldhelm. Without your assistance the Danes might well have taken all of us."

Brioni looked at the tight, little anxious face in front of her as she stood up, and smiled: "Oh, Judith, don't be so stiff and formal with me, I beg you. My brother was a great galumphing ox of a man who never thought further ahead than his next meal, or the next skirmish with the enemy, until he met you. I loved him dearly and he died with his wounds to his front and his sword in his hand. We are really sisters, you and I," she went on, holding out her arms. "You have nothing to fear from me, I promise you Judith. Quite the contrary, in fact, for I need your help badly!"

With surprise in her eyes, and a sudden rush of warmth in her heart, she stepped forward and the two hugged one another closely; joined as much by their loss as their isolation amidst so many male fighters.

"I don't understand, my Lady," she said, stepping back a moment later. "How can I help you?"

"Please don't 'my Lady' me," Brioni replied with a laugh. "'Brioni' will do well enough, I promise you, after all we are both Woden born. Gyrth told me all, and in this wilderness I don't need a title. What I need, is your help with Heardred."

"With Heardred?" the girl gasped, her heart dropping like a stone.

"Yes, with Heardred!" Brioni exclaimed firmly. "Look, come with me, Judith, and I will try and explain," she said turning away towards her own room, separated from the rest of the hall by a thick leather curtain, that she and

Leofric always shared. "This place is too crowded and what I have to say too private. Heardred is busy right now with his command and I may not have another chance. Bring one of those torches that Aetheridge has fixed to the walls and we can be more comfortable. I never have been happy in the dark."

Judith smiled and shook her head. Here was this extraordinary girl, half clad in hard steel, who led hardened warriors into bloody raid and skirmish, admitting that she was afraid of the dark. And plucking a crude pine torch from its iron holder, she followed Brioni away from the noise and crush of the main hall to her own private chamber.

Chapter Twenty Six

"What is it you want of me...Brioni?" Judith asked her, hesitating briefly over using her name, sitting down on the large box bed that dominated the room. "I don't know the young Lord well."

"I know that, Judith," Brioni interrupted her, urgently. "But I so know that you would like to. No, don't look so startled!" she exclaimed softly. "I could see it on your face the moment I walked in amongst everyone, your eyes never left him. Quite apart from the fact that Heardred was most concerned for you on the way back from the attack."

"Concerned for me?"

"Yes. For your safety, and that you might not be cared for as the grand-daughter of Earl Brihtnoth should be."

"As if I should have cared. It was enough that I was safe."

"And that he should have risked his life to make it so?"

"I'm sorry, Brioni," Judith said, dropping her head. "I did not mean to sound so selfish, especially towards someone to whom I owe my life. We only met a short while ago. He was mourning you and I was mourning Gyrth. We felt so drawn to each other, me particularly, I suppose," she added more quickly. "Suddenly there was hope, something else to look forward to, someone kind and loving to care for who needed me. After losing Gyrth that was a miracle, and we did not expect to meet you. But you needn't worry," she concluded, swallowing hard, her eyes suddenly filled with tears. "He is yours, and all men know it. I shall not attempt to stand in your way."

"That's just what I was afraid of, Judith," Brioni replied dryly.

"*What?*"

"Not standing in my way! I don't want him. That part of my life is dead, Judith. It belongs to a different age now, and so I have told him. I love another, and have given myself to him willingly in every way a woman can."

"The Lord Leofric?"

"Yes. Everything changed after Foxley."

"But what about Heardred? What about his feelings? Surely he has some say in all this?"

"No!" Brioni replied sharply, pacing across the room. "Our betrothal never happened. No promises were exchanged, nothing was ever sworn. I am not bound to him, except in his own mind. But as to his feelings? That is another matter entirely. At the moment he is hurting badly, but Judith," she went on earnestly, coming to put her hand on the girl's shoulder, "it is his pride that is hurt, not his heart. True, he believes that he loves me, but he is mistaken. I am not the girl of his dreams, far from it, and I cannot be what he wants. But unless you and I can convince him of it, then he means to challenge Leofric to a fight to the death. It is the Saxon way, as you know. And if that happens, then Leofric will kill him!"

"*Oh, no!* Oh, Brioni that would be terrible!" Judith gasped, putting her hand up to her mouth. "I couldn't bear another loss, Brioni. I couldn't!"

"So, you do care greatly, don't you?"

"Oh, yes," she whispered. "I believe I could make him very happy. He is gentle and understanding, and loving him would be so very easy."

"I knew I could rely on you," Brioni replied brightly, coming to sit beside Judith on the bed. "I am not often mistaken in people."

"Leofric must be a very special man, Brioni."

"He is," she replied, watching the light from the torches wavering and flickering in the draught. "Very special, and I love him more than my life. He was a wolfshead you know, and I so did not wish to spend the rest of my life on the run."

"So, you know about the pardon?"

"Yes, Aldhelm just told me. Directly from the King as they left Athelney a few days ago. The point is that Alfred abhors feuding. If they fight, and Heardred is killed, then the King will not forgive him, and everything I have dreamed of will perish. I vowed I would not marry Leofric without the King's pardon; that is what we have all been striving for these past months. Risking our lives to bring steel to Alfred's enemies and keep him informed. That, and the death of that evil, dark-souled bastard Oscytel are all that separate us. Now Leofric has a royal pardon, the rest will follow, I am sure of it," and she stood up and walked to rub her hands over the brazier that was in one corner of her room.

"Dear God, was there ever a more wretched situation? I had not expected to meet with Heardred again this side of Ecberht's Stone! Now everything hangs in the balance because of one man's misplaced sense of honour! Why can't men run their lives in a less complicated fashion? You know, Judith," she concluded with a broad smile, "I sometimes feel if it wasn't for us, nothing would ever get sorted!"

"Well, Brioni, I will do all I can to help, I promise you. But where 'Honour' is concerned men can be remarkably foolish. Heardred may decide to challenge Leofric anyway, just to clear his own name of a charge of cowardice. Of being declared *Nithing*, for standing back and doing nothing while another man goes off with his lady, even if he no longer really wants her.

207

But as for his heart? God willing it will be safe in my keeping I promise you, and pray God we can turn his mind."

"It is enough!" Brioni replied, coming back to take Judith's hand and raise her from the bed. "You are just the kind of girl he needs, Judith. Not a shield maiden like me, but someone softer, kinder and more loving. I am not surprised my brother fell in love with you, for you bring the protective side of a man's nature into the open. Be happy, my Lady," she added giving her a swift hug, "he will make you a splendid husband."

And with that she led the way back into the main hall, where everyone was now gathered, with the exception of Heardred, Siward and Trausti who were checking that all was well for the night before leaving their guards to complete the first watch. Thus by the time they re-entered the building, Brioni had joined Hugo and Maritia on the dais, ready to tell them all that had happened, while Judith was with Aelflaeda checking on the wounded.

*

*A*s soon as Judith saw Heardred walk in and throw down his weapons she picked up a bowl of thick stew that she had placed ready to hand, and making her way across to where he was standing holding his injured arm and frowning up at Brioni on the dais, she smiled gently and touched him on the shoulder.

"Here, my Lord, I have kept some warm food against your coming, for the night is chill and you must be tired."

He looked down at her, startled by her soft approach. He had not expected to be pleased to see anyone, yet he could not resist her quiet charm and lovely smile, realising with a sudden rush that he had missed her warmth and companionship.

"Thank you, my Lady," he replied with a rueful grin, taking the proffered bowl and spoon. "Truth to tell I could eat an ox, and yours is the first pretty face I have seen all day!"

"You are too kind, my Lord," she answered with a mock curtsey and a beaming smile. "But, 'Judith' please, Heardred. After all we have been through I do not need any 'my Ladying' from you. Here, come and sit by me," she went on brightly, finding a convenient bench and trestle table closeby, "you look exhausted, and that arm of yours must be very painful. Eat your fill while it is still hot, and there are some bannocks here to help it down," she added pulling a wooden platter of little rolls towards him. "Then I will have a look at that wound of yours. I have salves and bandages with me to make sure you are more comfortable," she added putting a big scrip on the table.

"In the meantime you must tell me all that has happened. I have missed you, and was in an agony of distress until I saw Brioni's command leading the way up the old chariot ramp. Then I couldn't see you or Swiftfire anywhere, and my heart dropped like a stone. I feared you killed, until someone shouted you were in the wagon, and I haven't had a chance to speak with you since you arrived in the hall."

And sitting opposite one another, while he spooned mouthfuls of Baldred's hot meat stew from the bowl she had given him, and chewed on a number of the fresh little rolls off the platter beside him, Heardred told her of all that had happened: the bitter fight with Steinar, the death of Swiftfire and how Brioni's crashing arrival had saved all their lives. And especially how shocked he had been at meeting Brioni again in such circumstances, and of his confusion at finding her still alive.

"Poor Swiftfire!" Judith said a moment later, reaching for his hand. "He was such a lovely boy, and you cast onto the ground and forced to fight Steinar still mounted? Dear God, you might have been killed. And to think it was the Lady Brioni who rescued you! You could not invent a more unlikely tale," she continued, looking into his face. "But tell me, truthfully, Heardred...was she really not pleased to see you? Was there really no feeling left for you to draw on?"

And looking into her eyes, he suddenly realised with an awful pang just how much his talk of Brioni, and his feelings for her, must have hurt, especially after the time they had spent together in the clearing after Medraut's death, and the thoughts and feelings they had then shared so happily.

"She railed at me, Judith," he answered her sharply. "Called me fool and dolt and bid me let her alone. It was such a shock to see her there. I felt..I felt..I don't know what I felt! Shock, pleasure, love? I thought she must care for me too, in the same way that I believed I cared for her. No! That I believed I loved her. Look, I am sorry if this hurts you, Judith, but I have to say it all. Have to get it off my chest, get the poison out of my heart."

"Poison? Can love be poison?"

"Yes! If it is unrequited and eats your heart away; prevents you from loving another; from living a happy life in someone else's arms."

"It's alright, Heardred," she replied softly, moving to sit beside him and put her arms round him, pulling his head into her shoulder. "I understand. Go on my love, tell your tale. You will not hurt me, not now, not ever!"

He paused then, aware of her nearness, of her heart beating strongly, the firmness of her breasts, the warm comfort of her arms and body. He had not been held so since he had been a child. Not even with Brioni, and it felt good to him, suddenly to be safe from the wild emotional turbulence he had been spinning through since he had met Brioni again. And as Judith's words finally caught up with him, he sighed deeply and put his arms around her in return.

Then, turning his head to look up at the dancing shadows on the roof above him, while the wind bustled across the reeds that covered it, he began to speak.

"She has changed, Judith. She told me she had, but I didn't believe her. Didn't want to, I suppose. But it's true. Once she was soft and gentle, like you." he said, turning to look at her. "Warm and loving; someone special to share little things with: a tree aflame with autumn's fire, a bird's song, a squirrel with a nut. Now she is like tempered steel, hard and unfeeling," he added, turning back to look up into the rafters.

"*Love me?* I don't believe she has a true understanding of the word," he snarled bitterly. "The man Leofric is welcome to her. But, by God, he shall answer to me for the dishonour to my name. Oh, Judith, I felt so wretched! So forlorn and rejected. I had carried such a picture in my heart of how things should have been that I couldn't believe what she was telling me. Couldn't take it in. I felt so certain that we would just fall into each other's arms, and everything would be just the way it was. That all my dreams would come true. But I was wrong, so very wrong!"

She held him close, feeling his pain as well as her own. Yet she felt exultant also, for if she remained close to him, and was there when he needed her, then she felt certain she could win his heart. Not straight away, maybe, but soon. With Brioni being cool and distant, dismissive of his deeper feelings…and herself being close, warm and sympathetic, it would surely not be long before she won him permanently to her side.

"What now, my Lord?" she whispered, still holding him close.

"I need time, Judith," he said, then sitting up beside her. "It's not that my feelings about you have changed, but I need to be certain that they are the right ones. All that I felt for you in the clearing is still real. But I believed I loved Brioni greatly and to turn those affections on you now, especially after what has happened, would be very easy. But it also might be very wrong. Please don't look so stricken," he said swiftly as he saw her face crumple. "I do care about you, my sweeting, I just don't want to bruise your heart because my own is aching. Please be patient with me."

"I will be patient, Heardred. Women are good at it, believe me!"

"Now I have hurt you."

"No, not hurt. Just frustration. But then you are probably right. Maybe my own feelings towards you are mistaken? Maybe my loss of Gyrth and yours of Brioni are both confusing us. Maybe we should leave each other for a while? Meet coolly as friends. Not as lovers," she ended, smiling quietly to herself in the flickering darkness.

"*No, Judith!*" he answered her vehemently, putting his hand on her shoulders, and looking into her eyes. "It is only by being together often that we can know each other better. My life has been as bitter as gall since Foxley was destroyed. Now, suddenly, it is changing. The drowning man has been offered a branch on which to cling. Don't I beg of you, take that away now and leave me to sink."

"Don't you trust me then?"

"Yes, of course I do. But I owe it to myself to make one more attempt to speak with Brioni about ourselves."

"You will only be hurt again!" she replied, tersely.

"Why are you so sure?"

"Because I am a woman, Heardred," she answered him firmly. "What she said to you this night was not lightly done. She has told you the truth. You do not form a part of her life any longer."

"You have spoken with her?"

"Yes! She came to speak with me while you were outside with Siward and Trausti, her big Danish second."

"No matter, Judith," he responded with a wave of his hand. "I have my Honour to think of. I cannot just let this business rest. That pardoned wolfshead still stands between us," he ended defiantly.

"Do you still mean to fight him then?"

"Yes, I do!"

"*But why, Heardred?*" She now questioned him fiercely. "If Brioni no longer loves you, and you are not bound to her by troth, then why, in God's name, shed blood over it. Yours or his, it makes no difference. Either way it is disastrous!"

"You don't understand, do you?"

"About the need to salve your Honour at the expense of everyone's happiness? No, I don't. It is like a squabbling child. You can't have what you don't want anyway, so you seize it and destroy it then no-one can have it. You are cutting off your nose to spite your face, and that is wickedness. It is senseless. How can you be so foolish?"

"Is it so foolish to want to save your face, and your family name?"

"Not always, of course not. A man has to stand up for what he believes in, or he is no man. But not in this case."

"Why not? What is different here?"

"*Because Brioni no longer loves you!*" she almost shouted at him in frustration. "She loves Leofric, and fighting over it will not help anyone. On

211

the contrary, Heardred, it will only make things much worse. Dear God, you big ox, isn't it bad enough that we have to fight the Danes without adding to the misery by fighting amongst ourselves? Am I so wretched a prize that you wish to spurn me so cruelly?"

"No, of course not, Judith," he replied swiftly, turning anxiously towards her. "I never meant that at all!"

"Well, that's what it sounds and feels like," she said in a small voice, pawing softly at his shoulders like a small kitten. "Now you have hurt me," she said, her eyes filling with tears. "Unlike Brioni, I am the kind that cries when I feel pain in my heart. Oh, Heardred, look at me. I need you alive to hold me in your arms and love me. How can you do that if you are dead?"

"I do not intend to die, Judith," he answered her firmly. "But that man took something from me that was not his to seize, and when he learns of it, he will expect me to challenge him...and if I do not then I am *Nithing*, and that, my darling, is worse than death for a man."

"And now I am your 'darling'! Oh, God!" she groaned, burying her face in her hands. "Why are men so stubborn and so wasteful of themselves? And how can you fight when you are like a bird with a broken wing? I want to love you, Heardred, and be loved by you also. I want to laugh with you, and lie with you, and hand you our child. Those are the things that warm a woman's heart," she flung at him fiercely. "Not bloody death and destruction!"

With his good hand he lifted her face and looked deep into her green eyes, now flooded with tears that spilled out slowly and ran down her cheeks.

"Judith," he said with a heavy heart. "I have no choice. Love you, or not, my little lady, I have to face Leofric with this matter, and I shall need your strength, as well as mine, to do it." And bending forward he kissed her softly, and then with greater passion, drawing her closely against him and wrapping his good arm so fiercely round her that she could scarcely breathe.

*

Away across the great room Brioni watched them both and smiled. Clearly young Judith had the situation well in hand, and it was with a much lighter heart that she went to her own room, stripped to her shift and lay down in the box bed on its great fleece-filled mattress, beneath cool sheets of Egyptian cotton, a brilliantly woven plaid blanket thickly on top of her, Bran and Utha panting softly in the darkness by her side, to dream of Leofric and the morrow when they would be together again at last.

Chapter Twenty Seven

*T*hat night an uneasy quiet settled on everyone.

Those who had been injured tossed and moaned with the pain and discomfort of their wounds, while others rose to throw more wood on the fire to keep the flames moving. Or driven by whistling draughts, gathered in small groups round the hearth to talk over old raids and skirmishes, drink a clack of ale and make new friends of those warriors who had come in with the Lady Brioni's warband earlier that evening.

But eventually all slept, men and women sprawled out across one another, arms and legs awry, heads pillowed on shields, rolled blankets, saddles or a friendly shoulder. Those in alcoves along the long walls of the hall lay on thin pallets with bolsters of rolled fleeces, covered with cloaks and brightly woven blankets.

Outside the guards stamped and blew on their hands, for though this was April the wind had an icy bite, and a fine frost rimmed the edges of their spear points, and ran hard white fingers along the palisade and across the wall walk that ran round the whole perimeter of the huge compound. Change and change about throughout the long night, as one guard took the place of the other, warming their hands on the great flares that ringed the fortress, while the wind, never still, soughed and bustled amongst them. And in the distance a lone wolf howled to the quartering moon, sailing silently across a sea of sparkling crystal lanterns.

Finally came the dawn, a lightening of the darkness into pale grey, broken by a tremulous tendril of golden light, and the duck-egg green of the early morning that faded into a roseate glow as the sun rose slowly to the horizon. With that came the first larks spiralling upwards from the huge pasture land within the ramparts, calling up the new-born day, drowned by barking dogs and the clonking bells of the cattle as their herdsmen brought them in for milking. And so the whole place suddenly came alive again.

The hidden dangers of the night were over, and Brioni rolled onto her side and groaned.

"Sweet Jesus, but I am stiff!"

"Nothing that a jar of spiced ale and a good rub down won't put right," Maritia said to her, flinging back the leather curtain as she came into the room. "And what about those other two, sweetheart?" she asked, jerking her head to where Judith and Heardred were lying wrapped in each other's arms across the hall.

"Well enough for the time being, I'd say," Brioni replied with a swift smile, sitting up and taking the warm drinking bowl from Maritia's hands. "But what will happen when he meets Leofric is anyone's guess."

Maritia sighed, and sat down on the edge of the bed. "God's death, Brioni. Was there ever more cursed fortune than that!"

"None! Leofric will eat him alive. And there's the rub. Aldhelm has the King's pardon with him, though I don't know all the details as he wouldn't let me read it."

"You can't blame him for that," Maritia replied with a rueful smile. "Alfred gave it to him to guard with his life. It carries the King's seal, and he was ordered not to hand it to anyone except Leofric. And Alfred doesn't know about you!"

"Silly fool!"

"Alfred?"

"No, Aldhelm. He defied me completely. I got quite angry."

"We heard you," Maritia said, grinning broadly. "Leofric would have been proud of him. I thought the poor man's eyes were going to pop out of his head. He did well to stand up to you. Hugo was impressed, and took him off to say 'Hello' to Oswald and sample some of Gilbert's finest barley spirit. Cheered him up enormously."

"Ah well, Sweetheart, such is life," she said, shrugging her shoulders as she struggled up and dashed water over her face from the wide basin in its stand in the far corner of her room. "It is no real matter, for doubtless we will all find out soon enough when Leofric comes in this morning. I tell you one thing, Maritia," she added with a broad grin, as she dried her face on a rough towel, looking across the hall to where Aelflaeda was beginning to see to her mistress's needings, "my brother certainly knew flesh from fowl. She is certainly a tasty morsel, young Judith of Southampton. Her breasts are enough to make strong man weep!"

"*Brioni!*" her friend gasped, appalled. "You sound like Bjorn the Ravager. You've been in the company of fighting men too long," she added with a cheeky smile and a light punch to the shoulder. "Such talk should make a maiden blush!"

"Spare me the compliment, Honeyone," she answered swiftly, giving Maritia a sharp dig with her elbow as she reached for her mailed trousers. "That part of my life died at Foxley. Now, if I do the cross-gartering, you can help me on with my byrnie, and hand me my baldric. Leofric comes in today and he will expect me to be properly dressed for war, not dancing. Then let's get this rabble on their feet. The sun is up and there is much to do. How is that great furry rogue?" she asked, hearing a distant roar, as Maritia eased her into her heavy armoured jacket. "I did not see him when I got in last night."

"Oswald? Full of himself as usual, and calling to get out of his new wagon. He so loves to show off his skills. I will bring him into the hall after everyone has come in and settled down. He wouldn't miss it for the world."

"Right! That's me done," Brioni said stamping down into her long boots and shaking her body to settle everything around her. "Let's find Bran and Utha, and then get out amongst the people. Leofric will expect to see them, just as much as I can't wait to see him. The hours cannot pass swiftly enough. Eh, Mari, but I have missed him so!" And giving her friend a swift hug, she left her room and strode across the hall towards where Heardred and Judith were standing just below the dais.

*

*J*udith watched her coming over, and felt her heart flutter.

She was such a fine sight, such a warlike, purposeful figure in her dented mail byrnie, thick mailed chausses, cross-gartered to the knee, her two swords hanging from her waist, that swung with every step she took, and her two great hounds by her side. Even in her belted armour there was little disguising the rich curves of her body, and without her helmet her short hair bobbed and shook to every step, making her look even fiercer.

Disturbed, Judith turned to look for Heardred, and found that he was standing close beside her, his eyes smiling and his mouth and eyebrows quirked in amusement at her obvious concern. His whole posture was protective of her, and her heart went out to him. He had understood her inmost anxiety, that somehow she was not good enough, and had come with his nearness and his warm smile to reassure her.

It was enough.

Brioni had been right after all. She was not for him, nor he for her, and as her mind cleared she drew her body together, straightening her shoulders to show off her figure to its best advantage, and caressing the thick long braids of her hair as she moved. So it was a much more confident lady whom Heardred left behind as he and Brioni clasped hands, and then moved outside to discuss the details of Leofric's return to Battlesbury from his broad sweep of the shattered lands around Bath and Warminster.

*

215

*I*n broad daylight, the whole panoply of Battlesbury Rings was doubly impressive from what little they had glimpsed the previous evening weighed down with injured men and stray mules and horses.

For years, centuries, the place had been left untended - as the legions had left it when the red-headed Celts, in their iron-wheeled chariots, thundering along the chalky trackways, had been defeated. When long-haired warriors in tartan breeches had splashed the hillsides with a shifting pattern of bright colour. Since then it had been left to the wild spirits of the dead, and the tinkling clamour of distant sheep bells. It had become a place of desolation and emptiness where fox and badger made their dens, and the ravens gathered to seek carrion. A place where time was suspended, where the wind moaned and cried through the fallen gateways and across the scrub-filled ditches, and the wolves howled their hunger in the bitter time, when the stars had talons and the trees were caged branches of iron.

Now, however, the place was like a crowded market town.

The great earthen ramparts had been cleaned and in many places refaced with stone and timber, and a huge pair of double gates on massive iron pintles had been hung to guard the way, with a locking bar that took six men on ropes and pulleys to lift into place. But, best of all, the whole place seemed to be filled with armed men; a great seething hive of steel-clad hornets whose steady hum came from every quarter of the massive fortress. In truth it was an astonishing sight, and Heardred and his men were open-mouthed at the industry and sheer organisation that such an undertaking must so obviously have taken.

"There must be a thousand men here, my Lord," Siward said after a while in an awed whisper.

"And their families," Heardred added, as a gaggle of women and children bustled across the trackway that led to the gates, now flung open after the nightly curfew.

"You do us too much honour, Heardred," Brioni replied laughing. "We do not have quite that many, though the families of three villages now live up here in safety, and they all add to our numbers. But more fighting men come into us every day as the word spreads of what we do here."

"I am not surprised," he replied, looking around him, at the incredible bustle of people, animals and goods in general that was to be seen everywhere, especially around the three forges that were in full operation. "With these numbers of fighting Saxons, I doubt the Danish army would relish an attempt on you. You must draw all true men to you like bees to a honey pot. The King will love you for it."

"Not me, Heardred," she said crisply, coming up beside him. "Leofric! This is all his doing. I merely help to keep the wheels turning. He and his officers make the fighting happen. They organise the practice of making war. I carry out his orders and work with the village headmen to make sure the fighters get all the support they need."

"And you lead his men."

"No, I lead my own warband. Chosen by me and sworn to me. Leofric and I are equals."

"Unheard of!"

"Nevertheless it is so. And has been since Malmesbury."

"I am stunned," he called to her over the wind gusting in his face as he stood and watched with amazement. "I had not realised there was such resistance here. It is truly wonderful news."

"I hope you will bear that in mind, my Lord, when you meet Leofric, now pardoned by the King," she said, turning to face him. "He is the leader of all these people. They have learned to look to us for help against the Heathen. The pirate Danes whom we have all been fighting since Foxley was destroyed and Alfred was forced into the wilderness. Neither his death, nor yours, will help the Saxon cause.

"All men know that you come from the King. Many are simple borel folk who know nothing of 'Honour', as you choose to call it; others are hardened killers who will only see their leader threatened. They will think that Alfred is to blame, and will desert his cause. Don't you see, you fool," she stormed at his suddenly closed-in silent and bitter face, "*your life is forfeit!* If Leofric doesn't kill you, the others will, and everything that has been achieved here will have been wasted!"

"Brioni, I have no choice in the matter," he snapped back sharply.

"Of course you have a choice!"

"*No!* Not as a man of honour."

"But, Judith…" she remonstrated, waving her hands in frustration.

"Judith knows the way I feel," he snarled in anger. "There is nothing she can say or do to alter the situation. My cause is just and my course of action charted. *Deus Vult!*"

"Don't mouth Latin at me, you clodpole," she raged at him then through clenched teeth, as people turned towards them, alarmed by the fury. "'God wills it' indeed! It is *your* selfishness that wills it, Heardred; *your* arrogance and hurt pride! And you represent the King? Alfred would be appalled at your behaviour; threatening to destroy everything he has worked for on the altar of your foolish pride. *Foh!*" she exclaimed in disgust. "And I thought you had a level mind. That between Judith and myself we could bring you to some state of understanding. Sweet Mary, you make less sense than a donkey in a hen coop! God aid you, Heardred, for you are now beyond my care."

217

And turning on her heel she swept away from him just as the horns blew and Hugo's buccinas blared a wild challenge from above the gates, followed by a great roar of acclaim as through them, on Wotan, his enormous stallion, rode Leofric. His armour flashing like silver in the morning light, his hair short, his beard neatly clipped, shield on his back and helmet tied to his saddle he was swiftly followed by his whole command, pounding up the old chariot way, spears, swords and axes waving, and smiles on their faces as they stood in their stirrups and shouted their joy at being safely home again amongst their families.

Brioni took one look at the leading rider as he burst through the open gates into the huge compound, and flung herself towards him, swiftly followed by Bran and Utha.

Leofric saw her coming and suddenly he too was off his horse and running, leaving Wotan to be caught and held by others, and within seconds they were in each other's arms, laughing and kissing at the joy and relief of seeing each other again, whole and in one piece. And while the men of his command tittuped and curvetted about them in the April sunshine, wreathed in smiles, her two great hounds leapt up on both of them. Great shaggy forepaws on arms and chest, tongues working furiously they bowled them over, sending them rolling together down the nearest grassy slope. Bounding after them with deep woofy voices and bright black button eyes they chased the rolling pair until eventually they came and stood over them panting heavily, tongues a-lol and wet hairy beards pushed into their laughing faces.

"Well," Brioni said, forcing the pair of them away from them. "At least they haven't forgotten you while you've been away. Poor things, they do hate it when they get left behind."

"Nonsense," he said laughing, ruffling Bran's great brindled face. "As long as you take them when you can, they can have no complaints. By the way," he continued, pulling her to her feet. "Who are those others with you? Wounded too, and women if my eyes don't deceive me. And what ails their leader? You looked to be having a real set-to with him. I have seldom seen so sour a face beneath a lark-filled sky."

Brioni dusted off her hands and turned to face him, while her two great hounds leaped and gambolled around them, her face suddenly tense and anxious as she said slowly: "It is the Lord Heardred, Leofric." And turning to look up at the fat clouds sailing serenely above them, before looking back into his gold-flecked eyes, she added: "He has come back into my life."

And there was silence between them.

"So," he breathed out deeply after a moment's pause, putting his arm over her shoulders, "it has come at last. It was bound to happen sometime, my

218

love. Still, he can have no complaint. You were never officially betrothed with oaths and promises before your father and the people of Foxley...nor was the church involved. Where in the name of the gods did you fall in with him?"

"He ran into one of Steinar's ambushes," she answered him, taking his hand as they began to walk up towards the track, Bran and Utha ranging wide before them. "Just before the bridges over the Wylye near Sutton Veny. We had been shadowing Steinar for some time, when he drew his men across the trackway right in front of Heardred's forces, who had a wagon full of women with them. Look, my darling, I know what your orders are regarding daylight skirmishes. But that pig's offal outnumbered them, and I couldn't just leave them to their fate!"

"So you waited until the fight started and then broke Steinar's shield wall."

"Yes! We slew a score of them between us, and drove the rest off. Heardred got his women and baggage away first, and then piled in. They fought like furies, but he was unhorsed and fighting Steinar from the ground when we burst in on them. I saw him just as we broke through. Dear God, Leofric, I was so startled I almost fell off Foxhead. I was never more shaken in my life!"

"What was his reaction afterwards?"

"White-faced shock! All these months he had believed me slain at Foxley. Found poor Agatha's body in my clothes, wearing his betrothal gift, too badly hacked about to be recognisable and thought it was me. Buried me, wept over my grave, and when he found me again believed that all would be as it was! Foolish beyond belief, and so I told him. Still loves me greatly, or so he thought yesterday."

"Yesterday?"

" Until I gave him the facts of life as they are now!" she said firmly, looking up into Leofric's face with a loving smile. "You are my Lord now, in every possible way," she added, reaching up to kiss him. "He is a foreign country, once loved, now left far behind. My life is bound up with yours, Leofric, and so I told him. And anyway, it is not me he loves, but the thought of me. He really loves another."

"Another? Where did she come from?" he asked, stopping to look into her face with eyebrows raised in surprise.

"One of the girls he rescued!" And while Trausti met up with Beornred, Leofric's shield bearer and huge Danish second, still leading the long column forward, and with Finnar Olafsson, Brioni told Leofric all that had transpired between herself and the Saxon war lord whom Alfred had sent to greet them: Medraut, Judith, the pardon, everything.

219

*

*E*ventually they sat down out of the wind that was a constant on the top of the Rings, and lay back on the sun-warmed grass that covered the hillside, looking out across the distant flash and sparkle of the Wylye and its tributary that wound its way around the base of the ancient fortress, from where the water to fill the cisterns was constantly drawn. Above them the sun shone in warming splendour, the clear blue of the spring sky decked with white fleeces that the wind shepherded in little gusts and sallies, their shadows swooping and rushing across the hillside. Far below them the trees in the valley clustered thickly, while a hidden cuckoo yodelled and called to them and fat bumble bees buzzed and fumbles amongst the flowers that nestled in the tough grasses.

The war had never seemed so far away, so remote.

Here was a place for love, where the gentle breeze could cool their heated bodies and they could lie naked together beneath a cerulean sky and savour the sun's growing warmth on their tingling bodies.

Leofric's nearness, the smell of his flesh, the sweaty tang of leather and warm steel were making her dizzy with passion. She wanted to forget their problems and offer her panting body to his caress, press her lips to his and have him take her as only he could. Fill her and ravage her as she so loved him to do; completely and utterly his to do with as he pleased.

She ground her teeth together and rolled away from him, sighed deeply and sat up with a rueful grin. Theirs should have been a hot steamy reunion in every possible sense of the word. They had the pardon they so desperately wanted and had striven so hard to achieve…yet now they had the needless problem of Heardred to contend with.

"So, he wishes to fight," Leofric growled, propping himself on his elbows as she leaned over him. "Despite the fact that he knows you do not love him, and he himself is strongly drawn to another. Loves her?"

"Strongly drawn? Yes. Loves her? Maybe. Wants to fight? Yes!"

"The man's moon-mad. What ails him?"

"A misplaced sense of honour and overwhelming pride. Alfred would be appalled. Honestly, my darling, is it all necessary?"

"If he challenges me directly, in front of all my people? Yes, my pretty. I am afraid it is. It is an ancient code that at the moment cannot be changed. It leads to endless feuding and blood-letting, but it cannot be avoided."

She turned towards him then and held out her arms.

"I love you, my Lord," she said softly. "Love you with all my heart. Hold me close and kiss me, for I am afraid."

220

Without another word he pulled her to him, wrapping his great arms closely around her, bruising her through her armour with the fierceness of his ardour.

"Eh, Heart of Mary, but I love you Brioni," he breathed into her hair. "Do not be afraid my little one. I shall not let anything harm us. Not the Danes, not the King and certainly not that puppy, Heardred of the Somerseatas! I love you with my whole being and in life or death I will never desert you."

"Oh, Leofric," she whispered, lifting her face for his hungry mouth. "Truly…" but she never managed to finish her sentence for he kissed her then deeply and thoroughly, and whatever other thoughts she might have had vanished in a wild spinning vortex from which she had no desire to escape.

Chapter Twenty Eight

*J*udith, who had watched their first meeting, turned to look at Heardred, but his face was set hard, and only the bright flitter of his eyes showed his emotion.

She sighed and looked away again, her heart choking her with its wild beating. She had tried to turn his mind and had failed. Now all she could do was support him with her love and understanding. That much, surely, he must be aware of? The fact that he was not fully in love with her did not seem to be important somehow. That was something she knew would grow given time. Just a little time! But here they were in the heart of a great bustling Saxon fortress, whose leader was the object of her man's distress...and time had suddenly run out. Life had a cruel habit of flattening those just on the verge of standing up.

She shook her head.

Well, the fiends take them all. She knew whom she loved and what she wanted. Somehow she would find a way to stop them fighting, or at the very least from killing one another!

Just then Beornred, Leofric's giant second, held up his hand and the whole column behind him jostled to a halt, as Trausti and Finnar came up to him.

Instantly his men dismounted, and were swiftly surrounded by people, many of them tall hard-faced veterans of the long Danish wars who were also part of Leofric's extended warband. But there were also a lot of much younger fighters and fyrdsmen from the three villages who had sought refuge with Leofric on Battlesbury Rings, and all the villagers as well, young and old, men and women both with their children and whatever animals they had managed to bring with them. For a while everyone milled around in whooping groups, full of chatter and much laughter, while horses were led away, saddles and tack removed and the pack horses at the rear were busily unloaded.

Everywhere she and Heardred looked there were armed men, either cleaning or polishing their weapons and armour, or sparring lightly with each other to test the mettle of their blades that rang and chimed in the bright sunlight, and their skill in using them. Shields blazed with colour and fierce design: here a wolf's head, there a badger's head with jaws agape. But most common of all was a fox's mask, teeth bared and ears laid back, surrounded by brilliant flashes of zig-zag fire.

This was no hotch-potch collection of displaced fighting men, wolfsheads and warriors from the scattered Saxon host...this was an army in training. Men gathered from all over that part of Wessex who had lost their homes, their families and their King, and who had come together under Leofric's leadership to fight the Heathen. Far and wide Leofric's name had clearly spread, and from tiny shattered hamlets and burned out villages, from the desolate wastelands, from the forests and the river plains they had made their way to the old British fortress on the hill. They had seen that Heathen men could be fought and killed. Their King had shown the way from the watery mires around Athelney, and Leofric and all those others who fought the pirates in their homelands had shown the Danes could be beaten. Now they were ready to do their part.

If only Alfred could be here to see this his heart would beat all the more strongly for it.

Heardred thought back to what he had said before they left Athelney and smiled: 'You will see a greater company of fighting men than even you could hope for!' It had been a bold promise. A thought to conjure with, and now that the reality was all around him, all the more warming for it.

Then, suddenly, he grimaced.

All this was the work of the wolfshead leader Leofric Iron Hand, Lord of Wimborne, whom the King had pardoned. The man who had stolen the heart of the only woman he had ever fallen in love with.

The man he had sworn to kill!

"What is it, Heardred?" Judith asked him, touching him on his shoulder.

"It's that blond-haired ravager, Leofric, they call the 'Iron Hand'," he snarled, shrugging away from her.

"Oh, Heardred, you saw how much Brioni loves him. You know what her feelings are towards you. She has told you to your face. Why can't you leave well alone? Fulfil Alfred's orders, and get on with your life. Instead of which you may only succeed in getting us all killed."

"It is the way of things, my Lady," he snapped back at her fiercely. "No man does me scathe and lives unchallenged."

"*Very well!*" she shouted at him suddenly, coming to a dead halt amongst the huge throng of people now making their way towards the great sprawling knock-kneed building at the centre of the vast compound, that served as Hall and Moot Place in one. "Make your challenge, you pig-headed Saxon lummox, and much good may it do you. But I will not be there to watch you!"

"But Judith..." he stammered, trying to stop her leaving him.

"Don't you dare '*Judith*' me, you..you great *lunkhead!*" she raged at him, her eyes filled with tears. "And leave me be!" she continued, snatching her arm away from him. "I love you, Heardred. Don't you understand what that means you stupid ox?" she added, her face flushed, her tears spilling down her cheeks. "I, the Lady Judith, grand-daughter of the Earl Brihtnoth, with Woden's blood in my veins, loves you, Heardred of the Somerseatas. But, apparently I am not good enough for you. My love is cheap!"

"It isn't like that!" he shouted, white-faced, his hands clenching and unclenching in his distress. "Your love isn't cheap. I thought you understood?"

"Understood? *Understood?* Is that all you can say to me? Oh, God, Heardred. How can you be so..so *blind?*" And stamping her foot in rage, she spun on her heels and ran away from him, forcing her way through the burgeoning crowds, her vision blurred with weeping, her heart aching for the great Saxon war-lord who preferred his damaged pride and selfish hurt to the warm, caring oasis that her love could offer him.

In stunned confusion Heardred watched her go, his mind in helpless turmoil. Then, before he had a chance to chase after her, he was swept onwards into the hall and seated, with the men of his own command all about him, on the long benches that had been swiftly set up, with a host of trestle tables, on Brioni's orders the moment Leofric had been sighted coming towards the fortress.

Siward, Clun, Aetheridge, Cenwald, they were all there with Baldred close by and Osbert and Wiglaf just behind. There were others of his warband also, but half carried wounds about their bodies, and of those who had set out from Athelney, eight lay cremated beside the road where Steinar's warriors had cut them down with sword and axe and flighted arrows. And the rest were in the care of the wise women of two shires, too badly hurt to move.

Last to enter the hall was Maritia with Oswald who came in wearing his scarlet jacket, freshly dressed with silver buttons, and sat on a great chair made from half an oak barrel of barley ale, and called to all he knew in that great room with coughing grunts, and swayed his head to the beat of music played gently beside him. He was as much a favourite as ever, and while Hugo came up to join the throng around the long table on the dais, many who knew the huge bear of old came and patted his massive shoulders, or rubbed his back in affection, or presented him with small apples that he crunched with evident enjoyment.

Food was brought forward and freshly brewed ale from great barrels that lay behind the bent and twisted building in which they were all seated. Brewed from malted barley rescued from ravaged steadings, barns and shattered halls across half of Wessex, it was a strong drink that could really slake a warrior's thirst, and Leofric had heady vats of it constantly preparing in the brew-house that his men had quickly built when first they had arrived upon the Rings.

It was brought through in long leather jacks and poured out into the eagerly proffered drinking bowls and decorated horns that each man carried with him, and with hearty cried of '*Wassail*' and '*Drink Hael*' they opened their dry throats and threw it down them. Up on the dais Gilbert offered mead to all seated there, and barley spirit in small flasks that made even Hugo gasp and splutter.

The steady drinking soon released the tensions of the morning, and the night before, and by the time Leofric and Brioni entered the building the whole of their command was getting into their stride, toasting each other's prowess in battle, Heardred's men calling across to those of Brioni's war group who had saved their lives. It was a noisy, cheerful revel, full of colour and movement: bright textured garments of wool and linen, tangy leather dark with sweat and spilt ale and the flicker of fire and sunlight off the mail armour that many still wore. Amongst the heaving male throng the village girls, in their brightest costumes, moved with cheerful quip and laughter, and a hefty smack for any cheeky warrior who presumed too far, as they carried food and beer from trestle to trestle that Brioni and Gilbert had ordered prepared against Leofric's return.

There was freshly baked bread in fat round loaves, with great pats of yellow butter to go with them, and a fine tasty pottage in thick gravy: beef collops and coney quarters with onions, barley kernels, parsnips and herbs. This was not a great feast in the accustomed style with roasted ox, venison and mutton, but a plain hearty meal for the returned warriors of the Lord and Lady, and the stern-faced young war-leader whom the King had sent to them from his secret base on Athelney, and the men of his command who had journeyed with him.

*

*F*or a while Leofric and Brioni watched them from a wide side entrance, Bran and Utha by their sides, their coats brushed until they shone, their fighting collars replaced with broad scarlet leather ones studded with glistening silver stars. Unwilling to spoil the enjoyment of all those gathered there, they put off their entrance, but in the end, with smiles on their faces they swept in, Leofric's thick cloak billowing behind him as he moved, Brioni close beside him, her two giant hounds padding softly beside her, sterns waving as they stalked in.

Their unheralded arrival was greeted with a great roar of approval, and the blowing of horns, the men of Leofric's close command and of his personal guard rising to their feet and stamping hard on the floor and on the wooden dais, where Hugo, Beornred, Trausti, Finnar and Raedwald all waited to receive them. A truly thunderous welcome as the men pressed back to allow the lord and his fighting lady to come through and take their places in the two high-backed chairs pulled back ready for them to be seated.

Here was the man who had led them the length and breadth of the land, and finally to the ancient British fortress of Battlesbury Rings on the edge of Wessex's heartlands; from one bloody raid and skirmish to another, ever onwards and upwards as they had flayed the Heathen of the Great Army, slain their crews, taken their silver and broken their communications...and they wanted the newcomers amongst them to know their feelings.

Past the lines of trestles and benches their leaders went, and up onto the raised dais of earth and timber that lay at the head of the crude building they went, through the cheering shouting crowds, and so to the rough chairs, arms and seats covered with plain fleece, that Gilbert and his men had placed there against their coming.

Heardred, deafened by the wild noise around him, and obscured by the pillars that held up the roof, caught but a glimpse of Leofric as he strode past, but he felt the man's presence nevertheless. Here was a born leader of men. A man, such as the King himself, who could inspire great courage and loyalty. A man whom it was good to be near when the war horns bulled, and the arrows began to fly. A man who would stay by you if you fell in battle and cover you with his shield; who would weave a pattern of whirring death above you with his bloodied steel until you could rise again.

Suddenly Leofric stood, held up his arms and shouted for silence, while his guard clashed their swords against their shields as if going into battle.

"*Aldhelm stand forth!*" he roared, pointing to a tall warrior holding a scarlet leather tube in his hands. "I believe you have a message from the King for me. We have waited long enough, my friend, now it is time to hear his true words, though many have said what they believe is in there, and revel in their meaning."

"You speak the truth, my Lord," the tall Saxon replied, rising from his place, as the violent noise around him stilled. "The King commends himself to you, and all who follow you, and bids me give you this."

And while everyone craned their necks to see, and drew their breath, Aldhelm strode to where Leofric was now standing near the edge of the raised platform and dropping down on one knee, he held out the roll of scarlet leather that Alfred had given him on Athelney.

226

In tense expectancy, almost silent except for Oswald's coughing grunts, all those who had managed to force an entrance into the twisted building waited to hear what Leofric had to say. Ever since word had crept out about the secret document that the King had sent the Iron Hand, the people had been gathering outside, and now it seemed the whole world waited for his proclamation.

With studied care, and gentleness, Leofric broke the seals, and with his seaxe he carefully slit the leather that held the rolled parchment in its grip, unrolling it and holding it up before him. Then there was an agonising pause while he read it through slowly, his brows taut with concentration as he traced the words with his eyes and fingers, and all held their breath in an agony of suspense.

Then, looking up, he raised the document high and shouted out: *"The King pardons us! He pardons us, Danes and Saxons all,"* he continued, his voice ringing clear across the packed hall, *"and names us Royal Companions! My lands and titles are restored to me and he promises compensation for all who have been wronged!"*

And with that the whole place erupted with sound as the people bayed and roared their commendation, leaping up and down, thundering their feet on the ground, hammering their fists on the tables and howling his name over and over again.

"See!" he bellowed over the wild rumpus, turning the parchment round. "It carries the King's own seal. I do not lie. This is the truth. He honours us. *We are all free men!"* And turning to where Brioni was now standing, her face alive, glowing with excitement, tears sparkling in her blue eyes, he picked her up and swung her round, while the people, leaped, and jumped and capered madly all about them.

Chapter Twenty Nine

Stuck behind his pillar, Heardred had listened to all that had been said with glowering face and panting breath, stunned by the reaction all around him, and appalled that Alfred had given Leofric and his men so much, despite all that they had done to grind down the Danes in their area and gathered so many men to his standard. Jealousy rushed through him in a poisoned torrent. It had been bad enough when Brioni had leapt into the man's arms outside, by the ramparts, and he had nearly spoken out then...but he had his injured arm to think of, and Judith had been with him.

Now it was different.

Judith had left his side and now his former love, his Brioni, was in another man's arms, laughing into another man's face as she was picked up and swung round. It was too much, his control broke, and struggling free of the press, shaking off Siward's arm as he valiantly tried to stop him, he lurched, red faced with fury towards the dais on which Leofric and Brioni were standing, arms wrapped round each other, and raised his voice in fury.

"*The King may pardon you*, Leofric Iron Hand," he bellowed. "*But I do not!* I, the Lord Heardred of the Somerseatas, the King's loyal companion and war leader call you *Nithing!* Stealer of women and oath breaker, *and I challenge you to defy me!*"

At the first sight of his frantic struggles and face filled with wrath, those around him had rapidly drawn away. And though Siward had risen to his feet, he did not attempt to follow him. So, when he railed against Leofric, his anguished cry cut through the romping hurly burly like a skinner's knife, and his last words rang round the suddenly silent room with awful clarity.

Up on the platform Leofric heard those fateful words and groaned, and letting go of Brioni he turned, stony-faced, to where Heardred was standing, flushed with defiance and swaying his weight from one foot to the other, his bandaged arm at his side, his sword held firmly in his right hand.

"What did you say, Saxon?" Leofric questioned slowly, coming to the front of the timber stage.

"You knew to whom Brioni was about to be betrothed when first you took her," Heardred raged, oblivious of the fury his words had brought to the building, of the shuffle of armed men around him and of the movement of Leofric's warriors to close off any exit from the hall. "You knew I was not dead; that the girl was distraught and stricken with grief at the murder of her family. Yet you cozened her none the less. You stole her from me, and now you must pay for your arrogance."

"How dare you challenge Leofric in his own hall!" Brioni shouted down at him, her eyes blazing fire at his words. "You, who have taken salt with him, are the betrayer. I do not love you, my Lord Heardred of the Somerseatas. Nor do I want to be a part of your life. I repudiate any claim you may have of me utterly. No oaths were taken, nothing ratified by the priest and no settlement was ever reached with my family. I want none of you. You do this out of pride and jealous spite!"

"Not true, my Lady Brioni," he snarled at her in spitting anger. "My challenge is not spawned by jealous spite, but Honour!"

"*Enough!*" Leofric roared out, holding up his hands. "Enough of this wrangling. You are a great fool, Heardred, and ignorant of all reasonable behaviour. Yet you are a brave man to challenge me direct in this my hall, when I have all my men and my companions clustered round me."

"I don't want your comments, Leofric Iron Hand, I want your blood," Heardred replied angrily, shaking his sword at him, while all around him men growled fiercely at his words and actions. "You have dishonoured my house, and for that I call you *Nithing!*" And all around him gasped at the foul insult to their lord.

"You are wrong in that, Lord Heardred," Leofric said calmly, stepping down from the dais, his armour shining silver bright in the shafts of sunlight that beamed from the open doors and unshuttered windows. "Here in the land of the West Saxons a lady has a free choice, and the Lady Brioni has made it. Take back your words and I shall spare your life," he continued, his voice dark with purpose, as he shrugged off his heavy wolfskin cape and drew his great sword clear of its scabbard of soft scarlet leather. "I have no wish to slay you, but if you press me now, I must, or be myself dishonoured."

"Do not play with me, you coward!" Heardred taunted him, throwing his cloak onto a nearby table, and gripping his sword more tightly in his hand. "I have had enough of your wriggling!" And leaping forward, he cut viciously at Leofric's unguarded head.

With a light jump, and a deft flick of his wrist, Leofric turned the blade aside, and coming down on his toes he feinted left and right before swinging his arm round and cutting hard at Heardred's neck.

This was no sparring contest, nor demonstration bout…this was to the death, and both men knew it as they stabbed, thrust and clattered back and forth across the hall, dodging and twisting each other's flashing blades and battering the tables in the way. All around them the people pressed back to give them room, roaring Leofric on as he forced his younger opponent to give ground before the practised fury of his attack.

Again and again the sparks flew from their tempered blades as they bit and screeched against one another, while Siward and the rest of Heardred's command, appalled by what was happening, stood grim-faced in a silent cluster beside the tables they had so recently been feasting at. Their lives hung in the balance, but they were powerless to intervene.

Bob, weave, cut and parry, their feet moved swiftly across the rush strewn floor, as Leofric hounded the young Saxon lord, now rapidly tiring, weakened and unbalanced by his injured shield arm that hung limp and useless by his left side. *Block!* in a shower of sparks; both men's faces inches apart, Heardred's white and strained, the sweat standing out on his forehead, Leofric's fiercely determined and frighteningly calm, treating his opponent's frantic efforts with disdain, as if he was on a morning's stroll, not fighting for his life.

Then away again in a flurry of vicious blows, Heardred becoming desperate as Leofric hunted him across the hall, flicking his attacks away with consummate skill and ease as he pressed him hard, first darting forward and then hanging back, letting the young Saxon war-leader exhaust himself against his ringing, driving blade that never wavered, no matter how swift or violent his enemy's attack.

Suddenly there was a wild commotion beside the entrance as a dust-stained messenger burst in, while a slight figure, in faded blue cloak and carrying a thick fur mantle, rushed through the crowd and flung itself on the swords both men had levelled at each other's throats, just as Heardred stabbed his blade forward once more.

It was Judith.

And as she leapt she screamed in pain. A wild shriek of agony, for even as she jumped in upon the two men, heavy cape held out before her, Heardred lunged and the biting edge of his blade sliced into her, ripping open her arm and collapsing her into a weeping bundle of arms and legs from which her blood was pouring onto the soiled ground.

Instantly Brioni was off the dais, her large scrip by her side, racing towards the place where the girl lay bleeding on the floor. But Heardred was before her. Dropping his sword to the beaten earth he rushed to Judith's side to staunch the flow of blood that coursed up between his fingers and across his hand.

"Dear God, what have I done?" he moaned, as he held her in his arms and tried to press down on her wound. "How could I have been so foolish?"

"Here. Move aside," Leofric rumbled softly, handing his own sword to one of his men. "Let me see the wound, it may not be as fearful as it seems. The blood is not gushing, though the flow is swift. Brioni," he called out loudly, "bandages and your wound wort!"

And while Heardred looked on in stricken silence the crowd fell still, many stretching their necks like eager turtles to see what was happening, as Leofric and Brioni worked on the wounded girl with swift skill and the calm of long practice and understanding.

At last, Leofric stood back, while Brioni finally tied off a bandage.

"She will live," he said gently, "but with a scar, for this is only a temporary dressing. Her arm will need stitches which my lady will put in shortly. Here, Trausti!" he called sharply over his shoulder. "Bring that trestle top and have her carried to our quarters. She will rest more easily there, and the Lady Brioni can more properly attend her."

"Where's Aelflaeda?" Brioni broke in urgently as Trausti and a small team bustled around her, lifting Judith with great care and laying her on the thick mantle she had brought with her. "The child is devoted to Judith, poor thing, she will be distraught when she hears what has happened."

"I am here, my Lady," a small voice said softly from behind her shoulder.

"Aelflaeda, your mistress has been sorely hurt," Brioni said gently, turning to take the young girl's hands in her own. "She needs your help."

"I know, my Lady. We planned it, she and I, to stop the fighting. Stop the Lord Leofric from a brutal killing. When I heard her scream I came as swiftly as I could. Oh, my Lady, is it very bad?"

"No, Aelflaeda, not very bad. But not good either. Lord Heardred's blade has raked her arm, and she must have it stitched. But my Lord Leofric says she will live, and so do I, and we are never wrong. Now come with me, sweeting, for I need your help."

"I will go with her also," Heardred said softly as he saw them all move off. "If you will give me leave, that is?" he asked of Leofric, as his foeman stood and brushed his hands together, now reddened with Judith's blood. Then, after a pause, while the great Saxon war lord just stood and looked at him, he dropped to one knee, and held out his sword in supplication.

"My Lord of Wimborne, I have done great wrong by you, and yours," he said humbly, blue eyes to gold-flecked. "My conduct has been a shame to you and all your people, and to my King, and I beg your forgiveness. Take this and break it if it is your will. I have done harm enough for any man this day."

Stooping forward, Leofric lifted the weapon from Heardred's hands and swung it high in a glittering figure of eight that sent the ruddy fire light flashing off its blade, ending in a lightning twist that finished with sword point in his hand and the heavy hilt and pommel towards its staring owner.

"Here, Heardred of the Somerseatas, take back your sword of me," Leofric said quietly in his deep voice. "It is ended between us as if it had never been. The King needs his war-leaders in one piece, and you fought well. Alfred should be proud of his chosen man."

"Now I know why so many follow you," Heardred said, rising to take back his sword and slip it into its sheath, while his own command clustered at his back, hugely relieved that Leofric had accepted their leader's submission with such grace and evident goodwill. "You are a fair man, slow to anger and generous to those who really care. It is a rare gift these days."

"You do me too much honour," the giant Saxon said with a laugh, clasping Heardred's arm firmly. "Now, away with you," he added, pointing to where Trausti and his stretcher party were carrying Judith away. "Your lady has need of you, and you have some humble pie to eat before her. It will do you no harm. I must go and see what all that commotion was about as Judith burst in on us. You and I will meet later."

And with a smile of deep relief on his face, Heardred turned and slipped away, his men following, as everyone else left the hall, while Maritia brought Oswald up the long table to join her father, now in deep talk with Leofric.

*

"So, you let that young puppy off the hook?" Hugo queried him, drinking horn in hand, sitting in a broad seated chair, his daughter nearby with Oswald, now collapsed in a monstrous furry heap, by her side and breathing deeply.

"He was carried away with false dreams, and spoke rashly," Leofric replied, reaching for his own gold-rimmed horn, now filled with heather beer. "He will be all the better for it, now it is over."

"You played with him down there, Leofric," Hugo rumbled at him, over his own beer, his periwinkle eyes twitching as he smiled. "You could have hacked him to ribbons."

"Of course he could," Finnar, said with a grunt. "I have seen him fight, and know how good he is."

"Well, maybe a bit," Leofric agreed with a grin. "But what was I to do? Split Alfred's chosen man in pieces because of his youthful foolishness? That way would only lead to disaster. I need the King's goodwill, and cutting young Heardred into bits would not have been the best way forward. But what a brave thing for that lass to do? She might have been killed!"

"Well, it certainly brought things neatly to a head. And not before time," Hugo replied pointing to a man still standing at the head of the table, dust covering his tunic and hose, a deep bowl of ale in his hand. "This man has come in with a message for you from Alfred, repeated from Odda of the Devonseatas, that he will give to no-one but you."

"What message is this, soldier?" Leofric asked then swiftly, holding out his hand. "Come, you are rested now. Who are you, and who has sent you to me in such haste?"

"I am Gilpin of the Devonseatas, my Lord. From Lynmouth, fyrdsman to Ealdorman Odda, and sent to you from the King with this message."

"From Alfred on Athelney?" Leofric questioned the man urgently.

"Yes, my Lord. The Danes are in turmoil. Everywhere there are men on the march and all streaming towards Chippenham. Our King prepares to march, and the men of the Shires are marching with him. In ones and twos, sometimes many more. But best of all, my Lord, the Heathen have suffered a great setback," and kneeling before Leofric he held out a rolled parchment in a linen cover, with the King's seal pressed onto it.

Swiftly taking it, Leofric slit the linen cover with a knife and peeled out the message which he fiercely read, his eyes flicking over the neat, precise words that Alfred's priests had written down, just as Brioni returned to his side.

"*Holy Mary, Mother of God!*" Leofric exclaimed a moment later, looking round at them all, astonished. "This is stirring news! Almost beyond belief! There has been a great battle on the north Devon coast. The Heathen came to Countisbury with twenty three war-boats and twelve hundred men under the leadership of King Ubbi of Ireland."

"Ubbi of Ireland?" Brioni queried.

"Yes! The last of the Sigurdssons, and one of the fiercest. The last great leader of the Great Army that came in '65 to be revenged on their father, the mighty Ragnar Lodbrok."

"The one murdered in a snake pit by the Northumbrians?"

"The same. This message says that he landed with his army, intending to join with Guthrum to seize Wessex once and for all. A pincer movement just as Alfred feared. Ubbi from Devon, Guthrum from Chippenham. Odda was in an ancient fort above the sea, called Cynwit, where Ubbi's forces had landed from Wales. Ubbi thought to trap them there, starve them and then destroy them. But Odda attacked him in the dawn. Rushed down on his Vikings and put them to the slaughter. Cut them in pieces! Slew Ubbi and eight hundred of his men, including forty of his personal companions, and burned most of his fleet. Only a handful escaped. It is a stunning result!"

233

"Eight hundred slain?" Hugo gasped, before burying his face in his horn. "That is a slaughter indeed. That will hit Guthrum hard."

"But not as hard as this!" Leofric replied, his eyes like stars as he waved the message in the air. "Odda has seized Landravager! The sacred raven banner of the Great Army! The Danes' magic talisman that they call 'Raven'"

"No!" Brioni gasped amazed, her hand to her mouth. "The one sewn in a single night by the daughters of Ragnar? The magic one whose fluttering wings signal a Danish victory?"

"Exactly that!" Leofric almost shouted. "It seems incredible, but it is true. Ubbi Lodbroksson's been slain, along with eight hundred of the best the Danes have, and their sacred banner taken. They must be appalled! Were you there Gilpin?"

"Aye, my Lord," the man replied with a smile, stepping forward again. "The Heathen came in a great fleet that darkened the water and made their camp by the shore. We were above them in the old fort of Cynwit. Not far from my own home. They thought they had us trapped. But Earl Odda roused us at dawn and we rushed them in the semi-darkness. Caught them unprepared, and slaughtered them; burned all their fleet. They fell like wheat before the sickles at harvest time. Heaps of them. We watered the ground with their blood, and when it was full light, and we searched amongst the bodies, we found their banner, close to where King Ubbi was slain, dark with his blood. It was a famous victory, Lord. And the King has sent more messages out to all who love Wessex to come to the muster at Ecberht's stone in Kingston Deverill on the 6th of May."

"Well done, Gilpin!" Leofric commended him with a shout of laughter. "A great victory indeed, but nothing to compare to the one that is coming when we bring the last of the Great Army to battle, and destroy them. Only then will we truly all be free!

"Gilpin, go and find Beornred, my second, and he will take you under his wing until you are properly rested. Then you can join my own fyrdsmen. They will be delighted to have you with them and you can tell all of the Battle of Cynwit, where you did such execution on the pirates."

"Come, my friends," Leofric called to all those gathered around the long table as Gilpin left to find Beornred, to Hugo, Maritia, Brioni and the rest: *"Drink Hael!* We march in ten days' time. The word is out already. We are going home!"

Chapter Thirty

*T*hose last few days before they finally left were some of the most intense and hectic that Brioni could remember, and some of the warmest.

From dawn to eventide the whole of that vast compound seethed with activity as Leofric and Heardred, their quarrel long forgotten, harried their people to be ready for departure. They must be gone on the morning of May 6th to Ecberht's Stone on King's Court Hill, near Kingston Deverill, to meet with the King. Not one stone but three, two upright and one capstone, placed there in the elder time where King Ecberht, Alfred's Royal forebear, his grandfather, held court and gave his dooms. Just six miles from where the Rings stood tall above the countryside, where the borders of Wiltshire and Somerset marched beside each other; the place of Alfred's muster to which all men who loved their freedom must come and pledge their allegiance to their King.

There was so much to do, and yet so little time in which to do it.

And all day the sun searched them out and sweated them as they toiled endlessly beneath an azure sky, turning the beaten earth into a choking dust that tortured their flayed skin and lined their throats with rasping powder. Only the constant wind cooled them, as they lay panting on their backs from yet another mock attack.

All day the smithies set up by Leofric pulsed with heat and sang with the constant ringing clash of hammers as Wiglaf, and Thurwold from Slaughterford, reforged old blades, and prepared new ones against the coming struggle. Bent spear points were straightened, arrow heads by the score prepared, horseshoes, dented helmets and worn mail, all came under their hands. Nor were they the only ones who worked in iron and steel for Brorda, Eadwine's smith from Ford, was also with them, and Arnwulf, Leofric's own farrier, noted for his cunning with hard metal worked amongst the men, as did Hugo the Bearmaster, who could twist iron with the best of them.

And every morning the men who had gathered to Leofric in those long weeks since Chippenham were put through their paces, chopping left, right and overhead at the rows of posts that had been set up for them to practise their skills, while Siward, Eadberht and Trausti bellowed at them to keep their shields up as they had at Brioni when she was going through the same process, and Finnar stood behind them with drawn sword to prick them if they faltered.

Or they practised the shield wall, the true measure of a warrior, where the battle would be decided and where the fighting would be at its fiercest, the most terrible; where the dead stuck in the lines with the living, and where the stench of blood, of torn offal, and of faeces, and the groans of the dying, marked a man for life.

Long lines of sweating, cursing warriors with sword, spear and battle axe, with Leofric and Heardred roaring at them: "*Shield wall! Shield wall!*" and hammering them into place, left shield edge locked into right, to make a solid wall of painted lime-wood that would front the enemy on the battlefield. A wall behind which the men would pile in six, eight, ten deep to take the battle to the enemy and break their hearts; a wall with axemen to pull down the Danish shields with their bearded axes, and sword and spearmen behind to stab the Heathen in the chest and throat so the blood would fountain in the air to fall like scarlet rain on friend and foe alike; a wall where the Saxon seaxe would do dreadful execution, the short thrusting blade like the Roman gladius, made famous by the legions many years before, that could pierce and rip the guts out of an army in bloodied coils.

Sometimes they practised the flying wedge, the boar's snout, with spears thrust out at every point like a great boar's spiky back, and shields held high, the fiercest at the very front, with special long spears with great leaf-shaped blades that three men held, the boar's tusks, sword and axe behind to smash their way through the Heathen, the whole driven at the run straight into the enemy's shield wall, to pierce it like a mighty javelin, then break it open and take their battle fury to the very heart of the fray. And sometimes they worked in open order, archers packed in behind the shields to lay down a barrage of flying steel, with spear-wielding warriors in their front to protect them against a mounted assault, and sword and axe men in support.

If Leofric had learned one thing from the heathen pirates, and Oscytel's war groups in particular, it was the importance of discipline and closely co-ordinated action.

Time and again the pagans had won against larger numbers of their Saxon enemies purely by virtue of their better organisation. It wasn't that Saxon men lacked courage, or ability. Far rather it was the simple fact that the Heathen were trained professionals, well-armed and armoured, and they had been together for years, many of them since leaving Frankland in '65 with the Sigurdsson brothers: Ubbi, Halfdan and Ivar the Boneless.

The bulk of the Saxon army was made up of the Fyrd: churls, free farmers off the land with sword and spear and little armour...and geburs, bonded farmers and labourers, with wooden helmets strengthened with iron strips, leather tunics and sharpened hoes and threshing tools in their hands, bill hooks, scythes and sickles, anything with which they could fight, even sharpened hoes and spades. Their lines strengthened by the thegns and their personal companions, the real warriors in a Saxon battle line. And curse as he might, Leofric was determined that whatever happened when the two armies finally met, the men of his command would stick together to the bitter end, and not become the fear-crazed rabble that had fled so many stricken fields and left the enemy to hold the place of slaughter.

So backwards and forwards he and Heardred and their commanders made them go, with the roar of "*Shields up! Shields up!*" ringing in their ears until their arms and shoulders drooped and their weapons felt like lead-lined coffins. And still Trausti, Siward, Beornred, Finnar and Raedwald shouted abuse at their gritted, red-eyed, sweat-drenched faces.

A swift raid, or a bloody skirmish was one thing...but the grinding, pulsing fury of a great battle was something else again. In a raid you could get out as swiftly as you had arrived, depending on the fleetness and fitness of your mount. But in a battle you left your horse behind in the hands of others, you drew your sword and gripped your war shield in your left hand, locked in with your neighbour's, and moved forward, and kept on moving until you were dead or victorious, or running from the field through your own lines of dead, and the howling wounded, with fear in your heart and terror in your heels.

When the war horns blew and the arrows began to fly there was no time for weakness.

For the Great Army never tired.

When one heathen warrior was down there were always others to take his place. The press and screaming rage of battle was no place to be craven, or fail a friend through weakness. So the Saxon leaders gave their men no mercy. And as the days passed so the weary soldiers became surer of their movements, more closely attuned with one another, hands and feet moving together as one as they advanced, withdrew, separated and came together again.

*

"Well, Heardred," Leofric asked him on the eve of the last day before they were due to leave, as they watched Beornred putting a large group through their paces, "what do you think of them?"

"I think they must be the finest Saxon warband this side of Ecberht's Stone!" he replied, smiling. "This kind of preparation is foreign to the Saxon host. We should all be doing it. I can see that now," he went on as the men finally packed up for the day, "especially after that fight with Steinar by the roadside. You have learned a hard lesson at Oscytel's hand, my friend, one we should all profit from!"

237

"I hope it will not be one they forget," he growled as Beornred sorted through his men, praising some and shaking others. "That man has been a curse on England and Wessex since first he came to these shores with his black clad followers, his Jomsvikings. Then he bore a charmed life. Nothing seemed to touch him. Even in the midst of death and carnage, with men falling all about him, no blade could do him scathe, no spear or arrowhead could dent his armour or pierce his flesh."

"The knife, *Sica*!" Heardred answered him dourly.

"You know about it then?"

"Yes, Leofric. Some from Brioni, but most from Trausti, her big second. It is a strange tale of a powerful talisman."

"Powerful and steeped in evil," Leofric replied darkly. "Bound up with Egyptian legend. But it does not give him eternal life. He can be slain, just that whoever holds the knife is kept safe from harm. His cause will always prosper and he will gain great riches."

"But there is a price to pay."

"Yes! The thing corrupts, eats away the soul until the real man has been utterly destroyed. Then it will change masters. It holds a fatal fascination for those who know its powers. But me it terrifies. I pray God I never have to lay hands on it."

"You mean you might seek to become its next holder?" Heardred asked, incredulously.

"No, I don't want that," Leofric went on slowly. "But it is supposed to have a will of its own. The legend makes that clear. I know that with it we might drive the Heathen into the sea. It might choose me!"

"Do you think Oscytel's power is weakening, then?" Heardred persisted as they sat in the bright sunshine, watching as Siward and Finnar put a different band of men to the sword of their determination.

"Yes, Heardred, I believe it is," Leofric answered him, watching as Siward bellowed at the men to stay in line and '*Keep your shields up!*' Finnar knocking sense into those who failed their orders.

"Ever since the Lady Brioni joined us his men have failed before our arms. Box, Bradford, Melksham; Brioni at Malmesbury, me at Bath; we have slaughtered his crews and taken his silver, and generally made an April Fool of him and his commanders. And Guthrum, when my men had to go in to Chippenham and rescue Brioni from beneath their Danish noses."

"I heard about that! Quite an event, Hugo told me; that giant bear in action as well. Tore the Danes to pieces! I wish I had been there!"

"Oswald was magnificent, terrified the bastards! And we fooled Oscytel brilliantly," Leofric added, sitting up. "Sent him off to make mincemeat of us at Swindon...while Beornred and I ripped the heart out of Bath and went off with all their plunder. And Hugo and Brioni burned down the King's Hall, and half of Chippenham as well for good measure. That's why I know that Oscytel's power is waning."

"Certainly seems to point that way."

"It does, doesn't it? His power fading while ours grows in strength from day to day. That's what those men are working so hard for," he went on, gesturing to where Siward, Finnar and now Beornred were yelling at the groaning warriors still training with them in the pluming dust. "With these men, and our new-found courage and discipline, I mean to cut through the heart of Guthrum's host. That's where we will find Oscytel, and that's where we will kill him!"

"You seem very certain."

"I am...but how it will happen and by whose hand I don't know. I want him for all the misery and the bloody killings and sacrifice that he and his men have carried out before their fearsome gods. But Brioni wants him too, for the destruction of her family and the fulfilment of her vow. Only then, my loyal Saxon Lord of the Somerseatas, will she feel herself again," he added, giving Heardred a light punch on his shoulder. "That man's shadow lies all across us, and until his blood has stained the soil, we will none of us be free!" And getting up, he strode back to the men who had now been dismissed at last, to praise and encourage them as they sat slumped in exhaustion on the bare parched earth over which they had just been pounding.

*

*H*eardred sighed as he watched him go.
For him the situation was so much clearer. He was the King's man, and had his royal master's ear. His estates around Taunton were unencumbered with debts or enemies. Judith loved him, came from a powerful family, and there was no hindrance to their betrothal and marriage. His way forward was simple. But for Brioni and Leofric the situation was still clouded. Leofric's own lands had long since been seized and distributed by Aethelwold amongst his supporters. Many of them with strong connections to the Danish host, who must first be defeated before any redress could be effected, despite Alfred's support,

And Brioni's life was burdened by her extraordinary vow, of which he now had full knowledge and understanding, and over both of them Oscytel's presence brooded with malevolent power. His evil had brought them together, and could still part them if coming events did not work out as they would wish.

The King's pardon had helped, but they still needed Alfred's personal commendation to make their future totally secure...and still there was success in battle to contend with. And for all Leofric's confidence, a battlefield was the very worst place to secure one's future. It still came back to the Black Jarl and the stone knife he set such store by, *Sica*, that had come from distant Egypt many centuries ago.

It was a situation that would daunt many lesser mortals than those two and he was hugely grateful that he had no such anguish of his own to weigh him down.

*

*A*nd with a lighter heart for his thoughts and contemplation, he too turned away and went in search of Siward, Baldred and Alfgar who were seated on the ground playing knuckle bones for a finely-chased hunting knife, more like a short sword, that one of Brorda's people had found in one of the great fosses that surrounded the whole encampment. Of Danish make it was a very handsome piece, the polished silver twists and whorls that ran down its tapering blade dazzling in the bright sunshine. Quite how Siward had come by it in the end he was not telling, but now he had wagered it against the last of Judith's honey-cakes that she had baked that morning, and it was a bright, uproarious group of fighting heroes that he found around his lady when he finally caught up with them.

"So, this is what my warriors get up to when they have nothing better to do." He greeted them with a laugh, throwing his arm around Judith as he did so. "A fine example of Saxon manhood you are to show your gambling skills before so chaste a maiden."

"Fie, my Lord Heardred," Judith replied archly. "They are after my honey dainties!"

"They had better not be, my jewel," he answered, eyeing them boldly and covering her breasts with his hands, "or else I will be forced to take my blade to them."

"You presume too much, my Lord," she answered him with a throaty chuckle, smacking his hands away as she dodged out of his grasp. "That kind of warmth I reserve for my own true love and not for some sweating, brute of a Saxon debaucher who just fancies a fondle of my wares! Besides which, Brioni, Aelflaeda and Maritia are waiting for me in the old hall. We have a great surprise planned for this evening and there is still some work to do before it will be ready," and pausing only to give Heardred a swift kiss, she whisked herself away before he had a chance to reply.

240

"I see she has your measure, my Lord," Baldred said laughing, twirling the fine weapon he had just won between his fingers.

"I shall deal with that one in my own way later," Heardred answered with a broad smile. "Right now I want to know how things are with us, for we leave tomorrow before mid-day, and I want to be sure all is ready."

"Well enough, Heardred," Siward answered him. "Wargeat and Hwicce are too injured to travel with us, and Clun, Wulfsi and Anlaf are in little better case, but sufficient to be walking wounded, and help in the defence of this place after we have gone. All the rest who took wounds are sufficiently recovered to make the journey with us. About a score or so altogether."

"What about our equipment?"

"Osbert has that all in hand. Packs and packhorses ready. Everything in its place and a place for everything."

"That is good, and I will thank Osbert when I see him. What about weapons, Baldred?" he asked next.

"All checked and finely ground. You could cut silk with your sword. Wiglaf and Brorda, the smith from Ford, have seen to all that. Our steel may not all be of the same quality as that of our enemies, but with good Saxon muscle behind them, they will cleave through their bodies with just as devastating an effect."

"And our mounts? We still have a distance to go and I don't want to lose a single man through a cast shoe or a lame horse."

"They have grown sleek on this upland grass, my Lord," Alfgar answered him. "Aetheridge and I have been over every one of them, and our beasts are in better fettle now than when we first set out from Athelney. They will all do well and Wiglaf has checked every shoe. I also have a fine bay stallion for you to ride, Irontooth. I had him from Julio, the Lord Hugo's own beast master. Less frisky than poor Swiftfire, but fully trained and ready to go. You will like him."

"For that I thank you hugely and will speak with the Bearmaster later today."

"Come, my Lord," Alfgar said then. "All has been checked and rechecked. We only await the dawn and then we will all be on our way. All our preparations have been completed. Surely now we can relax and enjoy ourselves in the last few hours we have left to us?"

"That was well said, my friend," Heardred replied, looking down at them all. "There will be a battle-feast tonight. Plenty of food, but not too much beer and ale eh? Otherwise no-one will be in a fit state to move come daybreak. It is as well that we do not leave here at first light. Come then and bring your spoils with you," he added with a grin, gesturing to the little pile of cakes that

Judith had left behind. "A pity about that blade though, I had a mind to it myself."

"It is yours, my Lord," Baldred said, handing it across to him with a grand flourish. "How could I deny my dear leader anything his heart so obviously desired?"

"For that, Saxon, I thank you most nobly," Heardred answered him with a mock bow. "There is someone I have in mind for whom this would be a great surprise."

"The Lady Judith?" Siward asked him.

"No, my friend, her little maid, Aelflaeda. She shuns the company of man anyway, after all that was done to her by Medraut's heathen, but since her mistress was hurt by my hand she has shunned me too, and spends her spare time with the Lady Brioni and her friend Maritia, and that giant bear of hers.

"They have taught her many things, but she lacks any kind of weapon to defend herself, and I thought just such a gift as this might show her that I understand her plight. Well, it is a chance anyway," he added ruefully at his men's quizzical amusement. "Besides, it will please the Lady Judith that I care about the child, and that has to be a good thing!"

And with their arms linked round each other's shoulders, they ambled slowly towards their own quarters.

Chapter Thirty One

*U*p at the hall the preparations for their final night were almost complete. Long rows of trestles and rough benches had all carefully been set up to accommodate the many hundreds who would gather together for the last time, while outside the great fire pits that had been dug for the roasting, flamed and sizzled as the beasts Leofric had ordered, and paid good silver for, were slowly turned on their long iron spits. Fresh bread was in abundance, and the air was filled with scents of baking and of meats roasting with herbs and seasoning. Large groups of people in their finery milled about everywhere, with laughter and good humour as they gathered for the feast, and there were as many seats and tables outside as there were within, as everyone had been invited, villagers from all about the compound, young and old, all bursting with pride and excitement.

Inside, the beams and rafters had been hung with newly cut greenery as though for a wedding feast, with great branches of May tied up everywhere, the air filled with the scent of their blossoms; while underfoot freshly gathered reeds had been thickly strewn across the floor. Mixed with herbs and lavender gathered from ruined halls and hearth places across half of Wessex, the whole building smelt of high summer after the rains had broken a long drought.

In her private quarters, Brioni, Judith and Maritia surveyed their secret handiwork and were hugely delighted with their efforts. Finding the right materials had been very difficult, and they had been forced to search far and wide for what they needed, and ask some of the accounted needlewomen amongst the villagers to help them. But now that it was all finished they wanted to crow with delight, especially as keeping their project safe from prying eyes, particularly Leofric's, had not been easy either. Now they couldn't wait to see his face, and those of all the men who would be there tonight when they showed everyone what they had created.

"Well, my love," Maritia asked, putting her arm around her friend, "is it what you wanted?"

"Oh, Mari, it is just beautiful," she answered softly, tears sparkling in her blue eyes as she gave her a close hug. "My father would have been so proud. Gyrth also," she added, turning to Judith beside her, and putting her arm around her shoulders. "It will put steel into the hearts of all our warriors who see it, and our enemies will quail before it. One man in particular will shake with unaccustomed fear. He believed all at Foxley to have been destroyed. Now he

243

knows different. With every strike at his men we have left a snarling foxhead badge to remind him of his wickedness. And when he sees what we have wrought together with our own hands, he will see his own death in it. I know it as surely as spring must follow winter, and I thank you from the bottom of my heart."

"Come then, Brioni," Maritia said with a smile. "My father is waiting to see us before the fun begins. Tonight the *Circus Maximus* will put on its best performance: tumblers, acrobats, dancers and the mighty Oswald in all his glory. Alfred will be astounded!"

"He travels with us tomorrow?" Judith questioned, astonished.

"Hugo persuaded Leofric to let him come too," Maritia said with a wide grin, "as the distance between here and the King is so little. Any further and he would have to have stayed behind, and that he would have hated. You know what he is like."

"Oh, Maritia, I am so glad. He was the reason we met each other in the first place. I am so glad he will be with us after all. And can I leave my two boys with you as well?"

"Bran and Utha? Do they not go with you to the battlefield?"

"No, my love. That would be far too dangerous for them. Leofric and I are agreed. Taking them for a night time attack is one thing. A great battle, with spears, arrows and hand axes flying everywhere would more likely be their death. No, they stay with you and Oswald. They have played their part. Now it is up to us to see the thing through."

"It will be a pleasure, Honeyone. But they will hate it! I can hear their howls now."

"Nevertheless, Maritia. Do all you can to keep them safe."

"Of course. The whole Circus Maximus will play their part," and she gave her a swift cuddle before turning to the others.

"Right! Are you all ready for this? Brioni? It will be a rare evening, I promise you."

"I can't wait! Now, let's go, for I know how much your father hates to be kept waiting," and all together they left her room, with its secret carefully wrapped on Brioni's great bed, laughing and chattering gaily, for all the world like any flourish of young maidens before a party. To look at them, now dressed in brightly coloured wool and softest suede, with matching half boots on their feet and long cloaks of russet, forest green and amber, no-one would have suspected that within a few days they would all be part of the greatest Saxon host ever mustered in Wessex, nor that one amongst them at least would be facing her mortal foe across her shield-iron, clad in ungentle steel with her long sword in her hand and Brain-Biter by her right side, while all about her was the screaming rage and bloody crush of battle.

*

*A*elflaeda, lying quietly concealed in her bed-place, heard Brioni and the others leave and smiled to herself, while in her hand she held the magnificent short-bladed sword that the Lord Heardred had just given her.

Soon the Lady Judith would marry, that she understood and was glad for, but then there would not be so ready a place by her side, for she would have her own handmaidens, and not need Aelflaeda in the same way as before. So, since the Lady's hurt at Lord Heardred's hands, she had taken to following the beautiful shield maiden whom the huge Saxon war-lord, with the blond hair and strange piercing gold-flecked eyes, loved so fiercely, the Lady Brioni. And when she went forward with her men to fight the Heathen pirates who had destroyed her family, then she, Aelflaeda, would find some way to join her. She had her own score to settle with the bloody pagans, and with Heardred's gift to aid her she meant to take full payment. The dark heathen war-lord might yet wish he never had been born.

And hugging her new weapon to her thin breasts she curled up in a ball, smiling and chuckling to herself as she pictured just what she intended to do to any wounded Danish warrior whom she might find stranded upon the battlefield. The wild, blood-filled images seemed good to her, and when she slept her dreams were filled with the bloodied agony of the dead.

*

*O*utside the daylight slowly faded as the sun was finally gathered into the west, spreading gold and crimson streamers across the darkening sky.

From edge to edge the heavens seemed on fire, the distant horizon rippling with incandescent flame that rimmed the clouds with scarlet, the afterglow edging them with purple as the night drew on.

Within the hall the crude tables were already filling with warriors, and their war leaders, who had been gathering on the heights since Leofric's messengers had carried the King's news throughout the neighbouring lands. Sometimes they had arrived in bristling armoured groups with their thegns beside them and their lord's companions in burnished mail and glittering helmets incised with silver, but more often they had arrived in ones and twos. For most were the Saxon men from the Dane-ravaged badlands who had made their way to the certain welcome of the Iron Hand and his veteran commanders, with little but their armour on their backs and their weapons over their shoulders. And while they began to call for beer and meat, so the rest of Leofric's men crowded in amongst them, some armoured up and ready for battle; others in a medley of coloured wool and leather, long wolfskin cloaks on their backs. And all eyes were bright with the expectation of battle, their hearts raised by the great company who had come in to take their war-lord's side.

Soon the twisted building was crammed with men, the villagers who had sought refuge within the ancient ramparts crowded in amongst them, or were gathered in lively groups outside it. And all the time the ale jugs went round to fill each proffered drinking bowl or deep horn, while the roasted meats were carved in thick juicy slices onto wooden platters, or great trenchers of stone-ground bread. The noise and clatter was enormous as all ate and drank their fill, shouting out their toasts and calling to their friends across the hall.

Suddenly the horns boomed, and Hugo's buccinas howled a brazen challenge as in amongst the throng came the dancers and acrobats of the *Circus Maximus*, whirling their long sticks with coloured ribbons of scarlet, blue and emerald on the end, while Julio, Marcus, Anton and all the others came leaping and swooping in twists and bounds, now on the ground and now tossed high in the air, and right at the back, in iron breastplates and scarlet jacket came Oswald. Led by Maritia in her Greek armour, her magnificent helmet and swirling cloak drawing gasps of astonishment and great shouts of appreciation, while he spun on his enormous feet to pipes and drums and tambourines, clapping his mighty forepaws together as he swayed and bobbed his head to the great crowd of people gathered there to cheer him on. Roaring his own appreciation, he swung his hips and walked towards the dais at the far end of the hall where Hugo the Bearmaster, huge in his own bearskin cloak, stood with arms wide to welcome him, the great bear's bucket of ale awaiting him beside the half barrel he always sat on.

Standing up, Brioni and Leofric shouted and applauded with the best of them, as the dancers and acrobats finally flew out of the building in a great swirl of colour and whoops of joy, to perform amongst the great crowd outside who greeted them all with more shouts and laughter.

On the raised platform Brioni and Leofric, hair and beard neatly clipped and brushed, his bare arms heavy with gold and silver rings, and dressed in scarlet, sat down again above the cheerful throng, surrounded by their closest friends and war companions: Finnar, Raedwald, Beornred, Trausti, Cadoc the Archer and many others; Heardred seated at one end, with the Lady Judith close beside him, her hand on his arm and Siward, Baldred and Aldhelm closeby. And at the other, Hugo, now with Oswald beside him on his wide barrel chair, and Marcus, Julio and Maritia together, her enormous Greek horsehair helmet at her feet, in laughing conversation about her escape from Alfred's burning hall at Chippenham.

They had all come together for one purpose, to aid their Royal Lord against his enemies, and not one of them that night but thought of the bearded, warrior King whom they would meet at Ecberht's stone the next day. Who had kept the fight for freedom alive when all around him had given up, and even now would be anxiously awaiting the results of the summons to arms that he had sent throughout his kingdom.

Finally, Leofric judged it time to speak, and rising to his feet he hammered the great table with his fist and roared for silence.

"Well, my friends," he said at last, when all had fallen quiet, every face towards him, "tomorrow we leave for the muster and our meeting with the King, who left Athelney some days ago with all his companions, gathering an army as he marches. A few months ago we were a hunted rabble, seeking shelter where we could find it, and fearful for our lives as the Heathen swarmed across our lands, burning our homes and butchering our families and any who had the misfortune to stand in their way. Not so today! Today the enemy are on the move, marching to meet the King in battle. Royal Chippenham is cleared of their pagan offal and their king has taken his power to destroy Alfred once and for all…"

"But he will not succeed!" Brioni interrupted, leaping to her feet, her russet cloak billowing behind her. "We have shown that the Great Army can be beaten. Alfred gave us the lead, showed us the way, and we have followed his example with a vengeance. But better than that," she continued, climbing up on her chair for greater effect, "they have lost their symbol! The great raven flag, Landravager, has fallen into loyal Saxon hands, their warriors slain and their ships burned. The last Sigurdsson is dead! King Ubbi of Ireland, Ragnar Lodbrok's son, has been slain, all his companions with him and eight hundred of his men. No more will their magic raven flutter its wings above their heads and lead their charge. *Its pride lies in the dust!"* she shouted.

And now she had the attention of every person in that whole great gathering, the people outside doing their best to crowd in through the double doors to be a part of all that was going on, as pausing only for breath, she went on: "Well, they may have lost their flag…but now I give you one for us!" And turning, she called to Judith and Maritia, who without a word rose from their places and moved away across the hall, threading past the tables and benches to where Brioni's quarters lay and disappeared, while everyone held their breaths and craned their necks to see just what would happen next.

247

A few moments later and they re-appeared, and all who saw what it was they bore between them leapt to their feet and roared their approval, stamping their feet and banging their fists on the tables in tumultuous applause.

Hand stitched in russet red on a shimmering golden background, with chest and whiskers in bright silver thread, black-edged ears laid back in fury, scarlet mouth drawn back in snarling rage across bared teeth of brilliant white, slitted eyes in iridescent yellow, was the foxhead symbol of her family on a great fluttering banner. And as the girls ran amongst them, every man rose to his feet with a great cheer to acknowledge it, while Leofric looked on his chosen lady with a greater love than he had dreamed possible to feel.

Coming to the front of the dais, where Judith and Maritia had now brought their banner up beside her, Brioni shouted out again: *"This is the flag my father would have borne to the King were he still alive!* It was the last thing that Alfred said to me before I left for Foxley after Christmas. 'Tell him that I shall look for his banner of the Fox's Head come the spring muster.' Well, Oscytel destroyed it when he pillaged my home and slaughtered all our people, but now I fulfil the promise to our King. And I vow before you all that it will be the last thing that Oscytel sees on earth before he dies beneath my steel!"

Then raising her voice once more, while Judith and Maritia held up the flag and shook it wildly, she shouted: *"For Leofric, Foxley and the King! Death to Oscytel, Guthrum and the Danes!"*

"Death! **Death!***"* came back the roared reply. *"Death to Oscytel, Guthrum and the Danes! Hail, Alfred, King of Wessex! Freedom!* **Freedom!***"*

And with their drinking horns held high, their beakers and their leather pots, they drank to the Foxley banner still waving to them from the front; to their King, now on his way to the muster, and their longed for freedom from the Danish curse that had held their land so long in thrall. With huge noise they bayed and shouted and stamped their feet in a spontaneous release of all their pent-up feelings, of the months of uncertainty and fear, the endless training and the bloody raids and vicious skirmishes that had cost so many lives.

They were fired up and ready for one last titanic struggle with the enemy, and as the hall began to empty and those warriors not sleeping in the building streamed out into the night, now clouded over and a warm wind blowing from the west, they left with the certain knowledge that they were going to win. They had fought and struggled hard for the heady scent of victory, and for their own self-respect; defeat now was unthinkable!

Watching them leave, with laughter and good cheer, arms across each other's shoulders, Leofric felt searing pride and great elation. He had started with a handful of warriors and a desire just to kill and take plunder, and an iron determination not to be defeated. But since the Saxon beauty by his side had joined his band from the stark wilderness, with a wounded soul and a burning sense of mission, everything had changed. Now he fought for Alfred and for Wessex, had received the King's pardon and won the right to call himself 'Lord' once again. He had made a real name for himself, and with his new lady had forged a weapon whose edge could not be turned. And as he gathered Brioni up in his arms, and held her against his heart, he knew the rightness of all they had shared and done together.

Looking up into his face, his gaze far away, Brioni asked meekly: "Was it well done, my Lord?"

"Very well done, my Lady," came the soft reply, his eyes full of love for her. "You held our hearts in your hand this night, and we all loved you for it, even Eadwine, whose son, Cuthbert, was proclaimed dead this morning."

"I heard. Slain by a raiding band of Danes out of Chippenham. Poor Aelfrid. He was her dearest, despite all his treachery. She let him out of the lock-up you know, and gave him a horse and silver. Couldn't bear to see him driven out with sticks and drums."

"Yet he got what he deserved, the treacherous little bastard, and has freed his father and Alfweald to fight for us against the Danish host. It all worked out in the end, though Aelfrid will never be my friend."

"Am I your friend, dearest of men?" she asked softly, putting her hands up to his neck.

"My friend always, Brioni of Foxley, and my lover," he added kissing her gently, passion making his throat rumble. My Lady, your Lord loves you well. Oh Heart of Christ, but I want you!"

"Then take me, Leofric Iron Hand," she answered, lifting her mouth to his. "I am yours to do with as you will. Now, tomorrow and forever. I need to feel your strength in me my love, for though I stand behind you in the battle, with my shield held high and my sword blade running red, I am still a woman with all a woman's needs. So, take me, my Lord. Match your fire with mine and we will burn on high until the morning brings us to our senses."

And burying his face in her hair, he turned and carried her away to their quarters, leaving everyone else behind, while those who had drunk too deeply slumbered noisily amongst the soiled rushes on the floor, and the firelight leapt and flickered across the stooping walls of the silent hall.

Chapter Thirty Two

They awoke to the soft purr and swish of rain that fell out of a grey cloaked sky in drifting curtains, the long unbroken days of sunshine ended at last. There was no horizon, only a continuous drizzling murk that clouded everything, the trickling water seeping through to the skin with persistent, chilling misery.

Yet despite the foulness of that early morning, everyone was up and about, coming and going through the hall as Gilbert and his team, helped by Leofric's cook-master, Aldred, prepared a warm broth from the meats left over from the evening. That, together with fresh baked bannocks and Gilbert's best spiced ale, mulled in great cauldrons hung over the embers from yesterday's fire in the long hearth, proved a most welcome start to the day despite the weather.

All morning Leofric's whole command gradually came together in the sodden compound for the last time, hundreds and hundreds of horses, most trained for war, their saddles thick with silver and hung with weapons and saddlebags, others carrying bulging packs and wicker panniers on wooden saddle trees, all with soft leather covers against the rain, packs to carry rations for the journey: soft flour and wheat kernels for grinding and crushed oats for the war horses, twice-baked bread, biscuits and weapons of every sort, especially bundles and bundles of spare shafts, the long arrows Cadoc and his archers would need for the coming battle. And as well as the horses there were also Arnwulf's's and Wiglaf's tilt carts with all their farrier's tools, fire beds and field anvils, sacks of charcoal, bellows, spare weapons and small pigs of iron.

But not all were mounted, for there were many who had come in to Leofric on foot, their only possessions slung from their spear shafts, their armour on their backs and their shields strapped firmly across their shoulders. Nor were they the only ones gathering around their leaders that morning, for there were many archers too. Men from the forests and wild foothills of the Welsh borders, men like Orn and Aelric, like Cadoc, who was in charge of them all; and those from the desolate Northumbrian hills, like Caewlin, Wybert and Cenhelm; Snorri, the sad-faced Dane out of Mercia and Kristian his brother. Men whom Leofric had taken in when their homes had been destroyed by drunken Danish Vikings; men who could split a peeled wand at two hundred paces and strike a flying mallard twice before it hit the ground.

They were the kind of archers that could shred a Viking charge before their spearmen could get close enough to make their cast. And as they stood clumped together with their long bow-staves in their calloused hands, tough leather jerkins covered with mail or hammered strips of iron, long boots on their feet, their strings safely in their hats out of the weather, and their long feathered shafts thrusting up thickly out of their quivers, Leofric felt pride swell up in him again.

He had been chided by many for the effort he had put into his bowmen. Archery in line of battle was not often used in the Saxon host, not in the way he had devised it, with blocks of archers protected by spear and axe men, who could deliver a devastating storm of arrows on the enemy before the shield walls closed in upon each other. But Leofric knew what a long-barbed shaft could do to a red deer stag at rutting time, and what could pull down a great 500lb beast in his fiery prime could just as easily slay a man in linked iron byrnie, or boiled leather breast plate. He smiled at the arguments that had raged about the table when first he had suggested trained archers to Raedwald, Trausti and Beornred. But time and again he had proved his point, like Malmesbury and Chippenham. And now they were all as pleased about them in their army as he was, for if well-handled they could help burst the stoutest shield ring asunder, or break the fiercest charge.

And as the morning wore on, steadily more and more of his command appeared until the whole area between the hall and the gates was crammed with armed men. Spearmen in bristling steel clumps, their shields on their backs and long spears to hand. Most carried long swords at their waists, but some preferred great war-hammers, lead-filled mauls of shaped stone on thick wooden staffs, and some there were who carried long-handled bearded axes, weapons that could shear a horse's head off with a single strike, could hook a shield down and split a man in two or hack a shield in pieces. All wore body armour of iron scales on thick leather, or riveted ring mail, on body and legs, with nut-shaped helmets, strengthened with steel strips and a strong nasal, and all had the long-bladed saexe on their right sides that could prove deadly in the close confines of the shield wall, when the enemy's breath was thick in your face and you could count his rotten teeth.

Then there were the mounted warriors who made up the core and backbone of his army. Now many hundreds of them, many who had been with him from the start like Ricberht, Hannes, Finnar, Sigweald and Jaenberht, all armed with sword and nine-foot ash spears at their right foot and shields on their armoured backs. And the men of Heardred's command, and Brioni's battle group: Aetheridge, Hathored and Cynric the Tracker and too many others to mention, together with those dispossessed thegns who had made it to this muster with their own household troops and loyal hearth companions, and others of the Saxon host who had come to the Rings in answer to Alfred's call to arms.

In link steel byrnies of finest mail strengthened with steel plates across back and chest, close-fitting helmets with hinged cheek-plates and thick chain coifs hanging from them, each carried a great war shield on his back bearing the foxhead emblem gaudily emblazoned on its taut leather surface. Without doubt they were the finest fighting men that Leofric had seen since Ashdown seven years before.

Finally he was joined by his own war leaders, by Beornred his giant Danish second, and Raedwald, Aldhelm and Eadberht; by Brioni with Trausti and Finnar; the Lord Heardred with Siward and Baldred his fire-master, and by Hugo with the Lady Judith, and Maritia with Oswald on his long travelling chain, still in his scarlet jacket and iron breastplates, who made up the last of the party.

By then it was midday and the weather had cleared before a brisk west wind, the clouds scurrying away to leave a rain-washed sky with bright May sunlight spearing down to lighten the mood of everyone gathered there. Swift to cast off the capes they had been wearing, and for the children to come out from the bothies and shelters that ringed the new defences, the people gathered all along the pathway to the huge gates, now flung wide before them, some cheerful, some weeping, hounds on the leash and wandering amongst them, as their men prepared to march out and make war on their Danish foes.

All were waiting for Leofric's word to move off, as he sat on Wotan in shimmering mail, burnished like silver in the fresh sunlight, with Brioni by his side on Foxhead, Bran and Utha closeby, their fighting collars firmly fastened and Hannes close beside them with the new banner, still covered, on a long ash pole fortified with metal so that it could not easily be hacked down.

Suddenly Leoftic stood up in his stirrups and looked across the mass of taut expectant faces, all flicking eyes and shuffling feet, and raised his hand above his head, his voice carrying to the furthest ranks despite the wind that swirled and scurried round them.

"The time has come, my friends," he roared out. "Our preparations are at an end and the enemy awaits us. We are the finest warriors this side of Ecberht's stone, and we ride to join the King. May God aid us for our cause is just. *Death to the Northmen. Glory to our King!*"

"*Death and glory!*" they bellowed back. "*Death to Guthrum. Glory to our King!*"

And with a great blare of Hugo's buccinas, and the deep *Hoom! Hoom! Hoom!* of the war horns, the horsemen thrust in their heels and spurred forward to the broad entrance of the ancient fortress that had shielded them so well. Squadron by glittering squadron they wheeled away in a wild scatter of flying sods, cohort by cohort, bristling with weapons, speeding through the gateway, while all those who had gathered there cheered them on their way, lifting up the children to see them go by and waving white and coloured favours in their hands.

Behind them came the fighting foot, the spear and axemen in their battalions, and the archers led by Cadoc, the whole army swinging through the great ramparts and away down the steep chariot slope that led south through ruined Warminster to Ecberht's stone on King's Court Hill beside the ancient village of Kingston Deverill, where Alfred had called his muster. Ahead went a great screen of scouts, then the vanguard and main body of mounted and heavy foot, while behind followed hundreds of pack horses and the tilt carts, with more mounted warriors bringing up the rear.

Leofric watched the vanguard disappearing in the front, and reined in to have a last word with Thurwold and Brorda whom he was leaving behind to guard the fortress, and were waiting for him beside the massive gates,

"So, it begins, my Lord," Thurwold said stiffly.

"Yes! And with God's will we shall make an end of all of them, and clear them out of Wessex once and for all!"

"What do you want me to do now?" he asked, eyes looking steadily at the great armoured figure above him on his massive horse.

"Keep everyone here. Close and bar the gates and let no man leave or enter, except it be by your personal wish or your command. You, Brorda, support him, but Thurwold is in command. I have left some men to guard you, though they still bear the marks of Steinar's steel. And keep a brave heart, Saxon," he added with a smile, "for the Heathen's days are numbered. And remember, bide here safely until I send you word, or my Lady tells you what to do. Come now, don't look so anxious," he ended with a laugh, as he reached down to clasp the big smith's arm. "The King does not mean to lose this throw of the dice, and neither do I!" And turning away again he dug in his spurs and flew off down the track in a spray of torn earth and wet stones, galloping past the long columns of tramping soldiery to the head of the line, where Brioni was waiting for him, Hannes beside her with the furled banner, and together they turned their faces to the south.

*

That day, despite the gloomy start, turned into a brilliant afternoon, the wind driving the rain and murk away from the hills to leave a May sun beaming down on them from a lightly cloud-brushed sky as they pushed south towards the Deverills. A day when they moved with less caution than before and with less urgency. They had made a good start and were only a half day's march from Alfred's muster, and Leofric wished to give his men, and his beasts, plenty of respite before bringing them before the King.

Now, too, there were more people on the move than they had seen in a six month. Sturdy churls with shield and sword and hasty bundles of clothes and rations over their shoulders; geburs, the peasant farmers of Wessex, with wooden helmets strengthened with iron strips, tough leather jerkins on their backs and armed with sharpened hoes, sickles, scythes and threshing tools with which to hack and beat the Danes to death. And there was the occasional thegn in chiming mail and boiled leather breastplate on a high-stepping charger, closed helmet with incised face plates, heavy brow defences and thick nasal, with his hearth companions well armoured, armed and mounted behind him. And all moving south-westwards to where the King had called his muster, Easter long behind them, and the enemy in front.

*

*I*t was an easy afternoon's march down the valley, with the huge escarpment of the long Waste Downs marching sternly on their right, solid oak and grey-trunked beech on their left. And as the sun warmed them, and the mists drew away from the Wylye, from river bank and sedgy marsh, so the men visibly relaxed and the pace slowed, their whole advance taking on a bright holiday air, with many songs and much laughter from the swinging ranks as they barrelled their way along the beaten trackway, pushing all in their path to the bush-lined verges with their cheerful swagger.

Then, suddenly it seemed, they were almost there, and Leofric halted the whole long column for an afternoon meal in a massive clearing, a time for the men to clean their armour of the morning's rain, and polish it until the sunlight burst off burnished steel in dazzling points of white fire, and to brush their beasts until their thick coats gleamed. Every man was ready and in his right place, and now for the first time since the last night in Leofric's hall, the golden banner of Foxley, with its snarling mask and piercing eyes, was unsheathed.

With stately grace Brioni rode with it rippling on Foxhead amongst the packed ranks of warriors, and as she moved she was greeted with great shouts of acclaim; until, with the afternoon breezes tugging at its shimmering fringes and long plaited leather tassels, she handed it once more to Hannes who was to be its guardian, and finally took her place between Leofric and Heardred.

254

"Today, is the sixth day of May," he shouted out, his voice carried by the wind to the furthest man in his host. "The hawthorn flowers in the wastelands and the cuckoo calls across the valleys. It is time to free our people from the foul yoke of the Northmen. It is time the Heathen pirates tasted Saxon steel in full. Not the light flavour we have given them so far. But the whole bloody feast! Today," he went on, waving his long-handled axe above his head, "we ride to meet the King. '*Long live King Alfred!*' he roared across the clearing, his voice startling the feather-legged crows, crowded amongst the trees, into wild tumbling flight. "Long live King Alfred! *Death to his enemies!*"

"Long live the King!" came back the tumultuous reply from a thousand voices. "***Death to his enemies!***" as Leofric, Brioni and Heardred dug in their heels and led their forces south to where the counties of Somerset and Wiltshire met, where the stone of Ecberht had been set up in the elder days, where the great Wessex King had held his moots and handed out his dooms, and where their own King had called for them to meet him in arms.

The second day after Whitsunday, the 6th of May, in the Year of Our Lord, 878, for the defence of his realm and the utter defeat of all his enemies.

*

*T*hose last few miles took them longer to cover than any had expected, for the lanes and trackways were crammed with troops as the southern shires responded to their King's desperate appeal: men from Wiltshire, Somerset and Hampshire, from Surrey and even from distant Kent came hurrying to Alfred's call. Seasoned warriors, and armoured fyrdsmen, the great peasant army of Wessex, all converging on the tiny village of Kingston Deverill, where the great stones that marked the boundaries on King's Court Hill had been soundly fixed. Two standing sarsens and one great capstone.

Nor were the men of Wessex the only warriors who came in to Alfred that day, for men came in from distant Northumbria in steel clumps and armoured battles, from Mercia and even from the shattered lands of the East Angles whose king, Edmund, had been so foully murdered by Ivar, son of the mighty Ragnar Lodbrok. And all were marching to greet the man who, alone in those early weeks of January, had kept the royal lamp of freedom flickering in the pagan darkness that had descended on Wessex when Chippenham had fallen. Now from east, west, north and south the fighting men of Wessex streamed in with joy in their hearts to greet their King and renew their oaths of loyalty and allegiance.

Yet of all the men who flocked to Alfred's standards that day, there were none so compact, nor so well accoutred for war as those whom Leofric Iron

255

Hand, Lord of Wimborne, and Heardred of the Somerseatas brought in to greet him. With horns booming, and buccinas shouting their brazen voices across the countryside to herald their approach, they came swaggering down the track to a great clearing at the bottom of the hill on which the Sarsen stones stood tall, the men's voices lifting on the breeze to the song of Beowulf, the foxhead banner of Brioni's House fluttering in their van, the stamp of their feet ringing on the beaten ground.

*

Standing by the rippling flag of the Fighting Man, with the great dragon banner of Wessex also curling above his head, surrounded by his priests in black, and with a corps of bishops, the Ealdormen of Somerset and Hampshire by his side, and with Earl Brihtnoth of the Somerseatas, Alfred watched their advance in wide-eyed amazement.

"Whose is this host that comes to the muster with heathen armour on their backs and Roman trumpets?" he asked the men grouped around him excitedly. "And with more horse than amongst my own companions, and five score archers in their train? I have not seen such a display, Aethelnoth," he said to the Ealdorman of Somerset, "nor so many well-equipped warriors since before Ashdown when my brother was still king!"

Then, as the wind, caught the flag that Hannes was carrying so proudly against his right stirrup, and stretched it fluttering against the sky, Alfred gave a great start and shouted exclamation: "Look, Brihtnoth!" he cried out, grabbing the older man firmly by the shoulder. "*Look!* Do you see? Surely my eyes must be deceiving me? That is the snarling banner of Wulfstan of Foxley!"

"Impossible, my Lord King!" the old Earl replied forcefully. "The man was brutally slain, together with his whole family when the Danes seized Chippenham, and all his people. Besides that flag is too new. Like, but unlike the one that we have seen so many times beckoning to us from the centre of the fray!"

"Well, my friend," the King replied with his usual good humour and throaty chuckle, and a wince from sudden pain in his bowels, "old or new, I'd know that bared mask and pinned back ears anywhere, though the face of he who bears it is unknown to me, as are the men who ride behind him. No! Splendour of God, that other leader is the Lord Heardred! Now, my loyal guardians of my lands, which one of you can read me this riddle? For I tell you, it is beyond my simple understanding!"

256

"There is one other thing that has escaped your notice, my Lord King," Aethelnoth said to him, stepping close. "Of those three leaders, one is a woman, of that I am certain!"

"A woman? How can that be?" the King said wonderingly, looking across the clearing from underneath his hand. "By St Cuthbert, I believe you may be right. There is more shape beneath that armour than a man should have. That other warrior beside her must be Leofric Iron Hand. I should have realised that the moment I saw Heardred amongst them."

"That must be right, Alfred," Earl Brihtnoth said, sharply. "We have heard that a woman fights beside him."

"The one who burned down my hall and half of Chippenham," the King grumped ruefully. "I had the reports."

"And slew a great pack of Danes, my Lord," Aelfric of Hampshire said with a grin. "And nearly took Guthrum out at the same time. Singed the Danes' beard nicely!" and they all laughed.

"So," Alfred said as the whole great contingent continued to advance towards them, "Heardred found the man after all. I knew Leofric had become a power north of the Avon. I have had his reports, and heard the stories of the fierce shield-maiden who shares his life and leads his men in battle. And I knew he had moved his command to the ancient fortress of Battlesbury Rings...but I had no idea he had so many warriors in his train."

"But why do they carry the banner of Wulfstan's House before them?" Aethelnoth queried, amazed.

"I don't know," Alfred answered the grizzled veteran. "But doubtless we shall soon find out, for they must halt soon and make themselves known to us. I tell you all this," he concluded through gritted teeth, "with men like that behind me last year, I never would have allowed that traitor Wulfhere to persuade me to disband our army before Christmas, nor left him in command of all my troops round Gloucester. Then the disaster of Chippenham never would have taken place! My life on it!" And leaving them all muttering beside his royal standards, he strode out to greet this man of whom he had heard so much.

Chapter Thirty Three

"Well, my Lady," Leofric said as he saw the King moving steadily towards them, "this is the moment you have been waiting for. How do you feel?"

"Very strange, my love," Brioni replied, raising her eyebrows. "I left Alfred just after Christmas as a young hand-maiden to his Queen, and busy nursemaid to his children. Now I return as a shield-maiden out of legend, with my sword well blooded in his service, having become the practised lover of a Saxon Wolfshead turned Royal Companion overnight. It couldn't be a more unusual home coming!"

"Surprised he may be, my beauty, but at least he cannot eat you! I cannot wait to see his face when he realises precisely who you are!" And with a great laugh he threw up his hand and brought the whole long column of men, horses and wagons to a jingling, stamping halt.

Swinging off Wotan, Leofric leapt lightly to the ground despite his armour and leaving his reins in Beornred's gnarled hands, he went forward to greet the King, while Heardred and Brioni dismounted and waited quietly beside their horses' heads, the shouts of the multitude of warriors, armoured fyrdsmen and peasants ringing in their ears.

Slipping his shield off his back, and laying it on the ground with his fighting axe, Leofric drew his sword and dropping to one knee he held it out in his hands before his King, bowed his head and then lifted it again to swear his oath.

"Alfred, son of Aethulwulf, of the right line of Cerdic, true King of Wessex, I, Leofric Iron Hand, Lord of Wimborne, offer you my sword, my life and the service of all who follow me. Pardon me and mine, Great King, and let us take our place beside you on the field of battle. If I break faith with you, may the green earth gape and swallow me, may the grey seas roll in and overwhelm me, may the sky of stars fall on me and crush me out of life forever."

The words were ancient and well known.

The form and manner of their speaking reaching back into the elder days when first the Saxons came to Britain and fought the Roman-British people for the island, and Leofric had given them much thought and care in practice for this moment. Now, as his voice rose deep and sonorous on the wind, all men waited to see how their King would receive them.

Alfred looked down at the giant Saxon warrior kneeling meekly before him and smiled.

Here was a man whom others liked to follow, whose strength and loyalty reached out and touched his heart. This warrior lord had done great things for Wessex already, despite his previous reputation as a rieving wolfshead and ruthless plunderer. He, and those who followed him, was just the kind of man whom Wessex needed to make her rich and powerful again. A man who would put on his war-harness to fight the pagan Danes, and with his hearth companions drive the Heathen from their lands. Bending forward he took the proffered weapon, and holding it firmly, he swung it around his head and back again in a glittering arc of steel, its polished blade sparkling in the May sunshine as he did so. Then, reaching for Leofric's right hand he pulled him to his feet, and holding the sword out carefully by the blade, he offered it back to the man who now stood towering above him.

"Take back your sword of me, Leofric Iron Hand. My pardon I have already granted, but now I offer you my friendship in person. If you will serve Wessex nobly upon the battlefield, and fight beneath the royal standards of my House, then come to me again and I will richly reward you as you deserve." And clasping his arms firmly about Leofric's shoulders, Alfred embraced him and the two men exchanged the kiss of peace upon each other's cheeks, while all about them the Saxon host stamped and roared out their approval.

Finally the two men stood back and looked at one another. Stern blue eyes studying the gold-flecked, emerald ones of the other; both steadily appraising, both looking for weaknesses in gaze and stature. There were none, and though Leofric was a head taller than the King, Alfred's long years with sword and shield on a dozen stricken fields had thickened his arms and shoulders, broadened his chest and given his face the firm cast of command that Leofric had hoped for.

"Well, Saxon, are you satisfied?" Alfred asked him quizzically.

"Yes, my Lord King," Leofric answered him, unabashed, his face breaking into a craggy smile. "I am pleased beyond measure to meet with you at last."

"You spoke the ritual words well," Alfred answered him. "I have not heard them all for many years." Adding with a grin, "I had not expected to meet with such polished speech from one more used to forest clearings, bloody raid and skirmish than the Courts of Kings!"

"I had a good teacher, my Lord."

"Ah," Alfred answered, knowingly. "The Lord Heardred."

"No, my Lord King," Leofric replied with a hint of mystery in his voice. "One much closer to you and your Queen than you can possibly imagine!"

And before Alfred could respond, he turned away and beckoned his two group leaders over towards him.

"The Lord Heardred you know of course, for it was he you sent to us. But this, my Lord," he added dramatically, "this is the Lady Brioni of Foxley!"

In awed amazement Alfred watched as Brioni pulled off her helmet and knelt before him, her cropped hair bobbing in the breeze as she did so,

"*The Lady Brioni?*" he asked, as a gasp of astonishment went round the men gathered behind him. "Brioni of Foxley? Thane Wulfstan's daughter?" he questioned her incredulously. "The sword-wielding Amazon who burned down my hall in Chippenham and left Guthrum and the Danish host in turmoil?"

"So, you heard, my Lord?" she replied, blushing lightly.

"Heard!" he exclaimed, throwing his hands up in the air. "I should think the whole of Wessex must have heard by now. You, archers and a bear, if all can be believed! I can't wait to meet that bear."

"Oswald, my Lord King. He is part of Hugo the Bearmaster's family. I met them all after Foxley was destroyed."

"Dear God, my child. I thought your whole family were slain when that hell-hound, Oscytel, destroyed your home in January. I had no idea that anyone had survived that awful shambles!"

"I alone, my Lord King!" she answered quickly, looking up into his eyes. "I witnessed all that was done there."

"All, my Lady?" the king asked, appalled.

"All, my Lord. And I can't tell you how terrible that was. It was after that I met with Hugo the Bearmaster and his daughter, Maritia, and then with my Lord Leofric, with whom I have been ever since."

"I am sure there is much you have not said," he replied looking at her face, and the unshed tears that shimmered in her eyes.

"It is a long story, and a bitter one. But I have had Leofric to lean on, and to comfort me, have made friends where I never expected to, and have had a burning mission to sustain me."

"Oscytel's death?" Alfred questioned her darkly.

"Yes, My Lord King. Oscytel's death at my hand. I vowed it in blood upon my father's body whom he butchered before my eyes. Only when he is dead shall I be free to marry Leofric at last, then I shall follow him wherever he may lead me. He is my man, my Lord, and I love him greatly."

Alfred looked at them both as they stood before him in their battle glory, shimmering mail, shields, weapons and close helmets and smiled softly. Such hopes, such determination, such ideals.

260

"That man will not fall easily," he said after a pause. "He has the Devil's own protection," and he crossed himself, while Oscytel's name rustled through the priests and bishops behind him.

"I know," she replied steadily, "the green stone knife, *Sica.* That evil talisman from across the seas, from ancient Egypt, that has been his source of strength for so long. Since he came from Byzantium; I have heard the tale. But now his power is waning; we who serve the Iron Hand all know that to be true. We have slain his crews, taken his booty and harried his messengers. We have humiliated him before the other leaders of the Great Army, and before Guthrum the High King of the Danes. When next we meet, my Lord King, then I shall kill him, of that I am certain!"

Alfred sighed and shook his head briefly, placing his hands on her shoulders as he did so.

"You have chosen a stony path to tread, young Brioni. That man has become a legend for evil in this land, and many finer warriors than you have fallen beneath his axe. You father would have been proud of you and I, your King, pay tribute to your bravery." Then, turning away towards his tall war-leader, he asked: "But what of you, my Lord Heardred? I understand that you were to be betrothed to this lady; yet you do not seem to be concerned?" he ended quizzically.

"It never happened, Alfred, as you know," Heardred answered smiling, coming forward to clasp the King's arm in welcome, "and I, also, have met another," and calling Judith forward, who had gathered beside Beornred on the track, he presented her to the King.

Alfred blinked at the sight of her, and his mouth almost fell open as gasps of surprise came from the men behind him.

"Well, well! It seems this is to be a day of big surprises. You also, my Lady, have been proclaimed missing, presumed dead or worse! I have your grandfather with me now. I pray God the shock of finding you alive and unharmed does not carry him off. You must join him shortly. Now, come all of you," he went on briskly, "there is no time now for all your tales, that will surely come later. Leofric, Heardred, billet your men where you can find the space. I have taken quarters in the village – they are not grand by any means, but at least they are dry and under cover. My bones ache these days if I spend too long on damp ground," he added with a wry smile. "Tonight there will be a meeting of all my commanders to which you are formally bidden to attend. Then it will be decided what next to do. Time, my friends, not the enemy is our most pressing concern. Now, bring the Bearmaster and Oswald to meet me. I must greet this bear who made such mincemeat of those Danes and wrecked my hall!"

261

And sweeping Judith up with him to join her grandfather, he turned and strode away through his entourage and his bodyguards, while a host of well-wishers jostled round to greet the newcomers who had arrived with such style and warlike mien.

*

No sooner had the King gone than the Lords Edwin and Harold came rushing up to greet Heardred, and exchange hard news of the war and their estates. It was the first time since leaving Foxley that the three of them had been together, so there was much to talk of, and leaving Siward to sort out his men, they bore Heardred off to their own encampment nearby amidst much laughter.

Indeed theirs was an emotional reunion, for both of Heardred's great friends had been cut off from actual contact with him for many months. The fighting in their area had been severe; they'd had to move more than once to avoid capture, and were both amazed and delighted to find their old comrade in such fine fettle. And as he told them of all that had happened since parting, about meeting up with Alfred, about Athelney, of raid and counter-raid with Guthrum's forces and the whole awful struggle throughout the last winter in the marshes, it quite made up for all the anxieties they had suffered on his behalf in the meantime.

Judith they thought an enchanting and lovely creature, and they cursed their own misfortune in not meeting up with her themselves and having the pleasure of putting an end to all Medraut's wickedness. But it was the tale of how he met with the Lady Brioni again that really stunned them both into almost silent amazement, especially to learn that the body they had buried at Foxley with so much sadness was that of her maid and not the girl herself! That really made them open their eyes and gasp, exclaim and roar with laughter before pledging eternal friendship, with the promise to stick together on the battlefield and fight to the death over the bodies of their comrades should they fall beneath fierce Danish steel.

It was all very affecting, and by the time Leofric and Brioni saw him again he was very much the worse for wear, tottering amiably about the sprawling encampment, waving his sword about and threatening the Danes in a thick ale-shotten tenor, when he wasn't singing the Lay of Roland at the top of his voice!

By then the sun had set in a blaze of glory, casting the trees that cloaked the village into stark relief and filling the sky with soft evening light.

"Just look at him!" Leofric exclaimed, laughing, as Brioni seized Heardred by the hand and dragged him over to where their shelters had been thrown up. "Alfred will be less than entertained to see him in this state. God alone knows what condition those other two are in, but we must see what we can do to bring him quickly to his senses before the meeting with Alfred later. Quick, Brioni, bring me that bucket of water over there and we'll give him a good sousing!"

It was as they were onto the second bucket that Brioni noticed two heavily-cloaked figures flitting silently through the darkened encampment, carefully avoiding the thousands of campfires that had sprung up everywhere, and the many bands of warriors who were grouped about them.

"Surely that must be Hugo?" Brioni said, pulling on Leofric's arm. I would know that huge shape anywhere. "But who is that with him? For it is not Maritia, she is with Oswald, I saw them together not long ago. Quick, Leofric. Go after him and see who it is. Bring them over to join us. I haven't had a chance to speak to the Bearmaster since we met the King."

"Leave him be, Brioni. He knows where we are and can come and find us anytime. He doesn't need a nursemaid."

"Go on, Leofric. Quickly before you lose him. That other one bothers me. There is something furtive about him!"

"Furtive?"

"Something not right, and why does he have a bag across his shoulders?"

"Is this another of your intuitions?" he asked her quietly, standing up and rubbing his hands together, Heardred still slumped in a groaning heap at his feet, Bran and Utha wuffling all over him.

"It's just a feeling, Leofric, but I would hate the King's peace to be disturbed by something Hugo took it into his mind to do."

"Like what?"

"Like bringing Oswald with the army to fight!"

"What? Even Hugo could not be that mad!"

"You know what he is like with that bear, and Maritia is little better. Now, go on, before he disappears amongst this throng."

But she was talking to his back, for Leofric had already made up his mind. He had learned to trust her long ago, and he now loped off after the two men as they made unerringly for the edge of the village, and the dark ranks of heavy timber and thick shrub-land that lay beyond. Looking back now and again to see if they were being followed, the sight of Leofric's towering bulk came as quite a shock, for the two gave a sudden start and immediately picked up their pace, so that now Leofric hurried in earnest to catch them up.

263

Then, suddenly, he was baulked by a rowdy group of thegns who clamoured for his attention, swiftly surrounding him with ale on their breath and shouts of commendation for his exploits against Guthrum…and by the time he had finally got rid of them the hurrying cloaks he had been following had disappeared. Search as he might he could see no further sign of them in the darkness, wishing he had taken the two great hounds with him, and shrugging his shoulders he returned to where Brioni was sitting, a swiftly sobering Heardred retching miserably by her side.

"I lost them! I was within forty paces of them when I was blocked by a group of Brihtnoth's thegns in rollicking good humour, and by the time I had got rid of them, they were gone. A strange business because those two were actually leaving the encampment, and I cannot think why Hugo would do such a thing. You must go and find Maritia, perhaps she would know where her father has slipped off to, and who was with him."

"I will do just that when you have gone off to your meeting," she said, mopping Heardred's face with a towel. "And you two can come with me," she said, ruffling the wiry muzzles of her two giant hounds as they pushed up at her.

"Well, it cannot be too serious," the big Saxon war-leader replied. "The perimeter guards would have seized them both, and there has been no outcry. Anyway, Hugo would do nothing to threaten our security. He is as solid for Alfred as you or I."

"I suppose so," she replied reluctantly. "Though with the enemy maybe closeby, I would hate to think of anyone hazarding themselves by leaving the camp in darkness. It worries me!"

Leofric smiled and gave her a quick squeeze, and then grabbing Heardred beneath his arms he hoisted him onto his feet, and to the accompaniment of sad moans and groans from a very whey-faced royal officer, he and Heardred stumbled across the busy camp to where Alfred had taken up quarters in the village.

*

*B*ut, to their amazement, there was no meeting with the King that night after all. Despite the words that he had said on their arrival, Alfred was absent from the Council. Priests, bishops and Ealdormen Brihtnoth, Aelfric and Aethelnoth of the Somerseatas were there, but not the King. And it was Aethelnoth with whom Alfred had fought the Danes since arriving on Athelney who addressed them all.

"Tomorrow the army will move up to Iley Oak near Sutton Veny," he told everyone, his lined face looking even more craggy than usual. "There the King will meet us in arms and give you all his orders," he added, looking distinctly uncomfortable as he did so. "The Heathen have left Chippenham. They have gathered all their men together from every corner of Wessex and are moving to cross our line of march. Our scouts are hanging on the fringe of their army, shadowing them as they advance so we know where they are, but our movements are hidden from them."

"So, where are the pagan bastards?" a burly thegn called out, followed by a collective murmur from all those gathered there.

"Approaching the Royal Lodge at Edington, where there is fodder for their horses and plenty of water."

"*Ethandun!*" Another called out.

"So some call it round here," shouted another. "I know it well; a core of buildings round a central hall, with ditches and banks around it, with the Waste Downs on its left flank and open land behind it all the way back to Chippenham if things go badly for them. They have chosen well!"

"But where is the King, Aethelnoth?" came the grumbled question from many voices.

"Aye, where is Alfred?" others called. "Many of us have come long distances to serve him, yet we see him not!"

"The King is about his lawful business," the Ealdorman replied, looking round at the Council.

"Then why is he not with us?" yet others called out, waving their hands and shuffling their feet in frustration.

"We are not at liberty to say!" Earl Britnoth said firmly, coming forward to stare down any dissenters. "The King's orders are clear," the old war-leader said, waving a sheaf of parchments in the air. "The army moves at daybreak. The whole host will move in column, mounted warriors in the van and at the rear, spearmen and axemen in their companies, with the Fyrd in the centre, archers on the flanks, scouts ahead and to the sides. It is all here," he said, fluttering the parchments at them again. "The King may not be here, but these are his orders, names, positions, everything. Do you doubt it?"

"*NO!*" came back the roared reply, with a thunder of feet.

"Very well, then away with you all. The King has given orders that you are all to be fed and watered at his expense, then go about your business and get your heads down. You will need it!"

And with that they all had to be content, though there was much good-natured banter and speculation as to Alfred's strange absence and the obvious discontent of his top commanders. Some said that he had gone to lie with his

Queen, others that he had gone to make his peace with God, to pray for victory at some special shrine as he had been known to do. They might not have liked it, those worthy thanes and thick-set warriors, that their King was not there to speak with them himself, but they could survive a night and day without him being amongst them. They had been glad enough to see him at the muster...and would be sure to welcome him just as royally again when next they met.

*

*B*ack at their own encampment Judith joined them from her grandfather's hearth, and with the help of Aldred and Osbert she and Aelflaeda set up the cooking fires and organised the men into collecting wood and drawing ale from the barrels that had been set up on the King's orders, while Leofric, Brioni and Heardred went from company to company to assure themselves that all was well.

No sooner had they settled, than the village folk of Kingston Deverill came crowding round them, eager to hear their news and share the food that Alfred had provided for the host from the Saxon commissariat. And with thousands of burly warriors lying in relaxed idleness all about the village and its green, along the roadway that ran right through the village, and in every hedgerow, it was not long before the local girls made their presence felt.

Dressed brightly in their hastily-donned finery, they flitted like gaudy butterflies from group to group with baskets of soft-baked scones upon their hips and spring flowers in their hair. Ale and beer was brought round and fuel for a great fire was quickly gathered. A fat heifer was throat-cut, gutted and spitted on an old iron axle; someone produced an age-blackened harp, an arc of bells was brought from the church, and others joined the throng with bagpipes, gittern, pipes and drums. And with that the dancing began, and while the guards who had been placed at all points from which the village could be approached, looked on in envy until it was their time to be relieved, Leofric and his command threw off their war gear and joined in the fun.

"Well, my beauty," Leofric said later, clutching a breathless Brioni tightly in his arms, "I haven't seen you dance and leap like that for ages!"

"Oh, Leofric," she laughed, face flushed from the heat and the excitement, "I haven't enjoyed myself so much since the Christmas Festival with the King's family at Chippenham. Before Foxley!" she added grimly. "We have spent too much time hunting, killing and just trying to stay alive, my love," she went on quietly, "that we have almost forgotten how to relax and enjoy ourselves. Look at them, sweetheart," she said, gesturing to where

266

Beornred and Cadoc were capering wildly round the fire, arms draped loosely about the shoulders of several of their men, "those grizzled veterans of ours are behaving like children on All Fools Day!"

"And we, my vagabond Saxon lady, are going to join them! Tomorrow we move up in preparation to meet the Danish host and crush them. Look and listen, they can smell victory, Brioni, and so by God and His angels can I! Come on, Brioni of Foxley," he added, picking her up and swinging her around. "You think they are like children? Until you have seen Leofric Iron Hand leap and shout you have seen nothing!"

And with a wild yell he threw her up onto his shoulders and ran out to join his companions who were reeling about in time to the wild music. There on the edges of the great blaze the men had built they found Judith and Heardred, now refreshingly sobered, arms linked with Siward, Trausti and some of the village people. Dropping Brioni to the ground they linked arms too, picked up the pounding beat of drums, buccinas and bagpipes, and kicking up their feet and shouting, they panted round the flames until exhausted, while the moon rose in silent splendour above them and the sparks leapt up like fireflies into the night.

Long after they had retired to their own quarters beneath their travelling shelter, the revels continued until every quart of ale provided by the King had been drained and the towering fire had been reduced to a vast pile of glowing embers.

Wrapped in each other's arms, their bodies pressed close against the chill night air, beneath Brioni's thick wolf skins on a bed of fleeces, and against their saddles for a bolster, they lay and loved with warmth and understanding. Each gave fully of themselves, bodies joined, hands and mouths together, while the stars wheeled overhead towards the dawn and Diana rode her silver chariot across the heavens.

*

*T*hat night the whole camp seethed with pent-up excitement.

Rumours about Guthrum and the Danish army flew round from tent to tent and shelter to shelter: they were two miles away and ready to attack; they had returned to their palisaded fortress at Chippenham; they had made one of their lightning moves across country and were back in Gloucester. But there were no calls to arms in the middle of the night, no pounding messengers came in with desperate news, no flaring beacons lit up the sky to warn of imminent attack, no cries and screams of terror destroyed the peace...and eventually everyone settled for an uneasy sleep, with one hand on their weapons and one eye on their mounts.

Chapter Thirty Four

*T*hey rose as the first larks spiralled upwards into a bluebell morning, their trilling voices calling everyone awake, and within minutes the whole great sprawling encampment had come to life. Cooking fires were swiftly kicked into new life, the horses led down to water from the River Wylye that almost ran right through the village, and those who had enjoyed themselves too freely groaned and cursed the world of which they had been forced so rudely to take notice as they dipped their heads in the crystal waters. The sun may have been gilding the new day with buttercup fingers and a glowing marigold eye, but they would much rather have lain still while the dark waters of Lethe washed over them than face his brilliant smile.

Then, all too soon it seemed, it was time to go, as the men's officers called them all to order, and from all over the village the men came together in their companies and armoured battles. Everything had been re-packed and stowed away; baggage wagons, tilt carts and trains of pack mules and sturdy horses all stood ready with their carters and riders, and the farewells of the Deverill folk both given and received with laughter and with tears.

Company by company, horsemen, proven warriors, bold fyrdsmen and archers all bristling with weaponry, helmets, shields and many armour-clad, moved out behind the royal standards, and their own: crosses, angels, prancing horses, stags, saints and the snarling mask, with pinned back ears of the House of Foxley, all waving and fluttering bravely in the morning breeze. Alfred himself may not have been in the van but his spirit was, and so were his war-leaders, his priests and bishops, and where the scarlet Wyvern Dragon and the Fighting Man of Wessex led, there all fighting men must follow.

Up the old road towards Warminster they swung with a shout and a wave to all who had gathered to see them on their way, clopping hooves and thumping feet stirring up the dust as the sun broke through the opaque shrouds of early morning to pour its heat out upon the ground, and by noon the host was sweltering. The men cursing their armour where it chafed their sweating bodies, and the horses tossing their heads and shaking their manes as they snorted to drive away the flies that gathered round their eyes and bristly nostrils.

But by then then they were arriving beside the great oak at Iley that gave the place its name, where there was an ancient earthwork to house the King's pavilion, and plentiful water from the free-flowing River Wylye close by for the thousands of horses that followed in the army's train. Sleek war horses, high stepping with iron hooves, and trained to fight with tooth and iron shoe; patient pack animals with heaped panniers of weapons, bags of oats and flour and mules, even donkeys...all close to Sutton Veny where there was a small church at which the King could pray. And just beyond was the great chalk escarpment that reared above all, that ran from the River Wylye at its feet near Warminster, on which the great fortress of Battlesbury Rings was built, to tower over the Royal Lodge of Edington, ten leagues further north, where the Great Army of Guthrum, of Oscytel and the Danes was busily assembling.

There, where the ancients had raised their barrows and built their tall stone circles; where the red-haired Celts had raced their chariots, and soaked the parched earth with the rich blood of their sacrifices; where the legions of ancient Rome had carried their eagles and driven all before them...there they would bring their pagan enemies to bay and there they surely would destroy them.

The great oak at Iley soared above the countryside and could be seen for miles. It was a mighty landmark that all men knew, to which those still marching towards the King could safely make. With water from the river Wylye right by its side, wood for cooking fires and warmth, shade from the sun for man and beast alike, it was an ideal stopping place from which to launch an attack. Though no men knew exactly what the enemy's intentions were, nor had the King made an appearance since the muster, there was a strong feeling throughout the army that the battle must be soon. While the enemy were all in one place and before the men of the Fyrd began to lose their courage and sneak away to their homes and farms. The longer the enemy could delay a fight, the greater was their chance of defeating their Saxon enemies, and Alfred's war-leaders all knew it!

*

*A*ll afternoon the men rested, visited the armourers and farriers who had set up their field forges with charcoal, bellows and anvils in half a dozen different places which both men and horses visited for hooves to be checked, sprung rivets to be hammered into place...and where weapons of every sort could be sharpened on grind stones in showers of sparks and an endless shriek of stone on metal. Many men had their own hand stones with which they honed their blades to incredible sharpness, sufficient to split silk if it was dropped across the edge.

As night drew on, the clouds thickened from the west and thunder growled and rumbled angrily, hammering across the heavens as great flashes of blue-white fire jagged down and lit up the hills. No rain fell, but the darkened sky was filled with menace and with crows and ravens flying home to roost, their mournful caarking dinning on the ears as they passed overhead going north. Many said they were pointing the way to the place of slaughter, where they could expect to feed on the eyes and entrails of the dead!

Here also, in a hollow close by the oak, was a curved earthwork, like an amphitheatre, and here the King's men raised a great pavilion with a rough timber dais at one end, and a host of benches and trestle tables, on a vast carpet of rush matting dyed in different colours. Strewn with herbs, and with iron braziers for warmth in every corner, laden with fruit wood that burned with scented smoke, the whole area was designed to make any man feel welcome, the leaping firelight and the lamps on every table driving back the shadows of the coming night.

And once more Alfred's call went out to all the thegns and war-lords who had assembled the night before, only this time the word passed by the King's messengers throughout the camp carried the certain stamp of the King's authority. From every corner of the host those leaders of his men who had been summoned streamed in, their minds alert, their senses raised for battle, and when they had all assembled, Brioni, Judith and Maritia amongst them, the King himself was there to greet them.

Behind him on the dais, on chairs and stools and benches around a long table laden with lamps and drinking bowls, sat his most senior war-lords, his bishops and Ealdormen, Heardred and Leofric amongst them and, to Brioni's great surprise, the huge figure of Hugo the Bearmaster at the end of the table.

Long they stood and cheered their King, stamping their feet and hammering their fists on the crude tables that had been set up for their comfort, shouting out his name and hooting and hurrahing him until the noise was almost beyond bearing. And all the time Alfred stood on the dais and marvelled at their welcome, until he raised his hands and slowly the noise subsided, while more ale was drawn from supplies brought in by wagon, until the King began to speak.

"My friends," he said, looking round the wide tented area before him, "Guthrum and the whole Danish host lie camped not more than ten miles from us at the foot of the Waste Down at Royal Edington...*Ethandun* as many of you know it. It is where we thought they would be," he continued, moving to the very edge of the timber stage, where he looked down at them all gathered before him, every face looking up into his eyes.

"Not at Bratton camp on the tops, where there is no water or sustenance for their host, and for the thousands of horses in their train; but at the bottom. There water flows freely, and there are ditches and banks for them to shelter

271

behind…and from where they can retreat back to their fortress at Chippenham with greater ease than ever they would achieve from Bratton, with its murderous drops and steep banks on every side."

"How do you know this, my Lord King?" a huge grizzled warrior called out to him from the floor.

"Because I have been into their camp myself, Wulfric," Alfred answered him, a bold smile on his face, to first a stunned silence and then a rising crescendo of shouts and cries of amazement and dismay. "I went there last night with Hugo the Bearmaster to meet with the one man who has been constant amongst the enemy since Chippenham fell, the Norse Skald, Grimnir Grimmersson. He has been my eyes and ears these many months, working with Hugo, and with Leofric Iron Hand whom you all know," he said, indicating Leofric now sitting astonished amongst the King's most valued warleaders.

So that was what Hugo had been doing last night! Sneaking off to see Grimnir with the King beside him! He was both amazed and appalled at the risk that Alfred had taken; no wonder his Ealdormen had been so unsettled at last night's meeting. They must have been absolutely horrified at Alfred's decision. Alfred *was* Wessex! Lose him and you lost everything. And it wasn't as if the Danes didn't know who he was either. He had negotiated with them face-to-face both at Wareham and at Exeter, and had fought them at Wilton first and then at Merton, and throughout the spring. The King had taken a shattering risk even approaching the Danish encampment, let alone entering it, even though he had been with Hugo.

"That is why I was not with you last night, nor during your march this morning," the King continued blandly as if he had done nothing extraordinary, while all around him gasped at his doing so dangerous a thing. "Instead we mingled with their warriors, joked and laughed with them, and listened to their hopes and dreams, and to their fears. And while Hugo and I were at their camp fires last night with my harp and his pipe and tabor, Grimnir was playing to their leaders in their hall.

"They are tired of the war; tired of having to fight and struggle and bleed for every foot of Wessex soil; for every beast they wish to steal and every chicken; for every wretched peasant's life they tear out and every house and hovel they burn down. They were planning to sit tight where they are, amongst the banks and ditches that surround the lodge, where they have plenty of water and good supplies…"

"Like Reading after Ashdown, my Lord King!" Heardred called out.

"And Wareham and Exeter," another added bitterly. "Where they can extract a bargain, and then move on again."

"What they always do!" Heardred added to a chorus of groans.

"Like Thanet, twenty years ago!" Brihtnoth said darkly. "And, as the Lord Heardred has said, they have been doing it ever since! Once they have settled themselves in, we have never managed to shift them by force of arms. Only by negotiation and the giving of hostages whom they later kill when they break their word."

"And once settled even the strongest warriors lose heart," Aethelnoth chipped in, "and the Fyrd pack up and go back to their farms, so that all that are left are the royal companions!"

"Those heathen bastards are snakes in every sense of the word," Aelfric of Hampshire added in his gruff voice, "and like snakes they need to be trodden on and destroyed, before they have the time to slip away!" And all those gathered there agreed, murmuring and nodding their heads at Aelfric's words until Alfred hushed them once more with his hands.

"You see?" Alfred questioned them all, hands on hips, head thrust forward towards them. "Lord Britnoth is right, so is Aethelnoth and Lord Aelfric. You all know it for a fact, that time is our greatest enemy! Time, not just the presence of the Great Army. If there is no battle soon, the bulk of our army will begin to melt away. Disillusionment will set in and those God-damned pagans will have won by default. So I went disguised as a gleeman, with Hugo to accompany me; to meet with Grimnir and see what we could do. He to play to the Viking lords, to their High King, Guthrum, and to the Lord Oscytel, king of the Jomsvikings, in their hall...and we to mingle with their army. I know all the old lays and the soft songs the Vikings like, and I can play the harp as well as any man."

"*A harper?* Our King disguised as a harper?" a great voice called out, appalled. "Splendour of God, Alfred, you might have been killed and all Wessex lost on account of it!"

"Yes, Aethelstan!" the King shouted back to the tall, gaunt warrior who had leaped to his feet. "I took a risk, that is what leaders do. And my Council were as horrified as you are. But someone had to go and find out just what the enemy were planning," he said, waving his arms in the direction of the Danish host.

"Do you know the old Norse Sagas?" he demanded, looking around at all of them. "The myths and legends of the Danish people? Their songs of home and hearth? No! Why should you? *But I do!*" he shouted out, tapping his chest. "I learned them when I was a young Aethling with little better to do. But not even I could rouse their leaders as they needed to be roused, and I dared not enter their hall for then I would have been recognised for certain. For that I needed an expert, a man they all knew and respected, a man who could

273

stir their hearts and souls like no other. Grimnir Grimmersson!" And turning he beckoned to the wide entrance of the enormous pavilion, and through the flaps came the slight figure of the famous Norse Skald, with his silver hair, scarlet boots and plaid cape, his green harp bag on his back, and all there stood up and shouted their acclaim.

"My Lord King," the little man said in his precise voice, when the noise finally abated, bowing deeply as he did so. "I am come to report as you asked me to. My time with Guthrum and the Great Army is now passed. I am yours to command as always."

"Welcome, welcome!" Alfred beamed at him, his eyes sparkling. "You have served me with great loyalty and boundless courage. Now I need you to tell my people what you know and how your performance was received," and turning back to his own great chair, he sat down, picked up his gold-rimmed drinking horn and supped deeply while Grimnir addressed the leaders of the army, who strained the heads to see him and their ears to hear his words.

"It is true what your King has said," he called out, looking across the mass of faces whose eyes were fixed on his. "A good player is always welcome, and the Danes like their music thick and strong, as you do. And it is true that the enemy are tired of fighting. Many just want to go home. The Lord Leofric, in particular, has wounded them deeply, especially the Lord Oscytel and his Jomsvikings. He has damaged their reputation as fearless warriors, slain his crews and taken his silver. As have many of you all, I know, since your King showed you the way.

"When I met with Hugo and Alfred the talk amongst the leaders was all of staying put. Of taking hostages and demanding tribute, the old story of Danegeld; the enemy know your weaknesses of old. They just didn't want to fight!" and a sigh of dismay went through the room like a winter's gust amongst bare trees.

"But with the help of the Bearmaster, and of your King, amongst their common soldiery outside…and my playing to their leaders in their hall, to Guthrum and the Lord Oscytel, with all my skill, we convinced them that this time they would win. This time they would defeat their enemies once and for all, and we left them stamping their feet, banging their ale pots and swearing vengeance and retribution on the whole Saxon nation and the disreputable, scruffy bog-wight they call a king!"

"*Me*, my warriors!" Alfred exclaimed loudly with a booming laugh, leaping up to join Grimnir at the front of the dais. "I, who have fought and wrestled with them from Athelney, with Aethelnoth of the Somerseatas and his thegns by my side; whom Leofric has tormented from Ford and from Battlesbury Rings; whom the Lords Edwin and Harold of Southampton, Earl

274

Brihtnoth, Aelric of Hampshire and many others have harried far and wide. We have brought the enemy to this place, and now, with Grimnir's help, and that of Hugo the Bearmaster, *they are coming out to fight!*

"They will move out from Edington at dawn to take the roadway to Westbury and meet us in battle at the foot of the downs, where they can anchor their line against that escarpment, with water for their men and horses and clear space behind to retreat to Chippenham should the day turn against them.

"But they do not know that we are so close. Their scouts have not come so far towards us. They are too confident; it is a failing of theirs. We will march out while the moon is still high and try and catch them in the open, in extended order; or stretched across our line of march, it matters not, for there we will defeat them!" And with a great belling cry that rang round the densely packed pavilion, he roared out to them: "*God aid us!* ***Death to the Danes!!***"

And their reply was as deafening and clamorous as anything he could have wished for. A huge howl of defiance, a paean of victory that carried beyond the tented walls to the thousands camped out all around it who picked up the cry until the whole Saxon host seemed to be baying for blood and stamping their feet. The sound went on and on in crashing waves that roared and seethed about them until finally it was swept up by the wind and vanished in the reeling darkness.

Chapter Thirty Five

With that all his commanders began to leave, streaming out into a night made sparkling by the myriad firefly beacons that lit each tiny campsite and shelter around the giant clearing where the King's pavilion had been pitched. Above them the clouds had parted, the dry storm of earlier blown away, and the moon shone bright. To the east all was dark and still, and there was time for just a few hours of sleep before the host must rise; to the west a faint tangerine line still showed where the sun had finally departed.

Time for Alfred's priests and bishops to break the host and share the sacrament with any who wished to confess their sins before going into battle. Time for the pledging of friendships and the swearing of vows, for making sure the charms one trusted in were safe, those little things that men cling to when the appalling furore of a bloody field bursts in upon the senses; when kill or be killed is the only thing that stands between life and death. Those brief moments when friendship and honour mean more than a whole skin, when flight becomes impossible and only death remains; when faith in your God and in your comrades, in the strength of your arm and the singing mettle of the steel in your hand, is all that stands between you and eternity.

*

Back at their own fireside, Leofric, Brioni and Heardred called all their leaders to them to tell them what Alfred had decided. And there Edwin and Harold came across to join them, with Judith, Hugo, Julio and Maritia.

"Well, you are a dark horse, and no mistake," Leofric said to the giant Bearmaster, easing himself down onto a canvas stool beside their own fire. "Brioni saw you just as you were setting out. Sent me to follow you."

"I saw you looking at me," Hugo replied, reaching for a bowl of ale from Maritia's hand. "And did my best to hurry the King forward. He so didn't want anyone to know what he was doing."

"I am not surprised!" Leofric exclaimed. "It was a crazy thing to do! Utterly reckless. If he had been caught, or slain, that would have been the end of everything! I am surprised his Council did not tie him up and toss him in a corner!"

"But he was right!" Brioni said, stooping to fill her own horn from the cauldron of spiced ale on the fire. "Someone had to go in and find out what those bastards were planning. And a gleeman was the perfect foil. As Grimnir said, 'a good player is always welcome', and Alfred knows the lays and sagas, and can play, while we all know how brilliant Grimnir is with his harp and clever words. That man could charm the birds from the trees; our own Orpheus!"

"Brioni is right," Hugo growled in his deep voice, pulling his huge bearskin cloak about his shoulders. "Our own Orpheus indeed, who lulled the monster Cerberus to sleep. Grimnir alone could make the leader's hearts swell with triumph. But it needed someone to be amongst the warriors around their campfires as well. Men who would not know the King from Adam; whose confidence was low, were thinking of home and sweethearts and living a peaceful life. Thirteen years the Vikings have been trying to seize Wessex, and it is still not over yet! Now they must fight for their leaders again. So, while Grimnir stirred Guthrum and Oscytel into coming out to fight...Alfred and I played and sang to their soldiers of their homes and of their families. The kind of sentimental songs that soldiers far from home love to hear."

"So, while their leaders were filled with determination and bruising for a fight," Edwin said, poking the fire with a stick, "their army was filled with melancholy and a desire to go home. Should make an interesting combination." And they all paused for thought, while the flames pulsed and flared before them, blue, green, orange and fiery yellow.

"Well, this is it!" Leofric said after a while, putting his arm round Brioni's shoulders. "This is what we have all fought and trained for. Ours will be the greatest single war-band, next to the King's personal guard, in the whole Saxon host!"

"Have any of you fought in a great battle before?" Hugo asked in his quiet rumble, looking round at them all as they lounged round the fire and supped their ale.

"No," Leofric replied. "I haven't. Heardred?"

"Me, neither. I joined Alfred's host after Ashdown, just before his brother died, and I was down with a fever at Wilton, and on detached duty at Merton."

"Well, I have been," the big man went on. "Against the Danes in Frankland, before I came across the water, I was a soldier then. If there is one thing you must do, apart from fight like demons, it is to stick together. Don't allow yourselves to be drawn too far forward. Keep your shields linked together and walk towards the enemy until the last moment, only then rush them. If you run too soon you will never last the day; and remember where your horse lines are."

"Our horses?" Brioni asked, surprised.

"Yes! Make sure your horses are kept close behind your battle lines, and in secure hands. You never know when you may need them. Either to follow up the enemy if they really break…or to escape if your own lines are breached and defeat seems inevitable. And don't let the Danes lure you into disaster. Watch them and beware. They are the masters of the feigned retreat! Keep your shields high and your heads down, and your short swords in your hands. Remember those rules and you should be alright. The shield wall is a terrible place, and a great battle is a terrible affair!"

"That is sound advice, Hugo, and I thank you for it," Leofric answered him. "We have practised building and holding the shield wall all spring. And have used it against Oscytel's Jomsvikings in more than one bitter skirmish, but never in a great battle of thousands.

"As for not being drawn too far forwards, the King means for us to follow them hard at every moment, and not let them get away from us as they have done in the past. As Hugo has said," he went on, looking across his own war-leaders to those others who had closed in on them while he had been speaking: to Beornred, Finnar, Trausti, Eadberht and Raedwald, "the Heathen are past-masters of the feigned retreat, running at speed for even a mile, without breaking their lines, only to turn round and face their enemies in full battle order when the Fyrd are strung out and exhausted, and can be cut down in their thousands and destroyed.

"That is what happened at Wilton, and Merton. They ran, our men got strung out, the Fyrd all over the place, many pausing to loot the dead, when the enemy stopped, turned, and charged back into a totally disorganised pursuit and our host broke and fled, leaving the Danes to hold the place of slaughter. Tomorrow it will be different!"

"Remember though, Leofric," Brioni broke in urgently, "it is Oscytel whom we want. Let others of Alfred's army, Aethelnoth, Aelfric and Brihtnoth, worry about Guthrum. Oscytel is the key to this battle, I am sure of it. If he falls it will break their hearts!"

"I am not forgetting that, my love," he answered her calmly. "You, me, Beornred, Trausti, Finnar and all the others know just what has to be done. So," he continued briskly, looking at them all clustered round the fire, "we will take the right wing, as the King has ordered us, with Cadoc and the archers immediately behind us to give us covering fire. You, Heardred, with Edwin and Harold, must take the flanks with all your companions and their men beside you. That way we will not hamper each other. Hannes will guard the

278

banner, and I will put a strong company of axe and spearmen to protect him. I want Aetheridge to organise our horse lines, with Osbert to help him, if you are agreeable, Heardred?"

"That's fine," the big Saxon war-lord replied. "But you will need more than two men!"

"That's right. One man to six horses, and when our advance begins they are to follow up behind. Not too close, my friend, but close enough for them to reach us quickly when the enemy line breaks down. Then we really will be able to hunt the bastards down. At Ashdown our warriors were too tired to follow the Heathen at their heels. This time there must be no such mistake."

"But that will mean over sixty men, Leofric!" Beornred exclaimed, shocked.

"That is a small price to pay for total success. And besides, it will give us a mounted reserve for us to call on should such a thing be needed."

"Won't people think you craven to have your mounts so near the battle line?" Judith queried anxiously, her hand on Heardred's arm. "Unnerve our people? Make them think we are going to abandon them?"

"Not so," Hugo interrupted. "Fighting on horseback is the latest thing. The Franks do it all the time."

"But this is not Frankland, Hugo," Brioni cautioned him. "Here we still fight our battles in the old way, on foot behind a shield wall. Raids and skirmishes are one thing, swiftly in and swiftly out again. Battles something else again."

"Don't worry, my Lady," Heardred broke in urgently. "The King means to do the same thing. So do the other lords. We have all better learned the art of war these past months. The Heathen are in for a nasty shock!"

Leofric laughed: "That was well said, my Royal Thegn. Tomorrow, Alfred will hold the centre, the Ealdormen the left wing and us the right, in the way I have just outlined. Now, off with you and get what sleep you can. There is nothing more that we can do until we have the men assembled. We meet again when the light is grey!" And taking Brioni by the hand, he rose and left the fire and together they walked slowly towards their canvas shelter, while all around them their men slept or quietly talked amongst each other, as men do before a great battle.

*

"How do you think it will go tomorrow, Leofric?" Brioni asked later as they lay quietly together.

"Honestly?"

"Of course, my love. Honestly," she replied softly.

"I think it will be a very hard struggle. We will be fighting a professional army, an army that has been together for many years, and one that is used to victory, with a host mostly of poorly-trained and equipped levies straight off the farms. Oh, the thegns and their hearth troops, the King's guards, our boys and those who are with the Ealdormen are as good as you will find anywhere. And as well-armed and armoured as any in the Great Army...but there are not so many of them!"

"Can we really beat them?" she asked anxiously.

"Yes, my darling, this time, despite the logic, I think we can. This time the men really believe that they will win, and we have learned, after Wilton and Merton, how to beat them at their own game. Alfred's fighting out of Athelney, and ours, and others, like Edwin and Harold, have shown that the Heathen can be beaten. He has given the people back their pride. They greeted him with great joy yesterday. You heard them! I am surprised the Danes didn't hear them their shouts were so loud. And who wouldn't follow a king who disguised himself as a gleeman and went into the enemy's camp?"

"That was an outrageous thing to do, sweetheart. Beyond foolhardy!" she exclaimed. "I couldn't believe the King would take such a terrible risk."

"But he did, came out of that unscathed and full of honour. He made our hearts beat higher. Even the fyrdsmen are boasting of what they will do on the battlefield tomorrow."

"And Oscytel?" she asked, raising herself up on one elbow to look down at him.

"Oscytel's time has come," he growled back at her. "Of that much I am certain, and I believe he knows it too. When he sees your father's banner, and all our shields with the foxhead surrounding him, he will read his destruction in their teeth and wild eyes. God alone knows when that will come, nor by whose hand, but be very certain, my precious heart, that before the shadows fall again we will hold the place of slaughter, and that evil demon will be food for the crows and ravens!"

"I feel it too, Leofric," she answered him, kissing him lightly. "But I feel the presence of Death as well. Hold me tightly, sweetheart, for I am afraid. I hear the voices of the Old Ones and of my family calling to me on the wind to honour my vow. And I know that I must...but how, in the press of battle and before such an enemy, am I to do that? I feel my courage slipping from me, and yet I know that somehow I must face him tomorrow and win!"

"Don't be afraid, my darling," Leofric answered her, gathering her into his arms and wrapping them tightly around her. "You will not be alone on that battlefield. I will be in front of you. Beornred, Finnar, Trausti, Raedwald, the whole war-band will be with you, our shields and our weapons will protect you, and together we will pull him down so that you can thrust cold steel into his heart. Oh, Heart of Christ, Brioni, I love you!"

And rolling over he held her close and pressed her head into his shoulder, rocking her as he would a little child until sleep claimed them both; while the darkness steadily faded in the east as the cold light of early dawn crept with pale, searching fingers about the whole encampment.

*

*T*en miles away, in Edington, Guthrum and his commanders sat with their drinking horns at a long table in the old Royal Lodge that they had taken as their headquarters, while servants moved amongst them with roasted meats and large leather jacks of heather beer. Legs stretched out, and bellies full, they were filled with determination, and the confidence given them from Grimnir's playing, to go out in the morning and finish the job of Wessex's conquest once and for all.

"By Odin, that was spirited music," Guthrum grunted, stroking his beard, his arms clinking with the gold and silver arm rings that almost covered them. "Just what I needed to hear on the eve of battle, that Grimnir is a magician. He could put heart into the dead! We will go out there today and slaughter them!"

"But that wasn't the plan, Guthrum!" objected Bjorn Gunborg, one of his most respected veteran commanders, from the end of the table.

"No, my friend, but this lodge is not the place to make a final stand. There are no real defences. We need to confront them across their line of march."

"We should have moved the army up to the heights; to Bratton fortress," growled Oscytel, sitting near the king in his black leathers, adorned with heavy gold chains around his neck, his hand on the golden hilt of the jade knife, *Sica*. "There are real defences up there with steep banks all round where we could have defied the Saxons for ever!"

"We have been through this before, Oscytel," Guthrum answered him sharply, his great beard bristling. "There is no water up there, and no supplies. We have thousands of horses and men to feed and water. Do you know how much a horse drinks in a day?"

"No, my Lord King!" the big Dane grunted, his brows furrowed.

"Up to ten gallons, my noble Jarl of Helsing," Guthrum replied bitingly. "And that's without riding them hard in battle. There's nothing up there, Oscytel! *Nothing!* We would simply be trapped until we starved. And how in Odin's name would we get five thousand men off that escarpment in a hurry if

281

we needed to, most of them mounted and many in panic? That edge is so steep we would never be able to get our men away if the enemy broke through as they did at Ashdown. There we were able to ride like the wind for Reading. Here it would be a massacre!"

"*If they broke through?*" Oscytel interrupted with a snort of derision and a wave of his hand. "That bunch of farmers and derelicts? *Sica* says they will lose and she has never been wrong!"

"Don't you dare quote that thing at me!" Guthrum snarled viciously across the table, with a great thump of his fist that rattled everything. "Since your murder of that thegn last January, my fine Lord Oscytel, your powers have waned! Your crews have been slaughtered, your silver taken and you have been duped. Remember Swindon? You set off to destroy that Saxon earsling who had been so tormenting us for weeks…that Leofric, only to find that he had tricked you! Your garrison at Bath was wiped out, my hall at Chippenham was set on fire by his damned doxy, my Guard Commander was slain and I only just got out in the furore that followed. *So don't try to tell me of your powers!*" he raged at him. "And don't forget Ubbi at Cynwit. He thought he had the bastards pinned down and beaten. But they destroyed him! Slew him and his companions and eight hundred of his best men, and captured the Raven banner!! So don't talk to me of farmers and derelicts!"

"They haven't met my Jomsvikings."

"No? Malmesbury, Box, Bradford, Bath? Didn't your men hold those places?"

"Yes, they did. But a battlefield is a very different place. There my men will be invincible!"

"There was a time when I would have believed you," the king growled at him furiously across the table, "But not anymore! We will fight this battle the way I want to. In the open where we have room to manoeuvre. Bratton is out of the question, however tempting it may appear. *Out of the question!*" he shouted, banging his hand down once more. "Here we have plenty of water, good supplies and space to move how we please. We will put our left wing against the escarpment, so that they cannot outflank us, block the roadway with our centre, and then, with our greater numbers, we can wrap them round with our right."

"What are their numbers, Lord King?" asked Olaf Thorhollur, another of his war leaders, just recently come in from Gloucester.

"Some four thousand, maybe a few more," Oscytel replied swiftly. "We outnumber them by more than a thousand. And we are all professionals. They are more armoured farmers than proven fighters. My Jomsvikings will make offal of them!"

282

"But they fight under the banners of their God," another said, looking round the table. "They do not fight alone!"

"Nor do we, you *earsling!*" Guthrum roared at him. "We have Odin on our side, Freya, Thor and Tyr. Odin's ravens, Huginn and Muminn, alone will bring us victory. Just pray if you fall tomorrow, Tostig Ránnulfr, that the Valkyries will carry you to Valhalla…and not take you to Freya's *Fólkvangr* amongst the shadows! Enough!" he shouted out across the table. "We will make sacrifice at dawn, the horses have been chosen, and the witches have cast their runes. Nothing has been left undone."

"Yet the men are fearful," Steinar said, quietly. "They say the thunder and lightning last night are bad omens!"

"Since when has Thor's hammer been a sign for the fearful?" Oscytel said with complete distain. "He is striking the ground to put terror into his enemies. They know that they are in for another beating, like Wilton and Merton. They will fall like grass before the scythes of my Jomsvikings. We will carpet the ground with their dead! We cannot be beaten!"

"Why are the men fearful?" Guthrum demanded sharply, glaring round the table.

"There were two gleemen in the camp yesterday. While Grimnir played to us, they were around the campfires playing sentimental songs. Reminding the men how long they have been fighting away from their homes and families."

"Where did those two come from?" the king demanded fiercely. "How did they get in?"

"They were just a couple of wandering players," Bjorn Gunborg replied, shrugging his massive shoulders, ignoring the king's rage. "One with pipe and tabor, one with an old harp."

"One great big brute, one smaller," Olaf Thorhollur added. "I met with them; they seemed harmless enough. And the men needed some music in their lives. And they like songs about home and family."

"*Sentimental rubbish!*" Oscytel snarled. "The last thing they needed, Thorhollur, was to be reminded of home, from which some have been separated by years! What they needed were good rousing battle songs to put extra heart in them, Beowulf and Grendel!" he exclaimed. "Who vouched for them?"

"Grimnir," Gunborg replied. "He said he had known them from before Chippenham, and I saw no harm in them. They were only here for a while, and it's not as if the enemy are closeby."

"Where is our little Norse Skald?" Oscytel asked, looking round.

283

"Slipped away last night. Off to see some light skirt near Bratton," Ránnulfr said. "You know what he is like."

"Well, have him report back to me when you see him next," Guthrum growled. "I don't want anyone leaving the camp until this business is finished. Then he can write a song to celebrate our victory," he boomed at them, with a great smile. "Raise the men at dawn, get them properly fed and watered and plenty of beer, they'll like that. Fill them with confidence and the will to fight, promise them booty and women in full. Lift their hearts to go out and destroy these Saxon earslings who have defied us for so long, then, when you have got them shouting and roaring, we will do the sacrifices. After that we will march out and form our lines with the men packed in deep, and hold the horses safe behind the shield wall."

"So, my Lord king," the Black Jarl of Helsing said, staring into Guthrum's eyes. "It will be tomorrow."

"Yes, my Lord Oscytel. It will be tomorrow, I can feel it in my bones. Tomorrow we will defeat this Alfred and destroy his army!" And getting to his feet he raised his great gold-rimmed horn and shouted: "*Drink Hael!* Death to Alfred! Victory to the Danes!"

And with a great whoop of excitement, his men leaped to their feet, stools and benches flying everywhere, all concerns wiped away, and bayed their answer: "*Death! Death, and victory to the Danes!*"

Chapter Thirty Six

*T*he Saxon army was roused while the moon still rode high in the sky to light their way, and before the first birds were awake. In mounted battles and bristling companies they marched up the Wylye valley and swung onto the old trackway that led through the burned out ruins of Warminster, past the distant fortress of Battlesbury Rings, now hidden in the mists, and so on to Westbury, Bratton and the Royal Lodge at Edington, *Ethandun*, where all their scouts and spies confirmed the Danes would be waiting.

A fine spring morning, the light turning from black to grey as the moon above them set, slipping below the horizon, everything around them opaque, the trees and hedgerows, magpies chattering in the trees, all shrouded in an early mist that hid the great escarpment beyond their right shoulders. There its wicked slopes and gulleys ran north-east to the Cheverells and Lavingtons, the great plain of Salisbury stretching across its top for miles, while the road at its base swept around its lofty contours to Royal *Ethandun* and the steep slopes of the chalk downs that reared above it.

It was the 8th of May, Thursday, the day named after Thor, that day in the ancient Saxon calendar especially set aside for the great Saxon god of war their ancestors had worshipped in the elder days. It was a day that none of them would forget.

In the van, Alfred rode with his back straight and his eyes constantly on the alert, his bodyguard around him; his priests and Bishop Aethelheah of Sherborne and Werfirth of Worcester close by. Far ahead of the advancing host, and to the sides, rode the scouts, superbly mounted on the best the royal stables had to offer, their mounts sleek and full of stamina, clearing the way ahead as they pushed forward.

He had brought them all together: thegns, companions and armoured Fyrd; proven fighters with byrnie, shield and battle axe, and farmers with leather jerkins, sharpened hoes and billhooks on sturdy poles of ash, the peasant army of Wessex. If they packed in behind the shield wall, and stuck there no matter what, then they would win. If not? He shrugged…then it would not really matter for he would be dead and Wessex would be just a memory. And his dream of a united England? Pouff! Into thin air, and he laughed. He was getting as fatalistic as his enemies, and that was no way for a Christian King to be in on the eve of the greatest battle of his life! And digging in his heels he made his horse prance and curvette across the track, before settling into a fast canter.

Today was a great day on which to be alive, and he laughed again for the sheer joy of it, for the first blush of colour above his head, and the first trill of song from all around him as the morning burst into life at last.

*

Right at the rear, amongst the baggage wagons and long strings of pack animals, mules and horses, rode Aelflaeda, her slight figure made bulky by an ill-fitting leather jacket that she had acquired after the skirmish with Steinar Olafsson, her head covered by a wooden helmet drawn from the common store, with crude iron strips across it, and a thick felt liner to cushion the knotted wood from which it had been made. Keeping such war-gear from the Lady Judith had not been easy, nor had joining the host as it marched out. But she had been helped by one of Heardred's men who had taken a shine to her, and in the shouted confusion of leaving, and in the semi darkness, she had managed to slip away; made easier as the Lady Judith was not accompanying the army, staying behind with Maritia and Oswald and Brioni's two hounds.

Today she would avenge her own torment for what Medraut's slavers had done to her on the wounded stragglers of the Danish host, and she fingered the long-bladed seaxe that the Lord Heardred had given her. Somewhere up ahead of her amidst the immense column of horses and swaggering warriors, beneath the banner now lost to view, was the Lady Brioni whom she had come to admire so much. She was the final reason that she was hidden there amongst the Saxon host.

If she, a woman born into a noble family, could shed a man's blood with the ease of the boldest warrior...then why not herself? Aelflaeda, maid and abigail to the Lady Judith? Her cause was no less just, violently raped, abused and almost left for dead. And she hugged the rightness of it to her heart, her eyes fixed on the endless serpent of spearmen, axemen, archers and mounted warriors in shimmering mail and closed helmets that wound along the roadway ahead of her. Great battalions of armed men, bristling with pointed weapons: with spears, scythes, billhooks, sharpened hoes and sickles; with iron spades and wooden clubs; with lead filled mauls of stone; with bows and swords and bearded axes.

Surely she had as much right to be there as they did, and she gritted her teeth with determination, even as loud shouts and cries rang out and

286

messengers galloped up and down the huge column of marching men and horses with orders from the King.

The enemy had been found.

Not in their line of march as had been hoped for, but strung out in battle formation across the road, barring the way forward and calling the Saxon host to battle.

*

*E*ven as she watched, the Saxon army began its final deployment.

Left and right the huge moving snake began to open out, as the sun broke free of the morning mists to shimmer off the myriad points of spears and hefted weapons, and off the polished mail and helmets of all who had been gathered there. In the van was a great force of mounted warriors to keep the Viking army from making a sudden move against them as the wings and centre formed. The King's banners steadily advancing until they halted some two hundred paces from where the Viking army stood, strung out in packed lines of armoured men.

Now, all who had ridden dismounted and their horses were taken to the rear, where they were either left with selected handlers, or tethered to long ropes staked out above the ground.

Company by company the men were checked and placed in position by their leaders. Thegns and armoured warriors in the front, their great round shields, iron-rimmed and leather-covered, locked in one to the other, left inside right all along the line, where their professional skill and better equipment could best blunt the fury of their enemies. The fyrdhood, and those largely unarmoured peasants who had joined the host, all densely packed in behind them, six, eight, ten deep, jostling, jumping and standing, their weapons in their hands, their hearts thumping; some drunk, some vomiting in fear, some urinating on the trampled grass as they waited for the orders to advance.

And here was the weakest part of Alfred's whole command.

So often many of the Fyrd gave up and fell away after the first charge. Some even ran before the first real contact was made. Ill-trained peasants of the fields do not make good warriors. It is not in their nature. They lack the fire and stomach of the true fighting man. Those who tend sheep and cattle and till the soil do not make killers. And it is killers you need in the shield wall. Brutal men who can thrust and twist their steel in a man's body, rip out a throat, spread a man's brains across the battle line, spill his guts and offal on the bloody ground, and not run screaming mad with fear to leave a gap that an enemy can fill with his own warriors and so break the line.

287

Today, though, was different.

Today, all who had gathered to the muster were grimly determined to see the thing through to the bitter end, to the deaths of all if necessary, and they stood and seethed in their ranks, feet stamping, hands gripping whatever weapon had come to them, eyes steady on their leaders, mouths sternly fixed.

The Heathen had made Free Wessex their plaything. They had exacted undue tribute, razed whole villages to the ground, burned the churches, slain the priests and monks, whored the nuns, taken the people as slaves, and raped and pillaged where they would. For months the borel-folk had suffered every indignity, every bestial usage; the merchants could not trade, towns had been wrecked, noble halls and rich manors had been burned and plundered...even their King forced to flee into the wilderness. Now he had returned, had called for their aid, and they meant to exact full retribution for all that they had suffered at the hands of the pagan Northmen.

*

Alfred looked up and down the long lines of men now standing waiting for the order to advance; looked back at the thousands of horses in his rear, some pegged out in long lines, others held by mounted warriors with a clutch of reins in either fist; looked up at his own great banners flapping and curling in the morning breeze and at the sky above his head now burgeoning with warmth as larks sprang up into the late spring sunshine, and swallows and martins miracled overhead.

And then he turned his face towards the enemy standing in massed lines of armoured men, jeering and shouting at the Saxon host; some hot-heads rushing out to offer single combat; some groups running forward and back again, waving their weapons and shouting curses; some even running out and baring their backsides while their friends howled with laughter and pointed, while swifts screamed over the untrammelled grass between the two armies.

Thousands and thousands of them were stood there beneath the spring sunshine, the whole Great Army, their war shields garishly painted with barbaric splendour in reds and greens and blues, some with strange symbols on them, some with the beasts of the forest: bears and wolves and lordly stags. And all along their lines were banners of eagles, wolves and ravens, and in the centre, beneath his own great raven banner, stood their High King, Guthrum, his bodyguard massed around him, and the bloody heads of two freshly slain horses on great poles on either side. Sheeted with silver and inlaid with gold, they reared up above the Danish host, the blood of their sacrifices still falling on those grouped closely by them.

Finally Alfred swung round towards the places where his Ealdormen stood in all their battle glory, helmets and armour shining, to Aelfric of Hampshire and Aethelnoth of the Somerseatas, their hearth companions clustered round them, their men packed in. Men from Wiltshire, Somerset, Dorset and Hampshire; even from Devon, whom Ealdorman Odda had sent to represent his county, while the rest of the Devon Fyrd guarded the open coastline. Bristling with weapons and filled with battle ardour, their banners of crosses, saints and angels fluttering above them, Alfred saw them all, before turning towards Leofric, Heardred, and all their company beneath the snarling foxhead banner the Iron Hand had made his own. And smiling, beneath his own great banners curling lazily in the early morning breeze, with a word to God on his lips, and the mingled prayers of his priests and bishops in his ears behind him, Alfred took firm grip of his shield, raised his long sword high above his head, and giving a great shout: *"Advance banners! Victory under God! **Death to the Danes!**"* he stepped out towards the enemy.

All along the line there was a rasp of steel and a violent quiver of movement as the Saxon host began its advance, the beauty of the morning broken by the shouts and battle cries of their Viking enemies as the solid Saxon lines approached the Danish host, flags and banners etched against the pale blue sky of the morning, their polished mail dazzling in the sun's fresh brilliance as it lifted itself above the horizon, the icy flitter of steel spear-points, sword-blades and axe-heads like wintry sleet across the battlefield.

In determined silence, save for the shouts of their commanders, they pressed forwards relentlessly, an endless tide of bitter men, rank after rank of armoured warriors and iron helmeted fyrdsmen, all following the streaming banners of their leaders, with the great scarlet dragon of Wessex, and the Fighting Man, rippling above the head of their King and of his royal companions.

Across the fields they went at a steady rush, over the gulleys and ditches that lay between, while their enemies bayed their defiance and hammered their swords against their iron shield rims to keep up their courage, for their hearts were dismayed by the terrible, silent anger of their enemy's swift advance.

Fifty, forty yards to go and the Saxon host paused once more to address its lines, to wait for any scattered forces to gather in behind the leading thegns and heavily armoured warriors of the front ranks. And all the while spears and hand axes were hurled towards them that they jeered and dodged, or batted down with their shields, while from the rear of the Saxon lines massed arrows flew up and fell upon the enemy with barbed fury, making their lines writhe and howl in agony as they burst upon them.

Then, with a great roar, like the booming surf on a storm-wracked shore, the Saxon host unleashed their vengeance and leapt upon their hated Danish foes. Spears levelled, shields locked together, stabbing swords held low, they raced the last few yards that separated them, and with a monstrous, grinding crash the two armies came together.

Toe to toe, Dane and Saxon hewed at one another in demented fury across the war-linden as they strove to hack, stab and thrust their way forward, while the arrows flew in dense barbed showers overhead, piercing soft flesh and thrumming into shield and link-iron byrnie alike.

Suddenly their whole existence had narrowed to a few yards before each man, to the companions who flanked him and the desperate, contorted faces of the enemy whom he was trying to cut down and destroy. Whose face was just inches from his own, whose stinking breath washed over him, whose spittle flew into his eyes as he reached up to pull down his shield with bare hand or bearded axe, so the man behind could thrust his enemy through the throat with spear or sword.

The need to slash, maim and kill was paramount, the only need that existed in the pain-maddened world incarnadine through which they moved, gargoyle-like, hideous blood-boltered caricatures of the husbands, lovers and family men they once had been.

Back and forth the lines swayed in roaring fury, the dead packed in amongst the living in the fierce crush and press of battle, their heads lolling like unmanned puppets, their bodies drunk with death. And overall was the fierce, monstrous music of the fray: the clash of arms, the ringing sound of steel on steel, the shouts and screams of the wounded, the howls of rage, the wild booming of war horns and the brazen scream of trumpets rallying and encouraging the 'dancers' as they leapt and twisted on the bloody ground.

As more and more of the Fyrd arrived and flung themselves in behind the warriors in the front line, thegns and royal companions struggling furiously beside their King against the Danish shield wall, so the pressure against the enemy front line increased. Foot by bloody foot the Saxon army drove the enemy back over their own dead; limbs hacked off, hands severed, fingers crushed, heads broken open in a spray of blood and shattered brain pan, the Danes fought furiously but were forced to give ground before the sheer violence of the Saxon assault, unable to stem the battle-fury that had so enveloped them.

Near the King the iron storm was fiercest as the Danes strove to cut him down, and tear the royal standards from their guardians' hands. Time after time the enemy swept up to the very feet of the thegns and loyal warriors who were grouped about him, only to be beaten back with howls of anguish and frustrated rage. Alfred was the rock upon which their fury burst, his sword and shield turning aside every assault, until his armour was sheeted with the blood of the enemies he had slain, as with bellows and shouts of encouragement he continued to press forwards towards their centre.

There Guthrum fought with the pick of the Danish huscarles all about him, the blood from the morning sacrifices still thickly congealing on his armour. Above him, high on their silver poles, the fat golden pegs that held them there winking in the bright sunshine, were the bloody heads of two noble beasts, their soft eyes glazed in death, their velvet nostrils black with dried blood and the busy flies that fed there.

All about him was the heaving, howling press of battle, both hosts tempest-tossed by the fury of it, and the sweat ran down his face as he strove to stem the tide of the Saxon advance, his axe-head scored and encrusted with the blood and hair of the many he had slain.

Away to his right the great Jarl of Helsing fought with all his usual skill and ferocity. Standing a head taller than most other men, his axe wove a bright, shining pattern of death that no man seemed able to withstand for long. Beneath his black samite flag, with its twin ragged knives in gold, and rimmed with scarlet, his black mail shimmering in the May sunlight, and with his whole war-band and all his captains close about him, he alone seemed to dominate the battle. He alone seemed to draw the most anger towards him, for despite the heaped bodies of those whom he and his men had slaughtered, the Saxons pressed ever more fiercely against his part of the line than anywhere else.

*

*F*orcing their way forward, swords stabbing out and swinging sideways, axes sweeping round and back to clear the way, Leofric led his men with the utmost ferocity into the heart of the battle-storm raging all around him. With Beornred at his side to shield him, Raedwald and Jaenberht with long spears just behind, he drove forward relentlessly, using his great bearded axe to tear down the shield of every enemy before him. Then the two men just behind him would thrust home with their spears, bursting heads and throats apart in wild spouts of blood and brains, shielded from attack by those warriors on either side of them. Nor were they the only packet of warriors driving into the Danish host, for Finnar, Eadberht and Sigweald were doing the same, leaving a bloody trail of butchered sword-Danes in their wake.

Behind Leofric was Brioni, Brain-Biter in her right hand, its pointed blade thickly badged with blood, her strengthened wicker shield in her left, with Trausti and Ricberht on either side, with sword and long spear, to keep her safe in all the screaming press of battle. And at their rear was Cadoc and his archers, pouring their volleys of barbed death into the Danish host with matchless power. Bending and loosing, bending and loosing until the sky above them was streaked with death, arcing their arrows up over the heads of the enemy to plunge down amongst all those who sought to bring them aid, and amongst their horse lines, and then point blank into their wild faces whenever a gap in their ranks made that possible. Thick volleys of arrows that drove the Danish lines steadily backwards in their sector, bursting throats and bodies at every strike, until they were likely to break and fall apart.

But, despite all their efforts, they had not managed to come up with Oscytel's own war-group, though they could clearly see where he was fighting. His head thrown back as he roared on his Jomsvikings in their distinctive black armour and black leather-covered shields, the shimmering black samite flag with its great golden zigzag knives fluttering boldly above his head

"'Ware left, Brioni!" Leofric called out suddenly above the raging press, as a Danish spearman rushed in upon her. "*'Ware left!*", but even as she brought her shield up to take the blow, Trausti cut the man down beside her, parrying his thrust and cutting down at his exposed neck, severing the thick corded muscles that bound his head onto his shoulders. The blood spurting out to cover them both with scarlet rain as the Dane fell with a wild shriek to the torn ground beneath them.

But before she could give her thanks, she was in action herself, leaping forward to drive Brain-Biter into a snarling Danish face that suddenly appeared in a gap before her. Leaping to fill it with shield and body, she thrust her blade into the man's open mouth to pierce him to the brain in a fierce spray of blood and bone, as their line lurched forward another pace and the man's body was trampled beneath their Saxon feet.

"*Back!* Back, my Lady," Beornred shouted at her, covering Leofric with his shield. "Sigweald, take her place. Trausti, Ricberht, cover her! Now, forwards, *forwards!*" he bellowed, as Leofric's axe swung once more into the faces of their Danish foes, hacking through shield and body-armour alike with terrifying force, until none there were in the enemy line who would face him, so he could step back while Raedwald and Alnoth the Swordsman filled his place, shields high and blades flashing in front of the enemy who flung themselves in fury against their shield wall.

"How's the Lord Heardred?" she shouted at him, as he slipped back from the front line, behind the standard that Hannes had kept flying high.

"Still on his feet, and fighting like a tiger. But he is making no better progress than we are. Our line is too broad, we need to try something else."

"The pressure is too great on our left," she threw back at him, breaking off abruptly to urge on her men. "The Danes outreach our line, but we cannot outflank them on the right, because of the escarpment. I can see that heathen butcher, but cannot bring our banner before him. Sweet Mary, Leofric, but he fights well!"

"So do all in the Great Army. But this battle is not going well for them. I don't believe their hearts are in it. Look how Alfred presses in on them. Their line must have been forced back nearly a hundred paces. We are making things too hot for them. You mark my words," he said as a fresh roar went up from all along the Saxon front as once more they pushed the Viking army back. "Any moment now they will try and break off. I can feel it in my bones. Never have they had to fight so hard since Ashdown."

"What then?" she asked breathlessly as Eadwine of Ford, with Alfweald beside him, led a fresh band of shouting fyrdsmen past them to pile in behind where Finnar, Eadberht and Sigweald were carving a space out of the enemy line.

"We do as the King has said. We follow them hard, they mustn't get the chance to run clear and face about. And we mustn't allow ourselves to get too spread out and separated!"

"And then?"

"And then it's as I said. Our front is too broad. As we follow them we will form the boar's snout! The flying wedge we have practised so often. Me, Beornred, Finnar and the others at the point, long spears out and shields on either side, more spearmen on the flanks; axe and swordsmen, with you, Trausti, Ricberht, Sigweald and every man we have packed in behind to give us weight. As you saw your father try and break out that awful morning…only we will be trying to break in!"

*

*I*ndeed, Leofric's judgement of the situation was right. The Danish host had no liking for such hard-pressed, bitter conflict. It wasn't that they were afraid - just temporarily outfaced by the ferocity of the Saxon attack. They needed time to sort themselves out; time to separate the living from the dead, to re-organize their lines and give themselves some rest. With swift, practised movements they suddenly pulled down their bloody devices, gripped their weapons in their hands, seized hold of their wounded, and giving a single great shout they turned their backs and ran.

For those who had not seen such a thing, it looked for all the world as if they had been routed, as if the Danish line had been broken and all were fleeing for their lives, as those who could mounted, and those who couldn't ran. But those who had fought in the long Danish wars and served the Wessex host before knew that this was a feint; a cunning ruse to draw them on, as they had been at Wilton and Merton; when the enemy, after a mile, had turned and charged back into the battle, catching the Saxons disorganised and spread out, and had slaughtered them. For this was no beaten rabble; most ran together in a solid black line, their ranks still packed together, their shields slung loosely on their backs as they raced away across the plain. And those mounted kept pace with the others, led by their king and his hearth companions, while many of his commanders like Steinar Olafsson, Bjorn Gunborg and Tostig Ránnulfr stayed with the men to give them heart and steady them when the time came to turn again and face their enemies.

But Alfred had not fought the pirates so many times for nothing.

As soon as he saw the dripping heads coming down he knew what was to follow, and roaring at his commanders to keep the front line steady, he chased after the enemy. A Saxon could run as well as any pirate. His men were hungry for victory, and no warrior can feel fear when the open back of his foe is fleeing away before him. So the Saxon army followed hard, and for once the Fyrd stayed with the armoured warriors who had shielded them so long. No man dropped out to loot the bodies of their fallen foes, or paused to wander across the littered field in search of jewelled swords, gold-encrusted axes, arm rings or great torques of gold and silver. Their courage was high, they would keep faith with their King.

And as they ran, Leofric and Brioni signalled Heardred and his men to move further over to the left, for Harold and Edwin to close the gap between them, and for Hannes to carry their banner closer to where the Black Jarl of Helsing had been fighting.

Chapter Thirty Seven

*A*t the rear Aelflaeda raced forwards with the best of them, flinging herself up on one of the spare horses as the thousands of chargers that were behind the Saxon lines were swept forward by their handlers.

Gone was her desire to wreak vengeance on those Danish huscarles too crippled with their wounds to run or stumble with their comrades. Instead she was now determined to find the Lady Brioni. In some strange way she felt strongly drawn to her. It was as if something deep inside her was responding to a silent call, and with her eyes immovably fixed upon the distant banner of the snarling fox's mask, she began to outstrip the men with whom she had taken station, her mount's pounding hooves and her panting breath one and the same as she followed the Saxon host as it chased after their enemies.

*

*J*ust behind her, unknown to all, their hard leathery pads flying along the track, mouths gaping, tongues free, bounded Bran and Utha, desperate to find their mistress whose scent they had followed since breaking free of Maritia's control.

Awoken before dawn when the army had left they had howled and called for Brioni with all their hearts...then torn, gnawed and worried at the tethers with which Hugo and Maritia had tied them to great 'U' shaped stakes near Oswald until they had burst free. And before Hugo, Marcus or Julio could stop them, they had leaped for the ruined trackway the army had so recently taken. Muscles bunched and hearts pounding they had followed the thick scent the army had left behind them with the ease of long practice, chasing after the Saxon host as if they were tracking a huge pack of wolves. And ever amongst them was the tantalising scent of the one they loved above all othes, to whose aid they had come in the ruined forge the night the wolves had attacked her, who had guarded her against the bear, and beside whom they had fought at every skirmish since.

Huge and powerful, their fighting collars armed with sharpened spikes of iron, they followed their bristling noses with deadly intent, covering the ground with dauntless ease, racing forwards to join the Lady of Foxley in her last desperate struggle against the Danes.

*F*or nearly a mile, eight furlongs, the Danish host rushed north towards the distant safety of their fortress at Chippenham as the Danes tried to free themselves from the Saxon battle line, but their enemies had no intention of giving them a respite. With an energy and determination few knew they had, the Saxons followed the hurrying Danes so closely that they were given no opportunity to break free, and eventually they were forced to turn at bay.

This time, as they re-planted the now foully stinking horse-head standards, Leofric noted immediately that they were only thrust upon common spear shafts. The famous totem poles in silver and gold that they had used to start with, now being carried by a number of different warriors scattered through their host.

"See that, my friends?" he roared out to his men as the Danish lines stabilised once more before them, their men beating their swords against their shield rims. "The Heathen are not so sure of victory now that we have chased them a full league or more. Look how they have hidden their magic poles. Now, gather in behind me as we have practised so many times, and follow the boar's snout to victory!"

With the subtle change in position that they had effected as they had run, Leofric, Brioni and all their men, with Heardred and Siward on their right flank, and Edwin and Harold on their left, were now almost opposite the place where Oscytel's giant figure was once again preparing to cause the Saxons the utmost dismay. Now, with their lines fixed, Alfred swept his army back into the fray, as baying like hounds at the kill, his Saxon host charged once more into their Viking foe with as much energy and fury as if the day had just begun.

With his Jomsvikings packed in all about him, the Black Jarl did not need a shield, for they covered him with their own, protecting him from arrows, hand axes and the fury of their enemies in hand-to-hand combat, freeing him to wield his great axe two-handed in a devastating display of battle fury. There were none who came within its deadly sweep who could long withstand him. Shield, helmet, ring-mail harness, all were cleaved through as though they had been paper, and the blood of his victims ran down his black armour in thick, steaming runnels. He was indomitable. None marked him or even dented his helmet or scored across his battle-harness, and no arrow pierced his flesh, though many stuck in his armour like the quills of a porcupine.

*

*P*ulled back some thirty paces or so from the main Saxon front line where the raging conflict had begun again even more fiercely than before, Leofric, Beornred and Finnar carefully made their final preparations. Drawing in their flanks to form an open triangle, spears thrust out along both sides, they armed the very point of their boar's snout with the special long spears that Leofric had ordered to be made. Nine feet long with great leaf-shaped heads and long steel shanks, these were the boar's tusks, each carried by three men, closed helms on their heads and shields on their backs. Close behind strode Leofric and Beornred his shield bearer, Finnar, Raedwald and all their shield companions packed in around them; Brioni, Trausti and her war-band in the centre, their fyrdsmen piling in to give them added weight. While the rear of their bristling wedge was filled with Cadoc and his archers, a single quiverful of barbed arrows across each shoulder, and all armed with swords and battle-hammers at their waists.

On either side Heardred, Edwin, Harold and their companions waited with their men, ready to rush in and exploit the breach that Leofric was intending to create as he burst through the Danish shield wall. This would be where it would all end, one way or another, and they took their time to ensure that everyone was in his place before readying themselves for their assault on Oscytel and his whole command. Meanwhile the Saxon host fiercely strove with Guthrum's forces, the howling frenzy of the battle now reaching a crescendo as both forces fought for mastery of the other, their lines swaying this way and that, as first one, and then the other drove themselves back and forth, and the bodies of the dead piled up amongst them.

Finally Leofric was satisfied, and strapping his war-shield firmly across his back, he picked up his fighting axe in both hands and flexed his shoulders once more to fight two handed, as did the dark-faced enemy whom he and Brioni had sworn to kill "God aid you, Brioni, my love," he said, drawing her to him, "and bring you safely through this bloody fray. Dear God, I love you so!"

Beneath the rippling banner of her father's House, he briefly held her to his heart and kissed her face. There, with the rage and torment of the battle all before them, he held her fiercely in his arms while their men shouted and stamped their feet, and arrows flew and flickered overhead.

Then he put her gently from him and moving past Hannes and all the warriors grouped about the standard, to where Beornred, Raedwald and the others were standing, he hefted his axe and cocked it over his shoulder.

"*At the run!*" he bellowed, without turning round. "*Advance the banner. Let the horns and trumpets blow. Death to Oscytel!* **Victory to the King!**"

And with that Hugo's buccinas pierced the roar of battle with a brazen paean of sound that few had heard before, while the horns blew, *Hoom! Hoom! Hoom!* and the whole armoured phalanx began to move, slowly at first then faster and faster as they neared the Saxon battle line fighting furiously to keep the Danish host from pushing forward once again.

Hearing the shouts and brazen trumpets, and the wild booming horns, the Saxon front line swept apart to let them through, and like a fiercely cast javelin Leofric and his men drove through the gap shouting like madmen and flung themselves at the enemy line.

From the moment the horns and trumpets blew, the Danes had little time to brace themselves before the boar's snout struck home, and the shock of the impact burst iron plates from their rivets, shattered bones and flung helmets to the ground as the Danish line reeled under the sheer violence of the assault. The great spears at the front pierced shields and men together, bursting through wood and armour, tearing men apart and spilling their offal onto the torn and bloodied ground. And now both sides struggled for firm footholds in the thick grass, slippery with blood and entrails. The earth steamed under the sun, the weapons clashed and the screams and cries of the wounded rose ceaselessly on every side.

At the very point of the crash, where the boar's tusks thrust out at the Danish shield wall, the carnage was indiscriminate, vicious and bloody as the Danish huscarles in their front line were hurled backwards and then hacked down. The Saxon spearmen on the flanks of the wedge did frightful execution on their enemies, both sides suffering terrible injuries: hands lopped off, shields and armour split through to the very backbones of those who bore them and heads struck clean off, the sagging trunks fountaining blood that splattered friend and foe alike. Some were crushed to death by the very shock of the charge itself, chests caved in and limbs all torn asunder. Yet others were spitted through the body, their life's blood gushing out upon the barbarous spear-points that had impaled them.

Left and right Leofric's hearth companions hewed their way towards the great rippling black standard that rose above Oscytel's head, led by Leofric, Beornred on one side with his great war shield, Finnar on his other, and by Raedwald and Sigweald with long spear and sword in hand. Shields held high they cut, stabbed and thrust their way into the very heart of the Danish host, while on either flank the remainder of the Saxon army, with Alfred at their head, flayed their enemies with hard steel, with sword, axe, spear and wooden club.

*

298

*I*nexorably Leofric's initial advance slowed as the Black Jarl rallied his forces and rushed to stem the flood of men and iron that now threatened his position. But with the swift arrival of Heardred, Edwin and Harold and their whole war-bands, the Fyrd piling in behind them as before, the added pressure forced the Danes back again, while from the rear Cadoc and his archers poured their last volleys of arrows into the twisted, feral faces of their foe, before dropping their bows and rushing in on their enemies with sword and war-hammer to add their fury to the battle.

And the noise was tumultuous, a howling cacophony that dulled the senses and brutalised the mind. The screams and groans of the wounded and the dying, the shouts of rage and hatred, the clattering of sword on shield, the thud of blows, the ring of tempered steel as blade met blade, the whole crashing, grinding roar of two great armies at each other's throats rising to a deafening crescendo as the enemy line first wilted, buckled and was finally torn apart.

They were through at last!

Now they could wrap up the enemy line, bring up their horses and harry a fleeing enemy across the countryside. And as the Danish shield-wall broke up into murderous confusion, Leofric, Brioni and the core of their command left the screaming mêlée and rushed on to face Oscytel. Nor did they have far to go, for the giant Danish war-lord stood not thirty paces from them where he was fighting a desperate rear-guard action to withdraw those of his Jomsvikings who had survived the Saxon onslaught.

He had seen their banner from afar and wondered at it, stirred by some distant memory. Next moment, even as he looked about him, he suddenly found himself surrounded by a sea of snarling masks, and the great banner itself, for every shield that faced him bore a gaping foxhead on its painted surface, and the banner itself was the same.

And in them he saw his death, for in that instant he understood.

He saw again the man whose living body he had so brutally dismembered, the burning buildings and the butchered corpses. For this was the same flag that had faced him then, whose devices now hemmed him in. And he remembered the tale of the curse that had been levelled at him by the girl who had survived his assault. In some way the man had stretched out his hand from beyond the grave to seize his enemy and crush him, and he fingered the great gem-encrusted brooches that he had torn from the Saxon's bloody clothing, while fear ran through him and his body trembled. Those standing nearby saw the hot blood drain from his face and cold sweat break out upon his brow and were dismayed. Suddenly the dark spirit of their lord was gripped in torment and all his forces quailed.

From the bleak lands of the Rus to the golden domes of fabled Miklagard he had fought and made his name. From the fog-bound shores of the great western ocean to the blue seas of the Grecian Isles he had brought terror and despair wherever he had passed. Now, in this fair green, rain-swept land of the West Saxons, with a clear sky overhead and a fresh wind blowing, it seemed that his gods were calling him away, that here it had been ordained that he would leave his bones.

He stood up straight then and laughed, throwing back his head amidst all the hell going on around him and roared out his mirth. No man had ever done him scathe, nor ever would so as long as *Sica* lay close to his hand. Gently he ran his fingers across the knobbled surface of her golden hilt and caressed the curved green stone of her blade where it lay secure against his chest, tested her eternal sharpness and loved the cold stone from which her blade had been made so many centuries ago. She was the source of his power. As long as she never left his hand all would be well, and he would live, even from this *débacle* of a battle that Guthrum looked to be losing. Perhaps now he would be named High King as he should have been from the start, and he laughed again as he turned to watch his enemy's approach, his huge bearded axe already swinging as he stalked forward to meet this new Saxon threat, loudly calling his men to him as he moved.

*

*J*ust once Leofric paused, and then with a great shout he led his men into the attack, Beornred by his side, Finnar, Raedwald closeby; Brioni just behind with Trausti, Eadberht, Sigweald and Hannes with the banner, and all that great flag's bodyguard clustered round them.

Up went Oscytel's blade, back and round his head, flashing in the May sunshine as it moved, a massive, swingeing blow that hewed Ricberht's shield from top to bottom and severed his arm, the bright blood spurting through his mail as he fell with a wild cry at Aldhelm's feet. And while Steinar Olafsson, Tostig Ránnulfr and Olaf Thorhollur his chief captains struggled on either side of him, Oscytel's rhythm never faltered as he prepared to carve his way to the rippling banner that mocked him, the badge of which had tormented him for so long. Left among the dead at every town and village his men had been defeated, it had galled him beyond reason, and now he would be revenged on those who held it once and for all.

Left and right he struck, each sweeping blow perfection as he turned his wrists and cut through his enemies with all the power at his command, the great curved head of his blade flashing in the bright sunlight as it turned and twisted in his grasp. So died Jaenberht and Sigweald the Messenger beneath his bloodied steel, hacked through their bodies as if their armour was paper, as did many others, their defence smashed to kindling, their weapons flung contemptuously aside and their armour hacked through in an instant. And ever he shouted as he fought, his axe-blade whirring and spinning round his head in a glistening, bloody figure of eight, the men he slaughtered falling like meadow grass beneath the reaper's scythe.

Thus was Raedwald slain, his shoulder cleaved through to his breastbone, his heart and lungs falling out upon the greasy soil, and Daegberht with him, his skull split open like a fat marrow left overlong to ripen in the sun. So also was Beornred cut down as he sought to shield Leofric from Steinar's fierce attack, his shield cut through and his ribs broken by a sweeping blow that left his shield arm hanging useless by his side. But even as he slumped down to the flattened turf with a dreadful cry, so Leofric stepped over him, shielding him with his armoured bulk, and with his own mighty war-axe with which he wove a shimmering pattern of death above his fallen friend, whom others reached and swiftly dragged to safety beneath their own shields.

*

And so they met at last upon the field of battle; the Saxon wolfshead leader and the Danish Jarl, and while their forces grappled to the death on every hand, they circled one another like dancers, each poised to make the first blow, each recognising in the other a master in the art of war.

Axe swinging easily in his hands, Leofric watched Oscytel move, watched his blade circling around his head and back again...and he watched his eyes, aware of Brioni behind him, shielded by Trausti and Finnar, while she and Aldhelm did their best for Beornred, his blood flowing freely over them both.

Suddenly the big Dane leapt forward, switching hands like lightning as he did so to cut down upon his enemy from the other side. Round his blade came, a blur of scything metal that no mortal could possibly withstand. But Leofric had seen it coming, had seen the steel eyes flicker behind the closed face-plates of Oscytel's helmet, saw the tension in his arms and legs, and bringing his own axe sweeping in reverse met blade on blade in a screech of tortured metal and shower of sparks and lightly sprang aside.

Sweet Heaven but the man was quick!

Too many like that and soon it would be he who would stretch his length upon the plain and not Oscytel. Still he believed himself to be the fitter, younger man, and grasping his axe once more firmly in his hands he sprang to the attack.

With that Oscytel also rushed to meet him and both men went for each other like rutting stags, their weapons spinning and weaving around their heads as they twisted and turned about each other, sometimes locked together, bearded axe head to bearded head, when a terrific pulling struggle would follow, each warrior doing his best to tear the other's weapon out of his hands, to kick and pummel him to the ground, bending and twisting furiously this way and that, to free their axe-heads and bring their weapons sweeping into play once more.

Again and again their blades met with a brutal ring of steel and shower of sparks, while Brioni watched in appalled fascination. Never had she witnessed two such expert axemen at each other's throats before, and she wasn't sure she ever wished to do so again – not when one of them carried her heart and all her hopes with him.

Watching his enemy and listening to his breathing, Leofric knew the man was tiring. Not moving so smoothly, his axe not holding its line with the same ease and power as when they had started. And so he began to press Oscytel harder, not content to leap and dance around him any longer, but now with each blow he advanced, forcing the big Dane onto the defensive.

Up, down and round his blade went, sliding his feet forward each time while Oscytel steadily gave ground, his movements becoming more jerky, less controlled, as he struggled desperately to keep up his defence, his neck muscles taut, his face full of rigour as the very real threat of defeat and death bore down upon his spirits. Never had he faced such opposition, never had his skills been so completely met, and he prayed to his gods to come to his aid.

To those who watched it seemed as if they were in the very eye of the storm, for though the battle raged all around them as Alfred's army burst through the Danish line in many places, here it had come to a temporary halt as these two giants of war fought each other to exhaustion, a brief circle of individual violence amidst a hurricane of desperate war.

Then, even as Leofric felt he had the man in his grasp at last, he suddenly stumbled. His foot slipped on some bloody foulness in the grass, his ankle turned and broke sharply beneath him, and with a wild cry he fell to his knees, his head bowed to the ground in his distress, his axe flat upon the bloody field where he had fallen.

Seeing him go down, Oscytel jumped towards him with a fierce shout of triumph, and raising his axe high above his head he cut down at Leofric with all his power, his blade a terrifying blur of steel as the warm air rushed past it. But at every strike, Leofric just managed to roll clear, his ankle flopping uselessly on the soiled ground, his face white with pain, his teeth gritted in determination. And every time Oscytel roared out in frustrated anger above him, for his angle of attack was not right, only the corner of the blade striking the ground, grazing Leofric's head each time to bury itself in the chalky turf.

Watching him collapse in agony, Brioni gave a desperate cry of horror, Trausti beside her standing still as death, as heedless of any danger she rushed out to protect her man, swiftly followed by her big second whose instant of dismay had allowed her to escape the shelter of his great war shield.

Shouting to attract the Dane's attention, they raced towards him, crashing their swords across their shields as they came on, and shouting out Leofric's name to give him some encouragement. But they moved too late, for even as they sprang forward, Oscytel finally trapped Leofric amidst the spray of bodies that littered the ground, and with a monstrous bellow he struck home at last.

It was a finely-judged blow that split the wolf's head Leofric wore on top of his helmet, splitting the crafted steel beneath down the centre to his skull so that the blood gushed out in rivers over his face, his body giving a final violent, convulsive jerk before remaining motionless on the bloodied ground.

*

*B*rioni, deaf to the tempest of blood and iron that was raging all about her, shrieked as she saw him struck and his body quiver and slump back into stillness, unable to believe that her splendid lover had been slain. And while Trausti knelt beside his fallen leader and chafed his hands, she flew at Oscytel, battling him fiercely, her shield held high as Trausti and Eadberht had taught her, Brain Biter weaving and darting in his face, while Finnar and Jaenberht raced to engage him at the same time.

She had seen the man she loved above all others hacked down and killed, yet she felt no sorrow and no fear. Instead she felt him all around her, his hand guiding her and his voice encouraging her every move. Nor was his the only presence that she felt, for she was aware of other, older spirits, at work within her and about her, and she fought as though she was on wires, her feet on springs and her sword fashioned of quick-silver.

And before her fury the Black Jarl's spirit flinched.

He sensed a power in this small warrior who faced him with such dauntless courage that made him screw up his mouth in fury, and he searched the face that bobbed and weaved before him until he caught the eyes, the flitter of movement, the long lashes and moulded lips and realised it was a woman whom he faced. The one they long ago had heard of, the one who had cursed him, whose father he had butchered that January morning when Guthrum was breaking into Chippenham. The one who had escaped Foxley, and had been leading the wolfsheads against his bases ever since; the one whose mate he had just slain and whose banner still mocked him. And he gripped his axe ever more firmly in his hands, sweeping aside the attacks of the two men who threatened him on either side, successive blows sending them spinning into the fray, their swords beaten down, their bodies flung facedown onto the torn ground.

But in her eagerness to shed his blood and tear his filthy carcase open, Brioni suddenly lunged too closely at his throat, just as he raised his axe high above his head to attack her. It was a fateful move, for with Trausti still vainly chafing Leofric's hands, Finnar and Jaenberht scrambling on their hands and knees where Oscytel's blows had cast them, she was without support and unable to retire quickly enough to avoid the swingeing reverse blow with the flat of his broad blade that now smashed into her.

She felt as though she had been struck by a ton of iron, or a falling tree. Her shield broke up and she was flung sideways in a wild sprangle of arms and legs, her sword flying out of her grasp, as she landed flat on her back, her arms spread wide with no breath in her left to speak and no strength left to move.

With a great crow of harsh laughter, Oscytel dropped his axe and leapt towards her, blind to everything that was going on around him as his Jomsvikings battled to contain their enemies, while Heardred, Edwin and Harold pushed in fiercely on every side. But Oscytel was indifferent to all else save the desperate need to slay this heedless creature who had caused him so much torment, whose bloody masquerade had brought such ruin to his hopes and to his standing in the Danish host. As he had gutted and dismembered the father, so now he would disembowel the daughter, and the whole family of Foxley would truly be destroyed.

And so he came and towered over her, and with dreadful purpose he drew *Sica* from her secret hiding place, from the black sheath he wore strapped against his chest, her handle rising up from the mail that covered him. For just a moment he paused as he drew her out, relishing the feel of her golden handle in his hand and the hard, green smoothness of her curved blade, then he fell to his knees and holding *Sica* high in his right hand he stabbed down at Brioni's belly, knowing that its immortal blade would burst through her armour as if it were no more than parchment.

Yet even as he moved, he saw a shadow flit across his sight and felt a searing pain run down his back, a pain so terrible that even as he cried out he could neither breathe, nor move.

*

*I*t was Aelflaeda who had attacked him!

Aelflaeda, who had ridden like the wind, sprung off her horse at the battle line and then run her heart out to bring succour to this woman whom she had come to admire so greatly. Who had seen her fall, had dashed on past all those whose death groans rent the air, and at the last had flung herself upon the armoured back of this man, above all others, whom the Lady had so pledged herself to slay.

The long blade that the Lord Heardred had given her raised above her head, she plunged it into his hard flesh where it peeped out from an unseen gap in his mailed back. A tear amidst the linked black steel that covered him, a fatal chink in his armour where several rivets had burst free, and with all her strength she drove it into his broad body. Like slicing apples in the autumn when their flesh is crisp, she thrust her sharpened blade deep into him, and like the storms that cast the apples to the ground, so too was she seized in an iron grip and flung about in the wild rage of his pain.

With red-eyed fury he turned from Brioni and seized Aelflaeda with his left hand, and grasping her by the throat he battered her face with his helmet and shook her like a rat held fast between a terrier's jaws.

Aelflaeda screamed and struggled desperately in his grasp but to no avail. She felt as though her body was being torn apart, her eyes bulging in their sockets, her face turning purple as he squeezed the air out of her. So she was already dying when, with a powerful twist of his wrist, he thrust *Sica* into her yielding body, piercing her leather jerkin right into her very backbone, her life blood gushing out across his hand as he did so.

Just once she screamed, her tortured shriek soaring high above the battlefield, then she was gone, for that one brutal thrust had split her to the core and burst her back asunder.

But in doing so, *Sica* stuck fast!

He could not withdraw her, she would not come out, nor show her jade face to him again. *Sica* had turned from him at last, had consumed his soul until nothing but a black husk remained, and now, in the manner of her former wanderings, she sought a new partner. A fresh vessel for her to drain, to

305

suborn with all the promise that her power offered the new hand bold enough to draw her out. He had stolen her from her golden casket in Miklagard, and she had served him well. Now it was over and she would not be withdrawn from the bones that she had shattered.

Gently at first then ever more fiercely, Oscytel tugged at the golden handle as blind fear and utter desperation assailed him, but nothing he could do would move the green-bladed knife whose jutting golden hilt seemed so cruelly to mock him.

From where she had fallen Brioni had seen Aelflaeda leap upon Oscytel's back, had seen the flash of steel as she had stabbed home and heard his desperate shout of pain, but had been powerless to move, all strength knocked out of her by Oscytel's blow. All she could do was watch this girl whom she had befriended die, and listen to her paralysing cries. It was only as he flung the young girl's body about that all life and movement returned to her at last. And as she saw him wrestling on the ground with Aelflaeda's body, heard him cry out in despair and stare wildly about him, eyes blank and terror in his face, fresh energy rushed into her. In a moment she was up and running to where her sword had fallen, point down in the earth as when she first had found it in the garth at Foxley, its hilt and pommel shining like beacons in reflected sunlight. Her Brain Biter.

The next moment she had it in her hand, and while Oscytel staggered on his hands and knees, his brain numbed by his appalling loss and scrabbling frantically for his axe in the grass where he had dropped it, Aelflaeda's dagger still fixed in his back, she smote him two-handed with all the force at her command. Round her head for speed and then down upon his neck, angled as Trausti had taught her to strike, just below his helmet, her feet off the ground to give herself more height and power.

And with a great shout of triumph, she struck him a fearsome blow.

She saw her blade hack into his flesh and heard him howl; saw his body lurch and stumble beneath the weight and violence of her attack; saw the wound gape wide, like some hideous mouth, and the blood spurt out in carmine richness across her face, and knew that he would die. With a sudden jerk she wrenched her sword clear and stepped back to watch him fall...only he did not!

Seeing her stand before him, even though it was just a blurred shadow that he could detect through the waves of pain and weakness that washed over him, he made one final effort to destroy her. And even as Trausti and the others reached her at last, he gave a strange and terrible bubbling cry and flung himself upon her, seizing her throat in both hands in a dying man's last desperate grasp, his great weight crushing her beneath him as he finally collapsed.

Above her the sun still shone brilliantly out of a clear blue sky, a heat haze beginning to shimmer over the distant heights of the giant escarpment that towered over the battlefield, the larks soaring upwards in endless trilling spirals, while beneath them the Danish host finally broke and fled, casting their weapons from them as their retreat became a rout. They had seen their champion fall, and now they swept all their leaders away in their frantic panic to escape. Guthrum, no less than the rest of his commanders, was carried away as his broken army sought flight on their horses, riding flat out, crouched over their withers in their desperation to escape the butchery and horrors of *Ethandun*.

And so, to the wailing shouts and cries of terror and despair, was added the countless thunder of hooves as the Saxon army mounted, and led forward by their King, with horns blowing, they hunted the pagans off the field of slaughter; to pursue them the fifteen miles to their fortress of Chippenham from where they had marched out in such fine style just one week before.

*

*B*ut of that Brioni knew nothing, for as Oscytel's hands locked tight in death around her throat, a numbing tiredness seized her limbs and darkness cloaked her senses.

All about her were fluttering voices, and the dim shapes of men made strangely distant by a cloying red mist that clouded her eyesight. She thought she saw her father, with Gyrth and Leofric beside him, and she tried to cry out their names, but found she could not move. She saw herself once more at Foxley, her breasts daubed with her father's blood and called out to God to keep her memory bright, and to the Horned One, and the ancients of her people, that she had kept faith, that she had honoured her vow and never been foresworn. She saw the skies open before her, and heard a roaring acclamation of her courage, her loyalty and her love. She felt the panting warmth of Bran and Utha's breath on her face, their eyes button bright, heard their deep growls and fierce snarling voices; the vicious sound of shattered bones, and endured a violent worrying that shook her body to the core...then blackness seized her.

Her heart was stifled, she had a last vision of her lover's face, the great Saxon war-lord with whom she had learned to laugh and love again, his face a bloody mask, his voice calling her name as his hands reached down for her...reaching...reaching...reaching - and then the darkness rolled over her once more, engulfing her, drowning her, and with a quiet smile her body lost its wild stiffness, and lay still.

Epilogue

*I*t was October, one of those glorious autumn afternoons when the air is like chilled wine and the sun beams down from a sharp azure sky with gentle warmth. When distant things stand out in sharp relief and you can see for miles, when the trees are great pillars of quivering flame, whole forests bedecked with autumn's fire, when the pheasant calls from the woodside, and the streams run fat and clear.

A man and a woman, brightly dressed in wool and leather, with wolfskin cloaks lined with scarlet, the woman's pinned to her shoulders by two great brooches of ancient gold, rode slowly towards the crest of a gentle rise. Their horses moved easily beneath them, while two huge hounds bounded ahead, their sterns bumping and waving as they hunted for rabbits amongst the tangled gorse and briars that rioted along the way.

Ahead of them, still holding the fringed banner as he had done in battle, rode Hannes, with Trausti beside him, Finnar and Eadberht, and an escort of a dozen mounted warriors led by Alnoth the Swordsman, and Beornred, his arm now recovered of its strength and his ribs mended, rode with them. Behind was a heavily-laden string of pack horses with a well-armed escort led by Cadoc the Archer, Rhonwen by his side. The men's armour shone silver-bright in the autumn sunshine, their spear shafts balanced carelessly on their stirrup caps, their painted war shields slung comfortably across their backs, swords and seaxes at their waists.

Behind them rode a further band of twenty or so warriors, closed helmets on their heads, shields on their left arms and spears firmly gripped, ready for instant action, all grouped about four groaning ox carts, two piled high with huge sacking bales, rustic crates and four deep iron-bound chests filled with treasure; one bearing two enormous blocks of rough-hewn stone on a thick bed of fresh straw, and the other piled with oak barrels, some filled, many empty, and all the equipment needed for Rhonwen's brewing.

And right at the rear, pulled by two horses, was Arnwulf's wide tilt cart with tall wheels, two horses in its traces, laden with spare weapons, forge equipment, tools, anvils, horse shoes, arrow heads, sacks of charcoal and pigs of iron. Driving it, swaying easy on the box, with Aldred beside him, Arnwulf sat with the reins loose in his hands, joking with the men ahead. All laughed amongst one another as their mounts ambled slowly on their way, the sound of their mirth bright in the autumn lands through which they now were moving.

And all but those about the lurching carts had their heads bare, their helmets hanging from their chin straps off their saddles, their byrnies unlaced, and a holiday atmosphere about all of them.

On his great charger, Wotan, the man turned his head and smiled, wincing slightly at the sharp pain that lanced through him, for he had been badly injured in the great battle that had crushed the Danish army, and at times his wound still irked him, and he had a slight limp where no such limp had been before.

Edington people were calling it; *Ethandun* in ancient speech, after the royal steading near which the battle had been fought, and which Alfred had promised to his wife in honour of his victory.

"They seem pleased with life," the man said with a laugh, reaching for his lady's hand, as her coal-black stallion, Foxhead, stepped neatly by his side. "Anyone would think they had no need to care."

"Nor do they, my Royal Thegn," the woman replied with a throaty chuckle. "Wessex is free of pirates at last, and this land," she added warmly, her arms sweeping wide about her, "is all yours, as far as the eye can see. Confirmed by Royal Charter, to add to those round Wimborne returned to you by Alfred before the battle. And you wear my father's ring in affirmation of your title."

Leofric stood and stretched his legs in his stirrups and smiled at his young wife who, with the Queen's help, had persuaded Alfred to grant Foxley to him directly, rather than to herself as the King had originally intended.

"It is you I have to thank for all that, my darling girl," he said flashing her father's ring in the autumn sunshine, "as much as anything I may have done for Alfred at Edington. Or any other of a dozen different places that have seen our arms this last spring! You are a saucy puss, my love," he added, making Wotan tittup across the track. "What choice did Alfred have, or anyone else for that matter, once you had set your big blue eyes to work on him. The poor man was potter's clay in your hands!"

"Tush!" she answered him with an arch look. "It was the least he could do for his Queen's most favoured handmaiden. And besides, I needed a dower suitable to the rank of the man who had claimed me for his bride."

"Brioni," her husband answered her, butting Wotan up beside Foxhead to squeeze her hand with sudden fierce passion. "You are as unprincipled as you are beautiful. I should have left that bastard to throttle you. Oh God and Saint Cuthbert, my love, I thought I had lost you! If it had not been for Bran and Utha leaping on him and tearing his arms off at the shoulder, we still might have done! They saved your life, my darling," he said looking at the two huge hounds as they rooted hopefully amongst the bushes and rabbit holes along the way.

"Yes!" she exclaimed, smiling into his face. "They broke free from Maritia's care. Gnawed through the leather holding them and chased after the army. Arrived moments after poor Aelflaeda had been killed. I felt their breath and heard their voices as something violently shook me."

"That's when they crunched that bastard's wrists and shattered his grip on your throat, before tearing his arms out of their sockets. Worried and wrenched them out of his byrnie; that's what shook you so strongly. You should have heard them! I left them with their trophies…I think they ate them!" he added with a wicked grin.

"They would!" she laughed. "They are my father's fiercest hounds. He loved them as I do. And that's not the first time they've saved my life."

"The wolves at Foxley?"

"They drove them off; the whole hunting pack. Without them I would not be here with you, my darling."

"It was after they'd broken his hold that I reached you."

"I thought you were a vision from the gods!"

"Quite right too, sweetheart! What better welcome could you have had?"

"Not the blood-boltered ruin I saw, Leofric, passed out on the ground when I had recovered, that's for certain," she answered him, with a shake of her head at the memory. "Your head must be made of iron to have withstood that blow."

"So Father Cedric was always telling me," he answered with a ringing laugh, "when he wasn't using a birch besom on my hide. I was a very bad pupil!"

Brioni chuckled at his nonsense, turning in her saddle to look at him as she did so, at the breadth of his shoulders and the easy way he sat his horse, at his craggy smile and gold-flecked green eyes, at the scar across his face and the startling white streak in his hair that ran down the centre of his head.

"You look like a shaggy old badger," she said with her throaty chuckle.

"That's Oscytel's handiwork," he replied, rubbing his head where the Dane's axe had caught him. "I had Arnwulf put a plate of tempered steel inside my helm, like a double skin, and a strip over the top as well. Those, and the wolf's skull that covered it all, saved my life. Without all that he would have split me like a squirrel shelling nuts. As it was his blade never cracked my skull, only scored it. But I bled like a pig at the autumn slaughter. I thought I was dying. If it hadn't been for Trausti's immediate aid, I don't know if I would have survived!"

310

And they were silent then, each reliving the desperate events of that bloody day, and the long weeks that had followed while he hovered on the brink of death, flitting in and out of consciousness, and his broken ankle mended, while the King had pitched his camp right opposite the gates to Chippenham and had besieged what was left of Guthrum's army.

Every Viking who was found outside their gated palisade was slain immediately, most hanged from the trees in sight of their comrades, leaving them naked for the birds to feed on. There was no mercy from the King in those early days. And when the weather turned, as it can in May, and there were days of freezing winds and rain, the Wessex host fed off the fat of their own lands under secure shelters, while the Heathen grew lean and pinched and cursed their gods.

Just fourteen days after they had fled the battlefield, brought to the extremes depths of despair by hunger, cold and fear, they had finally surrendered, their leaders staggering out from the gates with their saddles on their backs, seeking peace, bringing their sacred arm rings with them and a dozen noble hostages in token of their good intent. But, most amazingly of all, they came with the genuine desire on the part of their High King, Guthrum, to speak with the God people about the Christ child and of baptism.

It was a remarkable break-through, and three weeks later, to the little church at Aller, near Athelney, Guthrum and thirty of his most honourable leaders had come to be baptised, with Guthrum taking the name of 'Aethelstan', to whom Alfred gave many gifts of gold and silver. Then came the Treaty of Wedmore where the Danes promised to leave Chippenham and Wessex for ever. Where Alfred gave them leave to enter the shattered lands of the wretched East Angles, whose king, Edmund, Ivar had so foully murdered with arrows, in the early years when the Great Army had still been all together.

And twelve days later, as Guthrum had promised, the Danes had marched out of Chippenham for the last time, horse and foot together. Leaving all their booty behind them, they took the old Fosse Way out of Wessex to Cirencester where they would spend the winter before moving across plundered Mercia, to the new lands that the great King of Wessex had just granted them.

Wessex was free of the heathen pirates at last!

*

*A*nd all that while Leofric had steadily regained his strength, tended night and day by his lady, along with those of his warband, especially his shield bearer, Beornred, and many others who had been wounded; while those who had survived the brutal killing when they had punched through the Danish shield wall, had often come to visit.

And in those early days Aelflaeda had been buried, her poor broken body borne with full ceremony by the Lord Heardred and the Lady Judith to the still ruined chapel at Foxley itself, at the Lady Brioni's express desire. There she was properly interred, beside Agatha, Brioni's handmaid whom Oscytel had also brutally slain; the knife *Sica* still embedded in Aelflaeda's body, no-one willing to draw it out for fear of its hidden powers. But while she grieved, Brioni refused to leave her Lord's side until he was properly out of danger.

Finally, Alfred's own physician, the old monk, Simeon of Winchester, had proclaimed himself satisfied and sanctioned Leofric to be up and about at last.

He smiled to himself at the memory, as he looked round him, at the fields back under the plough, at the sheep and cattle grazing on the common land, at the villages struggling back to life after years of ruination. The poor man had not had an easy time of it, for as Leofric's strength had returned, so had all his fire and determination. Still, as he looked at Brioni sitting her horse beside him, calling out to Beornred and pointing to a cherished landmark and radiating peaceful contentment, he felt it had been time well spent. Time to learn to be at peace again after the long years of constant warfare and imminent peril. Time for old wounds to heal, for his ankle to regain its strength, and time for Brioni to re-learn the art of being a woman and not a warrior; to become more used to wearing a dress and not her leather hose and armour, a linen wimple and not a steel helmet.

They had been difficult days.

Oscytel's death had affected Brioni strangely. For many weeks she had seemed abstracted and withdrawn from everything, wandering long distances on her own, or with just Rhonwen or Maritia for company. Cadoc and Eadberht her constant escort because there were still many masterless men about, even some Danes from the battlefield still in hiding. And she mourned her family in a way she had not done before, struggling to find a steady purpose to her life now that Oscytel had been slain and all the fighting was over. But little by little she had recovered her spirits, visited Hugo and the *Circus Maximus*, now back in its great pavilion outside Chippenham, and delighted in seeing Oswald perform his tricks and dance to pipe and tabor; watching the King's Hall being re-built and learning from Rhonwen the secret of brewing fine beer. So by the time of her marriage she was completely recovered, and eager to face the world again with all her usual dash and fervour.

The last not without some fine scenes with the other ladies of the Royal Court who had been not a little frightened and overawed by her presence among them, and by her occasional outbursts that had made them run screaming from the handmaiden's chamber, their hands over their ears to block out the appalling language!

In the end Queen Ealhswitha had been forced to take her former bower-maiden in hand, and though even she had not dared to burn her leathers and cast out her helmet, re-inforced steel jackets and crotch pieces, she had at least persuaded her to have them set aside and crated, and her weapons handed to Leofric until after their marriage. Anything rather than have the wretched girl frighten the living daylights out of her other maidens with the sudden crash of steel on steel and the harsh, wild battle cries and fierce soldiers' language that she had used every time she became frustrated with her women's clothes and stitchery.

Leofric laughed heartily.

Brioni and needlework did not really fit well together! The gods aid any daughter they might have, for the poor girl would doubtless learn to use sword and shield long before her fierce Lady mother would introduce her to the gentle art of herbs and cookery, let alone the distaff!

"Why the sudden laughter, Leofric?" Brioni asked him, smiling.

"Just thinking of you and a distaff, my darling," he replied lightly. "That and those poor girls you so terrified at Court. No wonder Alfred was so keen to have you married off and out of his wife's blonde hair! You are a real termagant, my Lady, and by God I love you for it," he said, reaching out for her hand again.

"Silly things," she scoffed, rolling her shoulders. "Alfred called me his 'Iron Rose!'"

"So I heard," he replied with a chuckle, looking across at her on Foxhead. "Not bad, my love. Me, the 'Iron Hand', you, the 'Iron Rose.' It has some resonance don't you think?"

"Arrant nonsense! There's nothing 'iron' about me, my Lord as well you know. All soft, sweet-scented rose, me, albeit with a few thorns at times!" she added with a smile. "You only have to touch me, my darling to know just how soft my petals are beneath your hands," she said with a cheeky smile beneath raised eyebrows. "And what could a silly bunch of bower-maidens know about *that*?"

"Nothing, my Lady. Especially not had they seen you dressed for your wedding day in flowing linen, white as the lilies in your hands, and covered in silver lace, a gift from the Queen herself, looking so demure and untouched, with pink roses in your hands. Truly you were a vision of loveliness in the old church that morning."

313

"It was certainly a fine ceremony, my Lord," she answered him sweetly after a pause, with a further twitch of her eyebrows, while Bran and Utha came and pranced around Foxhead, eager for her attention. "And I thought you bore yourself with great dignity, despite your debauched goings on with Beornred, Trausti and half your war-band! A pity that Hugo and Heardred were roaring drunk before the service, along with Julio and Marcus, even poor Oswald with his pitchers of ale...and you lost your new hose in the herb gardens the night before chasing rabbits with Finnar and a pitch fork! And as for Oswald, getting loose amongst the bower-maidens, words fail me!"

And he threw back his head and laughed uproariously, Brioni with him too, unable to maintain her cool posture a moment longer as the many pictures of that lovely day ran through their minds. Truly it had been a lively and joyous occasion, the whole court en fête, and all their friends present, especially Beornred whom Oscytel had so brutally injured. But it was a sad one also, for there were many faces missing from their crowd, Jaenberht, Raedwald, Ricberht and Sigweald the Messenger to name but a few, and all had paused to remember those who had fallen to make Wessex free from the hated pagans at last.

Alfred had given her away and the old Archbishop, Aethelred of Canterbury, in his long robes and embroidered cope performed the ceremony in the ancient church at Sherborne, with Bishop Aethelheah beside him, whose name had helped her get into Malmesbury the day before she had assaulted it, and her uncle Wilfrid, the Abbot of Malmesbury, had given them both a final blessing. The sun had blessed that July day with warmth and overflowing brightness, the blue sky flecked with white clouds, the hedgerows filled with colour, flocks of little birds, robins, tits and finches flitting everywhere like flashing jewels. And great crowds in all their finery had whooped and called out as they had gone in procession to the feast hall afterwards, while the bells had rung out a joyful paean across the sleepy summer countryside filled with flowers and beauty.

That was when the King had called him out before all the company gathered there and named him 'Thegn of Foxley' to tumultuous applause, the shouts and thumping feet echoing round the great hall where the feast had been held. Where the King had given into his hands the parchments gifting to him all the lands and honours that Brioni's father had been entitled to, and when she had come to kneel before him to give him her father's ring to wear, that she had carried all those months on a golden chain around her neck, he had been overwhelmed. It was the greatest honour, and he had been deeply affected by it, and by his Brioni's obvious pleasure and willingness for him to be so signally rewarded.

And that night, as they lay and loved together with complete abandon, bodies pressed close, and hearts racing, he marvelled once more at the amazing strings that had brought them both together, the depth of love that he had found in the wilderness, and the wonder of knowing that no creature on earth could ever match the beauty of the girl in his arms who was now his wife. Truly he was the most blessèd man on earth.

*

*T*hen, suddenly, everything seemed to happen at once.

Hugo left for Frankland with Maritia and Julio, to whom she had at last been betrothed amidst much laughter and noisy revelry, taking Oswald and all the *Circus Maximus* who wished to leave with them. The whole great train of wagons, horses and mules leaving Chippenham with buccinas braying and horns booming, drums beating and music playing as the great Bearmaster's dancers and acrobats left the town for the last time on their long march to the coast. Leofric and all those who had come to know and love them well were devastated to see them leave, journeying with them for many miles, as promises were made to come to Frankland and be with them all again.

From the Rings all the people who had come up from Warminster returned to re-build their shattered homes, helped by Leofric with royal silver and the willing help of his men. While those from Ford, and Slaughterford also returned to salvage what they could from the Vikings' fury when Guthrum had torn the villages apart in his rage at being duped. Led by Eadwine, newly confirmed by Alfred as 'Thegn' of both villages, they all left for home at last. Accompanied by his family, by Aelfrid, Alfweald and Ethelinda, and by Thurwold and Brorda, they took with them the chest of silver Leofric had promised. Returning to search out the huge mill stones that they had hidden, to find what animals the Vikings and the wolves might have left when the two settlements had been destroyed, and to build a small memorial to their son, Cuthbert, whom his mother had never forgotten despite his wickedness.

Judith and Heardred returned with her grandfather to his son's estates to prepare for their own marriage, Ecbert having been killed in the final advance from Chippenham, Leofric and Brioni promising to attend. Edwin and Harold left to join the border-watching that Alfred had insisted on since the first days of the Treaty with Guthrum. Ever mindful of what had happened at Gloucester before Christmas last, they left with clear orders of what was to happen to any of their command who was not constantly alert to anything the Danes might try to do!

Finally, in a solemn ceremony at Winchester, before Werfirth of Worcester and Dinewulf of Winchester, the assembled Witan and the King, Wulfhere of Wiltshire was stripped of all his lands and titles. Many thought he was lucky not to have been hanged for his treachery, and his whole family destroyed. But Alfred was not a Christian King for nothing, was mindful of showing mercy where possible, and so complete humiliation was considered sufficient punishment for his crimes.

So, by the time all had departed: bishops, Witan and all their war-bands, the first hints of late autumn had crept over the land. The harvest safely gathered in, the swallows and martins wheeling on scimitar wings above the creaking wains loaded high with fat sheaves for the threshing floor were just memories. Soon the birds would mass for the long flight south, before the first of the winter's gales came booming up the channel.

The orchards, too, lay bare in the mellow sunshine, the pigs driven in amongst the trees to root for fallen apples, and into the empty woodlands for the acorns that would soon fatten them for the autumn slaughter. All around the ploughs busily thrust into the rich earth, the great teams of plodding oxen goaded by small boys, the long furrows filled with birds rushing to plunder the thick sods as they were turned. In the hedgerows the brambles hung heavy with glistening black fruits, the rose hips scattered amongst them like scarlet drops of blood beneath the flickering cuffs of the trees, gold-braided, yellow mixed with red and amber, as the first leaves turned and floated to the ground.

Above the empty fields, barn owls hawked for voles, while the moon rose in quivering golden splendour over the quiet countryside, and the trees breathed softly in the scented darkness. And, all at once, the long summer was over, the light changed, the air was crisp and the time to leave had come at last.

*

So they had all moved up from Winchester to Chippenham, to the King's Hall, newly built and smelling of fresh wood and paint, the whole royal court journeying with them. And with soft tears and loud farewells from Godric, and from Grimnir who was staying close to the King, and from Alfred and his family, they had taken the same road north that Brioni had travelled that winter's day when her father had sent Osric out to bring his daughter home for her betrothal.

Now, turning in his saddle, Leofric looked at his wife with deep concern. It was almost ten months to the day since she had last seen her home, and now as they crested the last rise before the river he was anxious for her happiness.

Sensing his glance and his concern she reached out with her hand again, a warm smile of acknowledgment on her face.

"It's alright, my darling. I know where we are and what I hope to find. I gave Almaric the job of re-building all he could, of cutting out what timber he would need for house and hall and palisade, for barns and sheds and forge, and for the chapel so beloved of my father. He and all the people from the wolfshead village should have banded together to help him. What has been achieved I do not know. But I am safe in your love and we are together. That is all that matters now. Foxley is yours by right, and so am I. Nothing can hurt us anymore."

He squeezed her hand, and together they rode the last hundred paces and drew their horses to a gentle stand. All around them, where the village had been burned out and ruined, new houses had sprung up with stockades for beasts and fences to preserve the many garden plots from wandering sheep and cattle. Geese waddled by the village pond, goats and sheep ran in small flocks across the track, pigs were herded, and everywhere there were people, children and their dams who flocked around them and shouted out a welcome home.

Laughing and almost crying, Brioni rode amongst them and touched many hands, Leofric smiling by her side, riding through the broad meadows until before them lay the river and the bridge, just beyond which, high on its ridge, lay the ancient manor of Foxley. Her home, that Oscytel had assaulted in January and left burned and shattered, great sections of its palisade torn out, its gates pounded and broken, its great hall and barns utterly destroyed. And she was amazed.

Though much still lay in blackened ruins, with the wild growth of summer covering the worst of its wounds in great swathes of bright flowers and waving grasses, the broken palisade had been restored with massive new stakes of ash, the ditches cleaned out of all the debris from the fight. And stark against the sky rose a great expanse of freshly thatched roof where a grand new hall had been built, blue smoke rising from beneath its covered smoke-hole, and the newly hung water gates opened wide, horns blowing from the shooting towers on either side, the space between them packed with men and women cheering and waving at their approach.

Turning towards Leofric, Brioni tried to look cross but failed completely, wagging her fingers at him as she smiled: "*You knew!*" she gasped at him, her eyes sparkling. "You clever dissembler!" she exclaimed, kicking Foxhead on, tears falling down her cheeks. "You let me think all was as it had been when I left, and all the time you knew that work had already started to re-build my home!"

317

"Our home now, my love!" he replied quietly, gold-flecked green eyes staring into sparkling blue. "And, yes, I knew that work had started, but I had no idea how far that it had gone. They must all have worked like Trojans to have achieved so much, and with the Danes still a real problem early on. But at least we shall not have to sleep in the open tonight. I gave orders that the hall must be the first building to be raised. See, Almaric awaits you. He is your first appointment, and he has not let you down. Come, my love, be brave, he will not look to see Thegn Wulfstan's daughter weep!"

"Oh, Leofric," she said with a sudden flashing smile as she dashed the tears from her eyes with the back of her hand. "I *do* love you so. These are tears of joy not sadness. I could not have borne to spend our first night within that ruined hearth place. You are a clever man!"

"Not just clever, my Lady," he answered her with a grin, as they stopped just before the long bridge over the Avon, springing off Wotan to lift her off Foxhead's broad back, and sliding his arm around her waist. "Dazzling! Why else do you think that we have been carting half the countryside along with us?"

"Those great chunks of stone you mean?" she asked, puzzled by his swift change of subject.

"I thought you'd never ask!"

"I didn't want to spoil your fun," she replied swiftly walking on, Foxhead following with nodding head. "My mind was elsewhere."

"They're part of Ecberht's stone!"

"*Ecberht's stone?*" she wailed, turning to him exasperated. "I don't understand. Oh, Leofric, please don't talk in riddles, not today of all days. I can't bear it!"

He grinned boyishly, moving Wotan aside to let their escort pass, the long line of troopers and wagons rumbling across the bridge and up towards the open water gates above them.

"When the Treaty was signed with Guthrum, Alfred ordered the stones to be moved from the hillside to the churchyard at Kingston Deverill, where the muster was before the battle."

"So?"

"So, my darling, the muttonheads who'd been given the order dropped the damned capstone as they were moving it and it broke apart. After our wedding, when the King had granted me your father's lands, and you had given me his ring, I asked Alfred if I could take some parts of it with us when we returned to Foxley."

"But why, Leofric?" she asked him, astonished, as Arnwulf's great tilt cart with all his tools and anvils went by. "Alfred must have thought you were moon-mad!"

"Well, he was surprised. But very pleased to say 'yes' after I had explained what it was I wanted them for."

"Go On! Go on! Tell me!" she almost shouted at him, jumping up and down with frustration, making Foxhead jitter across the track.

"One," he answered her slowly, "to make the foundation stone of the new church in the village we will build."

"That's good. And the other?" she questioned him sharply, almost stamping her foot.

"The other," he ended with a flourish, and a piercing look into her blue eyes, "is to fashion the font in which our child will be baptised!"

"Our child, Leofric?" she gasped, looking up at him and smiling shyly.

"Yes, my Lady fair, our child," he said, gently putting his hand across her lower stomach. "The son or daughter you are carrying in your womb!"

"How can you tell?"

"I know you too well, my beauty," he went on, wrapping his arms about her and holding her close. "Little signs, sweetheart. A certain bloom in your skin, your secret smiles when you thought I wasn't looking, an added richness to your breasts, you being sick these past few mornings...tell me, my darling girl," he ended softly, "am I truly right?"

"Oh, yes, Leofric, *you are!* But I wasn't sure myself until a few days ago. But the wise woman who attended the Queen's last birthing assured me it is certain."

"When, my love?"

"In April, my Lord," she said, looking up at him, Foxhead blowing in her ears. "In the spring, maybe in May, the eve of the battle. Are you pleased?"

"Pleased? *Jubilant, my Lady!*" he shouted, picking her up and swinging her around in sudden ecstasy. "No child ever born of woman will be more loved or cherished than ours. Foxley will rise again, my darling, but more magnificent and stronger than before, and the new church and village we will build will give the people room to breathe."

"And my parents, Leofric? And Gyrth and Agatha and Aelflaeda? What of them?"

He looked down at her anxious face and squeezed her shoulders gently.

"They will rest easy where they are, my love. We will repair your father's chapel, give it a fine stone roof, bring in craftsmen to put real glass in the windows and build a fresh stone floor, with incised flags to show all people

319

where they lie. And Bishop Aethelheah will come with Abbot Wilfrid to do the service and give the blessing."

"And Aelflaeda?"

"Rest safe, my darling. Her body will never be moved again, and no clear mention of the dark treasure that lies buried with her now exists. *Sica* has gone from us forever. That evil thing will not rise up to haunt us ever again."

"Oh, Leofric," she sighed leaning her head against his shoulder, as Arnwulf's cart bumped and ground itself along the trackway that led to the distant Watergates. "Leofric, I nearly lost you! Oh, God! I love you so. What would I do without you?" and swiftly turning he flung his arms round her and lifted her face for his kiss, his lips pressing hers fiercely as they came together, until she freed her hands and pulled herself into him, almost swooning on the sudden tide of his passion, her heart racing, her face buried in the thick fur of his wolfskin cape. It was over.

Oscytel lay dead and his bones picked clean on the battlefield; Guthrum had led what was left of his army out of Wessex for the last time, and her vow was completed. Leofric was healed, her marriage dreams fulfilled, her happiness secure at last with the man she loved above all others, her womb already stirring. The killing was ended and new life was begun.

With a loving smile he kissed her gently and let her go, and hand in hand, with Wotan and Foxhead clopping solidly behind them, they finally crossed the bridge towards all those who had gathered by the gates to welcome them in the afternoon sunshine. Their people now, laughing, shouting out and waving as they came flooding down the old track towards them, Almaric her reeve leading them, his face beaming, his arms outstretched.

She could feel Leofric's love and strength reaching out to her, his own grin and nodded encouragement pushing her, and dropping his hand, Bran and Utha stalking proudly by her side, she strode forward with a brilliant smile of her own to greet their waving cheers.

Brioni of Foxley, King Alfred's Iron Rose, was coming home at last.

08.35. 21/07/2015

The Lion and the White Rose

A Medieval tale by Richard de Methley, Book One of the White Rose Series, a vibrant tale of Love, Murder, Treachery and Adventure in the days of Richard Lionheart.

King Henry II: The Toulouse War, July 1159
Southern France, Siege of Cahors: First Attack.

D aybreak…and the mists off the river were opaque, cloudlike, filling the dips and vales around it so the great city seemed to float upon them like some vast stone vessel on a sea of steam.

Its fortress towers and battlements rose up out of the mists wraithlike, ethereal, their sharp outlines etched black against the lightening sky, itself pale as a mallard's egg in spring, just flushing pink and saffron with the dawn. And at that time of early morning beauty all was breathless, silent, save for the song of birds…until, with a roar of fury, a host of armoured men rushed howling out of the shrouded western greyness towards the city ditch, and the peace of all was shattered.

Bridged at that point with huge stones, rubble and tight bundles of faggots, topped now with doors and great timbers torn from house and stable by the king's sappers, the ditch was still a formidable defence. And as the first attackers reached the bridge…they baulked; dismayed, uncertain of its safety, until urged on by the fierce shouts and curses of their officers they poured across it in a wild torrent of steel and armoured leather.

And as the sun thrust its first spears of gold and crimson light across the eastern sky so, armed with sword, shield and gavelock, they reached the breach itself and hurled themselves onto the steep glacis of shattered masonry and coarse rubble that had spilled out of it like an avalanche. But swiftly as King Henry's men began to climb the huge slope of scree and scrambled ashlar that now reared up out of the mists before them, scrabbling on hands and knees for purchase…so did the defenders leap up in a rage of towering defiance to meet their enemy's attack.

In moments all order vanished as huge bales of burning straw were hurled down upon the heads of their attackers, together with myriad pots of sulphur, pitch and oil, each with a faint trail that sullied the morning sky with a lattice of smoky vapours. Bursting upon King Henry's assault troops in violent explosions and great gouts of oily smoke and flame, they crashed amongst the struggling soldiery like lava bombs. Many on whom they fell were swiftly encased in fire and rushed screaming off the glacis to plummet like flaming meteors to the great ditch below; others flung themselves to the ground wreathed in flames and writhed and howled and were consumed.

And with the fire-pots came spears, arrows and sharp edged stones; great baulks of timber studded with nails and sharpened iron...and huge chunks of jagged masonry. These, with a whistle and shuddering *bang!* they crashed amongst the enemy host scrabbling on the glacis, scattering a deadly hail of bitter shards as they shattered, that ripped into King Henry's soldiers and tore their flesh apart.

Yet still amidst the smoke and flames, the flicker of arrows, the shrieks and screams of the wounded and the groans of the dying, the attackers continued to fight their way upwards towards the breach horizon beyond which the city lay open to their lusts. Baying and roaring out their challenge, faces twisted with wild rage and feral hatred they stormed upwards, their dead and wounded strewn in bloodied heaps behind them...until two thirds up that brutal slope their whole charge stalled, checked by an appalling obstacle that lay stretched out across the whole of their assault.

A monstrous *Cheval de Frise.*

A vast tree trunk into which a terrifying hedge of huge iron spikes had been hammered into three sides and then fiercely re-sharpened, together with a multitude of piercing glaives of steel, like mighty sword blades, each honed to a razor's edge, the whole monstrous thing lowered down the slope and held in place by long chains of iron, each link hand forged, that no sword or axe blade could shatter. There was no way round it, the breach was too narrow; nor in that violent press was there any way of burrowing beneath it. The only way was over it, and in moments, as their officers and sergeants bawled abuse and encouragement at their men, it claimed the lives of hundreds more of Henry's soldiers as they hurled themselves at it again and again in a frenzied effort to move it...or to make of their bodies a pathway over which their comrades could still make good their fierce attack.

But those who did so were swiftly assailed by the defenders, who hacked and battered at them with every weapon in their armoury. Some were thrust through with swords and spears in a violent spray of blood and torn intestines; others were hooked aside with gisarmes, their bodies burst apart with the axe blade on the back of every wicked bill so that limbless, headless bodies soon littered the slope with crushed skulls...and shattered bone and shredded tissue was everywhere scattered with fierce abandon.

And always above them, in the smoke and screaming fury of that dreadful morning, with men being slain on every side by fire, and rock and sharpened steel, the defenders were hallooed forwards and encouraged by the roaring voice of a single mighty warrior.

Tall and broad of stature, clad from head to toe in shimmering mail, his great fighting helm of shining steel masking his face, the man stood at the very top of the breach like a giant of old and shook his great sword in a rage of battle-fury at the enemy toiling below him. Above his armoured head a vast curling green banner snapped and shivered in the morning breeze; the great head of a huge black boar, eyes, teeth and wicked tushes red as blood all deeply stitched upon it. The Boar's Head erased Sable, armed Gules on a field Vert…the House Flag of the Lord Baron Sir Thibault de Brocas, known to all as 'The Cruel'. Lord of Montauban, Narbonne and Gruissan he was, whose enormous frame seemed to fill the breach, and whose towering spirit of contempt and hatred for his enemies roared the defenders onwards and forced King Henry's assault troops to a shameful, desperate retreat.

Appalled and demoralised their courage melted from them, and in moments Henry Plantagenet's army broke apart as his men fled away from the horrors of the breach and its demon glacis. Hundreds of bodies lay scattered all across it as though they were toy soldiers scattered by a giant's careless hand: butchered, crushed, and burned, their blood drenched the stones on which they lay.

And ever immoveable, the great *Cheval de Frise* that had broken them, draped with a multitude of torn and rendered corpses, remained to mock their efforts. Mired in brains and offal it was as much a testimony to the courage of all those who had attacked there…as to the ferocious ingenuity of the Lord Baron de Brocas to deny them access to the great fortress city of Cahors.

As King Henry's attack force straggled back to their camp, dragging their wounded with them, so with a thumping crash and whistle, the three great trebuchets the king had built for his assault burst into action again. Their huge counterweights falling to bring their throwing arms sweeping upwards, each one the length and breadth of a mighty tree, the great slings at each end whipping over as they passed their apogee to hurl their three hundred pound stone balls high into the air to fall with a great whistle and an enormous, thumping *crash!* upon the already broken walls of Cahors.

If the breach had been too narrow for that morning's attack…it would not be so in three days' time!

King Henry's siege camp, Cahors, after the failed attack.

S prawled in a vast tented city that stretched right across the Northern end of the great curving River Lot in which Cahors was securely nestled, as well as on the other side of the river, King Henry Plantagenet's great armed host was drawn from all over his new empire.

Stretched from Scotland to the Pyrenees and even to the great Circle Sea of the Mediterranean, Henry's lands were the richest in all Europe and he had drawn from them widely. Fighting men in their tens of thousands, priests, varlets, cooks and drudges; kings, barons, knights and squires; butchers, bakers and candlestick makers; serving girls, camp followers, doxies and whores...all packed in together; the morning sky smirched by their cooking fires, vats and ovens, as well as by the dense twisting columns of smoke still boiling up from the failed attack that dawn.

The whole huge encampment hummed like a giant swarm of bees punctured by the dink and clatter of field forges, and by the sobbing howls and cries of the wounded, their screams rising like the shrieks of peacocks through the smoky air, itself thick with the stench of blood and vomit from the sick and wounded. And from the sordid piles of dung from man and beast alike that everywhere lay heaped, a vile miasma seethed with buzzing life, and all around was soiled straw, while from the fallen scraps of food and rotting meat the maggots writhed.

Amidst all rose the multitude of other scents that accompany a vast army encamped and waiting: sweat, horses, leather, cooked meat and boiled cabbage, hot steel, wine, beer, the muskiness of men and the sickly perfume from those ladies of the night, those 'night-moths', who flitted amongst the soldiery as they roistered, boozed and fornicated their time away.

And over all was the pungent richness of wood smoke, blue and wispy on the summer breeze; the sharp stink of stale urine, and from the wide grave pits into which more bodies were tipped each day, the gasping stench of death and slow decay.

Reviews, inspections, scouting patrols and foraging for food and booty...all had their part to play for the soldiers of King Henry's army that summer...as well as mounting horrifying attacks upon their enemies within the great fortress city that blocked the army's route towards Toulouse, and which King Henry Plantagenet of England had sworn to capture.

325

With a growl of rage Sir Yvo de Malwood withdrew from the assault and led his men in good order back towards his encampment. Many had fallen, and others were badly wounded, but at least they had remained under his control and that of their officers. Nevertheless it had been a bitter experience and he felt deeply bruised by their failure…and incensed by the man who had been the architect of it all….*That bloody bastard Thibault de Brocas!* he swore.

Of all the men this side of the Circle Sea it would have to be him. He was supposed to have been King Henry's leal man. Swore an oath of fealty to the King for his lands…on his knees! Now he had broken his knightly word and in return for Cahors and all its riches, he had taken oath of fealty to King Louis VII of France instead: an utter disgrace in itself, and foolish as well beyond all measure. Louis was not one half the general that King Henry was, nor were his promises worth spit either…*I might have guessed that bastard would turn his coat. But since when has a Brocas ever been faithful in anything?*…And he swore violently again, hacking a fallen helmet out of his way with his armoured foot, to send it spinning into a mass of thorns.

The family 'de Brocas' had been a thorn in the flesh of both his ancestors and those of his great friend, Sir Henry de Burley, for generations. They had all been neighbours in the old days, before Duke William had made England his own. All three families had held great lands around Montauban and Rocamadour along the Dordoyne valley in the region of Auvergne…now within the disputed lands of Toulouse.

Toulouse, the greatest single county in the whole of France, was King Henry's by right through marriage to Eleanor of Aquitaine, but Louis still claimed them as his own which was what this war was all about. But the old Seigneur de Brocas, Sir Hubert in those far off days of King Philip 1st, when the world was still young in the days of his great grandfather, had wanted all for himself and so a history of feuding had followed with raid and bloody counter raid as Hubert and his sons had fought to control that whole region of Toulouse.

So bitter had the fighting become that when Duke William of Normandy had called for men to carry their arms into England, Sir Yvo's great grandfather…Sir Gui de Valence in those times past…and his greatest friend, Robert de Riveaux, had left the lands of their fathers and thrown their hats in the ring for William's great adventure into England.

And they had been superbly successful.

His mind was full of it...*Hastings, ninety years ago!*...And at the height of the fighting, amidst that screaming, howling maelstrom of blood and steel, with men falling on every side as the Saxons fought like all the fiends of Hell to drive the Normans out...Duke William had so nearly been slain. His horse brought down with him upon it as King Harold's two brothers, Gyrth and Leofwyne, with stabbing scramaseaxe and great two handed fighting axe, had sought to kill him.

....*Hastings! Sweet Jesus but that must have been some fight? The greatest battle of all time they say; and great grandfather was there!*...Saved the Fighting Duke's life. Slew the Saxon warrior, Gyrth, while Robert cut down his brother, Leofwyne, before he could chop the Duke in half with his axe. And then he had thrust the reins of his own destrier into William's hands and bid the Duke mount and ride to show his face to his army before they fled the field in terror.

And his mind was filled with the images of that far off day as he stamped his way back to the encampment full of rage....*Dear God, how I wish I had been there! So Exciting! That was a battle full of honour and great deeds. This? This morning? This was a shambles...A butcher's bloody shambles! By God and the Pheasant, but someone should pay for this day's rotten work!*...And he hacked furiously at a broken helmet someone had dropped in his flight from the siege that morning, grunting with frustration as he violently kicked it into bushes just close by

...*Hastings had been nothing like this!...This bugger's muddle of a bloody siege!*...

And then, when the battle was all over, and night had finally cloaked the battlefield in darkness, encamped amidst the bloody carnage of the battlefield, William had called both young men to him and honoured them with Saxon fiefs in what was to become the King's New Forest, the greatest hunting lands in all the south of England. They had been the first of all his knights to be so rewarded, and with the lands the title of 'Lord Baron', and the Duke's orders to adopt for themselves the names of the new manors they had been given.

So...Lord Baron of Malwood for my Great Grandfather, and Lord Baron of Burley for his old friend Sir Robert. The title since passed on to my great friend Sir Henry...Together then... and still together now. Deus Vult...God Wills it!...

And he smiled and banged his hands together; for with their family's stars rising...those of Hubert de Brocas and his hell-born whelps away in Montauban and Rocamadour had faded away to mere glimmers...*Until today!*...Today Thibault de Brocas had repelled their attack. Sent Henry Plantagenet's troops fleeing in terror. Today he had shown himself as all men knew him to be: a formidable warrior…but also a lying, deceiving, treacherous turn-coat. As were all those who carried his name. He had accepted King Louis' bribe of Cahors and all its wealth and lands to change sides. And now if he could hold out until the French King Louis could come and raise King Henry's siege, then he would crow and crow and crow.

A true French cockerel to the last!...*And by God that sticks in my throat!...Fucking bastard Frenchman! And all because some fucking idiot told the King that the breach Vernaille had made in Cahors' walls was 'practicable'…Just wait 'til I get my hands on him and he will soon know what it is like to piss blood!*

And with a grunt of anger The Lord Baron Sir Yvo de Malwood, Lord of the King's New Forest, stumped into his tent at last and hurled his own helmet from him in disgust. Bouncing and spinning off his camp bed it flew into a far corner to clatter amongst a pile of spare armour, sending his squire, young Jonathan Romsey, leaping off to rescue it.

*

"**B**ad day then, my Lord?"

"God's Throat, it was a bloody shambles, Jonathan!" The burly knight swore as he lifted his heavy mail hood back onto his shoulders and fratched his sweaty head. "A bloody, fucking shambles! For God's sake, boy," he growled, thrusting his laden baldric into his hands. "Give me a drink. I need it!"

Of more than medium height, with black hair and piercing eyes like blue Damascus steel, Sir Yvo de Malwood was a master in the saddle with sword, lance and battle axe: and a terror on the ground. Now at twenty five, just two years younger than the King himself, he had enormous upper body strength as you would expect of a man who had carried his harness for a dozen years in all weathers, and was a classic product of his age: a brutal fighter in a brutal time, yet mild mannered and courteous when at rest, and a born leader to all who fought under his banner of the Scarlet Lion Rampant.

To those who worked his lands around Castle Malwood in the old Conqueror's New Forest, or who served his family well in any way, he was a good master, and his lands prospered under his hand. He was known to be firm but fair, with a voice that could be heard across a raging field of battle…when all around him knew it was time to jump, and jump quickly!...and he had a thumping fist to be aware of. But he also had a kindly heart, preferring to find good in people wherever possible, not evil. Yet God help those who mistook his kindness for weakness, because he could be ruthless where necessary or

328

where his honour, or the safety of his people, was concerned - and he was a determined and pitiless enemy. Fiercely loyal to his king, Henry II, and to the whole Plantagenet family; he was the king's Leal man for the vast royal estates and messuages that made up the king's New Forest, and was well trusted by the King's Council, which was why he was now in southern Toulouse fighting for Henry II of England against King Louis VII of France, in this the first major war of Henry's reign.

Sweeping away all that stood in his path since the raising of a glittering host in Poitiers on Midsummer's Day, it was Henry's aim to seize control of Toulouse, the greatest county in the Kingdom of the Franks, promised to him through his marriage to Eleanor of Aquitaine his gorgeous, clever wife...yet denied him by King Louis, her former husband, and his allies And now that swift advance was stalled outside the great fortress city of Cahors due to the stupidity and ignorance of his Lord Chancellor's chief engineer who had declared the breach in its mighty walls 'practicable'.

Only it needed a bigger breach to seize Cahors, than Rupert de Vernaille's Trebuchets had so far provided...*Not the fucking whore's crack Henry sent us off to assault this morning! Sod Sir Rupert and his bloody 'engines'! And sod the fucking King who should have known better than to send brave men to face certain death in an assault on an impossible breach he had left to his sodding engineers! So...sod all fucking engineers as well!*

And he hurled his sweat soaked woollen arming cap after his helmet.

"A complete, bloody shambles!" The big armoured knight swore again loudly as he ripped off his mailed mittens, the blood off his arms running over his hands as he shook them steel-free at last, before seizing the silver-gilt goblet that his squire handed him and emptying it in a few huge swallows. "The bastards were waiting for us of course, but whoever told the king that de Vernaille's breach was practicable needs his fucking brains examining...and after this morning I feel just the man to do it too!" Sir Yvo raged, shaking his empty goblet in the air. "Practicable? The thing was a bloody nightmare. Sodding engineers! Once let them in on a siege, young Jonathan," he said, shaking his goblet at him. "And you can be stuck outside for months!"

And holding it out for a refill of fine Bordeaux off a nearby chest, he kicked an innocent, unoffending wooden bucket with such sudden violence that it soared clear out of the tent making a distant camp varlet shout out in sudden alarm as it shattered into a dozen pieces on the rock-hard ground.

"Clarence Wigmore, My Lord. One of the Lord Chancellor's men," his young squire replied, watching with a grin as the bucket soared past him.

"*What?*"

329

"Clarence Wigmore, Sir Yvo," he said again, laughing as the bucket crashed to the ground and burst into pieces making a servant carrying a tray of wine cups throw them all up in the air with a wild shout. "The Engineer who advised the Chancellor, Lord Thomas Becket, who advised the king. About the breach, my Lord," the young man added…still chuckling over the camp varlet now being furiously berated with shouts and curses by the men he had been about to serve…while steering Sir Yvo outside his tent so he could be completely disarmed without pools of blood and muck forming on the tent floor any longer. "The king did not examine the wall himself, my Lord. He trusted others to do that for him."

"So I gather, silly ass! Well he won't do that again, that's for certain! Despite this morning's fuck-up Henry's no fool, but we lost hundreds up there, Jonathan. Bloody hundreds, and not once did we get to the top. A bloody great *Cheval de Frise* stopped us in our tracks. We lost hundreds up there this morning. Dreadful! Have you seen Sir Henry?"

"Sir Henry de Burley, My lord?"

"Yes, Jonathan. My long suffering and well beloved friend, Sir Henry!"

"Yes, My Lord. He was on his way to the horse lines with some carrots to see his charger, Alexander."

"*Carrots?* I swear he loves that bloody horse more than his latest lady-love! And 'Alexander'?…"

"Named after the Greek Emperor, My Lord."

"Yes, I know that, Jonathan," he answered swiftly, batting the lad's cheeky face at the same time. "But really! Here, boy. Give me a hand to pull off these damned boots," he said collapsing onto a stout wooden bench close by. "They're killing me! And what about our Spanish Hidalgo, Don Mateo…"

"…de Silva de Pamplona from Navarre!" came a merry voice as a tall, black-haired man with deep brown eyes in a face with fine cheekbones and a high domed forehead, sauntered up. Lightly dressed in scarlet suede leather chausses, with a fine Egyptian cotton shirt in brilliant vertical stripes of blue and green open to the waist, and soft purple leather half boots on his feet he was encumbered with neither armour nor his beloved twin swords that he nearly always carried strapped to his back, and paused with a look of mock horror at Sir Yvo.

Red-faced and sweating in gambeson and riveted mail armour, off which blood was still dripping, Sir Yvo de Malwood was not a pretty sight. His long white cyclas with its great rearing scarlet lion armed in blue, torn and holed in many places, was drenched in it and his chest was thick with the filth and human mucous of battle: torn flesh, brains, human faeces and shards of bone. The tall Spaniard's hawk-like nose wrinkled as he sniffed at him disgustingly.

330

"My dear, Yvo!" he exclaimed in his soft musical Spanish lilt, eyes sparkling with sudden mischief, while he bent to flick stray gobs of flesh and hair off his friend's chest with long delicate fingers: "You stink like a wild boar in rut! Whatever have you been doing? You look as if you have been...fighting?"

"Don't you start, Matthew!" The big knight growled, offering the man his campaign chair. "Some ignorant, fucking bastard of an engineer told Henry that Rupert de Vernaille's breach was practicable! One of Becket's men I gather from Jonathan, here: Clarence Wigmore; fucking lunatic! Told Becket it was practicable, and Henry, trusting his Chancellor had got it right, ordered us to assault it at dawn."

"Without seeing it for himself?"

"Without seeing it for himself, indeed!" His friend confirmed heavily.

"Not good, then," Don Mateo said indicating Sir Yvo's bloodied state and lack of good humour. "I heard you all go in...and then I heard you all straggling back. Bloody grim up there?"

"Dreadful, Matthew! A huge Cheval de Frise stopped the assault dead in its tracks. It was bloody hell up there...The lads kept attacking. Dear God, did they try hard...we lost hundreds! And guess who was roaring down at us from the top of that wretched slit of a breach? Our good and noble friend the Lord Baron Thibault de Brocas; Sir Henry's vastly unloved Uncle! That double dyed treacherous, lying bastard has changed sides...Yes! Well may you gasp lad!...and is now leading the defence, God damn and blast it!" He raged.

"Before my father's grave I swore to have that bastard's head after the Malwood Emerald disappeared when Henry's mother died. She was that murderer's sister, and one of the most beautiful women of her age, and a lovely lady too, the Lady Philippa de Brocas: wholly different from her brother, Thibault. Sir Ralf adored her. So did Sir Alun de Malwood, my own dear Papa, almost as much as he loved old Baron Ralf himself. Everyone loved the Lady Philippa, and so on their wedding day my father gifted her our family's greatest heirloom, the Malwood Emerald. A magnificent jewel of great size and beauty, in an ancient and intricate golden setting that my ancestor, old Gui de Valance, had found when Castle Malwood was being built. Roman I always understood. He gifted it for her lifetime the old rascal! And on the very day she died, it mysteriously disappeared! Vanished...and has never been seen since. But that bastard up there had a hand in it, I swear," he added gesturing violently towards Cahors.

"I know the story, Yvo," the tall Spaniard said in his soft, lilting English. "I have heard it many times from you, my friend. But this time that man has finally overreached himself. King Henry has declared the man a proven traitor.

I had it from Chancellor Becket himself not half an hour ago. That Man-of-Blood and Treachery is doomed. Whether we kill him, or he manages somehow to escape the city, matters not one jot. All his lands within Henry's dominions are to be held forfeit to the crown...Henry's crown. De Brocas will lose *everything*! So, my friend, let's get you out of this disgusting armour, washed and properly fed, and then Henry and I can tell you what plans we have formed for dealing with the *Cheval de Frise* that so halted your assault this morning.

Jonathan!" He shouted out to Sir Yvo's squire. "Come and give me a hand with this great lump of armoured humanity, then take his filthy clothes away and burn them. He cannot wear them again...they offend me! And then go swiftly and find Sir Henry de Burley. I last saw him near the horse-lines talking to that great beast of his he loves so well. Bring him to us here and tell my man, Hererra Alcazar, to join me here also and collect Sir Henry's young squire, Andrew Redlynch, as you return.

Once our fine Horatio here has bathed and changed," he added with a laugh as Sir Yvo finished off his wine again. "We will all eat here tonight, and you idle varlets can serve us as if we were all at home, and not out here in this appalling camp! Now, my friend," he laughed at Sir Yvo in his musical Spanish lilt. "Come on, on your feet my brave Caballero, and bend forward, and let Jonathan and me get all this stuff off you at last.

Sir Yvo de Malwood's campaign tent: The same night.

That night, despite the bloody carnage of the morning, Sir Yvo, Don Mateo and Sir Henry de Burley sat at ease amidst the cheerful ruins of their supper, while the sun sank to its rest in a blaze of glory and the warm dusk was filled with evening birdsong and the call of doves.

The Western sky, filled with great flotillas of scarlet and crimson cloud, burned amidst a shimmering sea of gold; while great clouds, rimmed with amethyst, sailed across the darkening sky. Settling like a warm blanket over everyone, King and camp and fortress city alike, the gathering night masked the horrors of the morning, blanketing the shattered glacis with summer darkness, the far western horizon still streaked with lines of red and orange fire.

Served outside their tent by their squires, they had dined alfresco style as if they had been at home. Laid upon stout trestles beneath spotless napery of

Egyptian cotton, it had been a joyous meal. Small chickens barbecued on long wooden spits, tender collops of beef from a steer freshly slain that morning; smoked meats and pickled vegetables, some in ginger, some in turmeric; crisp lettuce, cucumber and scallions…the whole was a pleasing end to a bruising day. And with crocks of yellow butter to go with the fresh baked bread, still warm from the field ovens set up by order of the king, together with fresh fruit and wine drawn from their own supplies and a fine St Nectaire cheese…all had eaten their fill with gusto and simple, rude enjoyment.

Finally Sir Yvo and his companions mopped their mouths with their knee cloths, sighed with pleasure and sat back in their chairs, cheerfully replete. The meal cleared away by camp varlets, their squires came round with steaming bowls of hot scented water for them to wash their hands, each youth with a clean towel over his arm on which his master could dry his wetted fingers. Meanwhile a handful of other servants brushed off the white tablecloth, scattering the meal fragments onto the ground, before leaving the three knights to mull over the day with refreshed goblets of wine and small bowls of goats' cheese and olives. Beside their table a cluster of flambeaux were thrust into the ground, their resin flames lighting up their faces, the scented flames flickering and flaring in the warm night airs.

By then the moon had risen into a star dazed sky, her silver light casting long shadows across the vast encampment, still watchful, wakeful and alive with a multitude of flickering camp fires, the soft night breezes full of its noise and bustle. Raucous bursts of laughter rang out from time to time from the thousands of men camped up all around them; the ring of hammer on anvil; the stamp and whicker from horse and mule; the bray of a donkey; the scream from a girl, or from one of the many wounded; the cry of a child, the barking of dogs.

"So, Henry," Sir Yvo said at last, stretching his great shoulders as he spoke. "Tell me what you and Mateo have cooked up between you about that bastard tree trunk with all its spikes and blades. The thing is enormous, and deadly. It stopped the whole assault this morning. That and the fact that the breach was impossible anyway! We couldn't shift it; far too heavy for one thing and it was held in place by bloody great chains for another, hand forged. Would need a blacksmith to smite them apart! I had thought that Vernaille's fresh bombardment might scupper it once and for all. But they were already drawing it up the glacis as we were scuttling away back down it. So next time it will be out there again for certain: maybe two of them if Vernaille's engines bring down a really decent stretch of their curtain wall. To conquer that breach we have to be able to overcome those obstacles!"

Sir Henry de Burley, unlike his great friend, was not so heavily built, being both taller and more willowy, moving always with a grace that his bigger, more solid friend could not manage. But both men had the same great upper body strength needed to wield their weapons and hold their places in the battle line if required and, like Sir Yvo, Henry de Burley was a bruising rider. Always his charge hit an enemy like a thunderbolt, and his sword could split a man from crutch to navel, spilling his guts steaming onto the bloodied ground and then take his head off with the returning blow as sweetly as you could ever wish to see.

On his cyclas he wore a great red stag's head with golden antlers on an ermine background...Stag's Head erased Gules, attired d'Or on a field Ermine...in recognition of his own forest lands. For Burley, like Malwood, was within the New Forest, though several miles apart, where their ancestors had settled on great estates gifted to them by the Conqueror for saving his life at the height of the fighting, when his horse had been gutted out beneath him and the whole of his Allied-Norman army believed he had been slain.

Since that moment, as much as from before, the two families had been inseparable: the sons of each doing all things together, as much 'Roland and Oliver' together, or 'David and Jonathan', as it was possible for two great friends to be in their day and age. So it was that night that Yvo listened to all Sir Henry had to say with real interest not just because he was his greatest friend, but because Henry was by far the better strategist...*For if Henry cannot see a way through this bloody problem, I am damned if I can!*

"Well, Yvo, the thing is a real sod and no mistake. And we have to find a way to deal with it if we are to gain the city as the King so wishes us to do. Firstly, we cannot move it while it is anchored. Secondly, you can't climb over it without being cut to pieces; your lot tried that this morning and it was hopeless. Thirdly, as for burrowing under it - forget it!"

"So?" Yvo asked sharply. "We know all that, Henry. Have you two come up with a solution?"

"Yes, Yvo, if you'd just be a little patient. God's Bones but you are impulsive! Just shut up and listen for once! Yes? Good! We have to do what the Romans used to do in these situations..."

"...The *Romans?*" Sir Yvo interrupted with a howl of derision. "God's Blood, Henry! *The fucking Romans?*" And he thumped the campaign table with his fist making everything jump about.

"Christos, Yvo!" Henry shouted out, leaping up and fiercely brushing at his clothes as he did so. "Now look what you've done, you great oaf...bounced the bloody cheese and olives everywhere! You would test the patience of a saint," he added as their squires rushed to sort things out. "Now! Please, will you shut up and listen?"

"I am sorry, Henry. Truly. But honestly, man. *The Romans?* Alright – Alright," he added swiftly holding up his hands to Henry's frustrated face. "I'll shut up and listen."…*Romans indeed. Trust Matthew; the man must be bloody mad!*…

"Right!" Sir Henry started, sitting again and giving his friend a fierce glare. "When faced with these situations the Romans used a battle formation called a 'Testudo'…a 'Tortoise', where companies of troops held their shields both across their front and over their heads so that enemy missiles just bounced off them as they advanced. As well as proving almost impossible to stop, under cover of the 'testudo' all sorts of other tasks could be carried out with minimum casualties. Yes? Good.

Now, our lads are not trained Roman legionaries, and they don't carry the great rectangular shields those boys did. But, if we can get hold of some mantlets, those great boards the archers shelter behind, cut them into thirds and put handles on all the pieces, we will have something like it and with a bit of practice I am sure we could achieve the same kind of effect. Then, if we get some good axe-men together and some blacksmiths with their damned great hammers and cold chisels, we could not only flatten or smash down those spikes and blades that did so much damage this morning, but also hack through those chains as well so that the whole bloody thing can be heaved out of the way. And while our blacksmiths are doing their bit for the cause, our axe-men could also have a go at chopping the bastard thing up into smaller pieces. What do you think. Yvo?"

The burley Lord of Malwood looked at his friend….*Sweet Jesus, he is bloody mad! Fitzwalter will have a fit!*…and grunted. "Henry, I think this is completely insane…" And then, he added with a smile…"But maybe just mad enough to work. 'Romans'?" He queried again, shaking his head in amazement. "God help us! The king will think we have all lost our fucking senses. I suppose the 'Roman' bit came from you, Matthew?" Yvo groaned at the tall Spaniard after a moment's silence, adding with a grin: "While our Henry has more brains than I do, not even he could have thought that one up! Though having got that far I can see his hand on the practical side of it: chopped down mantlets, axe men and blacksmiths. You two must be both fucking mad! How long do we have before Henry orders another go at that breach? One day? Two?"

"Two days R and R and attack on the third day." Don Mateo said, quietly. "I had it from de Vernaille. He wants the whole of tomorrow and the next day to finish doing a 'proper job' on that wall…and then Henry will order another attack. And this time there will be a decent breach for our lads to climb, so we should get in...but only if we can remove their *Chevaux de Frises*..."

"*Chevaux de Frises now?*" Sir Yvo interrupted, aghast.

"Yes, Yvo. We must plan for that. For with a bigger breach there are bound to be more than one of those bastards up on that bloody slope to deal with."

"Sweet Wine of Christ! Two days! And more than one of those bastard things up there by then?"

"So, Yvo?" His oldest friend asked him, his eyes ice-blue, fixed on him with a concentrated stare: "Yes...or no?"...*And you'd better go with this Yvo because I can think of nothing else!*

"Well, I think you are both demented. And it's a completely insane idea. Roman 'Testudo' indeed! But...it's the only idea we've got, and if it worked for the bloody Romans there's no reason why it shouldn't work for us. So we'll do it! Though what Edward Fitzwalter will have to say when I tell him what we need our lads to do up on that fucking glacis in three days' time, I'll leave you to imagine. He will think it as mad a scheme as I do!" And he laughed. "And while they are at it, have the lads paint their shields in violent colours. God knows what that will do to the enemy...but it will cheer the lads up no end. Make them feel invincible! Now...who's for another clack of this excellent red I picked up on my way here?" He asked grinning at them again. "I don't know about you two...but after that little revelation, gentlemen. I *need* a drink. God help us, you two. Everything forward and trust in the Lord!" And they all laughed.

Continued in Book 1 of the White Rose Series: The Lion and the White Rose